LANDFALLS

LANDFALLS

NAOMI J. WILLIAMS

Little, Brown

LITTLE, BROWN

First published in Great Britain in 2015 by Little, Brown

1 3 5 7 9 10 8 6 4 2

Copyright © Naomi J. Williams 2015
Map Copyright © John Gilkes 2015
Designed by Jonathan D. Lippincott

The following chapters have been previously published, in slightly different
versions: "Items for Exchange" (*Sycamore Review*), "Lamanon at Sea"
(*A Public Space*), "Snow Men" (*One Story*), "The Report"
(*American Short Fiction*),and "Folie à Plusieurs"
(*Ninth Letter*).

A CIP catalogue record for this book
is available from the British Library.

HARDBACK ISBN 978-1-4087-0576-6
C FORMAT ISBN 978-1-4087-0577-3

Printed and bound in Great Britain by
Clays Ltd, St Ives plc

Papers used by Little, Brown are from well-managed forests
and other responsible sources.

MIX
Paper from
responsible sources
FSC
www.fsc.org   FSC® C104740

Little, Brown
An imprint of
Little, Brown Book Group
Carmelite House
50 Victoria Embankment
London EC4Y 0DZ

An Hachette UK Company
www.hachette.co.uk

www.littlebrown.co.uk

In memory of my grandmother Kimi Kawabata,
who also loved maps

A good Land fall is when we fall just with our reckoning, if otherwise a bad Land fall.

—Captain John Smith, *A Sea Grammar* (1627)

Exultation is the going
Of an inland soul to sea,
Past the houses—past the headlands—
Into deep Eternity—

Bred as we, among the mountains,
Can the sailor understand
The divine intoxication
Of the first league out from land?

—Emily Dickinson

A man finds his shipwrecks,
tells himself the necessary stories.

—Stephen Dunn, "Odysseus's Secret," *Different Hours*

CONTENTS

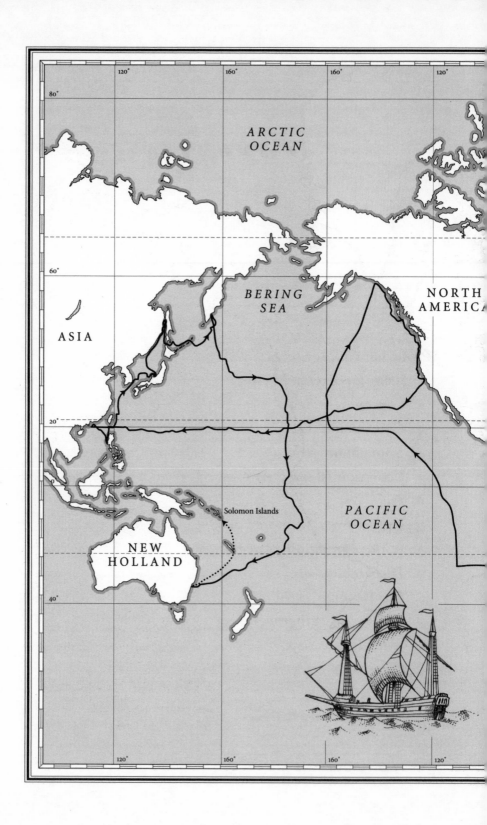

THE WORLD

*Lapérouse Voyage from France
to Botany Bay, 1785–88*

LANDFALLS

PROLOGUE:
GALLEY STOVES

Port of Brest, Spring 1785

No one knew what to make of the new galley stoves when they arrived. There were two—one for each ship—and they came by boat, first for the *Boussole* and then for the *Astrolabe*, disassembled into their cumbersome components and accompanied by a foul-mouthed shipyard locksmith charged with installing them.

"What is this?" the men asked as they watched the boats approach and again as they hauled the heavy iron pieces on board and laid them out on their decks.

The men had other questions too, questions that had gone unanswered: *Where is this expedition going? For what purpose? And for how long?* But this time, the captain of the *Boussole*, Jean-François de Galaup de Lapérouse, called down from the quarterdeck: "It's an English galley stove. A gift from the minister of marine." He laughed while the men grumbled about bringing English contrivances aboard, then instructed the head carpenter to keep an eye on the installation. "Make sure that locksmith doesn't damage my ship," he said.

The captain of the *Astrolabe*, Paul-Antoine-Marie Fleuriot, Viscount de Langle, didn't laugh. He clambered down from the quarterdeck, signaled wordlessly to his own head carpenter to join him, and followed the locksmith and the stove parts as they made their laborious way below. He endured the locksmith's epithet-laced bungling for two hours before dismissing the man and overseeing the rest of the installation himself.

Only a few months earlier, the *Boussole* and the *Astrolabe* had been humble naval storeships moving lumber or cordage from one known port on the Atlantic to another. Now they had been assigned to the mysterious expedition, reclassed as frigates, and given new, more respectable names. But they still had a storeship's dimensions, and the English stoves, no doubt designed for ships of the line, barely fit. On both vessels, men swore as they bashed toes and knees and foreheads into iron legs and doors and knobs.

They wanted to blame the locksmith, but the head carpenter on the *Astrolabe* reminded his shipmates that the blame lay with the minister of marine, who, from the comfort and opulence of the Hôtel de La Marine in Paris, had purchased two stoves he'd never laid eyes on for two ships he'd also never laid eyes on. This satisfied some of the men, who preferred blaming a distant aristocrat to a local man, and disappointed others, who'd looked forward to knocking the locksmith about the next time they had shore leave.

The head carpenter on the *Boussole*, an analytical man, added that he believed the stoves to be evidence of the expedition's importance. "The farther away the man making the decisions," he said, "the grander the mission." This pleased some of his shipmates, who imagined a long campaign that involved adventure, promotion, and money—but worried others, who imagined all those things too but preferred expeditions that brought them safely home after not too long away.

"Maybe it's war again," one of the men suggested.

"With who?" a shipmate asked.

"Does it matter?"

"We're not warships."

"Every ship in the Royale is a warship in time of war."

"But we're not *in* time of war."

"Maybe we're about to be, is what I'm saying."

Monsieur de Lapérouse happened to overhear this exchange and stopped before the men, whose names he couldn't recall. Everyone on board was new to the ship, including him. "No one's going to war," he said. "What made you say that?"

The assembled men looked at one another, then back at their captain, then back at one another, till one of them said, "On account of the minister's stoves, sir."

"The *stoves?*" the captain said. "Do you think hostile Englishmen might be hidden inside, ready to jump out in the night to take over our ships?"

"No, sir," they replied. Only one crew member, a petty officer who'd read the *Aeneid* as a boy, dared chuckle at the captain's reference.

As for the stoves themselves, they performed well—*quite* well—when only one person at a time used them. But when Monsieur de Lapérouse ordered a test in which every possible use of the stove was performed simultaneously, the results were deplorable. Add to the ship's cook the officers' cook and the captain's cook and the ship's baker and the expedition's chemist, and bread emerged from the oven burned on top and uncooked in the middle, pots boiled over or not at all, the alembic installed to desalinate seawater consumed far too much wood for the dribbles of fresh water it produced, and the chemist, rather belatedly, said he thought it quite lucky the galleys hadn't caught fire.

Monsieur de Lapérouse made light of the problem before the men, calling their new stove the "English baron." "It's fat, eats more than it should, and sits around all day smoking," he quipped. But urgent-looking missives carried by harried-looking messengers came and went from his cabin, suggesting that remote—and hence, important—discussions were taking place.

Meanwhile, on the *Astrolabe*, Monsieur de Langle had his carpenters remove their equally troublesome stove and replace it with a smaller traditional French stove. He then modified it himself to fit a new distilling device designed in Paris by Monsieur de Lavoisier, the famous chemist, and proposed redoing the test. He took the precaution of moving the *Astrolabe* to a less populated part of the harbor. ("In case we explode," one waggish crewman explained to Langle's cook, a thin, anxious individual who flinched thereafter at every sound from the galley stove.) The captain, undaunted, ordered up a large pot of peas, two loaves of fresh bread, a partridge for a captain's dinner, a pitcher of distilled seawater, and, for good measure, the heating up of some liquid-filled flasks as if for a science experiment.

Midafternoon, a skiff from the *Astrolabe* pulled up alongside the *Boussole*, where Lapérouse and his men awaited the results. "Well?" the captain demanded when one of Langle's lieutenants climbed aboard. The young officer presented a package that contained a still-steaming loaf of bread and a note. *Let us inform the minister that his stoves may be suited to an English sailor's lifestyle, but not to a Frenchman's,* it said.

"How do you know what it said?" one of the *Astrolabe*'s carpenters demanded of the assistant carpenter from the *Boussole* when he related this part of the story. "You can't read."

"Because the commander read the note out loud and we all laughed, he loudest of all," the young man replied. "And I *can* read, I'll have you know."

It was the following night, and they were at a watering hole in Brest favored by seamen. With Monsieur de Langle's design successfully implemented on both ships, the two captains had given their carpenters the evening off.

"So who says your Monsieur de Lapérouse is the expedition's commander?" another man from the *Astrolabe* retorted.

At this, the men from the *Boussole* burst into laughter. Of *course* their captain was in command—he was in daily communication with the minister, and Monsieur de Langle answered to him, not the other way around—had they not noticed? But *their* captain was a viscount, the *Astrolabe*'s carpenters said. Surely that still meant something. The debate threatened to become unfriendly till they spied a junior officer from the *Astrolabe* walking by and persuaded him to come in and settle the argument. The young officer diplomatically refrained from mentioning either captain by name and simply confirmed that, yes, the *Boussole* was to be the flagship and the *Astrolabe* her consort. By declining the drinks offered him by the *Boussole*'s men and instead treating the whole table to several jugs of the establishment's better wine, he also maintained harmony with his own shipmates and restored good cheer to the entire group.

"Can you also tell us where the expedition's going?" one of the men asked.

"*That* I'm not allowed to say," the officer said before heading out.

Rowing back to their ships that night, the carpenters found their way lit by an enormous full moon sinking into the ocean beyond the port. It cast a wide white ribbon of light across the water like a beacon. "One almost wants to row out forever," one man said, and they all felt it—that strange pull of the sublime inviting them into the unknown, into oblivion.

But they were practical men who could recognize a poetic impulse without acting on it. Tomorrow would bring another round of orders and dilemmas that demanded their attention and good sense. So they parted company from one another and from the beckoning light and returned to their ships.

ONE

ITEMS FOR EXCHANGE

London, April 1785

Plausibility

He always forgets how unpleasant the crossing from Calais is. He's never once made the trip without encountering inclement weather, contrary winds and tides, unexplained delays, seasick fellow travelers, surly packet captains, or dishonest boatmen waiting to extort the passengers ashore. This time it's all of the above. By the time he reaches Dover, he has, of course, missed the stagecoach to London. He spends the night at the Ship Hotel, where he endures a hard, flea-ridden bed and a neighbor with a wet, defeated cough.

It's not an auspicious start to the journey. But Paul-Mérault de Monneron is not given to superstition. The next day brings springlike weather, a passable meal from the hotel kitchen, the stagecoach ready to leave on time, and an unsmiling but efficient coachman who gives the correct change. The only other passenger inside the coach is a man Monneron recognizes from the packet; the poor man had been gray-skinned with nausea most of the way from France. "Well, I daresay we are being compensated for yesterday's horrors," the man says. Monneron nods politely, although he doesn't agree. For him, the universe is not given to compensating one for past miseries any more than it exacts payment for one's successes. But he is not immune to the pleasures of a smooth ride on a lovely day. The Kentish countryside, or such of it as he can see through the coach window, is charming. Once he points out the window at a large bird, white-breasted with black and white wings, perched atop a post. "Please—what do you call that?" he asks. "I do not know the word in English."

The man leans over. "That would be an osprey, I think," he says.

"Osprey." It's rare that he learns a word in English he finds nicer than its counterpart in French. But "osprey" is undoubtedly lovelier than "*balbuzard.*"

The brief exchange leads inevitably to an inquiry about Monneron's trip to London. Almost everything he says by way of reply is true: That he's a naval engineer, that he's leaving soon for the South Seas, that he's going to London to make some purchases for the voyage, that he was tasked with the errand because he speaks English—"Not that my English is so good," he adds, to which the man says, "Nonsense! You've hardly any accent at all." But part of Monneron's account is *not* true: that he's in England at the behest of a Spanish merchant, Don Inigo Alvarez, with whom he'll be sailing to the South Seas. Monneron will be sailing with neither Spaniards nor merchants. There is, in fact, no Don Inigo.

It's a French naval expedition he represents, a voyage of exploration meant to compete with the accomplishments of the late Captain Cook, a voyage that is supposed to be secret until it departs. This excursion to London is not just a shopping trip for books and instruments. He's supposed to find out the latest on antiscorbutics—scurvy-prevention measures—and on what items work best for trading with natives in the South Seas. For this he needs to find someone who sailed with Cook—someone both knowledgeable and willing to talk.

This is the first time he's tried the Don Inigo story on anyone. He's surprised by the fluency and ease with which he spouts the commingled lies and truths. He hadn't liked the idea of traveling under a pretext—had, in fact, challenged the need for secrecy at all, and when the minister of marine dismissed his query with an impatient wave of his beruffled hand, had considered turning the mission down. *Considered* it, but not seriously or for very long. There was no question of jeopardizing his place on the expedition. He would have stood on his head before the court of Versailles if required. Still, when the Spanish merchant ruse was first concocted, he'd burst out laughing. *"Don Inigo Alvarez?"* he'd cried. "It's like something out of a play." But the minister held firm: "People are inclined to believe what they hear," he said. "Speak with assurance, and no one will question you." So far, at least, he has proved right: Monneron's companion nods, interested, impressed, and apparently convinced.

Five Nights' Advance

The stagecoach arrives in London the following evening, and Monneron secures lodgings with a Mrs. Towe, recommended to him by his brother Louis, who often travels to London on business. The house smells unaccountably of stale cider, but it meets Monneron's most basic requirements—clean bed, convenient location, quiet landlady—and a couple of unusual ones—first, the absence of other lodgers, and second, a windowless storage room to which only he and Mrs. Towe will have a key.

Before going to sleep, he calculates his expenses since landing in Dover: a night's stay and meals at the Ship Hotel, then sixteen shillings and eight pence for the stagecoach, plus the fee for his baggage and a tip for the driver, not to mention a half crown for every meal and one night's lodging en route, and now, five nights paid in advance to Mrs. Towe. He's spent almost all of the English currency the minister gave him before he left. His first task the next day will be to go to the bank. So far he's had few choices about his expenditures, but now that he's in London, he'll be faced with myriad decisions, most of which will involve money. He can't spend too much, of course. But it might be worse to spend too little. He doesn't wish to squander the ministry's faith in him, of course. Above all, he doesn't wish to disappoint Monsieur de Lapérouse, the commander of the expedition. Staring up at Mrs. Towe's water-stained ceiling, Monneron reflects that there's still time to appoint another engineer—and plenty of ambitious young men of good family eager to take his place.

Costume

He wakes early, consumes without enjoyment Mrs. Towe's weak tea and cold toast, then faces the delicate task of getting dressed. For the past three days he's been hidden under an overcoat and top boots, but now he'll be entering establishments and homes, making impressions, gathering information. He doesn't wish to call attention to himself by looking too French, too naval, too fashionable, or not fashionable enough. Louis has advised him to dress more soberly than a gentleman his age in Paris might, but Monneron's not sure what that means. With all his years at sea, he's quite used to dressing himself—in uniform. Civilian clothes are another matter altogether. In the end, he puts on the plainest linen shirt he owns and a pair of ribbed white stockings, and over them a suit he's borrowed from Antoine, another brother who is the same height as he. The waistcoat, breeches, and frock coat are all of the same, dark-blue woven silk—even the buttons are covered. Then he dons wig, shoes, and overcoat, in that order. He hesitates before picking up the thin, tasseled cane that Louis had pressed him to take instead of his sword. "Don't carry a sword or a hat," his brother had told him. "They will mark you as a Frenchman and an effeminate."

On his way out, Monneron appraises himself in the smoky mirror in Mrs. Towe's entrance hall. He looks like a Frenchman who is trying not to look French, he thinks. And he hates the cane. What an absurd country, in which wearing a *sword* makes one effeminate but carrying a beribboned walking stick does not.

Letters

He steps out into the fetid, fog-drizzled streets and makes his way to the Bank of England, where he exchanges letters of credit for more cash than he's ever seen in one place, much less carried upon his person. He's grateful for Antoine's tailor, who's adopted the innovation of interior pockets in frock coats. It's a place to stow the money. Still, he hurries into a cab, afraid the smell of so many bank bills will attract every pickpocket in London, and asks to be taken to an address on Oxford Street.

Monneron has another letter with him that morning—a letter of introduction to John Webber, a painter who was the official artist on Cook's last voyage. Monneron would have preferred an introduction to *officers* who'd served with Cook, but according to the minister, most of the officers who aren't dead are at sea, and of the small number who are neither dead nor at sea, two live too far outside London and the others are too highly placed to approach without arousing suspicion. "What about Cook's naturalists?" Monsieur de Lapérouse had asked. "Can't we approach one of them?" No, the minister said. Solander was dead. The Forsters were both in Prussia. Only Sir Joseph Banks, the famous naturalist from the first

Cook expedition, was still alive and in London, but he was now president of the Royal Society and close to both the Admiralty and the king. "Don't underestimate the usefulness of an artist as a source," the minister said. Monneron and Lapérouse had exchanged a glance, neither man convinced. What would a draughtsman know of antiscorbutics or appropriate items for exchange?

The cab deposits him before a narrow, dignified residence on Oxford Street. The door is opened by a narrow, dignified servant. The man takes Monneron's letter of introduction and soon after escorts him into a parlor where a man in a silk damask morning gown with a matching cap is finishing breakfast. When he looks up, Monneron is shocked by his youth.

"You expected an old man," Webber says.

Monneron cannot deny it. It's been only five years since Cook's third and final voyage returned to England without him, but it has already achieved the status of legend, and yes, one expects those who sailed with him to be grizzled old men.

"I was only twenty-four when the expedition began," Webber explains. Monneron makes some mental calculations: Webber is younger than he is.

The artist invites his guest to sit down, then has his manservant bring another place setting. Monneron puts up only a nominal protest before making quick work of strong, hot tea, smoked herring, a slice of cold veal pie, and a roll with marmalade.

"So," Webber says, "you're going to the South Seas."

Monneron nods through a mouthful, then tells him about Don Inigo and the need for scientific books and instruments. Also, information on antiscorbutics. *And* advice about appropriate items for exchange with natives.

Webber nods. "How long are you here?"

"Till Friday."

"Friday?" The artist sets his teacup down before laughing. "You're going to be rather busy, Mr. Monneron." He meets Monneron's eyes with a look at once frank and challenging. "I'm not sure how useful I can be to you. I'm no sailor."

Monneron is inclined to agree, but doesn't say so. "I know you returned from the voyage with hundreds of paintings," he says, remembering what the minister said about artists. "You cannot have done so without learning many things."

Webber holds his gaze for a moment, then pushes back from the table. "Come with me," he says.

Knife

Webber's library is high-ceilinged, white-walled, lit by small windows above the bookcases. Books occupy the upper shelves; the lower shelves are filled with art and objects. "It's all from the voyage," he says. The drawings are his, he explains, sketches and paintings executed during the voyage; the rest are items he found, purchased, or was given.

Monneron steps forward to examine the drawings. They include land-scapes and topographical views, botanical drawings and sketches of birds and lizards, portraits of natives and studies of their homes and canoes, and numerous scenes—natives dancing, feasting, receiving Cook, burying their dead. The drawings are of various sizes, but many are larger than Mon-neron expected, some an arm's length across. He tries to imagine his silk-gowned young host working on the busy deck of the *Resolution*, or pitching about in one of its smaller boats, or walking around a newly discovered island, all the while managing these large sheets of paper and drawing supplies, perhaps an easel as well, and it seems at once impossible, comic, and noble. "They're marvelous," he says.

"You're very kind," Webber says. They're standing before a portrait of a native man. The man has something long and thin thrust through his upper ear. His hair is up in a sort of topknot tied with string, and he has copious, though close-shaved, facial hair; he looks like a pleasant crea-ture, except for the odd ear ornament. "He was from Mangea," Webber says. The expedition didn't land on the island, he goes on to explain, but men came out in canoes to trade with the ships, and this man— "his name was Mourua"—had been persuaded to come on board. "He was shaking with fright. I thought any moment he might fling himself overboard."

Monneron studies the painting a moment longer before venturing to say, "He does not *look* frightened."

Webber laughs. "That's because we gave him a knife in exchange for some fish and coconuts," he says. "That's what he's got in his ear. They all had these slits in one ear, the men of that island. Mourua slipped his knife right in like it had been made for the purpose." He suggests Monneron advise Don Inigo to take a supply of similar knives, as they had proved popular with all the islanders they met. "I can show you where to purchase them," he says.

Monneron turns to Webber. "You see? You are already helping me." He hopes he doesn't look as surprised as he feels.

Webber draws Monneron's attention to his collection of objects— a headdress, ornaments, carvings in wood and bone, Tahitian dresses. He remembers everything: the provenance of each item, the circumstances by which it came into his possession, the appearance and behavior of the natives there, what they were willing to trade, and for what. Monneron is amazed. If only he can keep himself in this man's company for the week, he thinks, his mission will be largely accomplished.

Their circumnavigation of the library complete, Webber opens the door leading back toward the parlor. On an impulse, Monneron says, "Do you still paint portraits, Mr. Webber?"

"My reputation is mostly in landscapes," Webber says, then watches Monneron's gaze travel around the room, taking in all the native faces. "Portraits of natives are really a kind of landscape painting too," he says. "Why do you ask?"

"I'm going away for so long—anything can happen—I thought—only if you have time, of course . . ." Monneron says, his discomfort entirely real.

"You want me to *paint* you?"

Monneron laughs, embarrassed. "It would be for my mother. But you must be busy."

"Not as busy as you this week."

Monneron's face warms. Indeed, he's just shared with this man a long list of tasks he has less than a week to complete; this request for a portrait must sound absurd and vain. "Perhaps something quick, just in pencil or pen," he says, "like one of these sketches from the voyage." He stops, abashed to think he's just characterized Webber's work as something one can simply dash off. He puts a hand to his forehead, aware that it's a nervous gesture people—women especially—find disarming.

Webber is smiling at him. "I'd be delighted to paint you."

Monneron laughs with relief. "I don't know how these things work," he says. "Is twenty-five guineas an appropriate fee?"

Webber shakes his head. "That's not necessary."

"It *is* necessary."

After some haggling, Webber reluctantly agrees to five guineas. He apologizes—he'd be happy to begin straightaway, but has engagements the rest of the day. Can Monneron return tomorrow?

"Come around three," Webber says. "The light is best in my studio then."

King's Ransom

Monneron has one more document on his person—a shopping list drawn up by Monsieur de Lapérouse himself. The minister had not been altogether pleased by it: "'English' does not mean 'better,'" he declared. "We have instrument makers in Paris!" But Lapérouse had insisted. "We bring no glory to France by traveling with inferior instruments made at home," he said. The minister relented, and now Monneron is on his way to the Fleet Street atelier of George Adams, Jr., to purchase several of the world's finest compasses.

Mr. Adams is a young man—not yet thirty-five, Monneron thinks—who inherited from his father both his business and his position as instrument maker to the king. Mr. Adams does not suffer from false modesty. Indeed, he doesn't suffer from modesty of any kind. He subjects Monneron to questioning as if to determine whether his new customer is worthy of his wares. "Inigo Alvarez?" he says with a sniff. "Never heard of him."

"Ah, but 'e knows of you, Monsieur Adams," Monneron says, exaggerating his accent.

The combination of flattery and Frenchness prevails, and Adams is persuaded to part with two azimuth compasses. They're beautiful in their simplicity, each hand-painted compass face with its durable steel needle seated in a glass-covered brass housing suspended from an outer brass ring, which in turn is affixed to a wooden box, all of it designed to withstand

the motions at sea. Unfortunately, Mr. Adams has no dipping needles—
used to adjust compass readings, essential on a long voyage into unknown
parts. Monsieur de Lapérouse has especially requested them—two, in fact,
one for each of the expedition's ships.

"I've had no orders for them in nearly a year," Adams says, peering at
Monneron with renewed suspicion.

"Do you know anyone else who—?"

"No," Adams says, apparently not given to recommending his compet-
itors even when he cannot meet a customer's needs himself.

The other instrument makers Monneron meets that afternoon are
friendlier and less inquisitive. Not far from Adams, in their workshop
behind the Sign of the Orrery, he meets the elfin Troughton brothers,
who cheerfully sell him a sextant and a pantograph for the expedition's
cartographers. At Nairne and Blunt's in Cornhill, he buys two of the most
beautiful and expensive barometers he's ever seen; they will please the
expedition's savants. Next door he finds hourglasses and magnetic bars.
And at the famed Ramsden's in Piccadilly, he leaves behind what feels
like a king's ransom and walks out with the promised delivery of two
theodolites, two night telescopes, four thermometers, one large sextant,
one small one, and four handheld compasses suitable for land exploration.
But alas, no dipping needles. "You'll want to see Mr. Adams for that," they
all say.

It's seven o'clock before Monneron returns, exhausted, cold, and
hungry, to Mrs. Towe's. The fire has gone out in his room, and supper con-
sists of watery boiled partridge and buttered potatoes so cold the butter
has recongealed. But he makes his own fire and shrugs his way through
the meal. He's eaten much worse in far greater discomfort. And he has
every reason to be satisfied with his first day in London: he's made contact
with a knowledgeable and forthcoming member of the Cook expedition
and procured nearly everything on Monsieur de Lapérouse's list. There's
even satisfaction in the knowledge that he's reduced the crown's coffers,
in one day, by more than three thousand *louis*. He's understood all along
that the expedition will be unlike any other that France has undertaken,
its scientific mission paramount, no reasonable expense to be spared. Today he's done his part to make it so.

He tosses a cold, butter-coated potato into the fire to watch it hiss and burn. If he could only find some dipping needles, he thinks, then throws in another potato.

A Treatise on the Scurvy

In the morning, the breakfast tray surprises by including a note from Sir Joseph Banks, the naturalist the minister said was too close to Admiralty and king to approach. It's a breathless, unpunctuated missive written in a hand more sure than legible:

> Sir
>
> having just learned of your presence in London to assist Don Inigo Alvarez in preparations for his upcoming voyage I take the liberty of proffering my assistance as Don Inigo and I are acquainted he having as you are no doubt aware a great interest in natural history and was once good enough to send me two Blepharopsis mendica for my collection
>
> would be honored if you would call at 11 o'clock for conversation of mutual interest and benefit
>
> JB

Monneron stares for several minutes together at the letter. He cannot decide which is stranger—that Banks knows of him at all, or that he claims acquaintance with the fictional Don Inigo. Banks must know on whose behalf Monneron is really here. But how? *Adams*, Monneron thinks, remembering the young instrument maker's disdainful, persistent curiosity. It must be. But what does Banks want? Does he mean to expose Monneron and embarrass the French government? And what is a *Blepharopsis mendica*?

The crux of the matter, however, is this: one does not turn down a summons from Sir Joseph Banks. As the bells of a nearby church toll the appointed hour, Monneron announces himself at Banks's residence at 32 Soho Square. Neither the square nor the house is at all what he expected for the president of the Royal Society: the neighborhood has the noisy, resigned air of a place abandoned by fashionable people, and the house, with its narrow three-story frontage of red brick, is nothing if not modest. But inside, the home is large and grand, and so is Banks—tall and stout, a perfectly fitted wig on his sizable head, a fur-trimmed robe adding to his overall bulk. As if to diminish all the largeness and grandeur, however, he shows Monneron into a small, dense library fitted under the great staircase of his home.

He motions for Monneron to sit on one side of a crowded desk while he arranges himself into a red leather chair opposite, then says, "And how is the good Don Inigo these days?"

Monneron eyes his host warily. "I found him very well the last time I saw him."

"Excellent." Banks slides a framed specimen display across the desk. The case appears to contain, pinned to the canvas, a few thin twigs with their leaves—some green and mottled, some brown and crinkled—but no, they're not twigs at all, they're insects, insects with long, jointed legs and triangular heads, very like the *mantes* Monneron enjoyed finding in the garden as a boy.

"The Egyptian flower mantis," Banks says. *"Blepharopsis mendica."*

*"Man-*tis," Monneron repeats under his breath, committing a new English word to memory. He stares at the insects and wonders if there might be a Don Inigo, after all.

"They spend their lives hanging upside down from tree branches whose leaves they resemble," Sir Joseph is saying. "Their prey crawl or fly by, never suspecting a thing till they're caught."

Monneron's attention swings back to Banks. "Caught?"

Banks smiles.

"Forgive me, Sir Joseph," Monneron says, "but I did not know Don Inigo had written to you about my visit."

"Oh, he didn't," Banks says. "I saw Mr. Webber yesterday afternoon."

"Mr. *Webber*?" Not Adams. Monneron feels a twitch of disappointment. He hadn't asked Webber to keep his presence in London a secret. Nevertheless, it feels . . . not like a betrayal of trust, exactly—that would presume too much of a morning's acquaintance—but like an assumption of openness Monneron had neither known about nor agreed to. "Mr. Webber was kind enough to show me some of his paintings yesterday," he finally says.

"He's a competent landscape painter," Banks says. "I must confess I don't think much of his portraiture." Seeing his guest's surprise, he adds: "They're pretty enough, but not very lifelike. His natives look too European. And his Europeans—well, they're a bit savage. He did a most unusual oil of Captain Cook and presented it to his widow. I certainly hope it did not compound the grief of the long-suffering Mrs. Cook. It bore little resemblance to the great man."

Monneron remembers the paintings and sketches in Webber's library, how very warm and human the man from Mangea looked, for all he had a knife stuck in his ear. Is Banks simply voicing his opinion, or warning him off? What is it that he wants, anyway?

As if divining his perplexity, Banks says, "Mr. Monneron, my sole purpose in making myself known to you is to offer any assistance it may be in my power to provide." The two men watch each other for a moment, then Banks says, "I understand you are tasked with learning about antiscorbutics." He reaches for a fat volume at one end of his desk and hands it to Monneron: *A Treatise on the Scurvy* by James Lind. "The most important contribution to seafaring physic this century," he says. "Take it. I have several copies. Be sure the ships' surgeons read it."

"Thank you, Sir Joseph," Monneron says, then, silencing a debate in his head between suspicion and expediency, adds, "There is something I would be happy to have your advice upon," and tells Banks about his unsuccessful search for dipping needles.

Banks closes his eyes, nodding as he listens. "I may be able to help you," he says at last, opening his eyes. "I'll send word."

When Monneron leaves 32 Soho Square, he's still not sure of the encounter. The least distressing conclusion is that Sir Joseph had prior intelligence of the expedition, has a purely scientific interest in offering his help, and is keeping up the pretext about Don Inigo to save Monneron from embarrassment. But how did Banks make the connection with Monneron through Webber's report? Unless Webber himself knows—no, Monneron thinks, calling to mind Webber's trusting, open face. He may know *now*, of course—which, Monneron reflects, pausing as he makes his way across the square, may make calling on Webber again this afternoon awkward. As for Banks himself, perhaps he's beguiling Monneron with attention and promises of assistance, waiting for a slip, an unintended revelation, some tidbit that will go straight to the Admiralty. But would a man who intends to expose you as a spy for the French Navy first press on you the latest in scurvy-prevention research?

Transparency

Back at Mrs. Towe's, he half expects to find a note from Webber regretfully explaining that urgent business will preclude them from meeting again. And when there is none, Monneron considers sending his own regrets, discovering a sudden compunction about having ingratiated himself with the artist under false pretenses. But Webber is too valuable a contact to give up over an uneasy conscience, and as Mrs. Towe's gloomy longcase clock sounds out two-thirty, Monneron sets out once more for Oxford Street.

The narrow, dignified manservant asks him to please wait in the library. Monneron paces the room, revisiting the paintings and objects that afforded him pleasure and instruction the day before, and looking in vain for evidence that Webber's natives look "too European." On a small table he finds the recently published official account of Cook's last voyage—*A Voyage to the Pacific Ocean. Undertaken, by the Command of His Majesty, for Making Discoveries in the Northern Hemisphere, etc.*—three volumes plus a folio volume containing maps and prints. Thumbing through the latter, he recognizes many of the pictures as engraved facsimiles of the paintings that surround him. The published images are very like the originals, but something is lost in the transfer of raw images produced in situ to engravings suitable for printing. The originals are in color and the engravings are not, of course, but it's more than that. Monneron closes the book and studies the nearest original, a painting of dancers in Tahiti. He can trace the creation of this piece from the first layer of pencil and chalk outlines to the washes and watercolor application to the final details added in ink. There's a transparency to the endeavor and its result that's missing from the published images.

"Mr. Monneron," Webber says, bursting in. He's dressed much as he was the previous morning, with the silk gown tied carelessly over faded trousers, stockinged feet shod in a pair of battered silk slippers. He crosses

the room and shakes Monneron's hand. "I'm delighted to see you again."
His smile is unchanged—friendly, artless. Monneron expects him to say
something about Banks—*I saw Sir Joseph yesterday and mentioned your
visit; he knows your Don Inigo, by the way; he said he would send—oh, he has
already? You've met him? Splendid*—but he doesn't, and his silence makes
Monneron diffident about saying anything himself. He'd like to know what
Webber said yesterday and what Banks said in turn. Was it "Don Inigo?
I'm acquainted with the gentleman. What did you say this Frenchman's
name was?" Or "Don Inigo? Ha! My dear Webber, your new friend is an
agent for the French Navy!"?

But Webber is showing him out of the library and down a corridor to
a bright room of north-facing windows. The space smells of canvas, wood,
paint, solvents, pine resin, and wax, and Monneron is reminded suddenly,
almost painfully, of being at sea. Then Webber surprises him by removing
his gown, then his vest and shirt. His arms are thin, his chest almost hair-
less, his belly just softening into middle age. "My painting costume," he says
offhandedly, grabbing a paint-splattered linen shirt from a peg. Monneron
doesn't know where to look. At sea, he's unfazed by other men's nakedness,
but on land, it's different. He wonders if Webber's lack of self-consciousness
is an English affectation, a product of artistic temperament, a habit from
his time at sea, or a more personal gesture.

Hostage

It's like being a boy in church—the more Monneron tells himself not to
shift about or scratch his head, the more he needs to. But Webber must
be used to restive subjects, for he tolerates it without comment. The studio is filled with unfinished paintings, and Monneron's attention settles
on a large oil canvas perched on an easel behind the artist. It depicts a
native woman, raven-haired and bare-breasted, with decorous tattoos covering her arms and a jasmine flower tucked behind each ear. A large white
cloth wrapped round the lower half of her body fails to hide the outline of
her generous hips. "She's very beautiful," Monneron says.

Webber turns to follow his gaze. "I'm finishing her for an exhibit at the
Royal Academy," he explains. "She's a Tahitian princess who sat for me on
board the *Resolution*."

Monneron regards the painting again. The princess is standing, not sitting, and appears to be ashore among heavy-fronded plants, not on the deck of a Royal Navy sloop. He supposes this license is allowed—perhaps even *expected*—of artists. "How did you persuade the natives to sit for you?" he asks.

"She was our captive and in no position to refuse," Webber says. He studies Monneron then turns back to his work. For a moment, the light scratching of pencil on paper is the only sound in the room. "Several of our men had deserted," he explains, looking back up, "and the islanders were sheltering them. The captain was compelled to take Princess Poedua"— he inclines his head toward the painting—"to press for the deserters' return."

"Did it work?"

"Of course."

Monneron looks again at the painting, at the princess's serene face, her pliant arms, the openness implied by her breasts, the nipples tipped slightly away from each other. One would never guess she'd been a hostage while this portrait was being done. Now he wonders—did she really have those flowers in her hair? That white cloth—did Webber add that to protect English sensibilities? And perhaps that's not serenity in her expression so much as surrender. He looks back at Webber, who's leaning in toward the paper before him with a piece of chalk, the pencil held between his teeth. He cannot quite admire a profession that allows so much dissimulation. His own engineering work demands meticulous calculation and is intolerant of error or alteration of facts. But then again, here he is in Webber's home pretending to be someone he is not. They are, both of them, simply doing their jobs.

Webber sits up and takes the pencil from his mouth. "If I may make so bold as to offer my views on something, Mr. Monneron."

"Please."

"One wants to find a middle way with natives," he says. "Neither too familiar nor too distant. Your Spaniards tend to be too harsh." He looks at Monneron, then back at his paper. "But we English have been far too familiar. I think the humanity we extended toward them lowered us in their regard." Monneron wonders how imprisoning native royalty constitutes overfamiliarity, but doesn't interrupt. "I believe it cost us the captain's life," Webber says quietly.

"Were you there when—when it happened?"

"No, I wasn't." He dips his brush into water, then paint, and gently draws the brush across the paper in short, even strokes. "But I did have to paint it. The Admiralty needed it for publication—*The Death of Cook*." He swirls his brush again in the water and leaves it there. "I had to read all the eyewitness accounts and talk with officers who were there, and—" He exhales. "It was like enduring it again and again."

Monneron knows what it is to lose shipmates. During the American War, when he served on the *Sceptre* with Lapérouse, their campaign in Hudson Bay and the subsequent crossing back to Europe had cost almost one hundred lives. But he's never lost a commanding officer; it would be akin to losing a parent. He's fortunate in not knowing that loss either. "I'm sorry," he says.

Webber looks up with a smile. "Well," he says, standing up. "It's not quite finished, but I think I can release you. What do you think?"

Monneron's never seen his own likeness before other than in a mirror, and he still remembers the moment—he must have been eleven or twelve—when he realized that since reflections are reversed, he would never see himself truly, not as others saw him. Now he bends over Webber's picture and regards the lines of his body in pencil, then chalk, watercolor washes indicating hair color and fabric. He's standing, not sitting, in the picture, and the background is still blank, which makes him look like he's floating. He does wonder about the proportions—he's always imagined himself a longer-legged man. Is that what Banks meant about Europeans who look like savages? And then there's the face itself, recognizable yet unexpected. It's an anxious face, the face of a lost child. "Is that what I look like?" he says.

Webber laughs. "No matter where I am in the world, everyone says the same thing: 'Is this really me?'"

Fishhooks

Webber insists that Monneron stay for dinner. By the time they've finished the codling, roast beef, potatoes in brown sauce, boiled cabbage, pudding, and a bottle of Graves, they've exchanged personal histories and dropped the "Mr." from each other's surnames. Monneron learns of Webber's early years in Switzerland and tells him in turn about his childhood in Annonay. He's about to regret that it's time he returned to Mrs. Towe's for the night when Webber offers to take him shopping.

"What? *Now?*"

"I promised to show you where to buy knives."

"Now?"

"It's London. Shops are open late."

Monneron accedes, and Webber takes him to an emporium of bladed and pointed things astonishing for the number and variety of its wares. Webber takes charge, collaring a shop boy on whom he loads samples for Monneron to purchase: small, cheap knives ("for your typical islander," he says, handing them to the boy); longer, sharper knives ("for your minor chieftains"); sturdy axes ("for your village elders"); and lances of different lengths ("be careful who you give these to"). Upstairs they sample ten different sizes of needles, then enter an aisle filled with fishhooks. Monneron and his brothers are avid fishers, so he knows the price of a fishhook; these English hooks are quite inexpensive. Even with shipping costs, it will be cheaper to import these. The shop boy gives way to the owner's son, who follows Monneron around as he orders "five hundred of these, a thousand of these, no, *two* thousand . . ."—almost eighteen thousand fishhooks in all, seventeen different kinds, to catch everything from smelt to shark.

It's nearly ten by the time they return to Oxford Street. Over a late supper of white soup with warm bread, Webber prepares a list of shops to visit the next day. Monneron watches him write, admiring the artist's pretty, precise script but also aware of a creeping impulse to snatch the paper away and make him stop. Instead, he tears at a ragged fingernail until it hurts, then asks, he hopes not too abruptly, "Webber, why are you doing all of this?"

Webber looks up, then turns his chair toward his guest and leans back in it with his long legs stretched out. "I'm happy if my experiences can actually be useful," he says. "Most people who ask me about the voyage only want to know if I met cannibals or slept with native women."

"Did you?"

Webber laughs. "No. Are you disappointed?"

A servant brings in plates of dried fruit and nuts and a bottle of port. Then it's nearly midnight, and Monneron is so relaxed and languid that when Webber invites him to stay the night, he allows himself to be led upstairs without protest.

Bolts of Silk

Some inchoate compunction alarms him into wakefulness, and without the fermented apple smell and watermarked ceiling of Mrs. Towe's, he can't at first place where he is. He turns over in the bed to make sure he's alone, and relieved on that point, remembers: Oxford Street, Webber, shopping, fishhooks, a bottle of port. A clock somewhere chimes nine, much later than he usually rises. He dresses quickly and heads down the stairs, but stops on the landing, accosted by a life-size oil of James Cook. He remembers again what Banks said about Webber's portraiture, and this time he sees it: a disproportion of parts, the head oddly simian, the wig looking outgrown and pinched, torso and thighs too thin, left hand too large for the arm above it, feet hidden behind a rock as if Webber didn't know how to render them. The late captain may not look *savage*, exactly, but he does lack dignity.

"Good morning, Mr. Monneron." The manservant appears at the bottom of the stairs. "Mr. Webber is in his dressing room and says you may join him there if you'd like."

No, he would *not* like, Monneron thinks, remembering the nonchalance with which Webber undressed before him yesterday. "I will wait for him in the library, if that is all right," he says.

Webber arrives five minutes later, dressed for another outing. "Monneron—breakfast before heading out?"

Monneron gets up with effort, suddenly exhausted by Webber's generosity, his indefatigable energy, the boundlessness of the man.

Webber cocks his head to one side. "Did you not sleep well?"

Monneron rallies himself to remember why he's there: the expedition, the minister, Monsieur de Lapérouse. He still needs Webber's knowledge, but only for one more day. "I slept very well, thank you," he says. "Breakfast sounds wonderful." He wills himself not to look away when he sees the relief on Webber's face.

After breakfast they venture into the city in a hired coach Webber has retained for the day. The artist has worked out exactly where to go, beginning at a notions shop for beads; then a foundry on Thames Street for unworked iron bars and copper sheeting; several grocers for samples of bouillon tablets, molasses, salts, preserved walnuts—all used as antiscorbutics on the *Resolution*; a brewers for spruce beer and essence of malt, a sickly sweet decoction Webber assures him is palatable when mixed with water or tea; and finally, back to Oxford Street for a fabric shop. Only then does Monneron understand that they have circumscribed a long, serpentine loop around London, a loop that will return him again to Webber's home for the night.

"Reserve these gifts for island royalty," Webber is telling him as he browses the display of silks and fine linens. "They're quite partial to red and gold—look at this, Monneron."

He holds out a bolt of silk taffeta, deep crimson shot through with gold thread. Monneron runs his hand over the fabric; its smoothness and color remind him of a well-dressed friend of his mother who visited Annonay one summer and was quite free with her favors. He has to clear his throat before saying, "It is exquisite," and when he looks up at Webber's smiling, oddly knowing face, he can feel himself flush. He turns away, oppressed by the man's nearness.

"You're tired," Webber says gently. "I'll take you home."

"Webber," Monneron says. "I must return to my lodgings tonight. I can take a cab from here."

Webber's face opens in disappointed surprise, and Monneron cannot suppress a flare of impatience. *I have spent a day and a half riding all over London with you*, he wants to say. *Is that not enough?* Instead he protests that he has much to do before he leaves, letters to write, accounts to check over—and it's all true, but still he sounds like a boor. "I am sorry, Webber," he says. "You have been so good to me." He does not add, *I no longer have need of you.* But the expression on Webber's face suggests he has heard it anyway.

He won't hear of Monneron taking a cab. They ride in silence to Mrs. Towe's. "I'll have your portrait ready tomorrow afternoon," Webber says when the driver stops.

Monneron gets out of the carriage, then turns around in the street. The portrait—he'd forgotten about it. And Webber can see that he has.

"I will come tomorrow, Webber," he says, then compelled by some need to address his indebtedness, says, "May I help pay for the driver?"

Webber looks stricken. "Please don't insult me, Mr. Monneron."

On a tarnished salver in Mrs. Towe's entryway lies a message addressed to Monneron. "It came yesterday," the landlady says from her parlor. The note is short and unsigned:

Sir

   have secured dipping needles for expedition which I should be honored to entrust to your safekeeping at earliest convenience

Influence

Sir Joseph receives him the next morning in the study under the stairs. He pats the top of a large box on his desk, then says: "On loan from the Board of Longitude."

Monneron sits up. The Board of Longitude? Clearly they are well past the fiction of Don Inigo. Sir Joseph opens the box, pulls out an instrument, and sets it on the desk surface. It's an odd apparatus, looking like a framed vertical compass set over an adjustable tripod. "There's a second one like it in the box," he says. He looks pointedly at Monneron. "They were on the *Resolution* and the *Discovery*."

The *Resolution* and *Discovery*—the ships from Cook's last voyage! Monneron breathes in sharply. "Sir Joseph," he says helplessly. "How—?"

Banks smiles. "There are quarters in which I have some influence," he says. Then more seriously: "We are honored to cooperate with your government in this."

Monneron cannot speak. He's struck, as he has not been before this moment, by the real importance of the expedition he represents. But also by the pointlessness of the secrecy he's been compelled to maintain—a secrecy that now seems like so much bureaucratic posturing.

Banks packs the dipping needle back into its box. "Take good care of these instruments," he says. "Discover much. Write everything down. And then, come back. It's very important that some of you come back."

Five Guineas

He's loath to leave Mrs. Towe's after depositing the dipping needles in the locked storage room. But he needs to collect the portrait and pay for it, and more than that he wishes to unburden himself to Webber, so he returns one last time to Oxford Street. He's surprised and vexed to learn that Webber is out. He has no right to his vexation, of course; he knows that. He's gone from expecting nothing helpful from the artist to having scruples about taking advantage of him to feeling smothered by the man's wanton availability to being, now, annoyed by evidence that he has other things to do. How can an acquaintance of four days have grown so tangled?

The dignified servant says no, he doesn't know when Mr. Webber will return, but there's a parcel for Mr. Monneron, if he would just step inside for a moment. This duty discharged, the servant doesn't invite him to wait. "May I—I should like to leave a note for Mr. Webber," Monneron says. The man returns with pencil and paper, then departs without showing him to the writing table in the parlor. Monneron leans awkwardly over a ledge in the entryway to write.

What he wished to say in person—about Don Inigo and Lapérouse and the minister, about Banks and the dipping needles—he cannot safely commit to paper. So he settles for thanking Webber—for the painting, for his hospitality, his time, knowledge, friendship. "I will think of you often on the voyage," he writes in French (English would take too long), "especially when we begin trading with natives." Then he places five guinea coins on the sheet and folds it up as securely as he can. The coins slide around inside, clinking with metallic vulgarity, but it's the best he can do. He's a little relieved, after all, not to have seen Webber again in person.

Back at Mrs. Towe's, he unwraps the portrait and looks at it by the late afternoon light. Webber has filled in the scenery around Monneron, who is now standing on a tropical shore. Palm trees and native huts grace the beach while mountains, ocean, and cloud-dappled sky fill out the background. His facial expression is also altered—or does it simply look different in context? He doesn't look anxious and lost now so much as surprised and curious. The painting is like a wish for a successful expedition: the young explorer standing amazed in a new place. On the right side, partly blocked by his own figure, Monneron can make out the image of a ship anchored offshore, a ship flying a white flag with three fleurs-de-lis. *So he did know*, Monneron thinks. He blinks back his regret as he rewraps the painting.

He can never sleep when he has to be up before dawn. He spends a few hours wondering if the stain above his head has grown, then gets up. By four o'clock, when Mrs. Towe knocks on his door, he's already dressed. The journey proceeds with clockwork precision: The stagecoach departs on time from the Golden Cross. They stop in Rochester for dinner, spend the night in Canterbury, reach Dover Saturday morning. He takes possession of his many purchases from the storehouse at the dock, pays the fees, watches everything stowed safely aboard the French mail boat, then takes his place on deck just as the right tide and a favorable wind arrive to speed the packet across the Channel.

In the past he's delighted in watching the approach of home. But today he keeps looking back at the receding white cliffs, fighting the sensation that he's left something undone. When England disappears in a veil of mist, the French coast comes at him too quickly, and he's astonished to find himself staggering on deck, dizzy and sick. A kindly crewman takes him below, murmuring that it's almost over, sir, some people are more sensitive than others, and Monneron cannot, dare not, open his mouth to put the man in his place, to tell him he's a naval officer, that he's about to circumnavigate the world, that he's never been seasick in his life.

TWO

LAMANON AT SEA

Tenerife, August 1785

It is the afternoon of August 26, 1785, and Jean-Honoré-Robert de Paul, Chevalier de Lamanon, has just returned to the *Boussole*, exhilarated and exhausted after a successful ascent of the Peak of Tenerife. Lamanon has two years, three months, and fifteen days left to live. He does not know this, of course. He has no inkling of what is to come: an uncharted cove in Samoa, an ill-conceived watering party, the misunderstanding over beads, stones overpowering muskets. Right now it is just three weeks into the voyage. The *Boussole* and her sister ship, the *Astrolabe*, are lying at anchor in the port of Tenerife. In two days the expedition will set sail across the Atlantic, away from the Old World and toward they know not what for certain. At the moment, however, Lamanon's chief concern is the safe retrieval of his supplies and equipment, which two crewmen are hauling up the side with altogether too much dispatch. The same two men just brought him up in the bosun's chair, and if their cheerful mis-handling of his person is any indication—

"Do be careful," Lamanon cries. "There's a Fortin barometer there, a gift from Monsieur de Lavoisier himself! Not to mention . . ." And then he goes on to mention the tripod and theodolite and glass sample bottles and his notebooks—oh, the loss to science if they should be dropped in the sea!

The crewmen do not know who Lavoisier is or why his barometer is so special, but they have safely delivered such objects before, to say nothing

of frightened livestock and sick passengers, or water barrels and carron-
ades that might kill a man if mishandled. "Your things, *Chevalier*," they say
with exaggerated flourish, placing everything on the deck.

Lamanon takes no notice of their flippancy. He likes to be called "chevalier." He is thirty-two but looks fifteen years older. He has the longest
official title of anyone on the expedition: Physicist, Geologist, Botanist,
and Meteorologist. "Four men of science for the price of one!" he is wont
to say, unaware that the comment does not endear him to his shipmates.

He walks with labored steps toward the companionway. Every part of
him aches with the effort of three days of climbing followed by two days
descending. He can look across to the island and see the mountain that
required so much of him. It looks so near, so gently sloped, so brown and
barren. It was none of these things. He would like to tell someone about
it—about the surprising ruggedness of the trail, the blue lizard he spotted
halfway up, and the clusters of violets and daisies he found at the summit, right next to a patch of snow. And most of all, the important scientific tasks he was able to carry out on the excursion. "I was just there!" he
says aloud, pointing at the peak. But no one is looking his way; they are
all busy with shipboard duties. No matter. He will have ample time to
record all of his observations tomorrow. Right now he wants nothing more
than to retire to his cabin and indulge in some reflective and self-satisfied
languor.

This is not to be, however, for here is the captain, Monsieur de
Lapérouse, informing him that a boat will be leaving the *Boussole* at five
o'clock, bearing letters for France. There will be no other opportunity to
send letters before they set sail, the captain adds; in fact, it may be three
months before they can send letters again. If Monsieur de Lamanon has
any letters to write, the time to do so is now.

Lamanon is displeased; this does not suit him at all. Not that he isn't
eager to depart. He cannot wait to see a place and a people untouched by
Europeans and their pernicious influence. Tenerife, for all it has been a
diverting and profitable port of call, is just another outpost of Spain, its
native people and culture and innocence erased. But writing a good letter
takes time, and naturally, he has several to complete ("*If* Monsieur de
Lamanon has any letters to write"? What an idea—so typical of the low
regard in which the expedition's savants are held!). They are not leaving

till the day after tomorrow. Why is *this afternoon* the last opportunity to send letters?

"Because I say so," Lapérouse tells Lamanon. A most peremptory and unsatisfactory reply, but this appears to be one of the many prerogatives of command. After three weeks at sea, Lamanon is learning that his preferences count for very little. He might not mind this so much if he could feel that logic and good sense prevailed on board. They do not. But there is nothing to be done, so he shrugs and makes his way down the companionway. He winces with every step, shins aching. Ducking his head to enter his room, he curses the poor light and bends over the slab of wood that passes for his work table. He assembles inkstand, paper, candle, sealing wax, and seal; they vie for space with one another and with the specimen jars, notebooks, and rocks that clutter the surface. Then there is Lamanon himself, not a small person (though he will steadily lose weight during the time left to him), with hands and elbows that must perforce be placed somewhere among these objects.

One of the items he must clear from the table is a small bag of white beans. Ah, yes, he thinks. He must not forget the beans. The beans are an achievement. In fact, his first letter ought to be the one that accompanies this bag back to France. The thought rallies him, and he picks up his quill to begin. Easily nettled, but almost as easily cheered. That is our Lamanon.

The letter is for the minister of marine, the bewigged and bemedaled Marshal de Castries. Lamanon writes to beg a favor of the minister, but it is the sort of favor calculated to impress more than impose. He asks the minister to send a bag of white beans, enclosed herewith, to his hometown of Salon-de-Provence. He reminds the minister that he, Lamanon, had been mayor of Salon-de-Provence before the expedition. (He does not mention that he had been so unsuited to the post that there was almost no complaint when he announced he was leaving after only four months in office.) Beans, he goes on to explain, are vital to the well-being of the peasants of lower Provence. The peasants satisfy their hunger with bean salads, which they carry with them into the fields. The beans not only strengthen them for their labors, but counteract the inebriating effects of the strong local wine, which they also tend to carry about with them.

In recent years, however, the bean crops of Provence have fallen prey to an infestation of rust, a problem he attributes to the "dry fog" of the summer of 1783. (This persistent haze, caused by a volcanic eruption in Iceland, had so darkened the daytime sky that for a few days Lamanon had been able to look at the sun through a telescope without a filtering lens. He does not clutter his letter with this detail, of course, but he does linger for a moment with the memory, feeling some nostalgia for that strange time.) At any rate, the fog and the resulting rust have rendered Provençal beans scarce and expensive. And no, he writes, anticipating an objection, potatoes are *not* a good substitute. Potatoes are bland. The peasants are not fond of potatoes. Potatoes do not go well with the local wine. "But I have had the good fortune to discover an excellent white bean in Tenerife," Lamanon writes. "With the introduction of this variety, it is hoped we may revive the cultivation of beans in southern France."

The ringing of the ship's bell reminds Lamanon that the afternoon is waning, although exactly how far gone it is he cannot tell. He is not yet used to naval timekeeping, to counting how many times the bell is struck or to listening for the helmsman's call. It amazes him, the way the common seamen can sleep through any bell except the one that announces their watch or summons them to dinner. His own pocket watch stopped working within days of leaving Brest, and he has not been sure of the time since. Now, wondering if it is two o'clock or three, or, God forbid, *four*, he hurries through the rest of his missive, describing briefly—*too* briefly—his just-completed trip to the peak. He concludes by assuring the minister of everyone's health and happiness. "We are as one big family," he writes, then remembering the captain's "Because I say so," adds: "Monsieur de Lapérouse is like our father." He likes this sentiment, and will repeat it in each of the letters that follow. He signs off in his usual fashion— "Chev^er de Lamanon"—and reaches for a fresh sheet of paper.

Alas, poor Lamanon! He does not know that the Marshal de Castries, minister of marine, will regard this letter with bemusement. Why, he will wonder, has Lapérouse's naturalist written such a long letter to him, a letter that sounds like a report to the provincial *intendant* or even the Academy of Sciences? And what is all this about a "dry fog"? The minister will not remember any such fog, although he should. Gray and malodorous and leaving a trail of fine ash in its wake, it had greatly aggravated his sensitive lungs through that unusually warm summer. What he *will* remember is meeting Lamanon, once, right before the expedition left, and how very loquacious the naturalist was. At the time, the minister had attributed it to a younger man's understandable excitement on being introduced to important people in Versailles. Now he will suspect that Lamanon is one of those people who will talk (or write) forever if you let them. The minister will especially puzzle over this passage on the culinary habits of Provençal peasants. What is it to him if peasants turn up their noses at potatoes, or need beans with which to balance their liberal consumption of wine? And this claim Lamanon makes, that the wine, thus paired, does not cause drunkenness: it is preposterous.

The minister does not know that Lamanon loves beans, that he has always loved beans. Lamanon's mother, who implored him not to leave on the expedition and whose heart will break when she hears about the uncharted cove and the troublesome beads, can attest to this. Even as a child, Robert was a great favorite with their cook, as he preferred the simple bean dishes she made for her own family to the more complicated dishes she prepared for the Lamanons. There was also their gardener, Jerôme, whom the young Robert liked to follow about the property. Jerôme knew a great deal about plants and insects and rocks and weather, and many afternoons he would take Master Robert along when he went to meet his own brothers and cousins out in the fields or orchards. The farmhands could always be counted on to share a bean salad in the shade of the olive grove, and they also thought it good fun to ply the future chevalier with wine. The minister does not know any of this, of course. Indeed, Lamanon's mother does not know all of this either.

And what *of* these beans from Tenerife? They are, simply put, the best beans Lamanon has ever tasted. Fat and meaty, they keep their shape when cooked and provide just a hint of resistance when bitten into. Redolent of butter and chestnuts, they are so flavorful they scarcely need any seasoning. After eating them one night at an inn in the port city of Santa Cruz de Tenerife, Lamanon pestered the innkeeper, and then the inkeeper's wife, and then the man at the market, until he was standing on a hillside verdant with vining legumes, persuading himself that the climate at that altitude was comparable to the climate in Provence, and then persuading the farmer he was with to part with a sack of beans for planting. This sack he is now preparing to send to the Marshal de Castries.

The minister is busy. He is trying to reform the French Navy during a time of shrinking resources and escalating court intrigue. He will pass Lamanon's letter and the sack to an underling, who in turn will pass the letter and beans to someone else. By the time the beans reach Salon-de-Provence, many months will have passed. It will be past planting season for beans. The man in the mayor's office who opens the sack will wrinkle his nose at the ammoniac smell that wafts out. He will inform the mayor that Monsieur de Lamanon has sent them a sack of moldy beans from Tenerife by way of the naval office in Paris. "What shall I do with it, sir?" he will ask.

"Get rid of it," the mayor will say. "I can smell it from here."

The mayor's name is Auguste de Paul de Lamanon. He is tall like his younger brother, Robert, but thin where Robert tends to fat, and bald where Robert tends to hair. The arrival of the moldy beans will vex him extremely. First, he does not share his brother's alarm over the state of Provençal bean production. Second, why did Robert not send *all* the beans directly to Salon-de-Provence by way of Marseilles? Several months earlier, a letter from Robert arrived for their mother, a letter that contained some beans that their mother and Jerôme have planted against a south-facing stone wall outside of the kitchen. Something small and green is now struggling there; his mother weeps every time she looks at it. Auguste has had to remain behind in Salon-de-Provence in order to comfort her. He also felt honor-bound to finish out his brother's term as mayor. Most of the time Auguste does not mind. But sometimes he remembers his resentment. This will be one of those times.

Meanwhile, back on the *Boussole*, on that warm August afternoon, Lamanon is writing a second letter, this one to the Marquis de Condorcet, the famous mathematician, philosopher, and soon-to-be revolutionary leader, who is, moreover, permanent secretary to the Academy of Sciences. Condorcet was the first to recommend Lamanon for the expedition, though it must be acknowledged that Lamanon asked him for the recommendation, and that Condorcet agreed to the request with some reluctance. It is not that Condorcet dislikes Lamanon; on the contrary, he is fond of the younger man and believes him to be a gifted natural philosopher. But appreciating the abilities of a fellow savant is different from believing that same man to be suited to life at sea. Who among us does not have the odd friend whose virtues we admire, but whom we do not wish to impose on others? Lamanon has no idea when he is giving offense and too little regard for authority. A few years ago, for instance, he began an argument with Buffon over the origin of fossils. Surely it was enough to publish his controversial ideas in the *Journal de physique*—that is what journals are for, after all. But what was he thinking, showing up at the salon of Madame Necker right afterward, knowing Buffon would be there, then heading straight for the old man and asking, "My dear Count, what did you make of my new piece in the *Journal*?"

Madame Necker, pale, powdered, and dressed in ivory, had turned to Condorcet and said, "Has your friend come simply to provoke my most distinguished guest into losing his temper?"

"No, madame," Condorcet replied. "He suffers only from an excess of enthusiasm."

Condorcet remembered this, and other instances like it, when Lamanon asked him to put his name forward for the Lapérouse expedition. But put him forward he did, because it is difficult to refuse a man who has eaten so much at one's table. Then it irked him—irked him exceedingly— to discover that Lamanon had also solicited a recommendation from the Duke de La Rochefoucauld, president of the academy and friend of Benjamin Franklin. It suggested, uncomfortably, that for all his apparent lack of social acumen, Lamanon had somehow sensed the halfheartedness of his friend's support. But worse, it suggested that Condorcet's influence in these matters might not be as great as he imagined it to be.

Perhaps this explains why Lamanon's letters will receive such scant attention from Condorcet when they arrive. Not only this letter from Tenerife, but the others—one from Santa Catarina Island in three months' time and another, much longer, written two years hence, from Macao— will elicit a slight frown, an impatient perusal, then consignment to a large pile of documents that the mathematician intends, one day soon, to go through with more care.

Condorcet's wife, Sophie, a beautiful and intelligent woman whose love for him will amaze him until the day he dies, will ask, "What news from the great expedition, Nicolas?"

Condorcet will reply, "Oh, it is all barometric readings and magnetic intensities mixed up with Lamanon's bombast."

"Just the thing to be read at the next meeting of the academy."

Condorcet will snort. "I would not dream of denying Lamanon that pleasure when he returns," he will say. And so Lamanon's letters and reports will remain on Condorcet's desk, read but not shared, and there they will remain until the Revolution upends everything, even mathematicians and their piles of paper.

This is all most unfortunate, as Condorcet's neglect will forever diminish Lamanon's scientific legacy. It is also too bad because Lamanon would be shocked to learn there might be cause for reserve between them. On the contrary, it pleases him to imagine Condorcet reading his letter. He can see the great man's distinctive dark eyebrows relaxing with delight when he sees who the letter is from, then contracting again with serious intent as he unfolds the pages and begins to read. Lamanon smiles as he leans over to conclude the letter: "We are like a big family on board, with Monsieur de Lapérouse as our father," he repeats. Then he folds the letter and affixes his seal to the back—he loves this part, the smell of the molten wax and its satisfying displacement under the weight of the seal—and moves on to write a very similar letter to the Count de Buffon. Yes, the same Buffon he provoked, first, with his disputatious paleontological *mémoire*, and then with his bad manners at Madame Necker's. But Lamanon does not worry if the count is still displeased, if, indeed, he ever noticed the count's displeasure at all; nor does he wonder if his letter will be welcome. He has an irrepressible faith in his own value as a man of science. And it is not always misplaced. Let us be clear about that. Lamanon will never know it, of course, but Buffon, still writing in his late seventies, will, in his monumental *Histoire naturelle*, refer to findings reported in this very letter from Tenerife.

As to the findings themselves, Condorcet is right that they have mostly to do with barometric readings and magnetic intensities. For Lamanon does not write to Condorcet and Buffon about beans. No. To these stalwarts of the French Enlightenment he writes about his ascent of the Peak of Tenerife. He and eleven other members of the expedition made the trip. It was the eve of the feast of St. Louis when they reached the top, where they drank to the king's health. "The highest elevation at which the feast day has ever been celebrated," he writes. He goes on to say that he and his friend Father Mongez, the *Boussole*'s chaplain and assistant naturalist, then settled down to serious scientific endeavor, collecting rocks, measuring air pressure with one barometer, then another, taking compass readings, noting the degree of magnetic inclination, counting their own pulses, and sniffing ammonia to see if it retained its strength at altitude. He is particularly pleased to report a new, barometrically derived measurement for the peak's height: 1,950 *toises*. He hopes this will be useful, as there has been little agreement on this subject among visitors to the island.

He does not mention that ten of his colleagues left the peak as soon as they had toasted the king, bothered by the sulfurous fumes that swirled about the mountaintop. Or that at one point he sniffed the ammonia to keep from passing out. Nor does he mention that barometric determinations of altitude are notoriously unreliable. Presumably his correspondents know the method's limitations and do not need to be reminded. He also does not write about how he and Mongez tried— and failed—to calculate the height of the mountain trigonometrically, a calculation that could have verified the barometric result. It was a discouraging setback. They had the views they needed—every landmark clear— and had just begun to set up the surveying equipment, when the hired guides refused to remain any longer on the mountain. Their mules were out of food and water, they said, and no amount of money would induce them to stay. So Lamanon and Mongez were obliged to pack up their tools and descend.

The marquis and the count will not hear about these troubles. Nor will they learn about Lamanon's altercation with Monsieur de Lapérouse right before the outing. How was Lamanon to know that the expedition would not cover the cost? He was taken aback when the commander informed him of this, especially as it was *one half hour* before the climbing party was scheduled to depart. Everything was in readiness—climbers assembled, guides present, mules packed with equipment, supplies, water, wine, bread, bean salad. A line from *Candide* sprang to Lamanon's mind at Lapérouse's announcement: "My friend," he wanted to say, quoting Pangloss, "this is not right at all. You go against the universal reason, and your timing is very bad!" But he saw the commander's round, unliterary face, blotchy with impatience, and thought better of it. "Sir, we were about to leave," he said instead.

"I am sorry for that," Lapérouse said, though he did not look very sorry. "If only you had informed me of your plans in advance, Monsieur de Lamanon."

Lamanon sniffed. "I understood this to be a voyage of *scientific exploration.*"

Lapérouse raised his eyebrows and asked what part of their scientific mission required six guides, twenty-five mules, and enough food and supplies for twenty people. "This could come to a hundred *louis,*" he said, and when Lamanon began to justify the expense (which, truth to tell, was somewhat *more* than that estimate), Lapérouse said, with quiet adamancy, "Monsieur de Lamanon, this island has been colonized for centuries, its every part mapped and explored. This excursion is an indulgence. You may not charge it to the king's expense."

Lamanon shrugged. "Very well," he said. "I'll sell my own account of the trip when we return to France, and reimburse myself from the proceeds."

At this, the other members of the climbing party, who had been staring at the ground or up at the sky during the uncomfortable exchange, came suddenly to attention. It was customary, and at times a contractual obligation, for members of such expeditions to delay publishing their own accounts of a voyage until after the commander had published *his* "official" account, a process that could take years. Lamanon's retort was very like a direct challenge to the commander's authority.

Lapérouse was not one to bristle over fine points of publishing protocol, however. He burst out laughing. "You won't be the first author ruined by a book," he said.

Thus forced to pay for the outing himself, Lamanon waved away two of the guides and half the mules. The rigors and delights of the ascent soon put the unpleasantness with the commander out of Lamanon's mind, although he was reminded of it three days later, when the guides insisted on leaving. The discomforts of the return trip did not afford Lamanon enough mental freedom to reflect that he was the one who had summarily dismissed the very mules carrying the extra food and water. As he and Mongez huffed their way down the mountain, he blamed Lapérouse for their misery. "My dear Mongez," he said at one point, "I could wish for a commander more sympathetic to the demands of science." Mongez panted back in reply, and they proceeded in silence, for it had grown hot and their water flasks were empty.

But in this, as in everything, Lamanon was not vexed for long. By the time he is back in his cabin on the *Boussole*, caught up in the demands of scientific correspondence, he has all but forgotten the dressing-down he received from Monsieur de Lapérouse, a dressing-down that would have mortified any other member of the expedition. He is immune to mortification, our Lamanon. He is happy to make his report and repeat the sentiment about the expedition being a happy family with Lapérouse as their head. He does not know that at this very moment, the "father" in question is scrawling a note to his own friend, the Count de Fleurieu, complaining about Lamanon. "As ignorant as a Capuchin!" Lapérouse writes. He regrets very much that one of their astronomers has been laid so low by seasickness that he is being sent home from Tenerife. "Oh, that it were Lamanon instead!" he says.

Lapérouse's frustration with him is understandable, but can we blame Lamanon for going through with his costly trip to the peak? Indulgent it may have been, but it was also a kind of test for the more difficult work ahead, and addressed many questions: What equipment does he need for excursions off the ship? How quickly can he pack? Do his knees hold up under the rigors of walking long distances over difficult terrain? Can he accurately detect the oscillations of a compass needle? How about the inclinations, declinations, and other "-ations" he is charged with recording? Can he take proper readings from a barometer? And most important: Which of the two barometers in his possession works better?

The matter of the barometers is not simply an academic question for Lamanon. His future reputation may stand or fall by his barometrical work on the expedition. Over the years, a number of scientists, including Newton and Laplace, have hypothesized the existence of atmospheric or barometric "tides" that respond to the same gravitational forces that create our oceanic tides. The academy has asked Lamanon to help settle this question by noting variations in barometric pressure over the course of twenty-four-hour periods. This work is best done at the equator, where the amplitude of any such variations, should they exist, is believed to be greatest. At Tenerife, the expedition is still twenty-eight degrees north of and a one-month sail from the equator. But Lamanon does not want to fail in the execution of his duties for lack of practice, and during the climb to the peak, he consulted his barometers as often as possible.

Nor does he wish to fail for having used the *wrong* barometer. He has two and has been taking readings from them every day since leaving Brest. To his great frustration, there is no agreement between them, ever, when they are at sea. An unhappy suspicion has formed in his mind that the English barometer is superior to the French one. The English instrument was purchased in London by the expedition's chief engineer, Paul de Monneron, a man more comfortable with objects than ideas, but competent enough for all that. The French barometer was made by Fortin and procured for the expedition by Monsieur de Lavoisier, the famous chemist. Lamanon knows he should rely on whichever barometer works best at sea, for it is extremely unlikely that they will be anywhere near land when they cross the line. He knows that the English barometer, made by Nairne, is similar to one used by Captain Cook, and that if it served Cook, it ought to serve him. But he has a prejudice in favor of Lavoisier's barometer, a prejudice that is entirely romantic.

He had gone in person to Lavoisier's residence to pick up the barometer. It was early May, about three months before the expedition left, and raining very hard. Lavoisier was not at home, but Madame de Lavoisier allowed him to wait in the laboratory while she herself sat nearby, quietly working at her own table. She wore a simple white dress, and her facial features were more pleasing than beautiful, but this effect of serenity was challenged by a mane of wildly curly hair that bounced with every movement she made and framed her head like an unruly helmet. Longer strands of hair fell over her shoulders and down her back, and Lamanon saw that she was actually sitting on the longest locks. Could she not feel that as she leaned over her work, he wondered, the pull at her scalp of hair pinned beneath her buttocks? But then the great chemist himself strode in, and before he noticed Lamanon, before his wife could warn him they had a visitor, he said, "Marie-Anne, come out in the garden with me. I want to see you soaked with rain." It was impossible to remain serious after that. The three of them gathered around the carrying case of the barometer and tittered while they examined the instrument—first Madame de Lavoisier, turning away to hide her mirth, then her husband, and finally Lamanon, all struck by the hilarity of the long, mercury-filled glass tube, snug in its velvet-lined cavity.

Lamanon has not stopped thinking of the Lavoisiers since. He dreams of them sometimes, of himself with them, of the three of them together, of the effect of rain on that white dress and the outrageous curls. But they are not just the subject of a lonely savant's fantasies. Antoine and Marie-Anne de Lavoisier held out for Lamanon the prospect of something he had not even known he was missing till that day in May—not so much marriage between equals, although that did seem true of them, or even marriage based on love, although that was obviously the case as well, but the happy union of science and humanity within an individual, and the joy that was possible when one person, so self-integrated, encountered another such person.

So he is loath to abandon the barometer that has for him such pleasurable associations. Yet now that he has taken both barometers to the peak and back, the verdict is clear. Lavoisier's barometer is fine for work on land, but will never do at sea. He is sorry, but also glad that he has been able to make such good use of the barometer at Tenerife. He feels he has discharged a debt of gratitude to the barometer, to its maker, to the generous chemist who obtained it for him, and to the chemist's wife who blushed and laughed when she saw it. It can now be left safely and without obligation in its case, where it will remain until they land someplace where an observatory can be established. Lamanon would like to write to the Lavoisiers now, to tell them how well the barometer performed in Tenerife, to remind them of that afternoon in May. But the ship's bell has rung at least twice since he began. He has time for just one short letter, and it will be to his mother.

What if, some two years, three months, and fifteen days after this afternoon of letter writing, instead of joining the men who leave the ships to collect water and stretch their legs at an unknown cove in Samoa, Lamanon were to remain safely aboard the *Boussole*? And what if, instead of foundering in a storm in the Solomon Islands the following spring, the *Boussole*, at least, were to make it back to France?

Two surmises come to mind: first, regarding Lamanon's scientific legacy, and second, suggesting a different sort of ending for him. As for his legacy, all that messing about with barometers and compasses during the voyage will yield two discoveries that properly belong to him. For the suppositions of Newton and Laplace were correct: there *are* atmospheric tides. And Lamanon, working round the clock with the English barometer every time the expedition crosses the equator (this will happen three times), will be the first to observe its twelve-hour cycles. Then there are his meticulous compass readings, which will lead to another discovery, this one establishing a correlation between magnetic intensity and latitude (intensity increasing with latitude, as one moves away from the equator and toward the poles). He will write up his findings with great care and send them to Condorcet, and we have already followed their fate there.

But now, imagine Lamanon's triumphant return to France. The Academy of Sciences will invite him to join their august body, of course. He will readily accept, and there will be ample time, before the National Convention abolishes all of the academies, for Lamanon to make several personal appearances to discuss his part in the great Lapérouse voyage. There will be time too, amid the social and political upheavals, to see to the formal publication of his own journals and letters. Will he do so ahead of Lapérouse, without the approval of the ministry, as he threatened to do at Tenerife? Probably. The revolutionary mood that greets him on his return will encourage the antiauthoritarian streak we have already seen in him. Indeed, when his friend Mongez remonstrates with him about this, and asks if Lamanon does not owe Lapérouse some consideration in this matter, Lamanon will retort with a quote from Rousseau: "My dear Mongez," he will say, "the family is the most ancient of societies, and the only one that is natural. But even there the children remain attached to the father only so long as they need him for their preservation."

The book will not be the financial success Lamanon hopes; but then, books rarely are. His scientific legacy, however, will be secure. Because the first publication on barometric tides will not now be authored by some Englishman called Horsburgh in 1805. Nor will it be the great Prussian naturalist and explorer, Alexander von Humboldt, a man with more than enough distinctions already, who first publishes the law of magnetic intensity and latitudes. It will be Lamanon, publishing in 1789 or '90 or '91. It will be Lamanon, no longer the unfortunate naturalist from the Lapérouse expedition killed by natives in Samoa.

Which brings us to our second surmise: a different death. Consider what happens to Lamanon's associates. Buffon will have died of natural causes in 1788, at the advanced age of eighty, thereby missing alike the thrills and the perils of revolution. By 1790, Madame Necker and her husband will flee to their native Switzerland. The Marshal de Castries, recipient of Lamanon's beans, his wigs and medals grown suspect, will join them shortly thereafter. The rest remain in Paris, caught up in the grand project of rebuilding society. But one by one they too will fall under suspicion. The Duke de La Rochefoucauld, Lamanon supporter and president of the academy, will be assassinated in Gisors in September of 1792. A year and a half later, it will be Condorcet, on the run from a trumped-up charge of treason but arrested in Clamart, those distinctive eyebrows giving him away. He will be found dead in his prison cell two days later, his body and the cause of death subsequently lost to a mass grave. And then it will be Lavoisier himself, tried, convicted, and guillotined on May 8, 1794—nine years after Lamanon's visit to pick up the barometer.

What would Lamanon make of such a future? It is tempting to imagine him asking Lavoisier's widow to marry him. But quite apart from the likelihood that she would refuse him (for she will remember that rainy afternoon only as an occasion when her dear Antoine embarrassed her in front of a guest whose name and purpose she cannot recall), there is the greater likelihood that Lamanon himself will end up branded an enemy of the republic. He might return to Salon-de-Provence to flee the unrest, but he will not be safe there. His brother, Auguste, will be arrested in 1793 and languish in prison for over a year before finally being released. Robert, with his closer association with the likes of Condorcet and Lavoisier, is likely to fare worse. Which leaves us to meditate on a question: Which is worse—violent death at the hands of natives whose language and anger you do not understand, or violent death at the hands of fellow citizens whose language and anger you thought you shared?

Lamanon's letter to his mother is brief and affectionate. He tells her that he is healthy, that he has friends, that his work is going well, that he thinks of her often, that he will write again from South America, that he will come home to her. He repeats that he and his shipmates are one big family, that Monsieur de Lapérouse is like their father. She will like that. She has felt, since the death of her husband ten years earlier, that her younger child has lost his bearings. He has reverted to his boyhood ways, wandering about collecting things; only now he wanders so very far and for so very long. It will cheer her to know there is a father figure on board, someone whose responsibility it is to steer her son homeward.

Lamanon decides to send her some of the white beans. "Have Jerôme plant them against the south-facing wall in the potager," he writes. "They are delicious. Think of me when you eat them." He signs the letter "Robert," opens the sack meant for the new mayor by way of the minister of marine, and counts out twenty beans. They make a dry, scattering sound as he drops them onto the paper.

His letters complete, he makes his way back up on deck (going up not nearly as painful as coming down) and delivers them—and the beans— to the officer in charge. Then he goes to the rail and gazes south through his spyglass. He is looking for the Tropic of Cancer. Some of the seamen, put off by his airs and amused by his gullibility, have told him the tropic is visible from here. "Like a green line straight across the sea, sir," they tell him. "It's a sight a scientifical gentleman such as yourself ought not miss." Lapérouse witnesses this from the quarterdeck and is tempted to disabuse him of the notion. He does not like to see his chief naturalist made a fool of. But he is still resentful about Lamanon's insolence over the excursion to the peak, so he leaves him be.

We do not have that luxury, but we will allow a pause. A pause to re-gard a man at the point of greatest optimism about the future, before the forces of history overwhelm him. A man who feels himself to be the most fortunate of men. A man who is exactly where he wishes to be. How many of us can say that, even once in our lives? Lamanon looks out for the green line of the tropic and thinks about the countryside near his home in France. How verdant the rows of healthy bean vines! How marvelous the possibil-ities of science wed to humanity!

THREE

CONCEPCIÓN

Concepción, Chile, February–March 1786

How strange that the town was not there.

Their maps, freshly minted by the Office of Charts, had guided them safely around the cape, past the eastern side of Quiriquine Island, and into Concepción Bay. They should have been in plain sight of the town of Concepción, a settlement more than two hundred years old, home to ten thousand people. A place they were counting on for fresh food, help with badly needed repairs, the company of other Europeans. They had consulted Frézier's 1712 drawing of the view from the bay, in which one could make out the whole breadth of the town and the spires of eight churches. Where had it all gone?

Lapérouse lowered his glass. He took in the expanse of shoreline before him, looking for the fort, the cathedral bell tower, some sign of habitation, a wisp of smoke, anything. Five of his officers were doing the same—scanning the coastline with puzzled faces, raising and lowering their own telescopes. Lapérouse handed his glass to his brother-in-law, Frédéric.

"See for yourself, Monsieur Broudou."

After a moment: "There's nothing there, sir."

"Indeed, there is not."

A voyage of exploration always entailed surprises, of course—interesting ones, like the discovery of new places and specimens and peoples, and vexing ones, like finding that an expensive barrel of wine in the hold had spoiled, or learning, too late, that the chief naturalist on board was an insufferable pedant. But this—the disappearance of an old Spanish town on the coast of Chile, a place that had been visited and mapped and described by other Frenchmen earlier in the century—was so entirely unexpected that it made one question the most basic verities, like whether or not one knew how to read a map or ply a sextant.

Lapérouse turned to look at their sister ship, the *Astrolabe*. Among the officers crowded at the port-side rail of her quarterdeck, he could make out his friend, Paul-Antoine-Marie Fleuriot de Langle, the captain of the ship. The peculiar way Langle had of moving, graceful and fussy at the same time, head held straight, hands never still, stood out from the other men even at this distance. Lapérouse considered shouting over to him to see what he made of the missing town, but no, better not to. His bewilderment, once expressed, might sow real consternation among the men.

"What has become of our port of call?" he heard, and turned to find Lamanon, the exasperating naturalist himself, climbing heavily up toward the quarterdeck.

Lapérouse made his way to the top of the stairs. "Monsieur de Lamanon."

"Concepción should be right *there*," Lamanon said, pointing to the southeast corner of the bay.

How did he know? He had not been included in any discussions about navigation—he had been specifically *excluded* from them, in fact. But of course: Lamanon probably had his own set of Frézier's *Voyage to the South-Sea, and Along the Coasts of Chili and Peru*. The man had insisted on bringing so many books that the carpenters had had to rebuild his cabin to accommodate them.

"We're still fixing our location, Monsieur de Lamanon," Lapérouse said.

"Perhaps we have stumbled upon the Roanoke of the Spanish empire, Commander."

"Doubtful."

"Maybe the Araucanians have finally prevailed over their invaders," Lamanon went on. "They are legendary for their long resistance to the Spaniards."

Lapérouse inclined his head in acknowledgment, glad he had skimmed enough of Frézier to recognize the name of the local Indians, and determined to avoid an argument. Lamanon was a committed Rousseauist. He had not yet met any natives, but that did not discourage him from holding forth on their superiority over civilized men. Lapérouse was tired of arguing about it.

An officer called from the rail: "Two small boats approaching, sir."

Lapérouse took his glass back from Frédéric. "Monsieur Broudou," he said, "please escort Monsieur de Lamanon back to the main deck."

Ten minutes later the boats were alongside. Lapérouse's officers pointed to where the town was supposed to be. "Concepción?" they asked.

The men in the boats—two in one and three in the other, all of them darker than the average Spaniard but not quite Indian in appearance—nodded. "*Sí.*"

"Where is Concepción?" the Frenchmen shouted down.

"*Sí,*" the men repeated, then proceeded with a stream of Spanish none of them understood, accompanied by dramatic but no less incomprehensible gestures.

"*Français?*"

"*Sí!*"

"Oh, for God's sake," Lapérouse cried. "Monsieur Broudou, find someone on board who speaks Spanish."

Frédéric grimaced apologetically when he returned, as behind him Lamanon made his labored and triumphant way up the steps.

The men were pilots, and they had been on the lookout for the French ships for the past month, ever since receiving official notice of the expedition from a visiting Spanish ship. As for Concepción—*old* Concepción, they called it—it had been gone these thirty-five years, destroyed by an earthquake and the enormous wave that followed. The *new* Concepción was inland, they explained, three leagues away, on the banks of the Bío-Bío River. Once they guided the French ships to safe anchorages in the southwest corner of the bay, they would send word to the governor. To the *acting* governor, actually, one Señor Quexada. The *real* governor, Brigadier General Ambrosio O'Higgins, was away subduing the Indians. But Señor Quexada would of course send word to Governor O'Higgins, who in all likelihood would return once he learned of the Frenchmen's arrival. For everyone in town was looking forward to their visit.

Lapérouse hardly knew whether to credit this story, told by all five men speaking at once while Lamanon gamely tried to interpret, but he allowed the pilots to guide them to a cove deep in the bay and ordered both ships to drop anchor. Through his glass he watched as the pilots landed their boats at a small village on the shore—it was called Talcahuano, according to Lamanon—then followed a figure as he rode off on horseback and disappeared into the hills behind the village.

"Is it really possible that a town of ten thousand people disappeared, and that a generation later, the best cartographers in France knew nothing about it?" Lapérouse asked.

Langle raised an eyebrow, considering. He had rowed over from the *Astrolabe* after dropping anchor. "The Spanish empire is well known for its secrecy."

"But a missing port is not something one simply hides."

"Perhaps no one outside the empire has visited since Frézier."

Lapérouse put his glass away. "That would explain their apparent excitement over our arrival."

The pilots' account was largely confirmed by Señor Quexada, acting governor of Concepción, who called on the ships the next morning with passable French, official welcome, more baskets of fresh food than could easily be stored on the ships, and a detachment of dragoons who were to camp at Talcahuano and place themselves at Lapérouse's disposal. A man with a mustache so stiff Lapérouse was tempted to tap it just to see if it moved, Quexada fairly beamed with delight at his good fortune to be the one in charge when the Frenchmen turned up. He pressed upon the expedition's officers and naturalists an invitation to town for a reception in their honor. "I hope you will come and stay awhile," he said. "Our best homes will be open to you."

Lapérouse thanked him. "I understand your governor, General O'Higgins, is at the frontier," he added. "Do you think we may yet have the honor of meeting him?"

Quexada's smile sagged a little. "I have sent for him, of course," he said. "He will return as soon as he is able. He is right now finishing a great peace treaty with *los Araucanos*, our Indians."

"We have heard something to that effect," Lapérouse said. He looked across the way and caught Lamanon's eye. Was it the pilots who had characterized O'Higgins's mission as "subduing the Indians," or was it Lamanon? The naturalist looked back at him with an ironic, answering gaze. Lapérouse could predict Lamanon's scornful reaction: "No doubt *peace treaty* is a local euphemism for *violent subjugation*." Lapérouse looked away. This is what happened after seven months at sea. One began to divine—or imagine one could divine—the very thoughts of the other men on board.

Lapérouse agreed to come in three days' time, once the most urgent shipboard tasks and repairs were under way, and he and Langle could decide who among the ships' officers and passengers could be spared for the visit. So it was that Monday afternoon, he, Langle, eight officers, Lapérouse's brother-in-law Frédéric, and all of the savants, engineers, artists, and clergymen, plus servants—twenty-eight men altogether—came ashore, climbed into carriages sent from the town to escort them, and made their way over hot and uncomfortable roads to the new town.

It did not *look* particularly new, Lapérouse thought when they drove through its dusty outskirts and into its even dustier central plaza. It was a wary place, made up of single-story buildings spread out over a wide area north of the Bío-Bío River. The dwellings were drab, their mud brick exteriors already worn by the elements, thin timber beams supporting faded tile roofs. It all wore an air of resignation, as if the inhabitants, knowing that forces deep within the earth could turn them all out at any moment, had stifled any impulse toward civic beauty or attachment.

They were met in the town square by Quexada and a Major Sabatero, a heavyset Spaniard with a red face whose active military service must have been many years and many meals behind him. The major led them to his house, a structure remarkable only for being wider than most of the other homes they saw. Inside, however, it was surprisingly cheerful, with whitewashed walls and ceilings; natural light from an internal courtyard; wooden furniture, old but solid, edges softened with use; family portraits, somewhat primitive in execution, whose bright colors belied the dour expressions of their subjects; and best of all, delicious aromas from an unseen kitchen. The spare, comfortable elegance of the interior put Lapérouse in mind of the Manoir du Gô, his childhood home outside of Albi, in the south of France. An austere stone house from without, it was, within, appointed with old family tables and settees and draperies that his mother professed to hate, but among which he had played wonderful games with his siblings in the years before he left for the naval school in Brest.

"It is humble, this house," Sabatero said in heavily accented but comprehensible French. Lapérouse and his men all hastened to exclaim their delight with the place. "Well, you have been at sea a long time," Sabatero said, laughing. "Any house looks good, yes?"

Five or six servants of uncertain racial extraction came forward, and Sabatero explained that dinner was not for another hour, and that his guests were welcome to make use of the spare bedrooms in the house to rest or tidy up. "My steward, José, will show the two captains to their room," he said, introducing a short, olive-skinned man to Lapérouse and Langle.

The steward bowed, unsmiling, and led Lapérouse, Langle, and their servants, Pierre and François, down the corridor. They passed several rough-hewn arched doorways, rounded one corner, passed more doorways, then turned again, finally stopping at an open door at which José waved them in. It was an immaculate room bright with sunshine and equipped with two of everything—chairs, beds, mirrors, washstands, wash basins, linens. As soon as José shut the door behind them, Lapérouse threw off his jacket and wig and boots, rebuffing Pierre's attempts to help him. He lowered himself onto the nearest bed with a groan, feeling at once relieved and repelled by the sensation of cooler air on damp armpits, head, and feet.

"Are you all right, sir?" Langle asked. He was removing his outer clothing, neatly folding each item and handing it to his servant, François.

"I am no longer accustomed to bumping about in a carriage," Lapérouse replied.

He sat on the bed and watched idly as Pierre and François fussed with their masters' wigs. Pierre was twenty-one and already a skilled captain's servant, while François was just a boy, and an awkward one at that. But one would never guess who was more experienced from the wigs they handled. Lapérouse's wig was in terrible shape, subject as it was to constant ill-treatment by its owner. François scarcely knew what to do with his hands, but it did not matter, as his master's wig—no doubt one of several Langle had brought with him—looked new. "That'll do," Lapérouse finally said, rescuing his wig before Pierre attacked it with another round of expensive powder.

He wanted nothing more than to close his eyes and ask to be wakened for dinner. But here was Langle, sleeves rolled up, bending over a wash basin to rinse his face. It would not do for the commander of the expedition to arrive for dinner unkempt and bleary-eyed. And it would not do at all for Langle, with his patrician bearing and manners and height, to be mistaken for the commander. Lapérouse heaved himself off the bed with a second groan and made his way to the other washstand.

An hour later, José announced them into the dining room: "Jean-François de Galaup, Count de Lapérouse, commander of the French expedition and captain of His Majesty's ship the *Boussole*, and Paul-Antoine-Marie Fleuriot, Viscount de Langle, captain of His Majesty's ship the *Astrolabe*." Or that was what he was supposed to say. He had obviously been taught the French names and phrases by rote that afternoon. Unfortunately, he had not first been taught any French.

Lapérouse looked over at Langle. "Did he just call me 'count'?"

Langle smiled. "It suits you."

Lapérouse shrugged. In truth, he was likely to be awarded the appellation when he completed the voyage, but officially he had no such title. He could hardly correct his hosts, however. Perhaps the Spaniards, unable to imagine a man in command over a viscount unless he was himself of higher rank, had supplied the title to preserve their own sense of social order.

The only lady present was a woman so much younger than Sabatero and coiffed so outlandishly that Lapérouse assumed Sabatero was widowed and the woman an unmarried daughter whose sartorial excess there was no mother to check. "My wife, Eleonora," Sabatero said, and Lapérouse had to stifle his surprise, not only at his mistake, but because of the resemblance to his own wife's name, Éléonore. The young woman curtsied, then sat at the opposite end of the long pine table, flanked by—how had this happened?—the least charming of the Frenchmen present: Lamanon and Frédéric on one side, and a glum naturalist from the *Astrolabe* called Dufresne on the other. Poor woman: accosted by excess of learning and false gallantry to her right, and an aggravated sense of personal suffering on the left. The more amiable Frenchmen present were all seated in a convivial group in the middle of the table. During the meal Lapérouse caught occasional bits of speech from the far end, all of it hyperbole—Dufresne exaggerating the discomforts of the journey, Frédéric exaggerating its dangers and his bravery in the face of them, and Lamanon declaiming—of course—on the splendidness of savages. Lapérouse wondered if Doña Eleonora understood a word of it. He rather hoped she did not.

At his end, Lapérouse sat between his host and Quexada and across from Langle, and enjoyed platefuls of seafood delicacies and glass after glass of surprisingly good local wine. He nodded politely through Sabatero's own version of the 1751 disaster and apologies for O'Higgins. "But it is your voyage we wish to know about," Sabatero said, so Lapérouse obliged him. The expedition just begun, of course, but a great success thus far: happy ships, the finest officers, the ablest crew, the savants both brilliant and personable; the passage out uneventful; rounding Cape Horn not nearly the navigational horror he had been led to believe; his men healthier now than when they left Brest, not one man sick. "We are truly the most fortunate of navigators," Lapérouse concluded. Langle raised his glass in concurrence.

"Not *one man* sick after so long?" Sabatero asked in surprise.

"Not one," Lapérouse repeated.

"Then you are indeed fortunate," Quexada said, raising his own glass.

Lapérouse nodded. It was true—everything he said—and yet he had a misgiving that he was not being sincere, as if he were reciting a prepared statement, or rehearsing a missive for the minister of marine.

After dinner, Sabatero invited his guests to enjoy more wine and refreshment in the courtyard while the dining room was cleared for the ball. "Count," he said—that title again!—"you will allow my wife to show you out?"

Up close, Doña Eleonora looked even younger than she had from the other end of the table. Her clothes and hair both seemed designed to distract the viewer from the real woman underneath. Tight black plaits of hair coiled around her head, giving her height she did not have; the striped silk mantle added width to her shoulders and the billowy skirt to her hips. But the hand she placed in the crook of his arm was tiny and soft, the stockinged calves that peeked out from under the skirt were the thin legs of a girl, and the serious face she turned up to him was round and pink with youth, though not, he observed, happiness. She was not yet twenty, perhaps not even seventeen. Young enough to be his own daughter. She smiled at him, then tipped a Chinese fan she was holding toward a set of open doors.

"A wonderful meal, Doña Eleonora," he said. Now he would learn if she spoke French.

"Thank you."

Anyone could say "thank you," of course. They stepped into a courtyard that looked like a stage, with its carefully placed plants and even more carefully placed servants. The lurid sunset sky looked unreal, as if painted in orange and red for the occasion. "I hope Monsieur de Lamanon didn't overwhelm you with his erudition," he ventured.

"Not at all. I found him very interesting."

"I'm glad to hear it," Lapérouse said. "And I hope Monsieur Dufresne did not oppress your spirits—he can be gloomy sometimes."

She nodded. "Some men are not so suited to life at sea," she said.

Excellent French. There was just a hint of those irrepressible Spanish *r*'s. She stopped a servant carrying a tray of wineglasses and handed one to Lapérouse. He had had several glasses already, but how to refuse this oddly poised girl, his hostess for the evening? The rest of the guests filled the courtyard, settling into jovial clusters, wineglasses in hand. He hoped none of his men would become foolishly drunk. During their time at sea, they had grown used to meting out their drink in sensible, barrel-conserving doses.

"I understand that I have the same name as Madame de Lapérouse," Eleonora said.

His face warmed at the mention of Éléonore. "Monsieur Broudou must have told you," he said. "He is my wife's brother."

"Do you have any children?"

Her directness took him by surprise, and he had no defense except to return candor for candor. "No—that is, not when I left France."

Her face opened into an artless smile. "You may be greeted by a child on your return?"

He laughed, flustered. "Perhaps." A letter had reached him in Brest right before they set sail. *It has been more than two months this time,* Éléonore had written. He knew not to count on it. But how to check hope? If she had been pregnant when he left, and all went well, the baby might have arrived already. He would not learn any news till much later, of course, when they reached another outpost of civilization—Macao, perhaps, or Petropavlovsk, or Manila—and crossed paths with another ship bearing letters from France. As for going home, that would be still later— sometime in 1789, most likely. Again, if all went well. In that time a child could be born, could cut its teeth, learn to walk, to babble prayers for an absent father. A child could also be carried off by fever, by measles, by accident. It had happened to seven of his own siblings.

He looked down to find Eleonora staring up at him with an expression that mixed curiosity with evaluation. "Doña Eleonora," he said, "you and Major Sabatero, are you blessed with—?"

"I have no children," she said. Her eyes strayed across the courtyard and toward the dining room, where servants rushed about rearranging furniture while musicians tuned their instruments. Sabatero stood at one of the open doorways, wiping his brow with a kerchief as he conferred with José. He waved when he saw them, gesturing that they were nearly ready to begin. Lapérouse nodded, delivered his empty wineglass to a passing tray, and offered his arm once more to Eleonora.

"You're young. You have time," he said.

For a moment her hand tightened around his upper arm; he could feel her fingers through the wool of his dress jacket. "That is what everyone says."

He led her back toward Sabatero and the warm light of the trans- formed dining room, relieved to deliver her back to her husband. There was something a bit overwrought about her. Perhaps it was just youth. He rubbed at the place above his elbow where she had gripped him. It did not hurt, but felt marked somehow, as if he would be aware of the spot all evening.

•

The distinguished citizens of Concepción began to arrive—retired military officers, members of the local council, magistrates, merchants; wives, many of them much younger than their husbands; some daughters and sisters; and priests, many priests. Lapérouse had never seen so many priests at a ball; it was possible he had never seen so many priests together in his life. He was aware of some hierarchy at work in the ordering of introductions, some complicated calculus of title, racial purity, and wealth, with the early introductions being generally for older, fairer-skinned, wealthier-looking individuals than the later ones. It was by no means straightforward, however. One of the first couples he met was a pompous old Spaniard weighed down by military medals whose wife looked for all the world like an Indian princess except for her startling blue eyes.

Seen now among her countrywomen, Eleonora looked less outlandish than Lapérouse had first found her. Nearly all of them wore the same pleated, bell-shaped skirts that ended just below the knee, displaying calves, shapely under striped stockings, and feet, some dainty, some not, in heavy, beribboned shoes. Like Eleonora, their upper bodies were draped with colorful mantillas, as if to compensate for the generous exposure of their lower extremities, and their hair was unpowdered and pulled back from the brow, arranged in those tight plaits, some coiled over the ears, some left to cascade down the back. It was a coiffure that worked better with some heads than others, but made all the women look like sisters. Then there were the headdresses, exotic and varied—hats, feathers, turbans, and flowers both real and artificial. Eleonora's head, adorned only by her plaited hair, seemed downright sober by comparison.

Most of the women fell silent as they entered the room and found themselves appraised by so many strangers. On being introduced, each woman shyly spoke a few words in French or Spanish, then retreated to the orbit of whichever man in the room she belonged to—husband, father, brother. It was an odd effect, the combination of apparel so gaudy and behavior so modest.

Langle leaned over. "You remember what Buffon said about New World birds?"

"You know I've never read Buffon," Lapérouse said.

"He said they were brilliantly feathered and largely mute."

"Perhaps he'd been here."

Gaspard Duché de Vancy, the *Boussole's* likable young artist, was standing nearby. "Monsieur Duché de Vancy," Lapérouse said, calling him over, "I hope you'll draw these people while we're here."

Duché de Vancy smiled. "I thought I was retained to draw flora and fauna, sir."

"Exactly."

The musicians were not so mediocre nor the music so antiquated as Lapérouse expected. "It's French," he said aloud, and Sabatero, standing next to him, inclined his head with satisfaction.

Langle was on his other side. "It's Leclair," he said, then whispered, "They know Leclair, who's been dead only twenty years, yet we had no idea their city had been destroyed and relocated years before that."

"The world will know more of them after our visit," Lapérouse said.

At a signal from Sabatero, the musicians embarked on a lively minuet. The company stirred: it was time to dance. Sabatero looked out at the room with a benignly expectant smile, too old and fat to begin dancing himself, his part in opening the festivities concluded. Lapérouse experienced a moment of silent panic. Was *he* expected to start the dancing? Pray God no. He did not mind dancing in a large crowd, the larger and less formal the better, where different social classes might mix and his lack of skill was apparent only to his partner. There had been nothing about dancing in the king's instructions for the expedition. He turned toward Langle: *he* could dance, let him begin. But his friend was diffident with strangers and hated being exposed to public view, and was even now quite refusing to return Lapérouse's glance.

Then rescue: the two La Borde brothers, officers on the *Astrolabe*, and their friend Barthélemy de Lesseps, the expedition's Russian interpreter, all three young and handsome and affable, their dress coats still unfaded, white stockings still white, caught Lapérouse's eye with a quick gesture that meant, undeniably, "May we, sir?" *Please*, Lapérouse mouthed back, and they were across the room to secure three of the prettiest dancing partners. Not to be outdone, the younger Spanish caballeros joined in, then more Frenchmen, even a couple of the more dapper savants, and the ball was under way.

Langle turned to Lapérouse. "Every day I'm glad I persuaded the Marquis de La Borde to let me bring his sons on the expedition."

"Very able officers."

"Quite." Langle cleared his throat. "In truth, I'm bending a promise I made to the marquis by letting them both off the *Astrolabe* at the same time."

"Oh?"

"Most mishaps on voyages occur when men leave their ships."

"True. But this hardly counts as a risky excursion."

"So I judged."

"Although I understand they have quite deadly earthquakes here."

Langle turned to him. "It's no joke. I considered that."

Lapérouse laughed. Ever the worrier, Langle. Only seven months into the expedition, he was convinced his water was going bad, that scurvy was about to break out among his crew, that their timepieces were losing accuracy.

Eleonora appeared beside them. "Count de Lapérouse, Viscount de Langle," she said, inclining her head in turn to each man, "may I consult with you on lodgings for your men tonight?"

The two men nodded in turn.

"You and the viscount and your servants will remain with my husband and me, if that is acceptable," she began. Lapérouse bowed. "I've placed most of the other officers with Señor Quexada, who has several extra rooms." They murmured gratitude for her kindness. "Your naturalists I assume will want to remain ashore for longer"—another bow—"so I've taken the liberty of housing them with various members of our Basque Society. That is our learned society for gentlemen," she explained. "They are very eager to make acquaintance with the savants on your expedition. Monsieur de Lamanon I've put with Don Mateo Moraga, the head of that society."

"You've seen to everything, Doña Eleonora," Lapérouse exclaimed.

She smiled. "What about your Monsieur Broudou? Shall I put him up with the younger officers, or would you prefer that he be here, near you?"

How had she divined so much about them in so short a time— Lamanon's need to feel valued and important, the savants' eagerness to get to their work, Frédéric's tendency to misbehave? And what *should* he do about Frédéric? He had acquitted himself admirably since August, but of course opportunities for gambling and whoring were limited on board.

He looked around for his brother-in-law, and found him, improbably, in conversation with one of the priests. He turned back to Eleonora. "I think Monsieur Broudou would be disappointed if he were lodged with two old men like Captain de Langle and me," he said.

"You and the captain are hardly old, sir," she said, looking up into their faces with an expression of friendly appraisal, "but I understand. We will find a suitable place for Monsieur Broudou."

He thanked her. She smiled, raising her fan to her lips. It was closed, but he could see that it was made of blue paper, with ivory or bone for slats. He wondered what it looked like inside, then held out a hand to her, acting on an impulse even as it was forming in his mind, an impulse that was absurd, for really, he could not dance well and was conscious of wanting to make a favorable impression—on the colonists, on his own men, on this young woman who was his hostess. But he stepped out onto the floor. "Will you do me the honor, Doña Eleonora?"

He was not one of those mariners so wedded to the sea that he slept better on board than on land. A capacious bed, solid ground, clean bedclothes, a quiet house—he found these things altogether conducive to long and restful sleep. When he awoke, it was into a yellow room flooded with sunlight and headache, and a long two or three seconds before he recollected where he was. He heaved himself out of bed, noticed that Langle's bed was empty, and roared for Pierre, wincing at his own noise. "What time is it?" he asked when Pierre appeared.

"Almost nine o'clock, sir."

"Nine! Why didn't you wake me?"

"You told me not to last night."

"Ah," he said, not remembering. "Where is Monsieur de Langle?"

"He got up early and returned to the *Astrolabe*, sir."

Lapérouse frowned, irked and disappointed. He had assumed he and Langle would be making the three-league trip back to the cove together that morning. It was a rare thing—a long trip on dry land, the two captains together, away from the eyes and ears of the men, a chance to talk unhindered and uncensored. And he disliked what Langle's earlier departure might suggest to others—that Langle was the more diligent and disciplined captain, back to work while the commander slept off an evening of too much wine. He dunked his head into the washbasin and subjected himself to a storm of toweling before letting Pierre help him get dressed.

A servant girl showed him into a drawing room, where Eleonora sat at a small table, the remains of a breakfast for two in evidence before her.

"Good morning, sir," Eleonora said, standing with a small curtsy before waving him into the other chair. It seemed impossible that Eleonora should look even younger than she had the night before, but she did. Her hair pulled back in a lace mantle, she looked every bit the girl playing at being the mistress of the house. His face warmed with the memory of dancing with her the night before. He hoped he had not looked entirely foolish.

"Are you hungry?" she asked, then smiled when he shook his head no and poured steaming water into a wooden cup with no handles. She stuck a silver straw into it and offered it to him. "Paraguayan tea," she said. "It is very restorative."

He thanked her and sipped at the tea, which was warm and smoky and tasted of some hybrid between tea and coffee. "The major, he is—?"

"I am afraid he is still asleep," Eleonora said. "The party last night, it tired him. I fear he is not that strong." She paused. "He was injured in a battle with the Araucanians."

"Recently?" It was hard to picture their host of the previous evening being spry enough to wage any sort of warfare.

"Oh, no," Eleonora said. "It was about ten years ago."

"I see." She had never known her husband in good health. At least he and Éléonore had had a few years together. Long-delayed years, granted, and years interrupted by several stints at sea, so that their total time together, really *together*, could be measured in months. But they were good months, when they were both young enough to enjoy each other. He looked at Eleonora again. Just how infirm *was* this husband of hers? She blushed under his gaze and looked down into her lap. There was a curious panel on the front of her skirt, a vertical seam that closed with three cloth-covered buttons. She was toying with one of the buttons. Why would a woman require such an opening in her skirt? He could not look away.

"But I am forgetting," Eleonora said, looking back up. "We received word from Don Ambrosio this morning."

Ambrosio, Ambrosio—but of *course*—Ambrosio O'Higgins, the governor of the town, for whose absence everyone had been so apologetic.

"He is returning from the front today."

"Wonderful news," Lapérouse said, then thought immediately of the *Boussole*. O'Higgins would almost certainly expect to be received on board, but the ship would be in an aggravated state of undress, half of the hold disgorged and sitting in boats, waiting to be restowed, sails and rigging spread everywhere, and sweaty, half-naked crewmen crawling all over with tools and tar and foul language. The officers still here in town would need to be summoned back to the ships. And he would need his cook, Bisalion, to feed O'Higgins and his entourage. Luncheon for we-do-not-know-how-many arriving we-are-not-sure-when. Bisalion was a high-strung individual. Paroxysms of anxiety would follow. "Doña Eleonora," he said, "I'm afraid I need to return to my ship immediately."

He stood, head pounding, and Eleonora stood too, and then the steward walked in. Lapérouse stepped back, startled by the man's sudden and silent appearance, thinking at first that it was Sabatero, finally awake. Indeed, the steward shared his master's short stature and wide shoulders. He stood before them without speaking, his expression blank, *too* blank, as if he had interrupted something between them. Eleonora spoke to him sharply in Spanish, which, Lapérouse reflected, tended to support that impression.

The man then addressed Eleonora. Lapérouse did not know what he said, but there was something about his manner—not exactly disrespectful, but offhand—that Lapérouse did not like. Their eyes met briefly, and then Lapérouse liked him even less. Hostility flared out from the man, and with it a hint of intelligence greater than the man's position required. Could the blood of the mighty, unbowed Araucanians flow through this man's veins? Maybe it was true what so many savants said—Lamanon himself was of this opinion—that when you mixed the races you degraded both, ending up with the worst of each. Lapérouse wondered how often Sabatero left his young wife alone with this mixed-blood servant.

"Monsieur de La Borde is here to see you," Eleonora said, translating for the steward. "He says it is urgent."

"La Borde?" He remembered the marquis and Langle's promise to him, their mandate to keep the brothers—or at least *one* of them—safe from harm. "Please, send him in."

It was the older La Borde, Edouard de La Borde Marchainville, looking windswept and harried, but not, Lapérouse was relieved to see, injured or panicked. "Madame, Commander," he said, bowing first toward Eleonora then to Lapérouse, "I'm sorry to burst in like this." He looked back at Eleonora, as if unsure whether to proceed in her presence.

"It's all right, Ensign," Lapérouse said. "What is it? Your brother?"

"My brother?" La Borde said. "No, he's fine, sir. It's—it's Broudou, sir. He never came back to the Quexadas' house last night after the ball. I've been looking for him, but, well—I don't know the town."

Lapérouse groaned.

Eleonora turned to the steward. They exchanged some words, her face troubled and stern, his wearing a wry smile. She turned back to her guests. "I am sure we can find him," she said. "Our steward knows the town very well. If Monsieur de La Borde does not mind having José for a guide . . ." Not at all, they assured her. They would be most grateful for the assistance. José bowed and left the room, then Eleonora excused herself to oversee preparations for the search party.

Lapérouse stood fuming. It was not the first time he had wondered how his gentle and scrupulous wife could have such a brother, but it was the first time he regretted bringing Frédéric on the voyage.

"Thank you, Monsieur de La Borde," he finally said, aware that the young officer was standing beside him in embarrassed silence. La Borde shook his head as if to say it was no bother at all, though they both knew it was nothing *but* bother. Lapérouse changed the subject: "You and your brother and Monsieur de Lesseps acquitted yourselves very handsomely last night."

"Thank you, sir."

"Do you and your brother share a cabin on the *Astrolabe*?"

"No, sir," La Borde replied. "My brother shares the council room with Monsieur de Lesseps and two other officers. I'm in a cabin with Monsieur de Vaujuas."

"I didn't see Vaujuas last night," Lapérouse observed.

"No, sir. The captain invited him, but he stayed behind. His servant has been quite ill."

"Ill?" Lapérouse felt a small shock. He thought no one was sick. The man was only a servant, but still— "What's wrong with him?"

La Borde seemed to realize he had said too much. "It's just a chest complaint. Vaujuas believes the sea voyage will improve him."

"Just a chest complaint?" Lapérouse cried. "Chest complaints kill people every day, Monsieur de La Borde."

"Of course, sir."

Eleonora returned to announce the readiness of three horses—one each for José and La Borde, and one for Frédéric when they found him. La Borde bowed and followed José out of the room, looking relieved to be on his way. Eleonora turned to Lapérouse: "Do not worry, sir."

"We've put you to a great deal of trouble."

"Not at all." She smiled and sat down. "It may be only a misunderstanding. He may have ended up with another family last night."

Lapérouse shook his head. "I know him too well to hope for that."

"Are you worried he may try to *leave* the expedition?"

"*Desert?*" Lapérouse laughed. "No. That would require some resolve. No, no, he's probably just found some—" He stopped, not wanting to subject Eleonora to a description of Frédéric's likely diversions.

She met his eyes with no hint of embarrassment. "You were eager to return to your ship. I have asked the groom to prepare a carriage to take you back, but would you prefer to wait awhile?"

"I hardly know," he admitted. "I'm afraid we'll leave your household with no means of transport."

She shook her head. "We have nowhere to go today. And it is only a humble cart. Nothing like your elegant French carriages."

He smiled. He could tell her that his life had not involved many elegant carriages; that his family owned only the meanest-looking phaeton and a cramped portable chair that still smelled of his grandmother; that he was not really so distinguished—not like Langle or the La Bordes or any number of the officers who served under him; that he was not a count, not officially, not *yet*; that he had not been born a Lapérouse, the name purchased to make him sound more noble when he decided to apply to the naval school in Brest. But she stood before him, the perfect, aristocratic girl-hostess, expecting him to play his part as the distinguished French guest, and he could not break the spell.

"You speak French better than anyone in Concepción," he said.

"Oh, the bishop's French is much better than mine," she said, but she was smiling, pleased by the compliment.

"Did you learn it at home?"

She shook her head. "I was raised in a convent school here. Two of the sisters were French."

"Ah." Could it be through such individuals, he wondered, that the colonists knew so much about France? "Doña Eleonora," he said, "we were surprised to hear the music of Leclair last night."

"Were you?" Her girlish mouth turned down into a concerned frown. "Is he not well regarded in France?"

"No, that's not it at all," Lapérouse hastened to assure her. "It's only that he was alive till quite recently, and here you are so far from Europe—"

She smiled archly. "Ships come from Cádiz at least once a year filled with news and books." She leaned a little toward him and whispered: "I have even read *Manon Lescaut*."

"Have you?" He could not help laughing and hoped she did not think he was laughing at her, although he was. "Did the nuns assign such texts at school?"

She leaned away, her lips pursed as if to protect her secrets, but her eyes were still smiling. "They were wonderful teachers. I was there until last year, when—" She stopped. "This house was my father's," she said at last, looking around the room with her hands held out, as if the fact surprised her. "When he died, I came here. My husband was a friend of his."

Lapérouse nodded. The revelation explained both too much and too little. Perhaps Sabatero had married her out of consideration for his friend, saving a young orphan from social isolation, from life in the convent, from rapacious suitors. Although it occurred to Lapérouse that a more conscientious friend of the family might have found a younger, healthier husband for her. Perhaps Sabatero had taken advantage of his position with the family to assume control of his friend's estate when he died. But no more conjectures, he told himself. There was unhappiness under Eleonora's studied composure, and he did not wish to discover it.

Eleonora turned abruptly toward the corridor, and then Lapérouse heard it too, a commotion at the back of the house. "Are they already back?" she cried. They followed the sound past the dining room and through a large kitchen, then out into a warm breeze, hanging linens, chickens underfoot, the smell of hay. A group of servants had stopped working to watch while José and La Borde hauled an inert body down from a horse.

"Oh, God," Lapérouse cried, running toward them.

La Borde turned: "It's all right, Commander. We found him right nearby. He's a mess, but he's fine. We'll clean him up—don't come any closer, sir."

Lapérouse did as he was bid. He had already caught a whiff of Frédéric's night on the town—a disgusting mix of cheap smoke, cheap drink, sex, piss, vomit. He took Eleonora's elbow and pulled her back into the house.

"I suppose that's the last time I'll ever leave the *Boussole*," Frédéric muttered from his side of the carriage.

"Most likely," Lapérouse said.

Frédéric was still drunk, but on the downhill side of it, belligerence and self-pity vying with each other for preeminence. "That's what I suspected from the start," he said, "so I made the most of it, you see."

"Don't be an ass, Frédéric."

The taunt rallied him. "Guess who showed me the sights last night, Jean-François—guess." When Lapérouse said nothing, he sidled over and whispered, "A *priest*."

Lapérouse looked away, repelled by the younger man's fetid breath, but also remembering his last sight of Frédéric the night before, talking to a priest at the ball, and how that sight had reassured him, allowing him to let Frédéric lodge elsewhere.

"Brother Marco, my guide," Frédéric declared. He tried to sit forward, but his inebriation was no match for the jostling of the carriage as it wound its way through the hills between Concepción and the bay. "He has a properly monastic cell with the Dominicans, but on the edge of town he keeps house with a fiery little mestiza called Clara. Cla-ra," he repeated, exaggerating the *r*. He laughed at Lapérouse's expression of disapproval. "They all do it, Jean-François."

"Do what?"

"Even this man O'Higgins, the governor, he keeps a woman in Chillán, he has a bastard son there."

"O'Higgins is not a man of the cloth."

"And Sabatero."

"What about Sabatero?"

"He has his own house in town with his Indian 'housekeeper.' She's borne him four or five children. He's installed the eldest in his home as steward."

"*José?*"

"I don't know what he's called, but he stands to inherit that big house and a great deal more if little Eleonora doesn't produce an heir."

Lapérouse called up José's face, the resemblance to Sabatero, his odd manner toward Eleonora, hers toward him, her strange eagerness when she learned about Éléonore's possible pregnancy, and he did not doubt the truth of Frédéric's information. He shook his head in dismay, wishing he had remained ignorant.

The younger man laughed sloppily. "Poor girl. Probably still a virgin. Marco says old Sabatero isn't up to the task anymore. Something about a well-aimed Indian arrow." He used his left hand to mime an arrow hitting him between the legs, then doubled over in mock agony. He sidled over again. "I saw you dancing with her last night, brother. Maybe you can help her. I won't tell Éléonore."

Lapérouse shoved him away. "I'm confining you to your quarters."

Frédéric laughed again, but with less conviction. "It's just like home here, Commander—or should I say 'Count'?" he said. "Just like Port Louis."

"I don't see the resemblance," Lapérouse said, although he did. Like Concepción, Port Louis in Île de France was a remote colonial outpost, a victualing station for ships headed elsewhere, a place ignored and looked down on by most Europeans. It was also where, more than ten years earlier, Lapérouse had first met Éléonore and Frédéric and the rest of the Broudou family.

"In both places," Frédéric began, "you have natives who hate you and Europeans with guns." He paused, as if recollecting his next point. "And then you have the *children* of the Europeans, who've ruined their morals and intelligence in the hot sun." He tapped his head as if offering his own case as evidence. "Or taken up with natives and bred mongrels. In any case they don't measure up, and have to watch while newly arrived Europeans"—he wagged a finger at Lapérouse—"drop in and take the best of everything—the best posts, the best land, the best women—like my sister."

Lapérouse rounded on him. "Mention Éléonore again and I'll have you flogged."

The watery smile on Frédéric's face wavered, and he slumped down in the carriage seat. He began to murmur about the unfairness of everything, about officers on the *Boussole* who had slighted him, then other men who had wronged him—in Port Louis, in Paris, in Brest; about his family, how they craved advancement for their daughters but cared not a whit for him; how things could not, *would* not, go on like this—society poisoned, festering, set to erupt.

Lapérouse looked out the side, waiting for the hills to give way to a view of Concepción Bay. He had had nothing to eat yet that day, and the bumps and twists of the road were making him ill. Frédéric's stink and talk were not helping. It was all nonsense, of course, every complaining word. Frédéric had never shown the slightest ambition for anything. The voyage was his best chance to improve himself—and more than he deserved. Indeed, had he not joined the *Boussole*, he would have been in prison. For years the Broudous had overlooked their only son's dissipation, debts, tavern brawls, even a duel. But when Frédéric waved a loaded pistol at his youngest sister, Elzire, their mother obtained a lettre de cachet for his incarceration at Mont Saint-Michel. It was to spare Éléonore, and not out of any regard for Frédéric, that Lapérouse had offered him a place on the voyage.

Surprisingly, his brother-in-law had done well on board until now, *very* well, quite beyond anyone's expectations, proving himself a quick study and a cheerful crew member. Lapérouse had been considering an official appointment for him. Maybe Frédéric was one of those men who withered in the wide open spaces of terra firma but thrived under the limitations of life on board. He had met such men before: men who craved discipline even when they raged against it. That revolutionary talk—where had *that* come from? Frédéric was not given to reading, and as far as Lapérouse knew, had never had radical friends, nor any inkling of philosophy or politics. Could it be Lamanon? Notwithstanding his much-vaunted democratic ideals, the fussy savant was not a likely companion for the likes of Frédéric.

In Talcahuano, the road smoothed out and the air grew cooler, with a hint of brine. Lapérouse could see the *Boussole* and the *Astrolabe*, almost elegant in their anchorages, and after another turn in the road could see crewmen he recognized, busy onshore, and several small boats at the water's edge, ready to ferry men back to the ships. He signaled for the carriage to stop and hailed the first officer he saw to take his brother-in-law back to the *Boussole* and place him under arrest for forty-eight hours.

"Do you want to transfer him to the *Astrolabe*?" Langle asked. "He won't have family to take advantage of."

Lapérouse shook his head. "He's my responsibility. You have your own troubles to deal with, no doubt."

"Yes, perhaps I have."

Lapérouse looked over at him. "Anything in particular?"

Langle nodded. "There is one matter."

"Vaujuas's servant?"

Langle's long, urbane face tilted in surprise. "You know about that?" Lapérouse nodded, and Langle sighed. "That's not what I was thinking of, but yes—Vaujuas's servant is sick. Consumptive," he admitted. "I doubt he'll make it many more months. I don't know how he passed Lavaux's physical exam in Brest."

"Vaujuas should never have brought him."

"Apparently he thought the sea voyage would improve the man's health. He's been with the family for many years. There's an attachment there."

Lapérouse shook his head. "Let's hope it's our first and only death." He watched Langle's eyebrows contract with a kind of anticipatory distress. "What's this other matter?"

But at that moment the man on watch called down to say some men on horseback had just arrived in Talcahuano. The two captains turned toward the rail. They were on the deck of the *Boussole*, waiting for

O'Higgins. A message from town that morning had told them to expect the governor around noon, and it was now nearly one, but Lapérouse did not mind. In general he preferred guests who arrived late to guests who arrived early. It had given everyone—especially Bisalion, who had worked himself into a state of shrill panic—more time to prepare for the visit. Lapérouse peered shoreward through his glass and watched as a contingent of mounted, uniformed men made their way to the water's edge. They were led by a large, impressive man on the largest of the horses, and followed by several pack animals bearing what were no doubt yet more gifts of food. He watched until they began to load themselves into the small boats. "Well. They're on their way."

"Good," Langle said. "It's been two days since I heard an account of the great earthquake of 1751. I am mad to hear it again."

Lapérouse grinned. He had felt gloomy ever since the ride back with Frédéric the day before, but standing on his deck with Langle, a light southwest breeze keeping them comfortable even in their dress uniforms, the deck newly swabbed, the crew washed and at the ready, his dark mood proved difficult to sustain, even while they traded complaints about their men.

"You were about to tell me something," Lapérouse said. "Not another illness?"

"No. It's Dufresne. He says he's bored to death and wants to disembark here, find his own way home."

"Oh, for God's sake. I didn't want to bring him in the first place!"

"I know."

"It was clear from our first meeting that the man had no idea what the voyage entailed."

"None whatsoever."

"His credentials as a naturalist were hardly impressive!"

"Hardly."

Lapérouse could not help but laugh. He wished he could soothe his friend's worries in the same easy way, but there was something entrenched about Langle's anxieties—they were more a state of mind than reactions to particular events, hard to read and even harder to address, hidden under his aristocratic polish.

"What did you tell him?" Lapérouse asked.

"I told him to write an official request to you and expect 'no' for an answer."

Lapérouse puffed out his cheeks. "God knows the other savants can be demanding and uncooperative. But at least they have some appreciation for the importance of the voyage. What is the matter with Dufresne?"

Langle shrugged. "He's been unhappy from the beginning. The others suspect him of being a spy from the Ministry of Finance."

Lapérouse snorted. "He'd be treated better if he were an English agent for the Royal Society."

Everyone on deck now came to attention as the bosun's chair rose into view, revealing a large man, his hat askew, clinging whitely to the ropes on either side of him. O'Higgins had looked imposing seen from a distance on horseback. But no one looked dignified hauled up the side in a chair. Lapérouse stood perfectly still and straight and straight-faced, and his men did the same, suppressing any impulse to laugh. O'Higgins was helped out of the chair and, finding his balance, stepped forward, every bit the impressive brigadier general he had seemed from afar—tall, with a large head and huge hands, his features Irish except for a Mediterranean arrangement of his mouth, no doubt the result of so many years speaking Spanish. He made straight for the two captains.

"Count de Lapérouse, Viscount de Langle," he said in French. His accent was thick and unplaceable. "Please forgive my tardiness. I welcome you—belatedly—to Concepción."

After introductions, after the obligatory retelling of the earthquake story, after the Frenchmen expressed again their gratitude for the colonists' generosity, after a tour of the frigate, after the Spaniards expressed their profound admiration for everything they saw—a windmill on deck! a cucurbit attached to the galley stove! how justly the French were praised for their ingenuity!—after all of that, O'Higgins and his officers and their hosts repaired to Lapérouse's stateroom for lunch. Bisalion looked as though he had had most of his blood drawn, but the meal was a success, featuring salt cod brandade with toasted triangles of bread, a pigeon tart, a dish of peas and mushrooms in a wine sauce, and fried cream sprinkled with sugar. O'Higgins's entourage included three officers who had been with him at the front. On the French side, Lapérouse and Langle were joined by the expedition's senior officers and by Lapérouse's chief engineer, Paul de Monneron, who was invited when they learned that O'Higgins himself had first come to Chile as an engineer.

"I am sorry our other savants are not on board to join us," Lapérouse said. "They are still in town, eager to take advantage of their furlough on land."

"But I have met them," O'Higgins said.

"Indeed?" Lapérouse said.

O'Higgins dabbed at his lips with a napkin. "A group of them came to see me as I was setting out this morning. A Monsieur—Lamanon, is it?—a man of great intelligence, he was their—how do you say it?—their speaker. They asked permission to explore the interior." He caught Lapérouse's eye as if to gauge whether or not this was news to the French commander.

"I see." So *that* was what had made O'Higgins late today—their own science delegation! Acting entirely on their own, ignoring the chain of command, not deigning to consult with their commander. Lapérouse said none of this aloud, but he could tell from the way Langle and the other officers shifted in their seats that he had not succeeded in hiding either his surprise or his annoyance.

"Unfortunately I had to turn them down," O'Higgins said.

"You turned them *down*?"

O'Higgins nodded. "I understand their desire to explore, of course." He took an appreciative bite of dessert, then went on: "A few years ago I myself went with two of our naturalists—Don Hipólito Ruiz and Don José Dombey—you have heard of them perhaps?—on an expedition to the interior. But today I cannot guarantee your men's safety outside of the area between here and the Bío-Bío River." His officers nodded in agreement.

Lapérouse said nothing, torn between grim pleasure that the troublesome savants had been rebuffed and dismay that the scientific mission of the voyage could be so easily dismissed.

Langle leaned forward. "We understood you had concluded an accord with the Indians."

"Indeed we have."

"It is still not safe to venture into the frontier?"

O'Higgins sat forward. "The Araucanians may not distinguish between a group of curious naturalists armed for their protection and settlers invading their territory and violating our agreement."

Lapérouse felt certain that, had he been inclined, O'Higgins could avail them of an armed escort for the savants, Indian guides, interpreters, introductions to tribal leaders. But he was apparently not so inclined, and Lapérouse was not sure what would be gained by pressing the point. The colonists had already done so much for them; the French would continue to need their cooperation while the frigates underwent repairs; and for all the secretiveness of the Spanish empire, Chile was already discovered—a land mapped, named, and conquered.

"We understand," he said, then looked over at Langle to secure his agreement. Langle nodded just once; it was a maddening way he had of signaling acknowledgment without acquiescence.

O'Higgins watched the exchange, then addressed himself to Langle. "There is still much to interest your naturalists within our borders," he said. "I know that the gentlemen of our Basque Society will lend every support to botanizing and other scientific endeavors proposed by your people."

Langle thanked him, and the conversation moved on. As if to compensate for his refusal of the savants' request, O'Higgins spoke very openly about the colony and the town. Lapérouse was left with the impression of a land of enormous bounty that profited almost no one. Isolated from the rest of the world, beset by the long-running and costly conflicts with the Araucanians, restrained by trade policies that favored Peru over Chile, and bloated by a large idle class that filled its convents and monasteries, the colony produced much, consumed much, and wasted much. "Every year we slaughter hundreds of bullocks just for their leather and tallow," O'Higgins said. "The meat has no buyers, you see."

"I fear we've taken advantage of your plenty and your lack of trade opportunities," Lapérouse said, thinking of the embarrassing quantities of food they had been given.

O'Higgins shook his head in reassurance. "You and your men have more than repaid us already. You may not understand how"—he searched for the right word—"how big, how *momentous*, your visit is for our people.

Most of them live long lives of comfort and boredom. They will speak of this for years to come. They will tell their children and grandchildren that they met the great French explorers Lapérouse and Langle."

Lapérouse felt his face warm with pleasure, and a grand notion suddenly formed in his mind. "Then we mean to make our stay truly memorable for all," he said. "I would like to invite you and all of Concepción society to a fête on the beach. French food, French music, and"—he looked pointedly at Monneron here—"a French spectacle." Monneron looked puzzled for a moment, but then his eyes widened with sudden understanding. "Say, in eight days' time?" Lapérouse concluded.

O'Higgins's face spread into a broad grin. "I accept with pleasure," he said.

They watched the small boat pull away from the *Boussole*, bearing O'Higgins and his party back to Talcahuano.

"I'm going to put Monneron in charge of the entertainment for the evening," Lapérouse told Langle.

"A good choice. He's a resourceful young man."

"Yes, he is," Lapérouse agreed. "He also happens to possess something that may serve well for the promised 'spectacle.'"

"I wondered what you meant by that," Langle said. "May I ask what it is?"

"You may not. It's to be a surprise." Lapérouse smiled, then let his face grow serious again. "I have to return to Concepción tomorrow," he said.

"To put Lamanon in his place?"

"Well, yes—to remind Lamanon and the others that they are sailing on His Majesty's frigates and bound by the rules and customs of His Majesty's Navy."

Langle pursed his lips for a moment. "Shall I go instead?"

Lapérouse frowned, unsure whether he welcomed or resented the suggestion. It was no secret that Langle got along better with the savants than he did. Langle was a man of science in his own right, a mathematician and member of the Royal Marine Academy; he had published papers on the longitude problem. The savants saw him as one of their own. Lapérouse was not jealous of these advantages; indeed, he was usually grateful for them. But today he felt Langle's suggestion was born of disappointment over Lapérouse's lukewarm advocacy of the savants over lunch. He was reminded of the rumors he had heard before they left France—that the ministry had been torn between offering him or Langle command of the expedition. Langle must have heard the same rumors. They had never spoken of it.

Lapérouse's gaze wandered from their departed guests, now nearing the shore, to the *Astrolabe*, where several crewmen were emptying water casks over the side. "What are they doing?" he asked, pointing across the way.

"They're draining out the old water to make room for fresh," Langle explained.

"Didn't you refill your casks in Santa Catarina?"

Langle was silent for a moment. "I refilled *some* of them. *That* there is French water, seven months old, hardly fit to drink." When Lapérouse said nothing, Langle said, "Sir, you know my convictions on this matter."

Lapérouse turned away from the rail. He hoped Langle's preoccupation with water would not become a chronic point of contention between them. His friend seemed to think that drinking old barrel water caused scurvy, but Lapérouse had never read or seen anything to support this idea. It was not a matter worth debating, however. Langle would grow heated and scientific. "Thank you for your offer, Monsieur de Langle," he finally said, "but I think I'll go into town myself."

Langle nodded so formally that Lapérouse felt compelled to say something to restore their usual amicability. "It's not just our savants," he said. "I am concerned for our hostess, Señora Sabatero."

Langle's face was blank for a few seconds. "Señora—you mean that tiny creature married to Sabatero—*Eleonora*?" He looked at Lapérouse with amused surprise, then laughed aloud.

"She is a very young person and not altogether happy," Lapérouse said, aware of sounding ridiculous, of blushing before his friend. But it worked: Langle was still grinning when he left the ship a few minutes later. Lapérouse made his way back to his stateroom and composed a message to Major Sabatero, requesting the indulgence of another night's stay in his home and the use of his drawing room to conduct some business related to the voyage.

•

In the morning, Frédéric was released from his onboard incarceration and ordered to report to duty. He did not apologize when he presented himself, but there was contrition in his washed face and neat dress and in his eagerness to return to duty. Even the strictly polite tone he adopted— "yes, sir," "of course, sir"—seemed an attempt to compensate for the monstrous overfamiliarity of two days earlier. Lapérouse felt a rush of pity for his brother-in-law: if only that desire to please were balanced by the ability to refuse a wrong thing now and then, he might make something of himself. When Frédéric left the room with a formal bow and a "thank you, sir," Lapérouse pulled a page from a letter he had begun to Éléonore the night before, a page that described in unstinting detail what had happened with Frédéric in Concepción, and tore it into small pieces.

A knock on the door brought Boutin, one of his ensigns, bearing a small package. "Today's reports and messages, sir," he said.

Routine communications, for the most part—a report from Langle on the progress of repairs on the *Astrolabe*; another from Dagelet, the *Boussole*'s astronomer, on the performance of their chronometers; lists from both ships of needed supplies—and then, as expected, a letter from Dufresne requesting permission to leave the expedition. A more self-pitying and lugubrious letter it was hard to imagine: he enjoyed the respect and friendship of no one on board, rued the day he ever consented to join the expedition, would consider himself a prisoner if his request were denied, and had nothing but days and years of unrelenting sadness to anticipate in that event. Lapérouse was hard-pressed to keep from laughing aloud.

"Monsieur de Boutin," he finally said, looking up from the table. "Please inform Monsieur de Monneron that I am ready to accompany him to town."

He had sent one of the dragoons ahead on a horse with their luggage, meaning to walk the three leagues to Concepción with Monneron. There was the spectacle to discuss, of course, a demonstration that required careful advance planning and allowed of no real rehearsal. But Lapérouse also wanted to get Monneron's assessment of the mood among the savants. By training, temperament, and formal appointment, Monneron straddled the worlds of naval officer and man of science. His views would be helpful to hear before Lapérouse confronted Lamanon.

But once again he was thwarted in his plan to have a long walk and talk with a member of his staff. O'Higgins had learned of his intention to return to town and came to meet him in person, riding the same magnificent horse he had the previous day, accompanied this time by a groom and horses for the Frenchmen. Lapérouse stifled a curse. He had last ridden a horse when he was a boy, and it had been a seat-bruising and humiliating experience.

If he embarrassed himself less on this occasion, it was due entirely to the skill and patience of the groom and the docility of the animal. Still, he did not feel at ease for any part of the journey, and barely attended to what O'Higgins was saying. "Ah!" he cried as O'Higgins pointed out the location of the old city on their left. "Indeed!" he said of O'Higgins's description of the Araucanians' equestrian prowess. Monneron, a more able rider, did his part to maintain their side of the conversation: Had Governor O'Higgins been in Concepción at the time of the great earthquake? (He had not. He was in Santiago then, or perhaps it was Cádiz.) Was it true the Araucanians drank horse blood? (The Indians themselves made this claim, but he had never seen it.) Would the governor oblige them with the story of how an Irishman had come to be a brigadier general for the king of Spain? He would and he did. The not uncommon story—an Irish family, its wealth diminished by Cromwell, its status tainted by Catholicism and an old loyalty to the Stuarts, forging a new life in Spain— brought them into town. O'Higgins conveyed them to the door of the Sabateros' house near the central plaza and left with a promise to see them at dinner.

The steward opened the door, his blank face betraying no memory of his last meeting with Lapérouse, when he had helped push a drunk and stinking Frédéric into the back of the family carriage. Lapérouse hoped his own expression was as mute, not only about the embarrassment with Frédéric, but also about his knowledge that José was Sabatero's natural son—a fact that now, looking at the man again at such close range, seemed entirely obvious.

Of course, most facts had that quality of being obvious once known, Lapérouse reflected as he followed José down the corridor. Everything was fraught with this knowledge: the defensive way Eleonora flicked open her fan when José entered the room; José's voice as he announced the guests, his tone polite but only just; and Sabatero's bland, unseeing benignity, dispensed with equal measure to his lonely Creole wife and the mestizo son poised to dispossess her.

Lapérouse bowed—first to Eleonora, who flushed prettily when she saw him; then to Sabatero, who looked, out of uniform, less florid than he had at the ball; and then to—well, here was a surprise—the discontented Dufresne himself, looking at once shamefaced and defiant in a corner of the room.

"We have had pleasure of Monsieur Dufresne's company from last night," Sabatero explained in his rough French.

"His host came down with a fever, and we thought it best he stay here," Eleonora added.

Lapérouse looked from the Sabateros to Dufresne, wondering how free the discontented naturalist had been in discussing his unhappiness with his hosts. "Well, Monsieur Dufresne," he said. "I'm delighted to see you here. It saves me the trouble of sending for you." Dufresne sank back into his chair as if the effort might render him invisible.

Eleonora stood up with a rustling of her skirts, drawing all eyes toward her. "Monsieur de Monneron, how nice to see you again," she said, extending her hand to the engineer. "Allow my husband and me to show you to your room, and then you must tell us about this party. It is all the talk in town today . . ." She reached her other hand out to her husband, who heaved himself from his chair and joined her.

Lapérouse bowed his thanks as Eleonora led her husband and Monneron out of the room. He was struck once more by her sensitivity, so far beyond her years, the promptness with which she cleared the room so he could confront Dufresne in private. But also—and this too not for the first time—how rehearsed both Eleonora and her husband sounded. Was it simply a function of speaking a language not one's own? Or had these people, with their long lives of relative ease and lack of diversion, steeped in their secrets and secretiveness, come so to excel in the art of the apologia that even simple explanations and exchanges seemed to hide something?

"You received my letter, then. Sir."

Lapérouse turned to find Dufresne, still seated, looking up at him through an unkempt fringe of hair that fell before his eyes. He looked every bit like the pupil who has not prepared his lesson and had absolutely counted on not being called to recite it.

"I did, this morning."

"Have you come all this way simply to refuse me in person?"

"No, Dufresne. You are only one in a long list of matters I have to attend to today."

Dufresne flushed and said nothing, as if unsure whether to proceed angrily or with contrition. "I'm sorry, sir," he finally said. "I know I have no one to blame but myself, but—*please* let me go. I should never have come. I plead my youth and inexperience."

"You'll find that youth and inexperience are rarely invoked in the Navy except when you are being refused a promotion."

Dufresne looked down, dejected.

"I *could* release you . . ." Lapérouse began, and Dufresne looked up, one lock of his hair stuck in the corner of his mouth. "But I think you would regret it."

"I've done nothing *but* regret since we left Brest." He was struggling not to cry.

Lapérouse sat down in the chair Eleonora had just vacated. It was still warm. "Monsieur Dufresne," he said. "This may go down in history as one of the most important voyages of the century. Do you want to be the man who left seven months in, witnessed none of the excitement in store, contributed nothing to its success, and missed out on all of its glory?"

"I'll be that man even if I stay on board."

"If you don't feel useful, it's no doubt because you haven't *made* yourself useful," Lapérouse said. "But that is about to change." He went out into the corridor and asked a servant to find Monneron.

"Ah, Monneron," he said when the engineer appeared in the drawing room. "You know Monsieur Dufresne, of course." The two men nodded to each other. "I believe you'll want someone to assist you with preparations for the spectacle next week," he said, "and Dufresne here is wanting more occupation. Please take him into your confidence and allow him to accompany you on your errands in town."

"Of course," Monneron said. His expression was not one of delight, but it also betrayed neither reluctance nor dismay. This even-tempered cooperativeness was one of the things Lapérouse most valued about his engineer. "Major Sabatero and his wife are helping me figure out where in town I might procure a few needed supplies," Monneron said. "Why don't you join us, Monsieur Dufresne?"

The naturalist perked up at the mention of Eleonora, and dutifully followed Monneron out of the room. His gait had a cheerful, ungainly bounce to it. Had he always walked like that, or was the promise of being let in on a secret and the continued company of a pretty woman enough to turn him around? This, from a man who had all but threatened to harm himself if he were not released from the expedition! Lapérouse watched him go, annoyance mounting. Sometimes the role of captain seemed to resemble nothing more than that of nursemaid.

He turned back toward the drawing room to find José standing behind him. The steward had also been watching the two Frenchmen make their way down the corridor. "Señor," José said, acknowledging Lapérouse with a perfunctory nod, one side of his mouth curling up slightly. But in the instant before that, when Lapérouse first turned around, he had caught José in an unguarded moment, and his expression had worn nothing of his usual forced politesse with its hint of contempt. No, in that second before he remembered himself, before he nodded his head and said "Señor," his face had been soft, collapsed by some distress.

Lapérouse held the man's gaze. Was it just resentment? More guests meant more work for the steward, of course. The presence of guests also meant more supervision and the necessity for a greater show of propriety. Or—here was an odious possibility—perhaps José suspected Eleonora's virtue. Or had been instructed to guard it. The very young and quite pretty wife of an old and possibly impotent man, playing hostess to young men, *French* men, men long deprived of female company and scheduled to leave again very soon. Or maybe José's vigilance was for his own sake. Perhaps he feared Eleonora might find a way to produce an heir, after all. Or maybe he was himself in love with his father's wife.

"I need to see Monsieur de Lamanon," Lapérouse said, speaking louder than he needed to. "Señor La-ma-non," he repeated. "He's at the home of Señor Moraga, Don Mateo Moraga. Can you send word?"

As the steward nodded his understanding and turned away, Lapérouse felt oddly as if he had bested the man in some unspoken contest.

•

Lamanon marched into the drawing room, breathing hard and already talking. "Monsieur de Lapérouse," he boomed, "I do hope you've prevailed on *Governor* O'Higgins to let us explore the interior."

He had a way of stressing a word—*Governor*—to show his contempt for a thing. Lapérouse felt draining out of his head every diplomatic intention with which he had armed himself for the meeting.

Lamanon was still talking: "I had to forgo an outing with Don Mateo to be here. He wanted to show me a porphyritic rock formation just outside of town."

"Sit down," Lapérouse ordered, pointing to a hard wooden chair opposite him.

Lamanon made instead for a stuffed chair farther away, and lowered himself onto it slowly, with a show of ruffled dignity. He was in his early thirties, but with his heavy jowls and haughty demeanor, the midcentury cut of his expensive waistcoat, and the top-heavy, weak-legged body typical of gout sufferers, he seemed closer to fifty. The chair squeaked under his weight.

"I'll not mince words, Monsieur de Lamanon," Lapérouse said. "Neither you nor any of the other savants have any business making, or attempting to make, your own arrangements for excursions off of the ships. Such discussions should be between the local authorities and me or Captain de Langle. At the very least we should be consulted first."

Lamanon raised his eyes to the ceiling. "Is that why O'Higgins refused us? Because we had not gone through established *military* channels?"

"Governor O'Higgins had his own reasons for refusing you, mostly having to do with your safety."

"This place is overrun with underemployed soldiers," Lamanon said. "Surely he could summon up an armed escort for us. Isn't that how colonists keep peace with natives, by making a great *show of force*?"

Lapérouse sighed. Few things were more distasteful than arguing against a position with which one essentially agreed. "The colonists have just concluded a treaty with the Indians," he said. "They do not wish to risk the delicate peace they now enjoy."

Lamanon snorted. "Since when have naturalists begun wars?"

"We have no choice but to respect his judgment, Monsieur de Lamanon. I am not going to argue with a man who has already shown us the greatest generosity."

"So you will not support us in this matter?"

"I already *have*. The governor's mind is quite made up."

"What does Monsieur de Langle say?"

Lapérouse opened, then closed, his mouth, fighting a rising swell of anger. The man was relentless—and that faculty for homing right in on elements of discord! There was something diabolical about that kind of intelligence. "Monsieur de Langle was at the same meeting with Governor O'Higgins," he finally said. "He too was disappointed on your behalf. But he understands there is more at stake here than scientific curiosity. It would be well for you and the others to do the same."

Lamanon leaned back in his chair. It squeaked again, and Lapérouse wished fervently it would collapse beneath him.

"Is that all, *sir*?"

"That is all."

Lapérouse listened as the heavy footsteps left the room, then rested his head against the tall back of his chair and closed his eyes. When he opened them again, his mouth had gone slack, and he was startled to find Eleonora standing before him.

"I'm sorry to wake you," she said, looking apologetic but not displeased.

"No, no, no." Lapérouse sat up, then stood, wincing at the stiffness in his backside. No doubt he was feeling the delayed effects of his horseback ride into town. "I was just resting my eyes," he said, blinking himself into greater wakefulness. He hoped very much he had not been snoring. At home, Éléonore would sometimes poke him awake during Mass or at a concert—and occasionally, at dinner with his prickly sister, Jacquette, and her family. "You're the only person I know who can snore sitting straight up," Éléonore once told him, half amused and half vexed.

"I'm sorry, Éléon—Doña Eleonora," he said, piling on his embarrassment. "You came to tell me something?"

Eleonora looked at him, eyebrows drawn in friendly concern. "You look tired, sir, if you will excuse my saying so. It is hard work, overseeing all of your people."

"I'm fine."

"You are an excellent leader to your men."

He laughed. "And how can you tell, Doña Eleonora?"

She raised one dark eyebrow. "Many ways," she said archly. "But here is an example: Monsieur Dufresne tells me you have denied his request to leave the expedition, yet he seems happier now than he was before."

He nodded. "All I had to do was insist that he spend more time with you," he said.

It was her turn to laugh—a girlish, spontaneous laugh he was thrilled to have elicited. She looked down, hiding a blush, and toyed with the tasseled ends of a blue silk mantilla draped over her shoulders. Complementing the mantilla was a pale gray skirt. It was as stiffly pleated and pouffed as the skirts he had seen her wear before, but the modest color made it seem less garish, or perhaps he was growing accustomed to Chilean habits of dress. This skirt too had buttons down the front—four of them, large and silver—holding closed a panel along one of the pleats. He was terribly curious about the buttons, about the need for an opening, *there*, but a gentleman could hardly ask.

"Sir . . ."

"Yes?"

"We are about to take a light lunch now. Would you like to join us, or do you prefer to remain here, where you can continue to work? I can send in a tray."

Lapérouse leaned forward. "Is Monsieur de Lamanon still here?" he whispered.

Eleonora smiled conspiratorially. "No," she whispered back. "It will just be the major and me."

"How about Monneron and Dufresne?"

"They left to run errands in town related to the fête. They would not allow either of us to accompany them."

"I should hope not," Lapérouse said. "We must be allowed a few secrets, after all."

She smiled with an apologetic shrug, suggesting that Monneron and Dufresne had already let on about the planned spectacle. He frowned. Was even a level-headed man like Monneron so susceptible to the charms of a pretty woman? Of course this was a young woman who had a particular gift for asking direct questions with disarming politeness.

"It is all right," she said. "I am very discreet."

"All women say that."

"Yes, but with me it is true." She gestured out into the corridor. "Shall we?"

He offered her his arm. She took it with a squeeze that delighted and confused him. He hoped she did not notice his hobbling, postride gait as they walked down the corridor.

They sat at a round table in a small, sunny room that Eleonora explained was where they had meals when "it is only us." The Sabateros' "light" lunch required two servants to dispense, and consisted of platters of olives and cheese, fresh fruit, three kinds of bread, smoked ham, a flagon of wine, and a savory bean dish the major said was the Araucanians' finest contribution to the local cuisine. José poured a light red wine for Sabatero, who took up the glass, sniffed its contents, took a sip, then handed it back, gesturing for the steward to try it. José brought the glass to his own lips and took a sip, then nodded and said something in Spanish. He took another sip before handing the glass back to Sabatero. They looked for all the world like two wine merchants, father and son, judging the quality of a new vintage. Eleonora wore a pained expression throughout the exchange, and Lapérouse found himself wondering what really happened when "it is only us." He imagined Eleonora subjected to meals at which José sat at table with them like an equal.

"This wine is from our own vineyards," Sabatero explained, motioning for José to fill the other two glasses. "I worried it might be too young. It is not suitable for a heavy meal. But José agrees with me it is fine for lunch." He raised his glass, then regaled his guest with stories of his exploits in the wars against the Araucanians. Eleonora listened intently at first, and Lapérouse guessed she was monitoring how well he told the stories in French. No doubt they had practiced earlier. The major acquitted himself admirably, however, and gradually Eleonora's gaze grew distant. She looked every bit the petulant young person bored by the too-oft-repeated tales of her elders but compelled to sit through yet another recitation. And then she came suddenly and terribly back to attention, her cheeks flaming and her eyes fixed and cold. Sabatero was relating an anecdote about a company led by a criollo who had been given the post against the better judgment of his superiors and then confirmed their misgivings by proving so incompetent that both the regiment and the man's reputation needed to be rescued by Sabatero. Lapérouse knew without being told that the story must be about someone Eleonora knew—her own father, perhaps. When a servant came to announce the return of Monneron and Dufresne from their shopping excursion, she said, "Excuse me while I go and see," and fairly fled the room.

Sabatero poured himself more wine and leaned over to refill Lapérouse's glass. "To our wives," he said.

Lapérouse raised his glass only as high as politeness required, then set the glass down.

"I understand, Count, you also are married to a Creole," Sabatero said.

Lapérouse looked over at Eleonora's empty chair. "Actually," he said carefully, "my wife was born in France."

"But not raised in France. Bourbon?"

"Île de France."

Sabatero nodded. "It changes them when they are not raised in Europe."

"I had not noticed that." What it changes, Lapérouse thought, remembering his family's long opposition to Éléonore, was their standing with other Europeans. He felt his face warm with resentment—both at the memory evoked and at Sabatero's assumption that they would share this contempt for their wives' creole roots.

Sabatero smiled a wide, toothy smile. "The criollos here, they make very much noise about purity—purity of their blood." He pointed to the veins of his forearm. "But this purity, it is a—how do you say it?—a fiction. My Eleonora, her family has been in Chile one hundred fifty years. What is the chance, do you think, that her blood is completely Spanish? Tell me, what do you think?" He leaned toward Lapérouse and raised his thick, wayward eyebrows, revealing watery, red-rimmed eyes. "That is right, sir," he went on, though Lapérouse had said nothing. "It is zero." He made the fingers of one hand into an O. "I knew Eleonora's grandmother. She was mestiza. Yes. Eleonora has an older sister—you are surprised, sir, she has not mentioned it, naturally. The sister is still at the convent. She is a bit"— he tapped his head—"simple, you might say. But the real problem: she looks too Indian. Her parents make her a nun. And I marry the younger one. She is a good wife. But she is a typical criollo, and she has her distaste for Indians where she should not."

He gestured for José to approach the table and pressed the wineglass to him. To José's credit, thought Lapérouse, the steward looked embarrassed and stood by Sabatero without drinking. Sabatero looked up at José with unmistakable pride. "This is a good man. He takes care of everything for us."

Lapérouse could think of no response, torn between discomfort and disgust. He reached by instinct for his wine, then set the glass down. A servant entered the room and announced the arrival of a Señor Delphin.

"Ah," Sabatero said, his face resuming a pleasanter, more businesslike expression, "this is the merchant Don Ambrosio recommends to you to supply your ships. His grandparents were from France, and he speaks good French, not like me. He waits for you in the drawing room."

Lapérouse required no second invitation. On his way out, he passed the larger dining room, where he could hear Monneron's voice. Peering in, he saw the long dining room table at which he had taken his first meal in Concepción. Monneron and Dufresne stood over it examining their acquisitions, which Lapérouse could see included a large coil of rope and a portable brazier. Eleonora stood opposite them, smiling at something one of the men had said. He wondered that her good humor could be so easily restored. He wondered that she had any cheerfulness left at all, living with an old man who held her in contempt and who, Lapérouse now suspected, might be pressing his mixed-blood bastard son upon her.

"But what if it catches fire?" she was asking.

"Then our demonstration will be brief," Monneron said. Dufresne and Eleonora both laughed.

He wished he could join them, could take part in their joviality and exorcise the strange and unpleasant lunch he had just endured. But the lives of more than two hundred men depended on his successful procurement of four months' worth of provisions, and Señor Delphin was waiting. Anyway, he knew his presence would alter the mood in the dining room. It was a peculiar isolation that came with command: one was forever excluded from easy sociability with others while still being at the mercy of highly placed bigots and pompous gabblers the world over.

He made his way down the corridor, picturing as he did the drawing room in his house in Albi and the untidy pile of books and sewing Éléonore always left by her favorite chair, a faded fauteuil she had had shipped from Port Louis. No matter how long he lived, he would never feel he had spent enough hours there. It was with some surprise that he turned into the Sabateros' drawing room to be greeted, not by Éléonore, but by a fast-talking merchant dizzy with delight over the largest sale of his career.

The evening meal was a happier occasion than lunch, as O'Higgins did most of the talking and Sabatero very little. Lapérouse was impressed: O'Higgins was a man who sought peace, not simply through a superior show of force, but by learning to talk with his adversary. He actually knew the Araucanian chiefs and spoke of them by name with what seemed like genuine respect. The problem with a fascinating dinner companion, of course, was that one listened, rapt, and ate and drank without moderation. And the trouble with eating and drinking too much was that although one fell immediately to sleep afterward, it was a sleep neither restful nor lasting.

Lapérouse came to in the middle of the night, feeling slightly sick and aware that he had spent much of the night in a restless half sleep as one document after another floated before his mind's eye, demanding attention: the bill of exchange he needed to write up for Delphin; maps of the Pacific Ocean, with possible routes plotted out between Chile and the Sandwich Islands, Alaska, China; his shipboard journal, almost a month behind; letters he needed to write to the ministry; the unfinished letter to Éléonore.

He opened his eyes and stared into the blackness. He could make out the shape of the window in the room, but nothing else. Somewhere in town, a confused rooster was crowing. Closer, he could hear footsteps making their quiet way across the courtyard. Another restless soul in the house. He wondered whom he would meet if he went out there. Most likely a servant making his or her rounds in the night. Perhaps the vigilant and ubiquitous José. The footsteps stopped nearby, and then he could hear the sound of a door—it was just a few doors down from his own—cautiously opening and closing.

Could it be Eleonora's room? He knew where it was—or he thought he did. Right before dinner he had seen her leaving the room two doors down from his. She had not seen him—at least he did not think she had. Now he imagined himself being the one walking across the courtyard, the one opening and shutting Eleonora's door, and discovering at last the purpose of those mysterious buttons: silver buttons that were cool to the touch and slipped right through their buttonholes, cloth-covered buttons that resisted, requiring force to pop off, giving way to fabric, soft and white, and then it was hands—his own, reaching through warmer and warmer layers of gauze, and hers, small and white, reaching out to him, then his own again, fingers running through the fringe of her mantilla and unplaiting her hair, long and black, spreading it like an open fan around her head. Ashamed, he tried to switch to Éléonore, remembering the last time they were together before he set sail, the time he might have left her with child. But she had wept that night, naked shoulders shaking in his arms. Their first time, then—but no, she had cried then as well—and he was back to yielding buttons and fabric and hair, groping in the darkness for her, for himself, desire prevailing for the moment over compunction, over memory, even over fatigue.

He rose to use the basin and looked through the window at the courtyard, a dark space barely washed in the pale light of what he knew was an almost-quarter moon. Once more he heard a door close, then light footsteps outside. A tiny, disembodied light appeared to the left and began to travel diagonally across the space. Lapérouse moved to the edge of the window, not wishing to be seen peering out in the dead of night. The light reached the center of the courtyard and stopped for a moment. Face lit briefly by the taper in his hand, the figure looked up with an expression of wonder at the southern sky. It was Dufresne.

The cold surprised him as he stepped outside. He looked back once at the house, where José stood in the doorway watching them. It was impossible to read his expression in the dark. Lapérouse turned away in relief and set off with Pierre into the streets of the still dormant city.

They found their way easily enough to the edge of town, footfalls echoing off the crumbling mud walls of the buildings as they passed.

Once outside of town, they occasionally exchanged nods with fishermen or peasants on their way to town with fish and produce. At the top of the first rise, they stopped and unpacked the parcel José had silently handed them: two flasks of water, two minced-meat pastries, and some jerked beef. Lapérouse took one pastry and Pierre the other. Looking back, Lapérouse could see the roofs of the dusty town below just brightening while to the east, the rising sun gilt the jagged line of the cordillera.

"Why did we leave so early, sir?" Pierre asked.

"We didn't," Lapérouse said. "I meant to leave at daybreak, and see?" He pointed to the mountains. "It's daybreak."

"It is *now*," Pierre muttered.

Lapérouse got up and set off again down the road. He could hear Pierre groan sleepily as he hoisted himself to his feet and followed his master.

By the time they crested the highest point in the road between Concepción and Talcahuano, there was enough light to distinguish three bodies of water: the Bay of Concepción to the north, the frigates just visible in their anchorages; the great Bío-Bío River to the south, marking the boundary between the Spanish colony and the untamed Araucanians; and to the west, still murky with night and unanswered questions, the Pacific Ocean. Lapérouse's heart lifted at the sight of so much water and at the mostly downhill path that lay between him and the *Boussole*.

He was not a man to obsess about a thing for too long. He knew this about himself and trusted it. Every step he took away from Concepción resolved some of the turmoil he had experienced during the night and restored clarity to his mind. He thought of Éléonore with a twinge of guilt, but he had not, after all, done anything wrong. He knew what Jesus was reported to have said about lust, how it was the same as committing adultery. But only a man who had never been with a woman could have believed such a thing. He moved on, down the steepest part of the pass, and welcomed the return of his usual yearning for Éléonore, a feeling painful in its way, but not intolerably so, and familiar for all that. Some mariners suffered acutely from lovesickness at sea, but seemed to enjoy *missing* their wives or lovers more than *being* with them. Not he. He thought of Éléonore every day, many times a day, but he remembered her equably, and did not allow his longing for her to distract him from work.

Every time he returned to her, she delighted him all over again and, he liked to think, he her, but it was never a surprise. It was simply what it was: happiness. Stepping carefully over the loose gravel on the road, he began composing in his head the next page of his letter to her: *Some of the husbands in Chile are so very much older than their wives that you and I would be considered quite contemporaries, my dear.*

They reached a flatter part of the road, and Pierre unwrapped the sun-dried beef and handed a piece to Lapérouse before taking a bite for himself. A large shadow passed over them, and both men ducked by instinct. Looking up, Lapérouse saw the most enormous bird he had ever laid eyes on. Two more flew in long, graceful curves, never flapping their wings. He was not much of a naturalist—one bird was much like another, to his mind—but these creatures could not fail to impress. "They must be the famous Andean condors," he told Pierre, who nodded. Lapérouse tossed his meat out into a clearing by the side of the road and waited to see if they would come down for it, but the wide gyres they traced in the sky were apparently focused on something else.

"Sir?" Pierre said, offering what remained of his dried beef. Lapérouse regretted the loss of his breakfast, but he shook his head, and the two men proceeded in silence.

The village of Talcahuano was already in full bustle when they arrived, but the sudden appearance of two dusty, rumpled Frenchmen coming from the direction of Concepción, one in partial dress uniform, surprised the inhabitants and soldiers they passed. Even more surprised were two other Frenchmen, who had just hauled one of the *Astrolabe*'s small boats ashore. "Commander!" one of them cried out when he recognized Lapérouse. It was several paces before Lapérouse recognized him: It was Tréton de Vaujuas, Langle's young ensign. The other man was middle-aged, pale, and very thin.

"Good morning, Monsieur de Vaujuas," Lapérouse called out.

"Good morning, sir," Vaujuas said, then looked around for a corresponding boat from the *Boussole*, and finding none, toward the village for a carriage or horse or some other explanation for the commander's appearance. "Where did you come from, sir?"

"Never mind that," Lapérouse said, feeling testy and enjoying it. "Just row us back to my ship."

Vaujuas held the boat steady while Lapérouse and Pierre climbed aboard, then helped his companion on with great gentleness, and pushed off. The other man sat in the back and did not help row. Vaujuas sat facing Lapérouse and took the oars. "My manservant, Jean Le Fol, sir," he said by way of introduction. The servant leaned to the right so as to be seen from behind his master, and inclined his head in greeting. It was the sick servant La Borde had told him about.

"And how do you fare, Monsieur Le Fol?" Lapérouse asked.

"I'm very well, sir," the man replied, but he shivered in the light breeze, and sweat beaded his pale forehead.

Lapérouse did not leave the *Boussole* for three days. Indeed, he hardly left his cabin, spoke to almost no one, and did little but write. He wrote to Major Sabatero, thanking him for his hospitality and apologizing for his hasty departure, assuring him that only the most pressing need could have dragged him from their gracious company and home. He wrote to Monneron, who was still in town, with instructions regarding preparations for the fête. He wrote to decline an invitation from O'Higgins to celebrate Mass on Sunday at what passed for a cathedral in Concepción, then sent a note to the *Astrolabe*, directing Langle and a few officers to go in his stead. He wrote to the minister, assuring him that they "had not one sick aboard either vessel." He remembered Vaujuas's servant as soon as he'd penned the line, but he didn't wish to cross it out. Langle would be writing his own report to the minister—let *him* mention the sick servant. He wrote to accept a subsequent invitation from O'Higgins to join an outing to explore the ruins of the old city. He drafted a bill of exchange for Delphin and a short speech to give at the fête. He caught up on his journal, had it copied, then corrected the copy. He struggled to finish his letter to Éléonore. It seemed thoughtless not to mention a child if there were one, but equally thoughtless to mention one if there were not. In the end he punctuated the note with numerous "my dears" and "my loves" and trusted to her affectionate understanding.

Every time his thoughts strayed back toward Concepción, to the Sabateros, the darkened courtyard, the floating light, he forced his mind to something else, and failing that, cast doubt on his memories. Perhaps

Dufresne had just stepped out for the night air or to examine the stars. Perhaps it had not been Dufresne, after all. Perhaps his own disordered state of mind had created recognitions and associations where there were none.

By the fourth morning, he was pale and ink-stained, and his right hand ached from the hours spent writing, but he had caught up with his administrative duties, and his mind and conscience felt clear and un-encumbered. Unfortunately, the day's reports challenged his hard-won equanimity, bringing as they did a second letter from Dufresne, request-ing once more that he be released from the expedition. Lapérouse tried to bring a disinterested reading to the request, to put aside his suspicions, his own antipathy to the man, but it was impossible. Whereas before the young man had seemed motivated by a strong sense of having made a mistake, of realizing he was not suited to life at sea, and simple home-sickness, in this new letter he was more polite, but also more assertive. He sounded as though he just wanted to be freed from the expedition to go his own way: as if, Lapérouse could not help but think, he had found a compelling reason to stay behind.

Lapérouse set the letter aside. He had no stomach for writing back to Dufresne, and indeed, was not sure how to respond. Losing Dufresne would have little effect on the scientific aims of the voyage, but it set a bad precedent, suggesting that the savants might come and go as they pleased. Lapérouse fingered a scratch on his bust of Jean-Jacques Rous-seau. He liked to think of himself as a man unswayed by personal pique, but he could not deny there would be some satisfaction to turning the man down and forcing him to leave Concepción and whatever attach-ments he might have formed there.

An urgent rap on the door ended his introspection: one of his lieuten-ants requesting that the commander "please intervene right now in a problem on deck." The problem turned out to be an argument between Bisalion and Langle's cook, Deveau. The two men had not had occasion to interact with each other before, but now they were both charged with cooking for the fête, and each man wanted nothing more than to feel superior to the other. Deveau, strangely thin for a cook, was older and claimed to have cooked for Bougainville during the American War. Bisalion, high-strung and prematurely bald, believed that his position with the commander made *him* the senior cook. Deveau had rowed over to the *Boussole* that morning to confer with Bisalion, but by the time Lapérouse arrived, a disagreement over the soup course had devolved into shouted accusations of incompetence, drunkenness, pilferage, and, less relevantly, bastardy and impotence. Lapérouse stepped between them just as fists were raised. Both men shrank back in chagrin when they saw him.

Lapérouse dismissed the seamen who had gathered around, then turned to the two belligerents. "You will prepare exactly what Monsieur de Langle and I tell you to," he said. "Monsieur Deveau, kindly tell your captain that he and I will be settling on a menu for the fête when I visit the *Astrolabe* tomorrow evening." He heard Bisalion gulp behind him, ready to protest the unfairness of being left out, and held up a finger to maintain both cooks' silence. "Neither of you will be present at the discussion. We will inform you of our decisions and of who will be making what."

The men continued to glare past Lapérouse and at each other. "Monsieur Bisalion," Lapérouse said, addressing his own cook. "You promised me eggs this morning, but I still haven't seen them." The cook strode off, red-faced with anger and shame. Deveau made the mistake of laughing at his opponent's discomfiture. "You may return to the *Astrolabe*, Monsieur Deveau," Lapérouse said, then left the deck so he would not have to see the way his men, naturally taking their shipmate's side, harassed Deveau as he clambered gracelessly over the rail and down into the waiting boat.

Deveau may have been physically excluded from Lapérouse and Langle's discussion the following evening, but he took full advantage of the meeting taking place aboard the *Astrolabe* to ensure that he and his skills were not forgotten. The captains-only dinner, an occasional event that alternated between the two ships, was usually a casual affair, but that evening featured plates of Chilean goat cheese, steamed mussels with garlic, a deliciously light onion soup, stuffed pheasant served with mashed potatoes piped into rosettes, and warm fig tarts topped with fresh cream. Surely it was not Deveau's fault if some of these items made it onto the final menu.

Over a second serving of tart, Lapérouse told Langle that he had received a second letter from Dufresne.

"I know," Langle said

"Why is it that the least valuable men on a ship always take up the most time?"

"Why don't we let him go, sir?"

Lapérouse sighed. They had already discussed the whys and why-nots of the matter. "Is he still staying with the Sabateros?" he demanded.

Langle's eyebrows flicked upward in mild surprise. "I believe so. He was sitting with them in church on Sunday."

"He *was?*"

Langle looked at him for a moment before speaking. "If you're concerned about it, sir . . ."

"What do you mean?"

Langle gently set his fork down on the table. "We have an old, not very attentive husband; his very young, very pretty wife; a commander who is—shall we say—*solicitous* of her; and their guest, a dissatisfied but handsome naturalist—"

"*Handsome?*" Lapérouse blurted out. "*Dufresne?*" Langle laughed, and Lapérouse found himself covering his embarrassment with a volley of words: "I am surprised beyond measure to hear you describe him so, Monsieur de Langle. God knows I am no connoisseur of male beauty, but to me the man looks sallow and underfed, with that weak chin and eyes that refuse to meet yours. Is that what women like these days?"

Langle was still smiling. "He's also tall, with a full head of thick, dark curls. And a carefully cultivated air of tragedy that some women might find irresistible."

Lapérouse frowned, annoyed by Langle's mirth.

"I can order him back to the ship tomorrow if you wish," Langle said mildly.

Lapérouse waved a hand in dismissal, then briskly suggested they have the table cleared so they could consult their Pacific charts. "I need to inform the ministry of our plans from here," he said. Langle called for François to clear the table.

To decide on a plan of sail for the coming months, they needed a firm departure date from Concepción. That date depended on the completion of critical repairs, and the work was proceeding slowly. Some tasks took time and could not be rushed, like the caulking. Some things turned out to be in worse shape than they had expected, like the rigging. Some of the men had been diverted from repair work to preparations for the fête. But the main problem seemed to be an excess of leisure. The long stay in Concepción Bay, with its clement weather, ample food, friendly inhabitants, and lack of urgency, had turned even some of the more industrious seamen into idlers.

"We could promise the crew time in town if they complete the repairs more quickly," Langle suggested.

"We could end up with two frigates full of Frédérics," Lapérouse said.

"Yes. Some of the men will debauch themselves."

"And come back unfit for duty."

"Or diseased."

"Or not at all."

But it *would* get the work done sooner, as they both knew. Lapérouse sighed. He wished they could do something other than appealing to the men's animal appetites, something that fostered the finer virtues—camaraderie, pride, loyalty. "What if," he began, toying with the edge of the chart, "on the night after the fête, we were to use the same location to feed everyone from both frigates? Someone in town will be only too happy to sell us an ox or two for the occasion."

"An all-hands dinner on the beach," Langle said, nodding his appreciation. "One is less likely to desert ship captains who treat you to such things."

An hour later, their course was decided: In two days, the fête. The day after, an all-hands feast in the same place. Meanwhile, they would make it known that everyone would be granted leave for one day if all the repairs were completed by March 12, five days hence. On March 15 they would set sail. As for their itinerary thereafter, they would head west for Easter Island, then north to the Sandwich Islands, and still farther north for the coast of North America, where they would spend the summer exploring. Tinian by year's end, Manila in February, Kamchatka the following summer. New Holland the spring after that, then islands and more islands in the South Seas—hopefully some of them new—and through the Endeavour Strait for Île de France by the end of 1788, and finally back into the Atlantic and north for home.

"We should be back in France by July of 1789," Lapérouse said.

Langle's forehead was furrowed, betraying his ordinarily better-concealed disquiet. "It looks so easy on paper," he said.

"It won't be easy," Lapérouse said, "but I have no doubt we can accomplish it."

Langle cast his eyes over their scrawled notes and ran one finger down the expanse of the Pacific, still open on the table between them. "I keep wondering where the unforeseen calamity will strike."

"Well, that's the thing about unforeseen events, isn't it?"

Langle's lips twitched upward in a half smile. He gathered up the notes strewn across the charts. "Do you never lie awake at night with thoughts like this?"

Lapérouse considered for a moment. "No," he said. "I have my sleepless nights, of course. But they usually concern problems already present or about-to-be." Or lonely young wives and their mysterious buttons, he thought with a rush of private embarrassment. "Surely it's not a foregone conclusion that we'll experience a calamity," he said.

"Isn't it?"

"I should hope not." Lapérouse stood, rolled up the charts, and handed them to Langle.

Langle returned the maps to a drawer under the table. "It was your optimism, you know."

"What?"

"*Optimism.* That's what the philosophers call it. A basic faith in the goodness and rightness of life and the world."

Lapérouse disliked it when Langle waxed philosophical on him. "Well, what about it?"

Langle opened the door to show him out. "It was why *you* were chosen to lead the expedition."

The next day they visited the ruins of old Concepción. Lapérouse had awoken with a headache. The promise of time ashore had indeed produced the predicted effect, and at first light men were running up and down the deck and ladders and rigging, shouting up to men aloft or down to men below, and wielding adzes, mallets, caulking irons, and other clamorous tools. It made his head ring, but he could hardly order them to stop. When Pierre brought his breakfast, Lapérouse barked at him to go away, then remembered the outing to the ruins and bellowed at him to come back. He would have to get properly dressed again, put on his affable French captain face, and decide which of his officers could be spared for the day (none of them could be spared, really, but that would not do; he would have to bring *someone* along). Oh, he thought, with an audible groan, to be at sea again, without these social obligations!

Stepping out of his cabin, he was greeted by a stinging aroma. "What the devil is that?" he cried.

Pierre sniffed. "Onions, sir, for tomorrow's soup. Bisalion and a couple of hands are cutting up a barrel of them right now."

Lapérouse blinked the tears from his eyes, ordered the small boat to be made ready, and called for Lieutenant de Clonard to join him.

"I really cannot, sir," Clonard protested. "Monsieur Delphin's delivery is coming this morning. I have to—"

"Where are the other officers?"

"They're all ashore, sir, requisitioning chairs and dishes in Talcahuano for the fête."

At the landing area he saw Monneron, but it was quite out of the question to ask him to join the outing. He was running back and forth along the shore overseeing three sets of men: the ships' carpenters and sailmakers, whose job was to construct the tent for dinner; half a dozen men charged with clearing and setting up a platform for the spectacle; and an even smaller group, selected for their ability to wield a brush, who were secluded inside a temporary palisade with Duché de Vancy and pots of blue and gold paint.

"Do you have enough men to help you, Monsieur de Monneron?" Lapérouse called after him.

"Yes, sir, I think I have."

"Is Monsieur Dufresne still assisting you?"

Monneron stopped short. "I believe he's going to see the ruins today."

"But he *has* been assisting you?"

Someone called to Monneron from the tent-building site, and he began edging toward it. "He was quite helpful at first," he said, "but he seems to be busy with other matters now." A loud crash and volley of cursing from the carpenters, and Monneron broke into a run. "Enjoy the ruins, sir!" he called over his shoulder.

Lapérouse felt an unpleasant return of suspicion and jealousy. "You're coming with me," he said, collaring the first officer he saw, a man barely visible behind the tall column of wooden bowls balanced in his arms. Fortunately it was Lieutenant d'Escures, an impulsive and cheerful man who rarely said no to an unexpected turn of events and was undaunted by his commander's brusque tone. He happily bequeathed his armload of borrowed bowls to a junior officer and joined Lapérouse at the shoreline. They were soon joined by Langle, accompanied only by young Lesseps. Apparently *none* of the *Astrolabe*'s officers could be spared. Lesseps's services as Russian speaker would not be needed for months—perhaps a *year*—but he was an affable shipmate, always willing to participate in the expedition's activities.

"A perfect late-summer morning," Langle said by way of greeting.

It was true. The sky was brilliant and clear, with the morning chill giving way to a light southwest breeze. "I confess I had not noticed it earlier," Lapérouse said, "what with all the din and poisonous onion fumes aboard my ship."

Langle smiled. "I'm happy to report the *Astrolabe* smells like a bakery."

Lapérouse frowned in mock offense. "Now I understand your cunning in assigning the soup to Bisalion and the bread and tarts to Deveau."

The party from Concepción now made its appearance in Talcahuano. Almost forty people: O'Higgins, the hardier dignitaries of Concepción, most of the Basque Society, all of the French savants, hired porters, a few servants, including one woman, and three heavily laden pack animals. Right behind them were the deliveries from Delphin, carts bearing wheat, onions, potatoes, salted meats, and wine for the next four months.

The simultaneous arrival of so many people added to the disorder at the beach, with boats of various shapes and sizes and ownerships coming and going and vying for space at the water's edge. A great deal of gesturing and shouting in both French and Spanish ensued. One misunderstanding resulted in food baskets intended for the trip to the ruins being hauled aboard the *Astrolabe* and another in a barrel of wine falling into the bay. Eventually, however, the people and provisions headed for the ruins were loaded onto three of the expedition's boats to proceed by water toward the site of the old city. The breeze made light work for the rowers, and they seemed to fly across the southern end of the bay. Seated at the tiller of his own longboat, surrounded by men of intelligence and curiosity, the prospect of seeing something new and quite interesting before him, Lapérouse felt the weight of his ill humor and headache lighten.

It returned with some force, however, when he disembarked and was accosted by Dufresne, looking droopily tall and simultaneously languid and anxious. He acknowledged the naturalist with a curt nod, then strode off toward O'Higgins, just disembarking from another boat. Dufresne followed a few paces behind. Lapérouse let him nearly catch up, then turned around. "Monsieur Dufresne, do I understand correctly that you are still at the Sabateros?"

"Yes," Dufresne said, flushing as he stammered out something about his original host suffering a relapse.

"I see. Señora Sabatero, she is well?"

Was it his imagination, or was there a flicker of suppressed pain at the mention of Eleonora? Dufresne blinked before replying. "She is, and— and sends her regards. Sir."

"And how are the preparations for tomorrow's spectacle?"

Another wave of color passed over his face. "Fine, I believe," he said. "Monsieur de Monneron has things well in hand."

"He always does," Lapérouse said. "He is a most reliable shipmate." He turned away and joined O'Higgins; Dufresne did not follow.

The group made its way up from the beach, following the one woman servant, a wizened mestiza who turned out to be their guide to the ruins. She had been maid to a family of some importance, most of whom had died in the disaster, and was herself one of the oldest survivors of the calamity. She carried herself with the dignity of someone used to living among the wealthy and prominent, and walked with the sure gait of a much younger woman. Following her up the dirt path that led from the beach, Lapérouse could see nothing that looked like the remains of a town. The area was utterly overgrown, the forest taking back its own. But the old woman picked her way around trees and shrubs, pointing to this and that and explaining it all in a crackly stream of talk that O'Higgins and Lamanon translated for the others. Here was the main road, she said, and here the old plaza, and there, the cathedral. See, under that vine, one could still make out some of the stonework. The bell tower had fallen right there and killed her mistress's brother. Behind that was the church-yard, buried in mud after the wave. If one were to dig there, she said, one might still find legible tombstones. And right here, she said, her voice going soft, was the home of Señor and Señora Gallegos de Rubias, may they rest in peace, whom she had served for many years. She and her mistress had fled uphill before the wave, but alas, her master and most of the household were lost when it came. As for evidence of the wave and its destructive force, she clambered nimbly uphill and showed them, nestled beneath a wind-twisted dwarf pine, a broken statue she claimed had orig-inally been in the Gallegos's courtyard.

Lapérouse was impressed by the woman's memory of the old town and by her ability to find traces of the life that had once bustled in this place. But most of all he was impressed—and unnerved—by the power of nature to undo human endeavor. An entire city, two hundred years in the making, complete with monasteries and schools, gracious homes and craftsmen's shops, erased in a morning. And now, only thirty-five years later, the era-sure itself erased, the scars of that violent unmaking hidden under trees and vines. His own endeavor floated upon the high seas on two wooden ships. How much more tenuous their hold on life!

The official tour at an end, the group spread out over the area to explore. Langle joined Lamanon in examining geological evidence of the cataclysm, while some of the other savants made their quiet way through the overgrown ruins, looking for plants or creatures that were new to them, and the porters and servants prepared lunch in a clearing. Lapérouse, wishing to rid himself of the ruins' gloomier associations, wandered to-ward the shoreline and was cheered to see the frigates, sturdy and whole in the bay. He turned toward approaching footsteps, and was relieved to see O'Higgins, not Dufresne, coming toward him.

"It is perhaps too sobering a place to bring guests," O'Higgins said.

Not at all, Lapérouse assured him; it had been a most instructive and enjoyable outing. The usual compliments were traded: It is wonderful for our people to have so many men of science with whom to enjoy such an outing. But you and your people have gone far beyond the call of common hospitality for us. The pleasure has been ours, and if there is anything at all I can do in these days before you depart—

"There is one thing," Lapérouse said. He lowered his voice, though no one else was by. "You are of course acquainted with Monsieur Dufresne, the *Astrolabe*'s naturalist who has been staying with the Sabateros?"

O'Higgins nodded yes, of course, a delightful young man.

Lapérouse cleared his throat. "Yes, well. He wishes to be released from the expedition and stay here until he can find passage back to Europe."

"I see." O'Higgins looked at Lapérouse as if trying to gauge what it was the commander wanted. "I can, of course, speak with Captain de Postigo. He sails for Cádiz—"

Lapérouse shook his head. He looked up toward the ruined town and could make out a few of the savants, though not Dufresne, clambering over boulders. "Governor, I hope I may speak frankly."

But of course.

"He is not an especially gifted naturalist nor a particularly amiable shipmate. Our scientific mission would not be much affected by his departure."

"And yet."

Lapérouse nodded. "I am concerned about establishing an unfortunate precedent among the scientific delegation, of—"

"Of surrendering too easily to their demands."

"Yes. And allowing them to take the expedition too lightly."

O'Higgins nodded. "Monsieur Dufresne *will* need official permission to disembark and remain here," he said.

"Ah."

"The Spanish empire can be rather jealous of its borders."

"Indeed," Lapérouse said, remembering the day of their arrival, and how they had looked in vain toward this exact spot for a city that had been gone for a generation.

"This permission may prove difficult to obtain."

"I understand."

"I will try, of course."

"I would be much obliged, sir."

After lunch, he found Dufresne, standing alone and staring moodily out toward the bay, and informed him he could leave the expedition. "As long as you get the local authorities' permission to remain here," he added. "I have made your case in person to Governor O'Higgins."

"Oh, thank you, sir!" Dufresne cried.

Lapérouse frowned, more irritated by the man's cheerfulness than by his petulance. "I cannot promise you'll get a favorable response, Dufresne. You know how these Spaniards are—quite jealous of their borders." He walked away before Dufresne could begin thanking him again.

Back in Talcahuano, Lapérouse and Langle and the savants thanked their hosts again and again, promised to see them all on the morrow, and watched them make their way through the village and back toward Concepción. When Lapérouse turned toward the water to return to the *Boussole*, he found Lieutenant d'Escures in earnest conversation with Monneron and the older La Borde brother. "What is it?" he called.

D'Escures broke away from the group and approached Lapérouse and Langle. "Apparently in all the chaos this morning, two men from the *Astrolabe* stole off, hidden in one of Monsieur Delphin's emptied carts."

The next day, while the late-afternoon sun cast longer and longer shadows across the beach, Lapérouse and Langle stood and watched as the colorful procession of people and conveyances descended from the hills above Talcahuano. It looked like most of Concepción was coming for the fête. Governor O'Higgins, splendid in gold stitching, red brocade, and starched ruffles, led the way, and the rest of Concepción society followed, each rank in its proper order. Most of the ladies rode in carriages and most of the men on horseback, but some of the younger caballeros came on foot, while a few of the older ones, like Sabatero, arrived in sedan chairs carried by Indian servants. Close on the heels of these worthies were the common people of Concepción, hundreds of them, bearing baskets of food and drink, prepared to claim a bit of beach and enjoy the event in their own way.

Langle had been nearly silent while they awaited their guests, and Lapérouse had the uncomfortable sense that he had somehow caused offense. They had last seen each other the previous afternoon, right here, when they had returned from the ruins and learned of the deserters.

"Your runaways—have they returned?" he asked.

Langle shook his head. "I sent three officers into town this morning to look for them, but they couldn't find them. O'Higgins has promised to help, of course, but"—he inclined his head toward the stream of colonists approaching them—"most of his people are on their way here."

"Who *were* they, the men who left? Just sailors?"

Langle paused before answering. "One was, yes, *just* a sailor. The other was a fusilier. Both quite able men, actually. I'm sorry to lose them."

"Of course," Lapérouse said. "But perhaps it isn't worth forcing unwilling men on a trip of this duration?"

Langle turned to Lapérouse. "This morning I received an official letter from some clerk in Concepción denying Dufresne's request to remain here or find a berth on a Spanish ship returning to Europe."

Lapérouse felt his face warm. So that was it. Well, O'Higgins certainly did operate with dispatch. "I see," he said. "How did he take it?"

"Very badly. I've had to confine him to his quarters."

The first guests were arriving, with all the commotion that entailed, as horses were secured, carriage doors opened and closed, and servants rushed about fixing mussed dresses and hair and reapplying powders and rouge. The only thing Lapérouse could think of to say was of a practical nature, and not likely to ease the tension between them: "We may have to cancel the day off we've promised everyone."

"Yes," Langle said. "What a way to repay the men."

"We still have our all-hands feast tomorrow."

"It's not the same."

"Perhaps there's some way to give them their day in town *and* discourage deserters."

"What do you suggest?"

He hardly knew, but now there were guests to greet and direct toward the dining tent. Many of the faces were familiar from the ball at the Sabateros', but he had not seen them out of doors, in the sun, and it was interesting to note how the daylight improved some people and not others. For some, the exertion of the three-league trip had brought out a healthy, windswept look that the hasty ministrations of servants had not been able to undo, while in others, the light revealed the thinning skin around a woman's eyes, the pallor of lingering illness, or the frayed fabric that spoke

of genteel poverty. And then Eleonora stood before him. He had not
seen her in nearly a week. She was dressed much as she had been at the
ball, but her cheeks were flushed and her face framed by wisps of hair
that had escaped their braids. A jaunty and somewhat mannish riding
hat sat atop her head. Lapérouse laughed aloud in frank delight at the
sight of her.

"Doña Eleonora," he cried, "did you ride out from town?"

She curtsied. "Alas," she said, "I was confined to a carriage."

Langle cleared his throat next to him, drawing his attention to Sabatero, red-faced and out of breath beside Eleonora, sweating through an
ill-fitting uniform. "Major Sabatero," he called out in greeting, then pointed
toward the entrance to the dinner tent.

The tent was a marvel of lumber and sailcloth that was more spacious
inside than one would have guessed from without. It took some time to get
all of the guests inside and seated. Only the highest-ranking individuals—
O'Higgins, Señor Quexada and his wife, Sabatero and Eleonora, the
bishop, a visiting Spanish ship captain—had reserved seats at the long,
narrow tables built for the occasion. Some anxious jostling ensued, with
the other guests vying for the best places to which rank or wealth or
lineage entitled them. It took long enough that Bisalion stormed over
from his makeshift beach kitchen to hiss at Lapérouse that he would not
answer for the results if the soup were not served *immediately*. But in due
course everyone was in place: one hundred and fifty men and women of
Concepción; twenty-five of the expedition's officers, savants, and artists,
diplomatically scattered around the room; and another contingent of Frenchmen, mostly able seamen overseen by petty officers, lining the inside
perimeter of the tent, and ready, at a signal from the commander, to begin
serving the meal. Lapérouse rose.

"We are so honored by your presence," he began.

He had practiced the speech with care, and the words came easily—
too easily, perhaps, for his mind wandered. He asked his guests' indulgence for what was bound to be a rougher and simpler meal than they
were accustomed to and thanked them for their openness and generosity
to him and all of his men. But he was distracted by the realization that
Eleonora had been seated next to him. His remarks concluded with a
glass raised to the House of Bourbon, toasting the health and long reigns

of the most Christian kings of France and Spain. Hearty applause followed. He signaled for the first course to be served and sat down, and instantly felt his more diffuse awareness collapse into a single point, with the very physical and arresting sensation of Eleonora's fan touching his right leg.

Did she—*could* she—know what she was doing? Lapérouse all but inhaled his onion soup, hardly able to regard O'Higgins, who waxed enthusiastic about the soup's velvet texture, its fine balance of sharp and mild flavors. Langle got up to say a few words himself, and the fan shifted downward, closer to the knee. It disappeared during the applause for Langle, and he had almost forgotten about it when it suddenly returned, brushing against his hip, distracting him from the fish course. The stuffed pheasant required both hands to enjoy, and then the fan lay on the table between them like a paper and ivory border. But after eating a decorous quantity of the dish and not one bite more, Eleonora flicked open the fan and waved it before herself a few times before shutting it and letting her hand dip once more below the table. Lapérouse braced himself for the touch, but it did not come, and now he was as distracted by the lack of sensation as he had been earlier by its errant presence.

He had to stop this, he told himself. It was all imagination—it had always only been imagination. Here she was now, deep in conversation with Langle, who sat across from her. They were discussing the windmills and ovens he had devised for the frigates. "Do you mean you have had fresh bread on board all these months at sea?" she asked, her face alive with admiration. "Your crew, they are very fortunate men." Langle looked down, embarrassed, pleased by her interest. See, Lapérouse told himself, she has this effect on everyone. He shifted himself a bit to the right, the better to attend to O'Higgins, who was saying something about their deserters.

"They have hidden themselves well, your runaways. I sent some soldiers to the typical haunts of sailors, and they are not there."

"I hope you will not expend too much time and effort to find them," Lapérouse said, then seeing that Langle was listening, added, "But we are most grateful for your help on this, as on so much else during our stay."

"Governor," Langle said, "what would happen to two foreign sailors who are discovered only after their ship has sailed away?"

"We take them into the army to fight the Araucanians," he said.

"Why, Monsieur de Langle," Lapérouse said, leaning over to refill his friend's wineglass, "I believe we may have found a way to allow our men their time ashore while guaranteeing their return."

Langle nodded in agreement, but there was no relief in his face. He turned toward O'Higgins again. "But you are now at peace with the Indians."

"For now," O'Higgins said. He went on to explain all the ways in which their current truce might fail, but Lapérouse hardly attended, for he felt it again, on his thigh, only this time he could not be sure it was a fan. The pressure was warmer, firmer.

He pushed back from the table. "Forgive me, Governor," he said. "I'm anxious to know how preparations for the evening's entertainment are coming along. Will you excuse me for a few minutes? Monsieur de Langle, I'm going to check on Monneron."

Langle looked up with mild surprise. "I can go if you wish."

Lapérouse shook his head. "I'll only be a moment." He turned back to his right. "Doña Eleonora, will you excuse me?"

She nodded, smiling—the same winning smile she wore every time they spoke, and that she had offered Langle just moments before. He bowed hastily to their other guests and ducked out of the dining tent, face burning.

He headed toward the water and ran along the shore, not from any real urgency so much as a simple desire to exert himself. Climbing the rise they had designated for the viewing area, he looked down toward a clearing where six men stood conferring over what looked like a pile of collapsed sails atop four barrels. A long rope lay coiled on the ground beside each barrel.

"Monneron!" he called down. "How goes it?"

Monneron looked up, putting a hand to his forehead against the glare. "Is that you, Commander?" he said. "We're ready, sir. The wind is picking up; we shouldn't wait much longer."

"Agreed. Do you have the men you need to manage the ropes?"

Monneron nodded, indicating the four sturdy crewmen around him.

"And the fireworks?"

The engineer pointed to the collection of longboats and small boats making their way out into the bay. "As soon as it's dark enough, sir."

"And the salvo from the frigates?"

Monneron drew out his telescope and handed it up to Lapérouse. "Monsieur Broudou is on the quarterdeck, watching for our signal."

Lapérouse put the glass to his eye and scanned the deck of the *Boussole*. Indeed, there was Frédéric, looking back at him through his own glass. His brother-in-law had been so dogged and faithful in his efforts since his onboard incarceration that Lapérouse had left him second-in-charge for the evening, under Lieutenant Colinet, and had already decided to allow him off of the frigate the following evening for the all-hands dinner. They stared at each other across the distance, then Frédéric raised a hand in greeting. By instinct Lapérouse did the same, but felt suddenly ridiculous, as if they were two boys signaling each other in a game of pirates. He handed the glass back to Monneron.

"I trust the signal wasn't for him to wave and for me to wave back," Lapérouse said.

"No, sir," Monneron assured him.

Lapérouse looked about, feeling superfluous. "Have you eaten?" he asked. "The pheasant is quite delicious."

Monneron smiled up at Lapérouse with something like brotherly indulgence. "Sir, we're fine. Everything is in readiness here. We just need you and your guests to finish dinner and make your way out here."

"Yes, of course." So that was that. Everything fine, competent men exercising their competence. He should return to the tent, to his guests, to Langle, who for all his urbanity was diffident around people he did not know well. And to the young woman who might or might not have been teasing him under the table with her fan.

Back in the tent, Lamanon was addressing the assembly in Spanish. His admirers from the Basque Society, most of them seated around him, listened with great and approving attention, but some of the others in the room were looking down intently at the crumbs left from their fig tarts, and O'Higgins and the other military officers sat stone-faced. Lapérouse shot a glance at Langle, who looked back with a raised eyebrow and a slight shrug. What was Lamanon saying?

Lapérouse hurried back to his place and clinked his glass. "Monsieur de Lamanon will excuse my interruption," he said, "as it is a matter of science to which I now wish to draw your attention." Lamanon stood still, cocked his head to listen, then sat down in his place without turning to acknowledge Lapérouse. "If you will all follow me outside."

There was a sudden hubbub of voices, of benches being pushed back and the rustling of skirts, and Lapérouse was afraid he might have unleashed a stampede for the exits, but O'Higgins stood up with quiet dignity and the commotion instantly died down. O'Higgins then nodded to Lapérouse, and they led the way out together.

"Governor, I am almost afraid to ask what Monsieur de Lamanon was saying when I returned," Lapérouse said as they walked out toward the viewing area.

O'Higgins waved a hand in generous dismissal. "He predicts independence for Chile within twenty-five years."

"Good God." Lapérouse shook his head. "My apologies, sir. He is a brilliant man, but can become carried away by his own ideas."

"You should keep a careful watch on him, Count."

Lapérouse smiled. "I won't deny he's proved a thorn in my side," he said, "but he's harmless enough."

They had reached the viewing area, and Lapérouse offered O'Higgins one of the seats set up for dignitaries and ladies. O'Higgins nodded, then said before sitting down: "Do not underestimate men of ideas, Monsieur de Lapérouse. I fear you and your countrymen may be too open to men like Lamanon. My adopted country has sometimes taken its fear of new ideas too far, of course, but I will say that Spaniards understand that ideas can lead to actions, and actions to consequences one cannot always foresee."

Lapérouse did not know whether to feel grateful or put upon by O'Higgins's paternal tone. "Thank you, Governor," he said.

Eleonora made her way into the viewing area, saw her husband settled comfortably onto a seat, and declined the seat offered to her. "I hope it will not be indecorous of me to stand," she said. "I have been sitting all day."

"Not at all, Doña Eleonora." He watched her hands as they fiddled with her fan and with the light wool mantilla she wore against the evening chill.

As the other guests filed into the space, everyone pressed forward, craning their necks to see the area below them, where Monneron and his men continued to stand watch over the barrels, the ropes, and the piled-up fabric. After two weeks in Chile, he had picked up just enough Spanish to understand some of the chatter around him: "What could it be?" people were asking each other. "I can't see anything," one woman said, and a man replied, "There's nothing *to* see." Eleonora turned to Lapérouse with a grin, as if to say, *See, I did not tell a soul.* But her expression seemed more pointed than that; he read reproof in it: *See, I would have been very discreet.* The crowd surged again and Eleonora was edged over till she was directly before him, so close he could smell her—the warm felt smell of her hat, and, below that, a sweeter fragrance—jasmine, maybe—mixed with sweat. His wife had always smelled very clean; if she wore scent at all it was a dab at the throat, a mild fragrance of—was it orange blossoms? He could not quite remember.

An inexpert but effective fanfare of horns and drums quieted the crowd, then Monneron lit a brazier of wet straw, and a plume of black smoke rose into the sky—the signal to Frédéric, apparently, for the frigates' cannons fired. The assembly saw the flashes from the salvo before they felt it, but then it came, rolling up from the frigates like thunder, rumbling through their bodies as the bay filled with smoke. Eleonora gave a small shriek and started, losing her hat. Lapérouse caught the hat, then reached out to steady her, one hand landing on a hip and the other grabbing a shoulder. She pulled away, flustered, then straightened her back and stood upright through what remained of the salute, not covering her ears or cowering against the noise, as many of the other ladies did, but watching with head raised, allowing each onslaught of noise and vibration to wash over her unchecked.

The sound and smoke dissipated, and Lapérouse took a slow, deep breath, feeling as if he had just come through a naval action. He had experienced only a few battles of much consequence, but afterward he had felt exactly like this—liberated, scoured clean, his sight clearer than before. He had thought it due to the shocking brutality of warfare followed by the surprise and relief of surviving when others had not. But now he wondered if it was partly an effect of gunpowder itself—its acrid smell, its deafening noise, its concussive power. He was grateful for the salvo; somehow the release of all that raw energy and tension dispelled the turbulence in his own mind.

She was so young, after all—young enough to have bony shoulders and hips, to shriek when cannons went off, to flirt with a ship captain at dinner. The realization felt like a return to sanity, and in a moment he could divine the hours and days just ahead: the spectacle, hopefully successful, followed by a makeshift ball on the beach with such musicians as they had at their disposal. He would dance with her. Afterward, he would meaningfully press her hand and look into her eyes before delivering her to her husband. The evening would end with fireworks. Then the colonists would mount their horses and climb into their carriages and, like so many Cinderellas, return to their homes. Tears would be shed. Goodbyes and good nights would be shouted until they could no longer see or hear each other. And then his attention would return, finally and completely, to the expedition. To the dinner with his men tomorrow. To their promised day off. To seeing them all back on board, and then the departure. He felt enormous—what was that word Langle had used?—*optimism*, that was it. He could not wait to resume the voyage. The best parts of the expedition were yet to come. He returned the hat to Eleonora with a nod, then drew himself up as best he could in the press of people and addressed the crowd once more.

"We promised a French spectacle to follow the French dinner," he cried. "This evening, our chief engineer, Monsieur de Monneron, and his worthy assistants"—he motioned down the hill toward Monneron and his men—"will attempt to re-create for you a demonstration made in 1783 before the king and queen of France. Some of you may be aware of the experiments conducted by the Montgolfier brothers." There was a gasp of recognition from some in the assembly. "From the courtyards of Versailles to the shores of Chile, we offer you—flight."

Lapérouse nodded to Monneron and felt the crowd lean into him as Monneron bent down and lit a grate set on the ground between the barrels. At first there was nothing to see except for the backsides of Monneron and another crewman as they tended to an invisible fire. Then white smoke appeared, curling out from under the pile. Lapérouse held his breath, forgetting even Eleonora's beguiling nearness, so anxious was he for the spectacle not to fail. After what seemed an interminable time, but must only have been a minute or two, there was a slight movement in the pile, as if something were inside and trying to come free, and then more movement, the pile growing larger over the fire, lifting itself. Now the uninitiated were gasping also, as the object took shape before them: a hot-air balloon. Made of tissue paper affixed to a double, inner layer of cloth, it was painted to resemble the Montgolfiers' famous balloon, sky blue and ringed with gold scrolling, fleurs-de-lis, eagles, and sun faces. Duché de Vancy and his team of painters had done a marvelous job.

The balloon filled with the heated air, rising until it was as high as a house, then higher, as high as five grown men one on top of the other, and still it expanded, until it was nearly as wide as it was tall. Then it lifted clear of the barrels, and the four men assigned to control it took hold of the ropes, grunting and shouting—"More rope there!" "Steady!" "Watch the fire!"—and holding it in place so it could fill completely. Then at a signal from Monneron, they let go of their ropes in concert, and the paper and cloth dome soared into the sky. Great roars of approval came, not just from their amazed guests, but from the commoners on the beach, and then, like an echo, from the men waiting to discharge the fireworks in the longboats and those watching from the decks of the *Boussole* and the *Astrolabe*. The balloon traveled straight up at first, then caught a breeze from the ocean and began to drift inland, still climbing, climbing, till it was a bright blue dot against the darkening eastern sky.

"What will happen to it?" Eleonora asked.

Lapérouse turned to look at her. Her eyes were very bright. "What do you mean, Doña Eleonora?"

"Will it keep climbing into the sky? Forever?"

"No," Lapérouse said, turning back to look at the disappearing spectacle. It took him a moment to find it—shocking, how much smaller it had grown in just a few seconds. "No," he repeated. "The air inside will gradually cool, or escape, and it will float back to earth. Sometimes they come down in one piece; but as often as not they are torn apart by winds, or snagged in high trees, or crash into mountainsides and are wrecked."

She nodded gravely. "So it will not come back."

"No," he said. "It will never come back."

Then, heeding the reedy call of strings and woodwinds played in the open, he offered her his arm and led the assembly down to the beach, where an area had been swept clear for their dancing pleasure.

FOUR

SNOW MEN

Lituya Bay, Alaska, July 1786

There is a big disagreement in my family about what happens if you drown and your body is never found. My aunts say that you are turned into a Land Otter. Land Otters come up out of the water, in the dark, and steal away the living. You cannot see them, but you can hear them—they whistle. We lie in our huts at night and listen for whistling, because we lost a canoe when we arrived for the salmon season, and afterward we found only four of the bodies.

My father and his brothers say it is true about the Land Otters everywhere else, but not here. Here, they say, if you drown you are turned into a bear and become a lookout for Kah Lituya. Kah Lituya is the jealous spirit of this place. He sleeps at the mouth of the bay and tries to capsize canoes when they pass. He turns the people who drown into bears and makes the bears watch for more canoes coming into the bay. The aunts say they know about Kah Lituya, they respect his jealousy, they just do not agree about him turning people into bears. Why, in this one place, they ask, would the power of the Land Otters mean nothing? My aunts want the bears to be just bears. They want the men to hunt the bears—there are so many of them—but Grandfather says no hunting bears this season because you do not know who you might be killing.

The argument was very noisy for a while, every night around the fire, the aunts and my father and his brothers, back and forth, back and forth, till one day Grandfather got so angry he made his slave smash up his best canoe to shame us. Then everyone was quiet, but they still disagreed. I never said anything, but I hope my father's people are right. I am less afraid of bears than I am of Land Otters. One of the bodies we never found was my cousin. I was supposed to marry him after the salmon season. If he is a bear he will be busy watching for canoes. But if he is a Land Otter he might come for me.

Then the Snow Men appeared, and new fighting began. The day they came with their two winged war canoes, we were still singing for our lost people, and that is a song you must never interrupt, but one person stopped singing, then another and another, and one of the children shouted, Look! Look! so of course we all stopped singing, and there in the bay were the largest canoes we had ever seen. Grandfather, who is almost blind, saw instead a giant raven, and shouted that it was Yehlh, the creator. We all ran into the woods, because you will turn to stone if you look at Yehlh with your eyes, and although we knew Grandfather could not see and that the canoes were canoes and not a raven, no one can say, Grandfather, you are blind, you are wrong.

I hid behind a rock and felt a tug at my back. It was my little cousin, pulling on my dress. I call him my little cousin even though we are almost the same age. He is always coughing, he is shorter than I am and much too skinny, and he has followed me around ever since his brother drowned, the one I was supposed to marry. He was holding a bit of my dress between his bony fingers and wheezing. I shook him off and punched him hard, in the arm. What was *that* for? he said, and his eyes got watery. I said, If you hang on to me or start crying, I will hit you again. So he stopped saying anything, and I was a little disappointed. I wanted to hit him some more. The aunts say I will have to marry this cousin now that his older brother is dead. But not till he is older. *If* he grows older. I am glad that now I will not have to marry till later. My other cousin was handsome and I felt proud to be promised to him. I just wished we could wait a little— maybe till next salmon season. My aunts laughed at me when I said so. Hush, they said, you are lucky to get a man like him, you do not make a man like that wait.

Now my little cousin stood trembling next to me, and I said, You need to think. My aunts are always saying this to me. You never think, they say, You need to think. But really, I am always thinking. What they mean is,

Do what we tell you to, do it more, do it sooner—which has nothing to do with thinking. But when I told my cousin to think, I meant it. I said, What did you think you saw, before Grandfather said it was Yehlh? Two giant canoes? You saw them with your eyes, yes? And have you turned to stone? Look at your hands and feet—see, they are fine. Come, we will have another look. And he shrank back, shaking his head, but I rolled up some skunk cabbage leaves and gave them to him. What are you doing? he asked. I showed him how to look through the rolled-up leaves. I had heard Grandmother say once that it is safe to look at spirits if you look through a cabbage leaf.

We crept forward, and when my older brothers saw me they did the same, staying just behind us. When I looked through my rolled-up leaf, I said, They are giant canoes with wings, white wings, and little ants crawling all over, and my brothers ran to Grandfather to tell him what I said, and he nodded and told them they were brave. My little cousin frowned and said, But *you* are the one who is brave, you are the one who looked, not them, and I threatened to punch him again if he was not quiet.

Then we heard Grandfather tell my brothers that the ants were not ants, but tiny ravens, Yehlh's helpers, who would fly here to peck out their eyes, and my brothers who were so brave ran shouting into the trees, and my cousin laughed and looked through his skunk cabbage leaf and said, They are not ants, they are strange people. So I looked again, and he was right—they were men, climbing over the wings of the canoes. My cousin dropped his leaf and ran to Grandfather, who stood looking out with cloudy eyes, scaring everyone with his words and never feeling afraid himself. Grandfather, my cousin said, they are canoes filled with men, we will not die from looking, and it is she who knew it. He pointed to me and tried to say my name, but he started coughing, and for a while he could not stop. When he finally caught his breath, he spoke the rest of my name, but I pretended not to hear.

The canoes were so large they were like floating villages. The women and children watched from the hill while the men went out to meet them, and they came back with black metal and colorful beads and white food that looked like maggots that no one dared to eat, and told us that it was Snow Men. We had all heard of Snow Men, but none of us had seen them before except for one of our slaves. He said Snow Men had visited his

people, and these men in the giant canoes looked like them, and he
warned us about a powerful Snow Man weapon that made a noise like
thunder and could kill a man a long way off. Grandfather was pleased
by the slave's knowledge and told him he would be freed at the next pot-
latch. Then the aunts were unhappy because the man was their best
worker, and the other slaves were jealous, so there was new unhappiness
right after the Snow Men arrived.

But the real fighting did not start till a few days later. At first we were
all excited. The Snow Men moved their canoes to the far side of an island
in the bay and camped there. Our men and the older boys followed them
during the day, and every night around the fire they would tell us what
they saw: Snow Men climbing the ice rivers or scratching pictures on
funny boards, cleaning their canoes or looking up at the sky through
hard, hollow sticks, and my brother made us laugh by making *shwa la la
la* sounds to imitate their talk. My other brother asked, What do Snow
Women look like? and my uncle said, They do not have women, that is
why they are here, to take our women. The aunts laughed and said, No,
they are on a great hunt and they do not take women on their hunts, just
like you. Then Father said some of the Snow Men go off into the woods
with the Eagle women on the other side of the bay, and my uncle said,
They are all ugly anyway, the Eagle women, and everyone laughed except
for his wife, because she is an Eagle, and she refused that night to sleep
by him, and then he was not laughing.

After a couple of days, though, the women became angry with the
men for not catching salmon like they should and for trading what they
did catch with the Snow Men for more beads and metal. The men started
gambling with one another for the metal, and fighting when they lost, and
spying on the Eagles across the bay, and getting angry when the Eagles
got something from the Snow Men that they did not, and then there was
fighting between our people and theirs. But when we were not fighting
with one another or with the Eagles, everyone complained that the Snow
Men were taking all of our fish and our otters without asking, and the
men bragged each night about what they took from the Snow Men in return. Then there was fighting over *that*—Give that back, I saw that before
you did, you stole it from under my mat, you liar, you son of bear-dung—
all for strange-looking things you could not eat or wear, things no one

knew how to use or what they were for. They even stole one of the Snow Men weapons—the slave was right, we saw them knock birds out of the sky, with a great noise—but no one could make it work.

One day, my brothers and some of the Eagle men snuck onto the island and came back with a large wooden container filled with juice that looked like blood and smelled like spoiled berries. The Snow Men drink this every day, they said, It may be the secret of their skill in canoe building. Your skin will turn white like theirs if you drink it, the aunts said, your hair will become wild and yellow. But my brothers and the Eagles tried it anyway. They spat it out right away—it burned their throats—but they kept sipping it little by little even when we told them to stop, and it must be poison, because it turned them all into noisy fools and then into retching fools.

I was tired of them all, so I wandered away from the fire. There is a rock I like, up the hill behind our summer village. You can look at the whole world from there. Standing high on the rock, I could see the fog over the ocean like a rolling plain of snow, lit from above by the sun. The Snow Men had come out of that fog, and I wished they would go back into it. The bay was purple below me. What was Kah Lituya doing down there? How could he not notice when the Snow Men came with their giant canoes? Why would he take one of our canoes and not theirs? Maybe it is not true about the bears, I thought. Or maybe the Snow Men's canoes are too big. Maybe Kah Lituya and his bears are afraid of the Snow Men.

I heard whistling behind me, and I spun around so fast I hurt my neck. I thought it was my cousin, the dead one, I even saw him for a moment, smaller than he should have been, but with the same straight nose and the eyebrows that came to a slight point over each eye. But it was just my little cousin. I had never really noticed before how much he looked like his brother. The setting sun made his skin look better. Did I scare you? he said. I wish you would stop following me, I told him. He climbed up onto the rock. We are supposed to marry, you know, he said, panting. So? I said. So maybe we should— he began. Should what? I said. I don't know, he said, Never mind. I scrambled down the rock and headed home. Wait for me, my cousin said, you are too fast. I never asked you to come along, I said. His wheezing grew fainter and fainter behind me as

I walked, and when I heard nothing, I got worried, so I stopped and waited till I could hear him again before moving on, and that was how we got home that night, with me always ahead of him but making sure I could hear.

The next morning Kah Lituya took two of the Snow Men's canoes. I saw it.

Their giant canoes had many smaller canoes inside, all different sizes, some with oars and some with wings and some with both. That morning three of their canoes came out to our side of the bay—two of them big enough for ten men each, and a smaller one that fit six or seven. They looked like they were fishing, dropping strings in the water, and we all laughed and said, What are they doing? They will not catch anything like that. But then the canoes started running, running on the water, running toward the ocean, and we all stopped laughing, and someone said, Kah Lituya. One of the larger canoes turned and turned in the water, huge waves filling it and soaking the men, and then we saw the other big canoe rowing to help them, and Kah Lituya caught it too. Only the smaller canoe got away. Even from the hill we heard the Snow Men screaming, but only for a moment because the water swallowed them so fast. And then our men—my brothers, my father, my uncles—raced to their own canoes, to go to the two giant canoes by the island, the floating villages, to tell the Snow Men what they saw.

A strange excitement comes over people when something very bad happens. It happened the day our own men drowned. I felt it too. Even while I was crying, I was excited. I was thinking, This is one of those terrible things that I will remember always, I will tell this story to my children and grandchildren. It happened again when the Snow Men drowned, but without any sadness—just the excitement. When our men came back, their canoes were filled with presents from the Snow Men—metal tools, more beads, pretty cloth. There is more if we find any bodies, my brothers shouted, then they were off again. Some of the children started playing with their toy boats, pretending to turn them over, making screaming sounds and then starting over. I went and kicked away their toys and slapped the biggest child. Stop that bad game! I shouted. The aunts came running over and pulled me away by my hair. What are you thinking? they yelled. They are only playing! They thrust a large basket at me. Make yourself useful, they said. Go fill it with berries. *Ripe* berries, they said. Our men will be hungry when they return.

I made my way down the hillside and through some thickets and ate almost all the berries I picked, and I knew I could go home if I wanted to, but I kept walking. I wandered out onto a narrow finger of land, with the bay on one side and the ocean on the other, and just a line of spruce trees growing in between. For once I was not thinking at all. I just kept seeing the Snow Men's canoes disappearing into the angry water. I kept hearing the screams before they all went under. And I kept saying, Oh, cousin, my poor cousin. I had not actually seen him drown that day. I was in the group of canoes that came after. We did not know what happened till we landed safely and found everyone else shouting and crying at the landing place.

Now I saw five men walking along the shoreline, and at first I thought they were the drowned Snow Men coming out of the water, turned into Land Otters. I was so frightened a little water leaked out of me and down my leg, and I had to set down my basket to make it stop. But then I started thinking again. It was daytime, and it was too soon, and Land Otters are supposed to be invisible. Also, after what I had seen, I knew it was Kah Lituya who ruled these waters. If I was going to see anything unusual, it would be bears. These were Snow Men, living Snow Men.

One of them was far ahead of the others and walked right past without seeing me. His clothes were so strange—dark on top and white below, and so tight on his body I wondered how he could have put them on at all, much less moved around in them. I also wondered how the white coverings on his legs could stay clean, but when he got closer I saw that they were dirty. The man was looking down, down at the ground and down into the water, and his face was so sad. I knew he was looking for his lost people. He bent over a dead gull washed up on the beach, and at first he looked relieved to see that it was only a bird, but then he uttered a loud, choking cry and kicked it hard into the water.

You will not find them, I said out loud, and I was surprised by my voice in the air. My voice often surprises me like this. My father says it has a spirit of its own, but my aunts say, Spirit? What spirit? She talks too much, that is all.

The Snow Man turned around quickly when he heard me, and for just

a moment I saw the wild unhappiness on his face before it opened into
surprise. Now that I saw one of them close, I saw that their skin was not
anything like snow, which is clean and bright. They should be called Raw
Salmon Men because that is what they look like, like salmon flesh before
we smoke it. The man was now smiling at me, and I did not like that.
Why would he smile, when two of his canoes were gone and so many of
his men? But his strange, pale eyes were still sad, and then he spoke,
and his voice was even sadder. I remembered my brother at the fire saying
shwa la la la to imitate the Snow Men, but it did not really sound like
that. It was more like the babbling of babies before they can talk. The
man touched his chest and spoke again, and I was afraid he was saying
his own name, which is something children do before we teach them
not to. He held a yellow stone in his hand, still wet, and I thought of our
boys—they also like stones, they fill their hands with them and save them
under their mats, and when their mothers and sisters and aunts sweep
the stones outside, they shout as if their best arrows have been taken
away. Maybe, I thought, Snow Men are people whose bodies grow big but
whose spirits stay small. This explained many things, like the way they just
took whatever they wanted.

The man stepped toward me, and I had almost decided to run when
he sat down on a low rock and spoke again. He held out his hands and
turned them over, and I knew he was showing me the canoes he had lost.
His eyes filled, which I could tell even though he took a flask from his
side and hid his face behind it. I wondered what was in the flask, if it was
the red poison water. But it wasn't. I could tell because he spilled some of
it. It was water, our melted ice water, the water our men said the Snow
Men collected in great round vessels and rolled onto their canoes. I could
not blame them for taking it. It tastes so good—better than the lake water
we drink at our winter camp—and there is so much of it. And then the
Snow Man held his flask out to me, but I did not need his water, which
was actually *our* water, and I stepped back so he would know.

He laughed then, either at me or at something he said—he was still
talking—and even as he laughed, he was still crying, and I felt ashamed
to be there, although he was the one who should have felt ashamed, crying in front of me, a stranger, a girl. I hate that—feeling someone else's
shame because they are not feeling it like they should. If he were one of

our boys instead of a giant Snow Boy, I thought, I would rap the top of his head with my knuckles and say, Come now, be a man! But he might not understand. Where he came from, a girl rapping on your head might mean something else. It might mean, Yes, I will marry you and have your babies. So I just stood there looking at his bent head before me, wishing he would stop but also wanting to touch his hair, which was the color of moose hair, but tangled, like moss. Some of it stood away from his head, floating in the breeze, and I could not help reaching out my hand. I must have brushed a few hairs against my palm, but they were so thin I could not feel them.

Then I saw, behind the man, one of the other Snow Men coming toward us. I pulled my hand away and stepped back, which made the first Snow Man, the crying man, look up and turn around. He called out to the man, who said something in return. The new man was very thin, which I could see even though his clothing was looser on his body, and he was carrying one of the Snow Men weapons in his hands. There was something scared and hungry about the way he moved that I did not like. I liked him even less when he looked at me. I saw in his eyes the same wanting that I sometimes see in our men when they look at women, and that I sometimes saw in my cousin, the one who drowned, when he looked at me. I used to get a strange, watery feeling low in my stomach when my cousin looked at me that way, but with the thin Snow Man, it was more like cold fingers against the back of my neck.

The two Snow Men talked to each other, and although I did not understand anything they said, I could see that the first Snow Man was chief over the second one. They should have been saying, Our people are dead, we cannot find them, let's go back to our canoes and leave this place at once. But the new man kept staring at me while they spoke, and then the chief Snow Man looked at me too, so maybe they were talking about me. I should have been afraid. I should have run away, snaking through the spruce trees and back up the hill to my village. I could have outrun them, the chief Snow Man in his tight clothes and the skinny Snow Man with his heavy weapon. But I did nothing. I just waited to see what would happen.

Once, when I was very small, I wandered in front of a large tree the men were felling for a new canoe. It started to fall toward me, and someone screamed for me to get out of the way, but I just stood there. I looked up and watched as the tree grew larger and larger. My father threw himself on me and rolled me away from the tree. That is the story everyone tells, anyway. I do not remember my father saving my life. I only remember waiting for the falling tree.

The chief Snow Man stood up from the rock, turned the other man around by the shoulder, and started walking away. The new man did not follow, though, until the chief turned back and said something short and sharp, like a bark.

Now that they were leaving, I was suddenly very afraid, afraid of what might have happened to me, stuck out on the spit with five Snow Men between me and our village, and I hid myself among the trees. My aunts would say, See, there you go, you always think afterward about what you should have done, when it is too late and no good. This time they would have been right.

The first Snow Man turned around once when he got near his canoe, and I thought he looked surprised not to see me anymore. I wondered if I should step out from behind the tree so he would know I was alive and not a spirit. But that might look like an invitation, and then maybe he would come back. Still, I was disappointed when I lost sight of him. This is what is wrong with me—I am always wanting and not wanting something at the same time. Like wanting to marry my handsome cousin, but also not wanting it. No one else ever seems to feel this way. But I saw it in this Snow Man, the way he leaned over the dead gull, hoping it was one of his men and also hoping it was not.

Then I noticed, on the rock where the man had been sitting, his flask of water. Had he forgotten it, or was it a gift? I picked it up—it was round and hard, cold to the touch, and closed with a stopper made of some kind of soft wood. I could see my own reflection in the side. It was like looking into really smooth lake ice. I was pleased to have it. I had never had anything so wonderful in all my life, not for myself.

Then I heard a familiar cough behind me. It was my little cousin. I could tell without looking. They are gone, I said, you can come out. I could have killed him, he said, I could have killed them both. How? I said. With your bow and arrow? I was sorry as soon as I said it. His aim is terrible, but it is not his fault. He is too sick to practice much. I was still watching the Snow Men, who were now getting back in their small canoe. I couldn't see their faces anymore, but their bodies still looked sad. They had not found any of their people. Would they worry now about bears or about Land Otters? I wish I could have asked them.

What do you think happens when you drown? I asked my cousin. He cleared his throat. I don't know, he said, but sometimes when I cough and I can't stop, I think it might be like that. He had not understood me, but I said nothing. I felt sad all over again for the cousin who drowned. I knew my little cousin was thinking about his brother too, and I wondered if love could start like that, with two people feeling sad about the same thing. I turned around to look at him.

I should not have laughed. But I could not help it. He looked so serious with his bow and arrows, which were so big on him. I am glad you did not try shooting, I said, You might have killed me too. His face turned muddy-red with shame and anger. I felt sorry right away, and was about to offer him some of my berries, but he pointed to the flask in my hand and said, You should not have that. Why not? I said. Everyone will say you are like the Eagle women who go into the woods with the Snow Men and come back with gifts, he said. I looked down at the shiny flask, then back at my cousin. He was still looking at it, not at me, looking at it with wide-open eyes, panting a little. I walked forward and thrust the flask at his chest, hard enough to make him stagger. The flask fell to the ground.

What is the matter with you? he cried. You were here, I said, You could tell everyone it was not like that. I picked up my basket and started back toward our village. Wait! he shouted, then started coughing, but it sounded like he was making himself cough. Wait! he said again, and then he called out my name. I stopped. I will turn around, I thought. I will turn, and if the flask is still on the ground, I will wait. If he picks it up and holds it out toward me, I will wait. If he says, I know you are not like the Eagle women, I will wait. But if he has the flask in his hand, if he is wiping it clean against his clothes, if he looks happy to have it for himself, then I will run home without him, no matter how angry my aunts or father or brothers will be. I dug my heel into the ground a little, to spin on it, then looked out across the bay. The Snow Men were in their small canoe, rowing back toward the island, but rowing slowly, hugging the coast, still looking for their lost people. Still hoping to find something, yet also hoping not to.

FIVE

CENOTAPH ISLAND

Lituya Bay, Alaska, July 1786

At dawn, Paul-Antoine-Marie Fleuriot, Viscount de Langle, stood at the stern gallery windows of his cabin and surprised himself by enjoying the view. To the east, the sun had already crested the great snowcapped mountains that overlooked the bay and gilt the edge of a glacier where it met the water. In the middle distance, standing like twin beacons, were the pine-covered promontories that guarded the entrance to the bay's inner basins. Directly below him, small icebergs bobbed in the water; calved off glaciers in those inner basins, they were now reduced to a flotilla of rounded, melting ice. And overhead, suddenly, a bird—a white-headed eagle—raced its own reflection across the water.

Only an anxious man would have chosen to see more peril than beauty in such a prospect. But Langle was that anxious man. Or had been. Every morning of the expedition Langle had stood alone at these windows and enumerated the myriad things that could go wrong that day—an outbreak of fever, an encounter with cannibals, uncharted shoals, winds that were too violent or too still. Water was always on his mind. It could run out. It could go bad. He was convinced stale water predisposed sailors to scurvy.

But now he stood at the expanse of windows before him and felt no compulsion to inventory the day's potential calamities. He knew why. They had nearly died yesterday, all of them—the men of his own frigate as well as the *Boussole*. Over two hundred men. Entering the narrow pass of this uncharted bay, the ships had been tossed around in a confusion of veering winds and crosscurrents. The *Astrolabe* had passed less than a cable length from the rocks on the southern headland; the *Boussole*, even closer. Then they had shot through the gap, and the stillness in the bay had been shocking. It was like the quiet after a death watch, only they were all still alive, hearts beating wildly in their throats.

Today he understood: there was no benefit in the rote exercise of expecting the worst. Yesterday morning, his windowside litany had not included being dashed upon rocks entering an uncharted bay. Yet the danger had arisen—and been averted—without his anticipation. His anxiety had been irrelevant. It was such a liberating thought that he laughed aloud. His servant, François, knocked on the door, calling in his squeaky voice, "Sir? Are you all right, sir?"

An hour later Langle left the *Astrolabe* and had himself rowed to the bay island beside which the frigates had anchored. It was a protected place, wooded and unpeopled—ideal for setting up an observatory for the savants and work tents for the sailmakers and blacksmiths. He intervened in a disagreement between the savants over the observatory's location, then made his way along the bustling shoreline in search of Lapérouse. He found the commander surrounded by men and canvas and ropes, briskly creating order out of chaos, his genial Languedoc accent easy to pick out among the other voices.

"Ah, Monsieur de Langle," Lapérouse called out. He signaled one of his officers to take over the tent building and drew Langle away from the hubbub. "Come explore this excellent island with me," he said.

The island was dense with spruce, its shoreline rocky and strewn with fallen wood. Lapérouse, short and a bit stocky, made his way with an agility that always surprised Langle. There was something of the mountain goat in his friend and commanding officer. They rounded a point and could see, to the west, the entrance they had barely survived the day before. From this distance it looked altogether still and safe. With their visit, the bay and its island and glaciers would be measured and mapped and would enter the register of known places in the world. He turned to marvel aloud over their good fortune, but the commander was still looking toward the narrow pass, brows drawn together.

"We had a very narrow escape yesterday," Lapérouse finally said.

"We did indeed."

"I could hardly sleep last night," he continued. "I kept imagining what might have happened." He squinted toward the pass. "I worry about getting back through when we leave."

"We'll have to watch carefully for the slack tide," Langle said.

"I thought we had yesterday."

"But we had no notion of the place then," Langle said. "Now we know something of its temperament, we shall manage better."

Lapérouse looked pointedly at Langle, as if searching for a shared anxiety and surprised to find none. "I hope you're right."

"Think not on the morrow, sir."

"The morrow?"

"For the morrow shall take thought for itself. Sufficient to the day is the evil thereof."

"Are you quoting *scripture*?"

"Our Lord himself."

Lapérouse shook his head with a bemused smile. "Pardon the irreverence, Monsieur de Langle, but our Lord could afford to ignore tomorrow better than we. He could come back from the dead."

"And walk on water."

Lapérouse laughed, then turned around to return to the camp. Langle followed, disappointed that their exploration should be so brief. It occurred to him that Lapérouse had sought him out expressly to share his distress over yesterday's near-miss and the looming necessity of going back through the same treacherous pass. Langle's composure had no doubt struck Lapérouse as a failure of understanding.

"Sir," he called out. "We'll have time to study the pass more carefully before we leave."

Lapérouse stopped and looked back out at the water. The entrance to the bay was now hidden from view. "Yes," he said absently, but the subject was now closed. He gestured outward. "I thought we might call this place Frenchman's Bay," he said. "What do you think? It might make an ideal trading post. I believe no one can lay prior claim to it."

"The name will make it clear enough," Langle replied. "And what about this island, sir?" he said. "What will you call it?"

"I may name it after d'Escures," Lapérouse replied, referring to his first lieutenant. The day before, he explained, it was d'Escures who had taken the *Boussole's* longboat and sailed around the island and found their current anchorage on its sheltered side. He had also sailed into the interior basins of the bay and reported them clogged with glaciers. The Northwest Passage, if it existed anywhere, was not to be found here. "But he did find waterfalls," Lapérouse added. "Ideal for refilling water casks. Both ships can easily replace their water." He turned to look at Langle. "It's the best water I've ever tasted."

This was good news. Water had been a source of contention between the two captains almost since they left France. Lapérouse stubbornly maintained there was nothing wrong with stored water, that in fact water *improved* in quality the longer it was kept in barrels. Langle had nearly lost his temper over the manifest illogic of it.

"I'm delighted to hear it," he said now.

"I thought you might be," Lapérouse said, then resumed walking. He looked back over his shoulder. "Don't say anything to d'Escures about naming the island," he said. "He's a good officer but apt to think too much of himself."

Eight days passed. July 13 was to be their last full day in Frenchman's Bay. At first light, Langle stood at his windows and reviewed the few official tasks that remained: fill and stow the last of the water casks; dismantle the observatory and work tents on the island; take soundings at the western end of the bay to complete the excellent map drawn by Lieutenant Blondela. It was not a fretful recitation; with sunrise so early at this latitude, clear skies today and no wind, natives who were inclined to petty thievery but not aggression, and competent officers overseeing each job, everything needful would be done by noon. Indeed, the commander had given most of the men the afternoon off to explore, hunt, fish, or trade with the natives.

Lapérouse and d'Escures had been right about the water: the most delicious water any of them had ever drunk fell straight down the cliff-sides into the bay. One had only to open the barrels beneath and they were filled within minutes. When the expedition set sail the next day, both ships would be laden with fresh water. They would also leave with a map of this coast; the naturalists' descriptions of flora, fauna, and people;

specimens of rocks and plants and native handiwork; artists' drawings; a thousand sea otter pelts to sell in Macao; and a claim on this bay for French trade in that lucrative commodity.

As to the otters, Langle had one of his own, destined not for commerce but for scientific inquiry. He turned from the windows and moved to the oak table that occupied the middle of his cabin. The otter, large and dead, was sprawled across it. He would skin the animal this morning. If he did well, he would send the fur back to France with the next dispatches, a gift for the queen. But the real goal was to have the carcass. He and the *Astrolabe*'s naturalists planned to spend the long summer nights ahead dissecting the creature. He sat down at the table and picked up his sharpest knife.

By midmorning, however, he had freed only the hind legs. It was slow work. The connective tissue on the animal was strong; every few seconds Langle had to stop to cut it away. And he had been interrupted time and again. First it was Lieutenant de Monty, the officer assigned to the watering party, reporting his readiness to depart in the longboat with six seamen and twelve barrels. Then the surgeon, Monsieur Lavaux, to discuss a sick crew member. And after that, the two La Borde brothers. Langle had assigned the older one to take the *Astrolabe*'s double-masted pinnace out for the soundings work in the bay and the younger one to help dismantle the observatory. But the younger was dressed, like his brother, for an outing.

"Ah," Langle said. "You want to go with your brother."

The younger La Borde blushed as if surprised by his own transparency.

"Please, sir," the older one said, "the commander said we may all go ashore once we finish, and it may be our only chance to go hunting together."

The younger one nodded hopefully. He had turned twenty just a few days earlier. The brothers' boyishness and obvious attachment to each other belied their aristocratic upbringing and their competence as officers.

"Who's going from the *Boussole*?" Langle asked.

Lieutenant d'Escures was taking the *Boussole*'s pinnace, the older La Borde explained, and Monsieur de Boutin was rumored to be coming as well, in the *Boussole*'s small boat. A party of thirty in three boats, commanded by excellent officers. Langle stood and looked outside again.

The sky was still cloudless, the water of the bay like glass. He turned back. "You may go, Monsieur de La Borde," he said to the younger brother.

The brothers were profuse in their thanks. "Maybe we'll bring back a bear," the older one said as they left the cabin. The younger one called back, "It's a nice otter, sir," and then Langle heard them laughing as they scrambled up the companionway.

François accounted for four or five additional interruptions. He entered noisily with the breakfast tray, then returned to collect it, then came back again to ask, because he'd forgotten, what the captain wanted for the officers' dinner that evening. On his way out he crashed so hard into the mizzenmast on the half deck that Langle left the cabin to make sure he was all right. And five minutes later he was back again, dragged in by the ship's cook, Deveau, who demanded to know "what this worthless boy can possibly mean about having poached otter for dinner."

"It was salmon, poached *salmon*," Langle said. He waved his knife at the pair to send them away.

It was no wonder he had made so little progress on the otter. With the hind legs and tail free, however, he could now try pulling the pelt up and over the animal, like a dress. The creature was so small beneath its skin. Langle thought suddenly of his wife, Georgette. Every time he undressed her he'd been surprised by how small she was under her clothes, and then by her unembarrassed carnality, so at odds with the proper Madame de Langle she was during the day. He shook his head. An unchivalrous train of thought: from dead otter to much-loved wife. Nevertheless, his hand shook with remembered desire, and he had to set the knife down for a moment.

He thought he could hear men running and shouting somewhere above. And then a knock at the door. François, again. "What is it now?" Langle cried. "Monsieur Deveau box your ears again?" Later he would remember these words and his own exasperated laughter and the brief silence before François said, "I think something may have happened, sir," and would feel a shamefaced nostalgia.

"What are you talking about?" Langle demanded.

"Please just come up, sir."

Climbing up the stairs, Langle guessed the natives had come back out in their canoes, hopeful of getting more iron, and that one or more of them had managed to clamber up onto the deck. Both he and Lapérouse had instructed the men to keep the natives off the ships that morning. While pretending to work out a trade, they would take things—axes, iron bars, rope, clothing, anything not lashed down. Too few men remained on board to guard against this right now.

But once on deck, he saw that that wasn't it at all. He joined a small crowd—everyone still on the ship—at the port rail and looked down. The *Boussole*'s small boat was pulling away from the *Astrolabe*. Langle recognized Lieutenant de Boutin. There were six other men in the boat with him, all of them soaked. Water sloshed in the bottom of the boat. Boutin had lost his hat.

"The soundings expedition," Langle said. "Back already?"

For a moment no one spoke. Tréton de Vaujuas, recently promoted from ensign to lieutenant, looked around as if hoping to find an officer more senior than himself. Finding none, he cleared his throat: "Sir, Monsieur de Boutin said they were caught in a violent outgoing tide at the pass."

"The *pass*? What were they doing there?"

Vaujuas hunched his shoulders as if to deflect the question. "He said the current drove them there. He managed to get free of it. But their pinnace did not."

Langle felt an electric surge of alarm. "It capsized?"

Vaujuas nodded.

"But its men—Lieutenant d'Escures—?"

Vaujuas shook his head.

"And *our* pinnace?"

Vaujuas shook his head harder. "Monsieur de Boutin lost sight of it in the confusion. He thought they might have come back before he did." He stopped, but as Langle continued looking at him, added shakily, "They haven't, sir."

Langle looked behind him, toward the southwest, the direction in which the three boats had gone that morning, willing the pinnace to reappear from behind the island. Perhaps the La Borde brothers and the seven crewmen they had gone with were still out there, wending their way back. Perhaps they had managed to help the men from the *Boussole*'s capsized pinnace. Perhaps in his distress and hurry to return, Boutin had missed all of this. But there was no sign of them. Instead, Langle saw a group of native canoes approaching—canoes rowed with great speed and urgency, the speed and urgency of bad news. No, he thought. No, make this not be. Turning back to the rail, he put his glass to his eye and watched as Boutin and his men were helped up the side of the *Boussole*. One sank to his knees on reaching the deck and had to be helped away. Boutin was the last to climb aboard. Langle watched as Lapérouse, his round face looking oddly deflated, stepped forward and grasped Boutin by the arm. In the moment before he led his officer away, he looked across and seemed to catch Langle's eye. Confusion, disbelief, dread, entreaty— was it possible for a single look to convey all that? Langle put the glass down. He wondered what his own face betrayed. The only sensation he felt was a creeping dryness at the back of his throat.

The natives arrived in their red cedar canoes, all of them talking at once in their highly fricative, sing-songy language that even the expedition's savants could make no sense of. But no interpreter was needed to read the horrified excitement on their faces. Their lithe hand gestures were clear enough: they'd watched from the shore as two boats capsized at the mouth of the bay. The same mouth that had nearly devoured both frigates the day they arrived—how was it possible? They all knew the danger. And the La Borde brothers—oh, why had he let them both go? Langle clenched himself against a dizzying wave of shock and anger and regret.

"Monsieur de Langle!" Lapérouse was calling over through a speaking trumpet. "Lower gifts to the canoes. Make it clear there will be more, much more, for the rescue of even one man!"

Langle shook off his torpor and motioned for Vaujuas to comply; the young lieutenant leaped into action, relieved to have something to do. Lapérouse called over again. He was sending the *Boussole's* longboat to search the southern shoreline. "Send your longboat to the northern side," he shouted. "Do you have an officer to spare for the task?"

"I'll go myself," Langle shouted back.

The entrance to the bay was now so still it seemed impossible that a disaster had just occurred there. Langle, standing at the stern of the longboat, felt his panic and grief evaporate strangely at the sight, as if the drama of the last hour had been so much playacting. He could see several native canoes and the *Boussole*'s longboat making their way along the opposite shore. With one of his own men bent over the side taking depths to ensure against running aground, Langle could almost imagine that they were in fact the soundings expedition, and that nothing was amiss.

"Sir, there's something over there among the rocks," one of his men called back.

Langle put his glass to his eye and scanned the area the crewman had pointed out. Yes, there was something there, something not part of the natural landscape. He felt a sickening return to the task at hand as he directed the rowers to approach the object.

"It's the grapnel from Monsieur de Boutin's boat," the same keen-eyed man announced. "Shall we try to grab it, sir?"

"Yes." Langle watched as the men wrestled the anchor off the rocks with a long pole and hauled it on board. Its cablet was still attached to it, and the men clucked in wonder as they examined the end that had sheared off the boat. Langle said nothing, but he knew what they were all thinking: only a boiling sea could have spat an anchor back out onto the rocks. He tried to imagine for a moment such a sea, the two doomed boats floundering in its waves, the cries of drowning men inaudible over the roar, their open throats filling suddenly and fatally with tide water.

"Captain de Langle."

He looked up; his men were waiting for him. "There's a convenient landing just ahead," he said. He chose four men to join him on foot, then instructed the men left in the boat to continue their search along the shore. They agreed to meet when the sun was directly south. He knew they would not be late; the fear of getting caught in the reverse current when the tide came back in through the pass weighed heavily on all of them.

He headed southwest with his men, toward where the northern side of the bay ended in a long, low spit of land. It curved in toward the mouth of the bay like a lupine fang, and was a place that might snag survivors, wreckage, bodies. They spread out along the bay side of the spit, and Langle found himself alone, with the silent bay before him and a narrow band of spruce trees separating him from the ocean on the other side. Sometimes a gap in the trees would let in a windy blast and the roar of the ocean. Langle stepped into the bay once, thinking a shiny thing he saw there might be a button from one of the officer's jackets. But it was a flat yellow pebble, rubbed perfectly round by its time in the sea. He pocketed it to send home to his son, Charles, who was almost two years old. By the time it reached him, of course, he would be closer to three.

He spotted something gray and rounded on the rocky shore, and his stomach contracted with dread and hope. But a step closer revealed that it was just a dead gull. He was relieved, but only for an instant. The only thing they had recovered so far was the anchor from Boutin's boat, the boat that escaped. An apprehension that they would find nothing—no one to bury, no mementos to send home, no spar from the lost boats, nothing even to confirm that the accident had occurred—grew in his mind. It would be as if two boats and all their men had simply vanished from the world. He kicked the dead gull into the water with a curse.

A voice made him spin around. A native girl, eleven or twelve years old, he guessed, stood under a spruce tree watching him. He didn't understand what she'd said, of course, but he did notice how the language that sounded so harsh spoken by the native men was less grating coming from her. She was barefoot, wore a sleeveless goatskin shift that hung unevenly above her knees, and at her hip held a small round basket filled with berries. An assiduous berry-picker, Langle thought, noting the twigs and leaves stuck in her black, shoulder-length hair. Her lips were purple. She had a drop of juice trapped below her lower lip—but no, it was a piercing. He wondered what she was doing there; the spit didn't seem like a place where berries grew. He smiled at her, but she didn't smile in return.

He stepped closer and sat on a boulder. She didn't speak again, but she didn't seem afraid either. Even in his distress he was pleased by this. He liked to think he was the sort of European who put natives at ease. "We experienced a calamity today," he said. He took his copper canteen from its pouch, pulled off the cork stopper, and drank a long, cool draught of water. "We're looking for survivors," he said, then took another sip. The girl watched him in silence, her eyes betraying nothing he could read— not compassion, not wonder, not understanding, not even curiosity. He offered her the canteen but she drew away, her purple lips thinning in what he guessed was disapproval.

"This water," he said, "it's the best thing about this sorrowful place."

He drank again, then found his eyes filling with tears. He was aware of the girl's nearness, and his body tensed with the certainty that she would touch him. But instead she stepped back, her eyes looking past him up the beach. Langle turned to see one of his men approaching.

"We haven't found anything, sir," the man said when he came within earshot. He looked wary, frightened even, but when he noticed the girl, he stopped, and his pale eyes widened in open interest.

Langle stood up and glanced behind him at the position of the sun. "We should go back," he said. "The tide will be in soon."

The sailor stood, still ogling the girl. Langle spun the man around by the shoulder. "She is a *child*."

"Oh, no, sir, I—" the man protested as Langle marched him off.

Langle looked back once, but the girl was gone. He was sorry. He felt sure she knew about the accident; perhaps she'd even witnessed it from this lonely strip of land. She must have surmised he was looking for survivors or bodies. Yet they could not talk to each other. Something about that—the shared knowledge and the inability to communicate about it—had been soothing.

They were in the longboat, rowing back to the *Astrolabe*, before he missed his canteen. The girl—she must have taken it. She had distracted him with her voice and her purple mouth and that dispassionate stare.

It could not be put off any longer: his next duty was to go to the *Boussole* and meet with Lapérouse. First he returned to the *Astrolabe* to wash up and put on his formal coat. When he entered his cabin, the sight of the dead otter on the table startled him extremely. Its exposed flesh looked painfully raw, like a burn. The whiskered face, so charming in life, looked cruel—one eye half-shut, the other open and staring, while the stiffened jaw muscles revealed a sharp row of bottom teeth. Had it only been that morning when he'd been cheerfully skinning the creature while disaster struck not one league away? He tried to swallow, but his throat felt sandy, his tongue large in his mouth. He moved to the wash basin and rinsed his face, then reached for his pewter water pitcher but knocked it to the floor.

"François," he called. "François!"

The boy appeared in the doorway, rubbing the back of his hand under his nose.

"Clean this up," Langle said. "But first, get me some water." Waiting for François to return, he watched the spilled water spread across the floor then sink into the grain of the wood, staining it dark. He imagined it melting from the snows and glaciers above the bay, then growing brackish as it flowed toward the ocean, brackish and turbulent, turbulent enough to drown two boatloads of men. François returned with the refilled pitcher, but Langle waved it away. "My coat," he said hoarsely.

A few minutes later, sitting in the *Astrolabe*'s small boat with only the silent boatswain's mate for company, his mind lulled into numbness by the rhythmic slap of the oars, Langle wished the short trip between the two ships could last forever. It wasn't that he didn't wish to see Lapérouse; he wanted—*needed*—to see him. Only with the commander, his friend since the American War, could he allow himself the luxury of grief. But he also understood that once they saw each other, it would become impossible to ignore the enormity of what had happened. The expedition would not sail the next day, of course. They would have to continue searching for the lost men, no matter how futile the endeavor. Then there would be the surviving men to console, burials for any bodies they recovered, a memorial for all the dead, the sale of the lost men's possessions, the reassignment of their duties, and afterward, reports for Paris, and—oh, God—letters to the families.

He thought of the powerful Marquis de La Borde, and his mind recoiled. The marquis had not wanted his sons to serve on the same ship. "An ocean voyage is still a dangerous endeavor, even in this scientific age," the marquis had said. Langle had promised to keep them safe. He'd specifically promised not to assign the brothers to off-ship expeditions together. That was when most mishaps occurred—when men left the safety of their ships. And until this morning, he had kept his word. But the brothers' request—it had been so reasonable! Refusing would have seemed churlish, arbitrary. But how could he explain this to the marquis, now that both sons were lost?

He sat in the commander's cabin, choking down a glass of wine. Lapérouse, never one to stand on ceremony, had forgone it altogether, doffing hat and coat as soon as they'd entered the room. His vest was unbuttoned, his shirt wrinkled and untucked, and his hair, just beginning to gray at the temples, pulled back in a careless knot at the nape of his neck. He paced the room, tears spilling from his eyes as he railed against d'Escures.

"I told him to avoid the pass if there was any danger at all," Lapérouse cried.

"Boutin says they were driven there by the current," Langle said.

The commander shook his head. "Boutin's asked to write an official report on the incident. He's the most senior survivor, so it's right he should do so. But he's also trying to protect a dead friend from blame. It's no use, however." Lapérouse handed a piece of paper to Langle. "I gave d'Escures explicit written instructions before he left this morning."

Langle scanned the writing: . . . *Monsieur d'Escures is forbidden from exposing the boats to any danger whatsoever, or from approaching the pass if it is rough. If the ocean is not breaking over the pass but the water is turbulent, he will put off taking soundings, as the work is not urgent. I ask again that he exercise the greatest possible caution* . . .

Langle found himself wondering if the commander had written out the instructions *after* the accident in order to protect himself. They had, after all, sent three boats toward a pass they knew to be dangerous. Langle touched his thumb to the paper to test the ink. It felt dry, yet the suspicion persisted.

"Was I not clear enough?" Lapérouse demanded.

"Absolutely clear."

"Do you know what d'Escures said when I gave this to him?"

Langle shook his head wearily. Lapérouse's anger, so pointless now, exhausted him.

"'Do you take me for a child?' he said. 'I have commanded the king's ships,' he tells me. And now twenty men are drowned, five of them officers!"

"Twenty-one," Langle said.

"What?"

"*Six* officers."

Lapérouse stopped pacing, and stood before Langle. "Who else was in your boat?"

Please, sir. It's our only chance to go hunting together. Maybe we'll bring back a bear. "I let the younger La Borde join his brother."

He felt Lapérouse's hand on his shoulder, then its weight increase as the commander lowered himself to the floor and crouched beside him.

Lapérouse looked up at him; the anger had left his face. "Paul," he said, dropping the formality between them. Langle covered his face and wept. Lapérouse remained at his side, saying nothing. Langle finally sat up and emptied the wine in his glass, but it tasted spent and moldy. He coughed a few times, afraid he might retch. He wanted Lapérouse to stop looking at him; the pity in those searching eyes unmanned him completely. Lapérouse took the wineglass from him, then stood, buttoning the top of his vest, as if to signal his resumption of duty, as if he knew to relieve Langle of his sympathy.

A few hours later, the officers of both ships ate in near-silence aboard the *Astrolabe*. Langle pressed the side of his fork repeatedly into his fish, separating it into many small pieces that he did not eat. It was poached salmon, just as he'd requested of Deveau that morning. Cooked to pink perfection, it was served alongside sorrel they'd found in the woods.

Lapérouse cleared his throat. "Tomorrow," he whispered, as if testing his voice, then louder, "*Tomorrow*—we'll move our anchorage away from the island, and closer to the entrance of the bay." There was a ripple of barely suppressed reaction down the row of officers, shorter now by one table length. Lapérouse looked up from his plate and the men stilled themselves. The urgency that had fueled their earlier exertions in the bay had given way to exhaustion, sadness, and fear. No one wanted to spend time near the site of the disaster.

Langle knew he should say something. He understood the need to continue searching, how important it was that the accounts they sent back to France leave no doubt about their conduct in the hours and days following the tragedy. But it was already hopeless. He continued to shred the salmon on his plate, his mind pitching between fretfulness and grief. Something struck the back of his head, and he lurched forward.

"Oh, Captain de Langle, please excuse me!" It was François, holding a carafe. "More wine, sir?"

"For God's sake," Langle cried. "Go away."

François stepped back into the shadows, but not before Langle saw how his nose had pinked with shame, and that his eyes were red from long crying.

Across from him, Lapérouse took a great bite of salmon. Langle felt a flash of contempt. Only a man of shallow feeling would be able to eat with such relish after losing so many of his men. At least François, for all his ineptitude, was showing proper emotion. But as Langle watched, he saw how his friend labored to get through the mouthful he'd assigned himself, his jaws working with grim determination. Ashamed, Langle brought a forkful of fish to his lips, then another and another. He stumbled into his cabin afterward, feeling almost drunk with grief. The musky smell of the otter carcass assailed him; he couldn't help but look at the dark mass of it lying on his table, then rushed to a basin to be sick.

The fair weather held the next day. They paid the natives to guide them around the headlands, and searched all day along the rocky, oceanside coast outside the bay. The search continued the next day under overcast skies, and the day after, with more wind, and then for two days in the rain, a nasty, changeable rain that seemed to drive at the men's faces no matter which direction they turned. They found nothing and no one, and Lapérouse announced that the sixth day would conclude the search.

That morning Langle rose at dawn and left his cabin, only to trip over someone lying in front of his door. "What the devil!" he cried, grabbing the figure and heaving it to its feet. It was someone thin and light, and for a confused moment he imagined it was the native girl he'd met out on the spit. Maybe she'd come back with his canteen. But it was François, sleepy, embarrassed, and dressed for an outing.

"Oh, please, sir," François said, "may I go with you today?"

"Go where?"

"To— to help look."

"Don't you have duties on board?"

"Yes, sir," François said. "But I haven't left the ship forever. Please. I'm about to jump overboard."

Langle let go of the boy and sighed. He didn't want him along. He was likely to chatter inanely, make mistakes, and irritate Lieutenant de Vaujuas, who was joining Langle that morning. But François looked so earnest and desperate that he couldn't refuse.

Vaujuas raised an eyebrow in surprise when François climbed down into the small boat, but he was too well-bred to comment in front of the captain. Seated aft, Vaujuas steered the boat away from the *Astrolabe* and toward the northern side of the bay. Langle and François sat across from him, watching the *Astrolabe* and *Boussole* grow smaller then disappear behind the island. Beyond the bay, the sun crested the craggy mountains to the east, revealing a fresh layer of snow on the peaks.

"It doesn't feel like summer, does it, sir?" François said. He'd been much quieter than Langle expected.

They drifted along half a league of shoreline. As had become habitual with all of them when navigating this part of the bay, Langle turned repeatedly to check for breakers near the pass, and also watched their speed relative to the shore, to be sure they weren't getting caught in a fast current. Meanwhile he let Vaujuas decide where to pull in close, which small coves to explore, how long to examine a spot of beach through his glass before moving on. Of all the men on the *Astrolabe*, Vaujuas had been the most untiring in his search efforts, insisting on going out every day. The older La Borde had been his cabinmate. And then there was his servant, Jean Le Fol. He'd been ill since leaving France but had fallen into a rapid decline after they'd entered these northern latitudes. Whenever he wasn't attending to his duties, Vaujuas had been at Le Fol's side, trying to entice him to eat or carrying him up to the deck for fresh air.

"I'd like to see what that is, sir," Vaujuas said now, pointing to a dark mass in the water. They approached the object until the boat bumped bottom. He sighed. "I'll get out and take a closer look."

François stood, jostling the boat. "I'll go," he said, then clambered overboard, landing thigh-deep in the water. He gasped at the unexpected cold, but waded out to the object, then placed his hand on it. "It's just a rock," he called back.

Langle puffed out his cheeks. He was growing numb to the demands of the search, the impulse to mistake every rock for a corpse, every piece of driftwood for wreckage from the lost boats, the constant immixture of relief and disappointment. But Vaujuas breathed jaggedly next to him, and Langle realized the younger man was trying to stifle his sobs. Langle laid a hand on his shoulder, at which Vaujuas gave way completely. François stood on the shore, lanky and damp, and looked toward the boat, unsure of what to do. Langle motioned for him to wander off. François walked a few steps away, then picked up some rocks and began tossing them in the water.

"You've done your utmost," Langle told Vaujuas.

"We've found nothing, sir. Nothing," Vaujuas said. "How can that be?" He pulled away from Langle, and for a moment Langle thought the lieutenant was calling him to account. For how could it be that twenty-one men should perish on a calm, clear morning? How was it that he and Lapérouse had not foreseen the danger? But Vaujuas went on: "Every night I return to my cabin, and there are all of La Borde's things, just as he left them." Another sob overcame him. "He was so untidy," he finally said, then regarded François, who was now trying to skip the stones. "That boy has no idea how it's done."

Langle watched too as François flicked stone after stone in the water, each one sinking as soon as it struck. "That's enough, François," Langle called. "Come on back."

The next day, Lapérouse ordered the ships back to their anchorage by the island, and required all but a few soldiers ashore for a memorial service.

Langle dressed carefully for the occasion. With no bodies to inter and only a crude stone cenotaph to mark the event, attending the service in full naval splendor was the only thing in his power to do. He called François to help him dress; the boy worked in silence, bringing in warm water for Langle's shave, laying out his clothes, polishing his shoes. Langle watched as François fussed over his wig on the oak table, and suddenly noticed what was missing from it.

"What happened to my otter?" he demanded.

François swung around, his face flushing. But his voice was steady when he replied: "It was beginning to rot, sir, so we had to discard the innards. Also the entire head, I'm afraid. You hadn't skinned that part yet. But Monsieur Dufresne saved the pelt for you, sir. Minus the head, of course. He said to let him know when you wanted it back."

Langle nodded. When had François managed it? The otter was still there when he turned in that first night after the accident, but he had no recollection of it thereafter. Watching—and smelling—it decompose in his cabin would have depressed him extremely. François must have sought out Dufresne's help to save the pelt. An unhappy member of the expedition, Dufresne wasn't the most approachable of men. It would have taken courage. Langle buttoned up his crisp white shirt. "Thank you, François."

"We will call this place Cenotaph Island," Lapérouse said as he opened the memorial service. His voice shook as he read out the names of the dead. The written notice was placed in a bottle and buried beneath a stone memorial they erected. A small group of natives stood among the trees just outside their circle. Langle found himself scanning their faces in search of the girl he'd met, but only men had come to witness the strangers' death ritual. They scattered into the trees when the cannons on the ship went off to mark the end of the ceremony.

And now the expedition could leave, but a gale blew in from the west, preventing their escape. A ship in readiness for departure but not leaving—only a dead calm might be worse for the morale of a ship's company already affected by grief and fear. Langle himself was hard-pressed to contain his own desperation to be off. All of his old anxieties had returned. Every day he tasted the water from his pitcher, swishing it about in his mouth, testing it. He imagined daily that it declined in quality, yet found himself drinking it from morning till night, as if it were liquor and might help him forget. The pitcher was never empty, and one sleepless night it occurred to him that François was keeping it full, making sure his captain never had to ask for more. The boy deserved an increase in pay. He would remember that in his next dispatches to France, dispatches he would be sending from Monterey in Alta California, their next destination. The crew were relieved to be heading south, to warmer weather, well-charted coastline, and Spanish hospitality. But the prospect of relief eluded Langle. Lapérouse would expect him to arrive in Monterey with completed condolence letters. *My Lord, It is with unutterable regret that I write to inform you . . .*

The wind finally shifted, and at slack water on the afternoon of July 30 the order to weigh anchor was shouted over from the *Boussole*. More than a fortnight had passed since the tragedy. They had been in the bay almost a month. The crew let out a collectively held breath when the *Boussole*, going first, passed safely through the narrow entrance. Langle piloted the

Astrolabe out himself, grateful for a task to occupy him as they left the bay.

As they passed the spit on the starboard side, he looked over. He had walked that beach in search of survivors or bodies or wreckage, and found instead a dead gull, a rock for his son, and a girl who stole his canteen. He knew the girl would not be there again but looked for her anyway.

Of course she was not there. But standing on all fours at the point, facing the ship, was a large brown bear. Many of the men had seen bears onshore, gorging themselves on salmon along the streams, but this was the first one Langle had ever seen. Two weeks earlier the sight would have thrilled him; he would have described it in a letter home, urging Georgette to tell Charles that his father had seen the greatest beast of North America. But the creature appeared indifferent to the sight of two frigates passing before it, and Langle felt he would like nothing better than to shoot it right there where it stood. He turned back to the wheel to make a small correction, then looked back toward the point again, but they had now passed through, and the bear disappeared from view.

SIX

FOG

North American Coast, August–September 1786

White everywhere. Mist so thick it obliterates colors and edges. Up on the quarterdeck, our captain looks like an artist's afterthought. He stands on the port side, gazing out toward the North American coastline. But it's all one whiteness—sea, sky, and land. We can hear the flagship's bell but cannot see her.

I climb partway up the steps and wait until he notices me.

"Monsieur Lavaux," he says, inviting me up. When I reach him, I see his face, drawn and thin. François is right: the captain hasn't been sleeping or eating.

Of course, all of us have lost sleep and weight since Alaska.

"How is your patient?" he says.

I shake my head. "It won't be long."

One year into the campaign, and I have but *one* patient. That's never happened to me before. When I served under Admiral d'Orvilliers during the American War, the fleet lost almost a thousand men to dysentery and typhus. A *thousand*. In less than four months.

We've had no new sickness since leaving France. My current patient, a servant with one of our young lieutenants, was already ill when he joined the expedition. I still don't know by what subterfuge the lieutenant managed to sneak him aboard. The servant will be our first death from disease. I might reasonably feel proud of this. But twenty-one men drowned three weeks ago—eleven from our ship, ten from the flagship. The calamity has made pride impossible.

"And the rest of the men?" the captain asks.

"Minor complaints—a sprained finger, one deeply lodged splinter, a few colds. Their spirits are still subdued, of course."

The captain says nothing.

"Sir," I finally venture. "May I offer you anything? A sleeping draught, perhaps?"

The captain turns to me, searches my face for a moment. "No, I thank you, Monsieur Lavaux," he finally says. He turns back to studying the fog and its phantoms.

Below, I make my way to the cabin of our chaplain, Father Receveur. He's waiting with François, who's stooping awkwardly in a corner.

"Well?" the priest says.

"He looks exhausted," I acknowledge. "But he refused my offer of a sleeping draught."

The priest nods, unsurprised. "Look what else François brought," he says, pointing to papers spread out over his cot.

He holds up a lantern for me as I look over the crumpled sheets, each containing just one or two lines of writing:

My Lord—

My Dear Lord— It is with great regret

My Dear Lord, it is with the greatest regret that I write to report

My Lord, it is with a heavy heart that I write to inform you of the ~~death deaths~~ *death of your sons.*

I draw back. "We shouldn't be looking at this." I turn to François. "Where did you get it?"

The boy tries to shrink back and hits his head on the shelf over the priest's bed.

Father Receveur interjects. "It's his job to sweep up the captain's cabin," he says. "These papers were strewn over the captain's floor this morning."

"Well, he obviously meant to discard them," I say.

"He's writing to the La Borde brothers' father," the priest says.

"I can see that."

"The Marquis de La Borde—"

"Yes."

"—one of the richest, most powerful—"

"I *know* who he is."

"You know about the promise the captain made him?"

"I do." I look back at the scraps. "A terrible letter to have to write. No wonder he hasn't been sleeping." I turn to François. "Has he finished it?"

The boy blushes before speaking. "He has some sealed letters on his desk," he says. "I don't know who they're for." He blushes again, and then I remember: the boy cannot read.

"What can we do?" I say.

"I don't know," the priest says.

It's pleasing to hear the chaplain say for once that he does not know something.

In the morning I make my daily tour of the ship, greeting the men, looking and listening for signs of illness. On deck, I can't help but regard the fog as a miasma that might infect us all. The officers murmur that we've advanced only sixteen leagues in three days and complain of the worthlessness of the Spanish charts on which they're obliged to rely. Alas, I have no remedy for frustration. Midafternoon, a break in the mist allows them to get their bearings and observe the lay of the land as it spreads southward before us. But no sooner do we approach the shore than we're surrounded again—clouds, rain, then a pallid, clinging mist in which we are becalmed for two days.

The only change is in my dying patient. He wakes in greater pain each morning, his breathing more labored, weeping to discover himself still alive. I administer laudanum—more and more each day—and try to ply him with spoonfuls of beef broth, which he ingests less and less of each day. He asks me to bleed him. In my experience, men who are bled die faster. Perhaps I should accede to his request.

The young lieutenant, his master, is busier now than ever, as he must make up for the loss of three officers in Alaska. But he spends a few hours each day by his servant's side.

"I think he's better today, Monsieur Lavaux," he says, looking at me, eager for confirmation.

His servant lies insensible on the pallet, his feverish skin looking more like rain-beaded marble than the sheath of a living man. But I don't disabuse the young lieutenant of his hope.

François is waiting for me outside of my cabin. "He's still not sleeping or eating," he says.

"Who?"

"The *captain*," he says, eyebrows raised in impatience. "And I found more of these." He offers me a fistful of wastepaper.

I uncrumple one. An ashy bootprint over the handwriting:

Please understand, My Lord, there was no wind that morning, nor a cloud in the sky. The water of the bay was like glass.

"You shouldn't be showing these to anyone, François."

"I'm not showing them to 'anyone,'" he cries. "I'm showing them to *you*." He bows his head, embarrassed by his own vehemence.

"What can I do?" I say.

He bites his lower lip. "I was wondering." He clears his throat. "Could you give *me* the sleeping draught—just a little—and— and— I could put a few drops in his water at night."

I stare at the boy, horrified and amused and impressed.

"He always drinks water at night," he adds.

When he leaves, he ducks his head to clear the doorway. He's grown tall in the year since we left France. Someone needs to teach him how to shave.

At last, a clear day with light, variable winds. I watch our captain and the young lieutenant work together to determine the sun's altitude then check the ship's chronometers. Father Receveur, who imagines himself a savant, joins them, but he spends more time looking at the captain than at the sky. Another officer is occupied draughting the contours and visible high points on land. The sailors take advantage of the sun to clean: Some swab the decks while others do laundry. Clothes flutter from the lines like comic signal flags. The flagship is in hailing distance off the starboard bow. Her outlines are so clear now it's hard to imagine we couldn't see her this time yesterday.

Father Receveur joins me on deck.

"How is he?" I say.

He nods. "Fine, I think," he says. "Everyone looks happier today. Even the animals." He indicates the three sheep we have left from our time in Chile.

"Spoken like a true Franciscan."

He spreads his arms out before himself. "As you see," he says, then adds: "I wonder if people recover from grief more quickly in warmer climes."

"I was wondering the same." In fact, I'd been enumerating in my mind the needed elements: light, warmth, visibility, colors.

"Our captain looks better rested too."

"Mm. Yes," I say. I do not confess to him my arrangement with François.

Just before nightfall, a strong wind from the west-northwest pushes before it a wall of white that overtakes the ships in minutes. We also encounter strong crosscurrents suggestive of a nearby bay. I've sailed enough to know the risks: we may be driven ashore and run aground, or driven into a gulf and embayed. As expected, a hail from the flagship and a command shouted across to veer back out to sea. Before long we are pitching about in the relative safety of the open ocean.

The servant dies during the night. In the morning, I wake the young lieutenant, who weeps when I tell him. He'd still believed the man might recover. I used to think that people suffered more over sudden, unexpected deaths than over long, protracted ones, but I no longer think so. Grief always lands heavily.

I make my way to the captain's cabin. He calls "Come in!" but his face falls when he sees me. "Is he dead?" he asks.

I ask when we might expect to make landfall for a burial. Not for a month, he tells me. Not till we reach Monterey. He absently places a hand on what looks like a stack of correspondence.

"I'm afraid it means another condolence letter, sir."

He takes his hand back and looks up at me, eyes narrowed. "Not at all," he says. "This man was not my responsibility." It's the young lieutenant, he says, who has the difficult letter to write.

"Of course," I say. We should bury the man at sea, I tell him. This practice, common in French ships, of keeping corpses on board till they can be buried on land, is repugnant and insalubrious.

He agrees, then instructs one of his officers to find a carpenter and sailmaker to help the young lieutenant prepare his servant's body. An hour later the captain arrives on deck, hails the flagship through the mist to report that we've had a death on board, then summons all hands for the service. Father Receveur has the perfect, sonorous voice for the office. The fog renders everything and everyone less corporeal; it's as if the priest were consigning us all to the deep. But it's the servant's body that's dropped overboard. He vanishes before we hear the splash, the mist swallowing him whole before he hits the water. The captain runs a hand roughly across his face as he turns from the burial of the man who was not his responsibility.

For the first time in my long career as a naval surgeon, I am without patients.

François finds me again. "He's still at it," he says, clutching more pages.

My Lord, I hardly need tell you of your sons' superior qualities as officers. Had they been spared, they would have had brilliant careers.

Indeed, I begin to wonder how I can come home when they cannot.

"I need more laudanum," François says.

"Shh!" I command. Our cabins' walls may be made of thick planks, but there are gaps. I fix the boy with what I hope is a hard stare. "You're not using it yourself, are you?"

He shakes his head, eyes wide with surprise and insult.

"Is he eating?"

"Mostly broth and bread."

"His cook should—"

"It's what he *asks* for, Monsieur Lavaux."

Laudanum and broth. The consumptive servant's last diet.

"You have to *do* something, Monsieur Lavaux," the boy says. "He's going to die."

"Nonsense," I say sharply. "The captain is in perfect health."

But I see no sign of the captain for several days. The officers don't say anything in my hearing about it, but I sense among them an underlying anxiety.

For a week, we alternate between white calms and white gales.

Then, a clearing. The crew pours onto the deck, starved for sunlight.

We can see for leagues in every direction. Great snowbound peaks in the eastern distance. Lush green islands dotting the coastline. A bay opens before us, too deep to see to the other end. The officers note its position, but we sail on without exploring it, our orders to reach Monterey before mid-September. Father Receveur joins me again at the rail.

"Perhaps that was the Northwest Passage," I say as the opening recedes from view.

"There is no Northwest Passage," he declares.

"You know this for a fact."

"Not for a *fact*—not a geographical fact, at least," he says. He avidly scans the wide view before us as if to make up for the days when there was nothing to see. "I suspect this continent was not created for the convenience of European commerce," he says. "There's no easy way here—no short cuts." He breaks his outward gaze and looks over at me with a grin. When he smiles one can see the youth that's usually hidden under his cassock and behind that clerical certainty.

"Father," I say suddenly. "What if we wrote that letter for the captain?"

He turns to me. No longer smiling. "You cannot be serious."

We retreat to the privacy of his cabin.

My Lord, it is with the most painful regret that I inform you of the loss of your sons in a tragic and unforeseeable accident in Alaska on July 11, 1786.

I have asked that the official report from the flagship be forwarded to you so you may see for yourself the precautions we took. Not one of us had any presentiment of danger.

"Too defensive," I say.

"He has to assure the marquis that he didn't wantonly throw his sons into danger."

"Too late for that."

I hope it may be of some consolation to know that your sons were lost while heroically, though unwisely, trying to aid another boat in distress. Sadly, both boats and all 21 men aboard were lost in the violence of the currents in which they were caught.

"Is that actually consoling?" the priest says.

"I don't know. Is it?"

The moment we learned of the accident, Monsieur de Lapérouse and I ordered search parties to find and help survivors. Indeed, I myself directed one such party in the area of the bay where the boats were lost. Alas, we found no one, not even one body, despite many hours spent searching in the days following the tragedy.

"Now that *is* defensive."

"Can it be helped?"

We were obliged to delay our departure as a result . . .

"*Obliged?*" I say.

"What's wrong with 'obliged'?"

"It sounds as if we begrudged the time spent looking for the lost men."

Indeed, we delayed our departure by two weeks in the vain hope that someone would turn up alive or that we would find at least one body to properly mourn and bury.

"That's better."

Neither of us wants to write out the final copy, but I prevail. "Medical men can't write anything decipherable," I say. He agrees to play scribe if I deliver the letter.

I find François in the galley, drinking with the captain's personal cook. "You do realize that if you turn this boy into a drunkard, there will be less for you to imbibe, Monsieur Deveau?" I say as I draw François away. I take him up on deck, where the fog has enfolded us again, curling around the masts and sails and men like tentacles. "Don't give it to him directly," I say, handing the letter to François. "Just place it discreetly on his writing table." The boy wanders off unevenly. After he disappears into the mist, I look up and watch while thin, wet ribbons of cloud rush overhead, distorting the light of the quarter moon.

Dead calm the next day. Midmorning, I'm alphabetizing my collections of remedies and liniments when I hear a commotion outside the infirmary. I open the door to the young lieutenant holding up a bloodied and dazed François.

"What in God's name?" I cry.

"He did something to greatly displease the captain," the lieutenant says.

"The *captain*?" The captain has never struck a crew member before.

The lieutenant shrugs unhappily. He looks at François with such angry bewilderment I'm afraid the boy may sustain more blows.

"Go get Father Receveur," I tell the lieutenant, then take the boy into the infirmary. "What did you do, François?"

"What did *you* do?" the boy shouts back.

He is a mess of tears and snot and sweat, but the physical injuries are relatively minor: a small contusion on the back of his head, some bruises and lacerations on his arms and legs.

Father Receveur rushes in. "My dear boy, what happened?"

François regards us both with aggrieved belligerence. "He held up your paper and kept shouting, 'Who did this? Who did you talk to?'"

The priest and I look at each other. The priest's usual confidence drains out of his face along with all of its color.

"What did you tell him?" I ask François.

"You'd like to know, wouldn't you?" He juts out his chin then grimaces in pain.

"Yes, we would very much like to know."

The boy sneers at us and at our patrician fear. "I didn't say anything," he says. "Pretended I didn't know what he was talking about. That's when he shoved me into the wall."

"You could have offered us up, my boy," the priest says. I roll my eyes. Ex post facto declarations of selflessness: so typical of the religious.

"Could have," the boy says. "But didn't. Anyway, he's finished the letters. He put his paper and quills and inkpots away."

The priest and I exchange glances again. *So it might have worked*, our raised eyebrows seem to say. We don't *know*, of course. Maybe he sealed up our letter and added it to his stack. Maybe he copied out our words in his own hand. Maybe the fact that someone on board felt compelled to compose it for him spurred him to complete his own letter. Or maybe the new letter isn't to the Marquis de La Borde at all but to someone else—the minister of marine, perhaps—complaining of interfering crew members, asking that François's pay be cut—or requesting that his chaplain and surgeon be transferred from the ship at the next port of call.

I clean the boy up and send him to his berth for the day.

"We should teach that boy to read," Father Receveur says. "He might make something of himself."

I knock on the captain's door, dread knotting up my insides. But when I see him, I realize his dread has been worse than mine. His face is pale with misery. "Is he all right?" he says.

"He'll be fine," I say. "But if he could be relieved of duty today—"

"Of course."

"Is there anything I can do for you, sir?" I ask.

He shakes his head at first, then says, "A few weeks ago you offered me a sleeping draught—"

"I'd be happy to help with that, sir."

"Thank you, Monsieur Lavaux."

"Sir—"

He looks up, wary and ashamed, but I can see that his anger is not yet spent.

"He's very devoted to you, you know." It's not what I meant to say.

The captain blinks hard as he waves me away.

I go back out on deck. I'm needed below—a short-lived but quite unpleasant stomach ailment seems to have broken out among the marines. But first I stand gazing out into the blankness around me. I look down over the rail and am surprised to find dark shapes below—seabirds of some kind. From their postures I can tell they're sitting on the surface of the water. But the water on which they bob remains invisible, overlaid with mist and opaque to the sky. The birds seem to float, unmoored, in midair, like magical creatures who know how to hold themselves in suspension.

SEVEN

LETTERS FROM MONTEREY

Excerpts of dispatches sent on the Spanish corvette La Princesa in October 1786, from Monterey, California

I. *The report of Lieutenant Estevan Martínez, commander of the supply ships* La Princesa *and* La Favorita, *to His Excellency Don Bernardo Galvez, Viceroy of Mexico, Mexico City*

Excellency, I have the honor to report our safe arrival in Monterey on August 16 and the successful delivery of supplies for both the presidio and the mission. There was of course a disagreement between Governor Don Pedro Fages and His Reverence Fray Fermín Lasuén over the proper distribution of the wine, and when I produced the official order from San Blas showing that both men were overstating their due, they turned their dissatisfaction from each other to me. It happens every year.

The three new priests I also saw safely conducted to Fray Lasuén's custody, and glad I was to be free of them. One was seasick the entire voyage, the second relentlessly preached damnation at my men, and the third, a young man of excellent family who was a pleasant enough passenger at first, over the course of our voyage fell into a state of such severe melancholy that my officers took it in turns to watch him lest he throw himself overboard. I communicated my anxiety about this young man to Fray Lasuén, who is of the opinion that once the man is settled in his work at the mission, he will recover his spirits. I had occasion to see my former passengers once or twice before our departure, and I am happy to report Fray Lasuén's wisdom confirmed in this, as Fray Faustino Solá, the young melancholic, seemed much improved.

Your Excellency will remember that right before my departure, you informed me of a dispatch from the French consul at Cádiz requesting consideration for a French voyage of exploration planning to visit our settlements in Alta California. How fortunate we were to receive this news when we did, for it was not one month after my arrival that two French frigates appeared out of the mist—a circumstance that might have caused alarm had we not been forewarned. I lost no time in sending pilots to guide the *Boussole* and the *Astrolabe* to safe anchorages in the bay and also had chickens, cheese, wine, and fresh vegetables delivered, as I suspected the Frenchmen had been many months without civilized food. I had the great honor to be the first to welcome the Count de Lapérouse and his second-in-command, Viscount de Langle, to Alta California, and to introduce them and their officers, artists, and men of science to the governor and to their reverences the fathers of San Carlos Mission in Carmel.

Indeed, I believe the Frenchmen's pleasure was no less than ours, as every hospitality was extended to them during their ten-day stay. They were fêted at the governor's house, which is by all accounts a happier place than it was last year, and at the mission, and finally aboard *La Princesa*. In the days before their departure, I made my men available to assist them in the loading of fresh water, food, and wood. Everything pleased and interested them, and I am confident that the letters I now convey from them to their friends and superiors in France will tell of the warmth of their reception.

The count is a man of great understanding. I had occasion to speak with him at length about their exploration of Alaska this summer. They suffered a terrible calamity there, so the subject was a painful one. But it is the count's belief that the Russians are expanding their activities in this part of the continent. Upon my return to Mexico, I will propose to Your Excellency an expedition to Alaska to establish and confirm Spanish claims and interests there . . .

II. *From Pedro Fages, Governor of Alta and Baja California, to His Excellency Don Bernardo Galvez, Viceroy of Mexico, Mexico City*
. . . I thank Your Excellency most particularly for the news of the French expedition, for they arrived on September 14, only a few weeks after your letter. My wife and I had the honor of opening our home to the Count de

Lapérouse and his entourage. A more courtly and cultured group of guests we are unlikely to host again while we are here.

The visit was a source of great solace to my wife. Your Excellency knows she has suffered under the privations of life in Alta California. You may not know that we lost a child in May—a girl, only eight days old. We were heartbroken, and for my wife I feared another visitation of the dangerous excitability she exhibited last year. But the arrival of the Frenchmen revived her spirits enormously. I was anxious that when the frigates sailed away, she would fall again into despondency. But the memory of the honor and pleasure bestowed on us by their visit seems to sustain her still. One of the expedition artists was kind enough to paint her portrait. It now graces a wall in our home, a memento of our refined visitors and the pleasure of their society.

My only regret is that we were not able to enjoy the company of these excellent men a little longer. His Reverence Fray Lasuén and his priests invited them to the mission, so we were obliged to escort our guests to Carmel after only two days. Indeed, their reverences vied with us for the Frenchmen's attentions from the moment they arrived, hurrying hither as soon as they heard the news. Glad I was that day for the distinctions of dress! Captain Martínez had already met the count and strutted over his introductions as if he were an intimate of the French court. Fray Lasuén was little better. If not for his brown cassock, he might have been mistaken for the governor!

When they first arrived, our guests were still mourning the loss of some twenty crew members killed in an accident in Alaska. I believe that their time here proved of great comfort to them. There is nothing quite like the company of other Europeans and Catholics. Indeed, the visit was of much benefit to all concerned, with gifts and friendship freely exchanged. The count insisted on paying for provisions we would happily have offered as gifts. The Viscount de Langle, his second-in-command, also a man of refinement, gave to the mission a small millstone to assist in the grinding of corn.

It brings me no pleasure to end this letter with unpleasantness, Your Excellency. However, I must bring to your attention a grave matter concerning His Reverence Fray Matías Noriega, the priest who serves under Fray Lasuén. Fray Noriega has always been harsh in his treatment of the neophytes, but lately his punishments have grown excessive. My soldiers in Carmel are unsentimental men who have no particular love for the Indian, but they have asked to be transferred. His Reverence moderated his punishments during the Frenchmen's visit, but has, since their departure, applied them with redoubled violence. He recently abandoned the traditional leather whip in favor of chains. I fear lest these excesses incite a revolt among the Indians.

Last week a female neophyte, age about twenty-five, died two days after being punished. She had run away from the mission for the third time in as many months. My men found her and delivered her to Fray Lasuén's custody, but she was turned over to Fray Noriega. My men report that His Reverence compelled one of the younger priests, newly arrived with Captain Martínez, to witness and assist in the discipline. This man has since fallen prey to fits of madness.

I know that in making this report, I may appear to be vindictive and ungrateful. The mission's numerous complaints about the conduct of my soldiers are well-known. So is the great service their reverences—and Fray Noriega in particular—rendered to me last year. I have appealed to Fray Lasuén, but Fray Noriega is by all accounts prodigiously skilled at appeasing his superiors. Given this state of affairs, I have ordered my men at the mission to ignore henceforth any request from their reverences to retrieve runaways. My men are charged with the protection of the mission and its inmates, not with hunting down unwilling converts and delivering them to death . . .

III. *From Eulalia Callis de Fages, wife of Don Pedro Fages, Governor of California, to her mother, Doña Rosa Callis, Mexico City.* [Editor's note: The text rendered in italics is in a different ink and hand from the original; the fading of this ink over time has revealed some of the original text.]

My Dear Mother,

Last year I was not ~~permitted~~ *able* to write to you from the mission, where I ~~was held against my will, away from my children and friends,~~ *stayed* until I agreed to ~~submit to~~ *reconcile with* my husband, ~~recant my accusations against him,~~ thus restoring his honor *and my own.* This I eventually did, for ~~as unhappy as I was with my marriage,~~ a cold, damp cell is no place for a lady, and I grieved for my children, who were without their mother ~~for three long months~~. Don Pedro welcomed me warmly ~~enough~~, and before long I was with child again. Don Pedro was delighted and said the child would symbolize our renewed life together. She was born in May, a beautiful, dark-eyed girl with black hair, but eight days later she was gone. I asked my husband, "What does she symbolize now?" but he ~~made no answer~~ *only wept.*

For a long time—all through the foggy summer here that is more like winter—I did not speak another word. But one morning my Indian girl woke me and said two French ships had sailed into the bay. I think the mandate of hospitality must course through our Spanish blood, Mother, for the urgency of welcoming these visitors from Europe pushed back my grief. All that day I prepared to receive the French explorers, for that is who had arrived. The servants and I—and even Don Pedro—cleaned house and tidied the garden, mended our best clothes, slaughtered lambs, stirred soup, and baked bread. I was ashamed of the meanness of our dwelling, but Don Pedro assured me that after so long at sea, the Frenchmen would deem our home a small palace. It was ~~the~~ *such a* kind~~est~~ thing he said to me ~~in so long~~.

The next day two French captains and assorted officers and naturalists came to the presidio and then to our home for a reception. I wore my black polonaise over a gray silk underskirt, which felt in keeping with our recent bereavement without being gloomy. I had not used French in many years, so at first I was shy, but during the evening many words and phrases came back to me. ~~Don Pedro's French is very poor, he needed everything translated.~~ I could scarcely stop talking. I had not spoken to anyone in so long.

Our visitors were men of great refinement and kindness. The commander of the expedition, a Count de Lapérouse, is not a good-looking man but laughs so easily that one is charmed. They must eat very well aboard French ships, for he was surprisingly stout for one who had been so long at sea. His friend, the Viscount de Langle, who commands the second ship, is taller and thinner and more classically handsome but was quiet, almost grave. The officers were all young and so beautiful in their dress and manners. The men of science—they call themselves "savants"— intimidated me, but the junior botanist asked me about my garden, and poor man, I ended up telling him my entire life story! Then the most dashing member of the entourage, a young artist, asked if he could paint my portrait. It flatters me more than I deserve, but how I wish you could see it, Mother.

Don Pedro and I were more united in those days than we have been in many years. ~~In the end, it was not the priests' harsh intervention, nor even the birth of another child, but the introduction of some society that made all the difference. It confirmed for me what I've said all along, that if only we could live in a civilized place, we might be happy.~~ But rest assured, dear Mother, that all is ~~as~~ well ~~as can be expected~~. I still long for the day when I may return to Mexico City and see you again . . .

IV. *From Fray Fermín Francisco de Lasuén, President of the California Missions and Head of the Mission of San Carlos Borromeo of Monterey in Carmel, to the Reverend Father Guardian Fray Francisco Palóu, Guardian of the Apostolic College of San Fernando, Mexico City*

Dominus det tibi Pacem. I thank Your Reverence for the letter of April 20 and congratulate you on your election to the guardianship of the college. I thank you also for the supplies, especially the books. They will be my boon companions this next long year.

The three new priests also arrived safely. I will confess that at first I felt considerable unease as to their fitness for life in California. Fray Faustino Solá gave me most cause for concern. I know he left Your Reverence and the College filled with faith and confidence in the love of our Lord, but he grew strangely dejected during the voyage from San Blas. Captain Martínez told me that his officers feared for Fray Solá's sanity, although the good captain is inclined to exaggerate. It was true, however, that Fray Solá arrived looking like a haunted and hunted man. Several weeks after his arrival, he had progressed no further than taking solitary walks in the mission gardens and was unable to perform any priestly duties. I had nearly determined to send him back to Mexico with the supply ships when an event occurred that was a source of delight and novelty to everyone in our mission community and that effectively distracted Fray Solá out of his torpor.

This memorable event was the visit, in September, of a French scientific and exploratory expedition commanded by the Count de Lapérouse. When the news came that two French frigates had sailed into the bay, we hurried to make our humble mission as presentable as possible. Even the Indians, usually so indolent, bestirred themselves to greater industry. Fray Matías Noriega informed me with joy that he hardly needed the lash at all in the weeks before and during the Frenchmen's visit, as the Indians attended Mass more faithfully, ground more corn than their daily quotas, and repaired and swept out their dwellings when they saw us attending to ours.

The mission soldiers were not at first inclined to escort us to the presidio to meet our guests when they arrived, saying they had no orders from the governor to do so. But their own curiosity to see the visitors prevailed, so we—Fray Noriega, the three new priests, and myself—were on hand to greet the commander and his officers when they came ashore. Don Pedro was not altogether pleased to see us, particularly as it meant he was then bound by decorum to invite us to the reception at his home that evening. Even less happy to see us was his wife, Doña Eulalia, who was, as Your Reverence will no doubt recall from last year's dispatches, a most unwilling inmate of our mission for some months last year after her scandalous and insubordinate behavior.

Under ordinary circumstances we would have declined such a reluctant invitation: indulging the pleasures of a table overseen by one of the most impudent, stiff-necked women in all of Christendom can edify no one. However, these were extraordinary circumstances. I wished to learn in person what spiritual or material needs our guests might have and to ensure that the mission was not denied the opportunity to extend Christian hospitality and assistance to them. They readily accepted our invitation to visit the mission. Their eagerness to see for themselves our work among the Indians was naturally gratifying to me and the other priests. It also had the salutary effect of calming the almost unseemly high spirits of Don Pedro and Doña Eulalia. One would never have guessed that only a year earlier their home had been riven and shamed by a discord so public and indecent that all of Alta California fairly buzzed with it. Curiously, they are like patients who resent the doctor who has healed them. Indeed, their hostility toward me and even more toward Fray Noriega is so marked that it will not surprise me if Don Pedro acts against us in some

way. If this should occur, I hope I may rely on Your Reverence's interces-
sion on our behalf.

But to return to my account: two days after the reception, we were
honored by the arrival of the French delegation, consisting of the count,
his senior officers, and a distinguished group of savants that included
astronomers, physicists, botanists, linguists, and artists. Among the naturalists were two priests who, I fear, regard themselves as men of science
first and men of God second, but for all that, they were men of breeding,
wit, and generosity. They expressed the most kindly interest in our endeavors, applauded our spiritual conquest of the Indians, and did not balk
at the primitive conditions in which we currently live. I was nevertheless
grateful that their visit so closely followed the arrival of the supply ships,
as it meant we did not want for wine or cheese or candles. The demands
of hospitality will necessarily mean some privation for us later, especially
as we were compelled once again to accept a smaller share of wine than
was our due from the supply ship, but I cannot regret sharing our bounty.

For all their suavity, our visitors carried with them a great burden of
grief over the loss of twenty-one shipmates killed in Alaska in July. Several of the officers and even one of their naturalists sought me out, desir-
ous of confession or spiritual solace. One young officer had lost not only
his cabinmate in the accident in Alaska but, during the subsequent passage south, his servant, a man who'd been at his side since infancy. He
attended Mass every day.

The ministry was not one-sided, however, for the visit raised our
spirits as well. The most notable change was, as mentioned earlier, in Fray
Solá, who, after meeting the Frenchmen, seemed suddenly to remember
himself, becoming the amiable and energetic man described in Your Reverence's letter. He befriended a young botanist from the expedition who
expressed interest in our gardens and in the native plants of the area. Fray
Solá gave him a tour of the gardens he had come to know during his con-
valescence and even organized a botanizing expedition outside the mission. The next day he performed his first Mass. I rejoice that the Lord in
His infinite mercy has seen fit to restore this young and able priest to the
right use of his faculties. Most recently he has been ill, but Fray Noriega,
who has taken upon himself the role of spiritual adviser to our new arriv-
als, assures me that it is but a minor stomach complaint and will soon

pass. It is my hope that once he is fully recovered, he may serve in San Luis Obispo.

The Frenchmen left us with many tangible gifts as well. The young botanist gave us plants for our gardens—seed potatoes, grapevines, fig trees, and seeds for celery, artichoke, and melons—all miraculously preserved for over a year in the hold of his ship. The expedition artist completed a pencil drawing of their arrival at the mission and was kind enough to present it to me. Another gift came from the Viscount de Langle, who donated a small grinding stone to ease the work of the neophyte women. Regrettably, Fray Noriega reports that the women refuse to use it, preferring their traditional method of grinding corn, although it is more laborious and less effectual. I am no longer surprised by the neophytes' ignorance, but I find I am not yet inured to disappointment.

With this I conclude my report. I have enclosed a list of our requests for next year. May God our Lord keep Your Reverence many years in His holy grace.

V. *From Jean-François de Galaup de Lapérouse, Captain of the* Boussole *and Commander of the Expedition Ordered by His Majesty King Louis XVI, to his wife, Éléonore de Lapérouse, Albi, France*

My dear Éléonore, tomorrow, if the winds are in our favor, we leave Monterey Bay in California, a place of unmatched natural beauty and abundance. The bay teems with life: indeed, right now outside my window, I see lines of pelicans flying low over the water, and earlier we were entertained by a group of curious sea otters that had gathered around the ship. The land is no less fertile and is home now to some fifty or sixty Spanish colonists as well as several hundred Indians. The Spanish reputation for hospitality, proven once already during our time in Chile six months ago, has been doubly confirmed here. The soldiers and missionaries in this remote outpost of New Spain have little of their own but give generously of it anyway. We leave with so much fresh livestock, vegetables, and grain that I fear we are leaving these good people to suffer later for their magnanimity. It was with difficulty that I persuaded them to accept payment for the provisions.

Here too I am called "Count"—indeed, I grow quite used to the title!

Langle and I spent our first two days ashore as guests of the governor, Don Pedro Fages, a genial, urbane man in his fifties. In this newly conquered place it is a rough mud dwelling that passes for a governor's house, and though it was clean and furnished with taste and comfort in mind, there was no hiding the rough-hewn floors or the windows, which had no glass, only bars to keep out intruders and stretched hides to keep out the elements.

As is so common among Spaniards, Don Pedro's wife is nearly thirty years younger than he, younger even than you, my love. Sadly, Doña Eulalia's beauty and charms, which must once have been considerable, have been worn down by tribulations and discontent. Her hardships may also have eroded discretion, for by the end of our first night ashore, when the governor hosted a reception in our honor, we knew altogether too much about this woman and her sad life. I will not sully this letter with a recitation of the more scandalous tales we heard, some from her own lips. Suffice to say that she misses the comforts of life in Mexico City—as indeed, what civilized woman would not?—and has lost two of her four children, one to a miscarriage suffered en route to Monterey four years ago, and the other, a newborn daughter, just a few months ago. This excited our compassion, of course, but we could not admire her. She seemed to have no friends among the wives of the men who serve under her husband, and fairly threw herself at each of us in turn, eventually landing on my botanist, Collignon, who had no underling on whom to fob her off. I persuaded our artist, Duché de Vancy, to offer to paint her portrait. She sat for him for an hour while he tried valiantly to impart to her a grace she no longer had. The poor woman was pathetically happy with the result.

After two days, we were quite ready to accept an invitation to visit the Franciscan fathers at the nearby mission. There are many such establishments up and down the coastline of California. They are the bases from which the missionaries work among the natives, providing sustenance and employment to converts. It sounds noble enough, and I wish I could say the result was such as to make me glad to be a Christian. But alas, it reminded me too much of the sugar plantations in Île de France, only with lower productivity and more morose slaves. On our arrival, we were warmly greeted by the pealing of bells and the five priests who are currently in residence. But the Indian converts were also arrayed before us,

compelled to be there, I suspect, for a more listless group of human beings I have never before beheld. They showed neither surprise nor interest
when we arrived, although I was given to understand that we were the
first non-Spanish Europeans they had ever seen.

The good fathers are not content simply to convert the Indians. They
demand a level of piety from them that no French priest would expect of
a congregant raised in the faith from birth. The converts are whipped for
missing daily prayers and whipped harder if they try to leave the mission.
Father Lasuén, who is not only head of this mission but president of
all the California missions, assured me they discipline the Indians with
the same gentleness a father would use on his child. (I was put in mind of
some ferocious beatings I've seen men administer to their own children,
but did not say so.) He also told me, candidly and without bitterness, that
the Indians are ignorant and childish, often behaving in ways contrary to
their own betterment. The lack of any native religion or system of gover-
nance among them, far from making them tractable, renders all but a few
of them unable to understand authority or consequences or to plan for even
the near future, much less eternity.

I came to respect and admire this humble, thoughtful man who has
devoted his life to the nearly hopeless task of improving the lives of these
people. But there is a medieval quality to the endeavor that I could not see
without dismay. The mission is unnecessarily impoverished: They conduct
farmwork with primitive—even broken—implements. The Indian men,
who entertained us by demonstrating their ancient hunting techniques,
are rarely allowed to leave the mission to use their native skills to procure
fish or game. As a result, nearly every meal is a thin gruel made of corn,
and people go hungry in a land of astonishing plenty. The women spend
all day grinding corn between two rocks, a time-consuming, wasteful
process, and are punished if they fail to meet their daily quotas. This last
defect at least we were able to address. Monsieur de Langle gave them
the spare millstone from the *Astrolabe*, and he and Collignon spent an
afternoon demonstrating its use to the women and to the priests who oversee their work. In these small ways we hope to fulfill the king's directive
to benefit everyone we meet.

If you've read my letters in order, my dear, you know of the calamity
we suffered in Alaska. Only to you can I confess how much this loss

continues to weigh on me. It is my last thought when I retire at night and the first when I awake. I had expected this stay among other Europeans to console me, but, if anything, it has had the opposite effect. Sailing on the open seas, away from Alaska, my grief had been held at bay; indeed, I could imagine that the accident had not happened at all, that the absent men were simply elsewhere on my ship. Here, however, I have had to relate our misfortune to solicitous men who sympathize with our loss and wish to ease our grief. Yet this telling and retelling only makes it more real. Every reception held in our honor reminds me of the men who are missing, men who charmed the colonists in Chile only six months ago and are now gone. I am grateful for the kindness of our hosts, but I will be even more grateful when we sail away. Oh, my love, if only I had some words from you to comfort me in the dark night! But the earliest I can hope for a letter to reach me is in Macao, or perhaps even later, in Petropavlovsk . . .

VI. *From Fray Faustino Solá to his brother, Pablo Vicente de Solá, Sergeant, Free Company of Volunteers of Catalonia, San Blas, Mexico*
Brother, I worry you are no longer in San Blas but have been sent off someplace to wage war in the name of His Most Christian Majesty and that this letter will never find you. It seems years since you saw me off as I boarded *La Princesa*. Perhaps it *has* been years. I can scarcely remember the voyage except that I expected every day to be drowned, and once I arrived, I was taken to my cell, where I expected every night to be murdered in my bed by Indians. I don't know how many days I lay in that state. But by and by even one's dreads begin to bore one, so I made my way into the mission gardens. I wish you could see them. We have olive trees and roses, and it reminds me of Mondragón and the villa where we grew up. As a boy I liked to walk in our gardens and pretend I was in the first garden, in Eden, and I do that here as well. Sometimes I am Adam, sometimes Eve, and sometimes the serpent.

But then the visitors arrived and it was no longer practical to pretend, as they seemed very real, with their scientific instruments and their notebooks and their curiosity. One of them became my friend, and when he left my heart ached, for I am sure we will never see each other again, but now I can recall neither his name nor his face. Is that not odd? He was a gardener, and we looked at plants together, both here and outside the mission, and I could not help but pretend we were in Eden, he and I, but I did not alarm him by saying so. One Sunday I was recovered enough to take part in a baptism, and then I was Adam, for the neophytes were brought forward one by one, and it was my duty to name them.

You have always had an appetite for salacious stories, brother, so here is one: a man at the presidio violated an Indian girl who worked in his home, a child of only eleven, and his wife, discovering them, made the matter public. But her husband is a powerful man, so when he asked the mission priests to help him regain his honor, they did, even though they usually complain about the soldiers' licentious behavior. Fray Noriega, who is as ugly a man as I have ever seen, denounced the wife from the pulpit, and then she was taken bound from her home and held at the mission until she took back her accusations and returned home. I saw them, husband and wife, at a reception for our visitors, and they looked happy enough, but I could barely contain myself, for whose honor had been restored? On our way home that night I asked Fray Noriega what had happened to the Indian girl and he said, What Indian girl? The eleven-year-old Indian girl, I said, the one who was violated. There was no proof of that allegation, he said, and then he laughed and said that eleven-year-olds were quite capable of lasciviousness. All night long I lay sleepless on my pallet, plagued by foul, unbidden images of the man and his wife and the Indian girl. By morning I was sure they had placed me in the same cell that the woman had occupied. I could hear Fray Noriega exhorting her to forget her claim and threatening her with whipping if she did not, and I could *smell* the woman and her discharges of anger and hopelessness. I can smell it still though I have several times washed down the walls and floor.

When the visitors came to the mission, I began to see through their eyes our shabby mud church and dwellings, the gardens that are pretty but too small to feed our community, the squalid Indian huts, the neophytes in stocks for missing Mass, the children running around naked, most of them coughing infectiously, and the adults shuffling with expressionless faces to their tasks, and I felt weighed down with terrible shame.

One of the visitors saw how the women struggled to grind their corn, and he brought us a millstone to ease their work. He and the gardener whose name and face I can no longer recall asked Fray Noriega and me to help show the women how it worked. Remarkable, how quickly it reduced a basket of corn to usable meal! The women, who at first seemed resentful of our intrusion, began to smile and laugh. But Fray Noriega grew quieter and quieter, and some days later, after the visitors had sailed away, he bade me join him after Mass. We set off in a cart with two neophyte men from the mission and rode in silence till we stopped in gathering darkness at the top of a hill that pitched steeply away from us into the ocean. There the neophytes unloaded something from the back of the cart, and I saw it was the millstone. Fray Noriega made the two Indians roll the stone to the cliff edge, then bade me stand by it.

Fray Solá, he said, do you remember what our Lord said of the man who brings offense to these little ones who believe in Him? He pointed to the two neophytes when he said "little ones." I did indeed remember, but before I could reply, he said, quoting the Gospels, It were better for that man if a millstone were hung about his neck and he were cast into the depths of the sea. And then he fixed his gaze on me, and I cried, Oh, Father, how have I brought offense? but he would not answer. I had been afraid till then, but now I saw that he meant for me to die, and here at last was the cause of all my fear, and a strange calm came over me. I knelt to the ground and embraced the stone and prepared to fling it and myself over the edge, when Fray Noriega leaned over and said in my ear, Just the stone, Fray Solá. You are still needed here, whereas the stone will encourage indolence among the women. You must cast all your earthly attachments over with the stone. So I rolled the millstone, the visitors' gift, into the darkness yawning at my feet, and I could neither see nor hear it when it landed.

And now I must conclude, brother, for I am nearly late in meeting Fray Noriega. He has told me to meet him behind the granary with a length of chain. The granary is where we take the women to be punished, away from the others, where their men will not see or hear their cries. Fray Oramas told me this morning that the soldiers have brought back a neophyte woman who ran away. No doubt Fray Noriega means to punish her. Perhaps he means for me to punish her. Perhaps I will be the Lord this time, driving Eve out of the garden she has failed to appreciate. Or perhaps I will be the angel with the flaming sword, barring the way to the tree of life.

EIGHT

A MONOGRAPH
ON PARASITES

Macao, January 1787

They did not even get his name right when they came to apprehend him.

"Monsieur de Lamanon?"

"It's *Lamartinière*." Oh, how many times had he corrected them in the last year and a half? Even Captain de Langle had done it a few times. Lamartinière looked around the paneled meeting room in exasperation, looking for a sympathetic face, but found none. They had all just met him, after all, a few junior traders and the staff of the French consulate, compelled by their superiors to attend a visiting scientist's lunchtime presentation on marine parasites. They looked more interested now that he had been interrupted than they had for the previous fifteen minutes. "La-mar-ti-nière," he repeated to the young officer who had called him Lamanon.

"Of course," the officer said, unembarrassed and unapologetic, as if Lamartinière's insistence that he was not Lamanon were an idiosyncrasy that they all indulged. "We need to ask you to come with us, sir."

"Why? What's happened?" Emergencies flashed through his mind: his collections on board, lost or stolen; the captain dead, or the commander; a declaration of war—with Portugal, Spain, no, England—naturally, it would be England; letters from France, *finally*, but with bad news, his *mother*—

"Nothing's *happened*, sir," the officer said with a smile that was neither reassuring nor friendly. "But we do need to return you to your ship."

"On whose authority?" He took a step back and looked at the delegation before him—the young officer, whose round face he recognized but
whose name he did not know, accompanied by two armed, nervous-looking
marines he did not know at all. "You're not from the *Astrolabe*."

"We're from the *Boussole*," the officer said. "Commander's orders."

Lamartinière felt the heat rise in his face. "You're *arresting* me?"

"You can call it what you like, sir, but we still need you to come
with us."

"Are you sure it's *me* you want and *not* Monsieur de Lamanon?"

"We're collecting both of you."

"*Both* of us?" A niggling misgiving he had been trying to ignore all day
suddenly bloomed into full-blown dread. He looked around again at his
audience, eleven men seated around a great mahogany table. A few looked
toward him with regretful bemusement; others looked down, embarrassed
by the scene unfolding before them; and a couple of men stared with
barely concealed glee, delighted that something unusual was afoot. The
consul himself, Monsieur Vieillard, a wheezy, red-faced man who had been
nodding off during the lecture, now pushed himself to standing and shook
his guest's hand as if this were an ordinary leave-taking. "Thank you so
much for enlightening us about—" He stopped, clearly unsure as to the
subject of his enlightenment. "Yes, well," he rasped. "We're sorry you cannot stay longer, Monsieur de Lamanon."

"It's *Lamartinière*!" He scooped up his notes and drawings and stuffed
them into his leather document case, then followed the officer out of the
room. A Chinese servant with a black cap and a long braid down his back
hastened to shut the heavy oak door behind them, but not fast enough to
muffle the laughter of the traders and consulate staff.

Out in the street, the genial Macao breeze and the bustle of humans
unconnected to his plight softened the edge of his angry confusion. "Forgive me," he said, turning to the officer, "it's Ensign . . . ?"

"*Lieutenant*," the officer said. He set off in the direction of the Outer
Harbor. "Lieutenant de Boutin."

"Ah, of course." Lamartinière hurried to keep up, determined to walk
next to Boutin rather than being escorted between the lieutenant and the
marines like a common criminal. "Monsieur de Boutin, can you please
tell me what this is about?"

"You'll have to discuss it with Captain de Langle," Boutin replied, neither slowing down nor turning to look at his charge. "My orders are simply to return you to the *Astrolabe*."

A cluster of food stalls narrowed their passage, forcing Lamartinière to step back into the officer-prisoner-guards alignment he had wished to avoid. They attracted little enough attention from the diners, Chinese men dressed in the loose cotton clothes of porters and houseboys. Seated at round tables under bamboo umbrellas, they scarcely looked up from steaming bowls of noodles to watch the foreigners pass. If he had not been under duress, Lamartinière thought, he would have liked to sample the wares, which smelled delicious.

He caught up with Boutin when the road widened again. "How about Father Mongez and Father Receveur?" he asked. "Are you rounding them up as well?"

Boutin opened his mouth to reply, seemed to think better of it, then shrugged and said, "Yes. It's the four of you."

So even the priests were in trouble. He was beginning to understand. Oh, they should never have sent that second note to the commander! He *had* advised against it. But no one ever listened to him. Even in Brest, before the expedition left, his altogether reasonable request for an assistant had been overruled by the commander, who sided with a common gardener over the claims of a proper botanist. In that disagreement he had lost not only the assistant but his berth on the flagship. As it happened, he preferred Captain de Langle to Commander de Lapérouse, but the snub still rankled. Especially as on the *Astrolabe* he was crammed into a space shared with three other men, none of whom he liked. Things had started out well enough; the four men had even called their shared space the "Savants' Quarters." But Lieutenant d'Aigremont had turned out to be a stupid, talkative bore; the other naturalist, Dufresne, a melancholic who knew nothing about science; and Prévost, the ship's artist, a grouchy sluggard who refused to draw anything other than flowers. No importuning could persuade the man to draw the marine creatures Lamartinière had discovered in Alaska. In the end he had had to do his own drawing, a time-consuming task at which he did not excel.

And now this—whatever *this* was. His stomach grew heavy as fresh resentments formed and swirled over the older, more chronic disappointments of the voyage. An unlucky step on a loose cobblestone sent a spray of muddy water over his shins and shoes. Even his case was not spared.

Stifling the urge to swear, he let out instead a plaintive whine. His escorts ignored him, but a group of Chinese children stopped and stared, and above him he could hear a window opening and the rustle of a bamboo blind being raised. By the time the street ended, dumping them suddenly onto the Praya Grande, the wide crescent-shaped beach that faced the principal harbor in Macao, his feet were wet, his stockings ruined, and he, close to tears.

They made their way to the water's edge, where Boutin greeted a second, more senior officer, another man Lamartinière recognized but could not name. The two men leaned over to talk with the female drivers of two sampans drawn up to the shore. A moment later a wooden stool was lifted out of one sampan, and then a Chinese boy with an umbrella.

"We're likely to be here awhile, Monsieur de Lamartinière," Boutin said. "You may wish to sit down."

He drew himself up resentfully. Stool and shade indeed! He was just a few weeks shy of his twenty-ninth birthday, surely no older than Boutin. "No, thank you," he said. But within minutes he began to sweat under his hat and wig, and then to wonder just how long "awhile" might take. Where were the others? Why had he arrived first? He looked anxiously out at the harbor, filled with sampans, junks, the occasional European boat, and farther out, numerous ships at their anchorages. A low haze obscured details like flags, and he had no idea which ships were theirs. Not that he was eager to return to the *Astrolabe*. The tedium of the long Pacific crossing that had brought them here had nearly driven him mad. Still, it was disquieting to not recognize the ship that had been his home for seventeen months. A bead of sweat traveled down the nape of his neck, and the metal handle of his case dug painfully into his bent fingers. Nodding sheepishly at the boy with the umbrella, he ducked under its shelter and sat down.

At length another officer and two marines appeared on the Praya Grande, this time flanking a sedan chair carried, with noticeable effort, by two Chinese men. Lieutenant de Boutin advanced on the group and spoke briefly with this third officer before returning with a frown. "It's Monsieur de Lamentation himself," he said to the others. Hearing it, Lamartinière laughed; he hadn't heard Lamanon's nickname before. But the officer went on: "He kept them waiting at the house for twenty minutes before he would agree to leave, then demanded they call him a sedan chair because of his 'gout.' Now he's insisting we pay for it."

"For God's sake," the senior officer said. "Tell him no."

Boutin returned to the group and expostulated with the unseen Lamanon. Lamartinière watched the inaudible interaction and swallowed hard, his amusement over the nickname dissipated by a new resentment. They had found Lamanon at home in their rented lodgings? But Lamanon had told Lamartinière just that morning that he couldn't attend the presentation at the consulate because he was being taken to see "an unusual rock formation" that afternoon. Never mind that Lamartinière had dutifully attended Lamanon's presentation to the same group just a few days earlier. Or that he might have enjoyed visiting a rock formation himself. And to arrive in a sedan chair! The man did not have gout any more than he had a goiter. Just yesterday the four of them had climbed up to the Guia Fortress, the highest point in Macao, and Lamanon had suffered no more than a rare, brief spell of silence brought on by shortness of breath.

The sedan chair porters having been paid—Lamartinière could not see by whom—the group, led by Lamanon, who was taller and broader than the rest, made its way toward the water. One of the porters followed behind with what Lamartinière recognized as Lamanon's valise. Lamartinière groaned with the realization that he was leaving the peninsula with nothing but the clothes on his back and the drawings and notes in his case. Most of his wardrobe and books remained—safely, he hoped—in the rented house. He leaned forward and squinted. Was Lamanon *limping*? A fresh heat rose in Lamartinière's face despite the shade of the umbrella.

"Lieutenant de Clonard!" Lamanon cried, addressing the senior officer when he came within earshot. "Now we're rounding up savants and priests? What will the minister say when he learns of this? Or His *Majesty*?"

Clonard regarded his charge with what looked like forced impassivity. "No doubt they would agree with the commander that insubordination cannot be tolerated aboard His Majesty's ships."

"We are none of us actually *aboard* anything at the moment," Lamanon said.

"This is exactly what the commander is talking about, Lamanon." A muscle twitched in the lieutenant's cheek.

Lamanon shrugged and looked over at Lamartinière, taking in, it seemed, his colleague's sodden stockings, the mud-splattered document case, the stool, and the umbrella, before looking back at Clonard. "Where are Mongez and Receveur?" he said.

"*Fathers* Mongez and Receveur are saying Mass with the bishop," Clonard replied after a pause. "They'll be here soon."

"*So,*" Lamanon drawled, "a natural philosopher's rare opportunity for experimentation is interruptible, but religious rites that happen every day the world over are not."

What experimentation? Lamartinière wondered. Since landing, Lamanon had busied himself organizing outings for the four of them, ingratiating himself with local dignitaries, and writing up his findings about "atmospheric tides" to send to Buffon and Condorcet. What could he have been up to just now? Lamanon caught his eye and, as if reading the inquiry there, raised his eyebrows in an exaggerated leer. *Oh!* Lamartinière shrank back into his shade, suppressing a cry of dismay. Surely he did not mean Sophie, the woman they had discovered living in the rented house?

The house, a narrow three-story structure wedged in among more luxurious dwellings on the Rua de São Lourenço, had previously been occupied by another Frenchman, a longtime functionary in the consulate called Thérien who had shot himself just a few months earlier. The man's Portuguese landlord had been delighted to find short-term tenants, as potential local renters were unnerved by the house's association with a suicide. Indeed, Lamartinière and the two priests had exchanged uneasy glances on learning the house's history, but Lamanon had been all bluster: "*Every* house is witness to human misery," he declared. "That's what a house is *for.*" Father Mongez timidly inquired if the unfortunate gentleman had died *in* the house? "No, no," the agent for the landlord assured them. He mimed shooting himself in the head. "At the water. The beach."

"We'll take the house," Lamanon had declared.

Lamartinière could hardly object when the priests remained silent. The whole venture was Lamanon's idea, after all. He was also covering most of the expense. He had invited his particular friend Father Mongez, the *Boussole's* chaplain and occasional naturalist, who in turn invited Father Receveur, Mongez's counterpart on the *Astrolabe*, who invited Lamartinière. The unspoken hierarchy, from Lamanon at the top to each invitee in turn, governed everything that followed.

The house came with a watchman, a cleaning woman, a cook, and a comprador who bought their food and anything else they required. Their first night there, the watchman, a tiny, ancient man, also introduced them to "Sophie," who lived in a small room in the back and "do whatever you want very nice." She stood before the four astonished men, a lovely, slender woman in a blue European dress remarkable only for its very low-cut bodice. Her coral lips were smiling, but her large brown eyes, with their hybrid Chinese and European qualities, stared back at them with a languid defiance that Lamartinière found both stirring and unsettling. Mongez and Receveur explained that they were priests and that she had nothing to concern herself with during their stay. But she either did not understand French very well or did not see how their being priests made any difference, for she continued to stand and smile before them. Lamartinière could not tell whether she was relieved or disappointed when they finally persuaded her to leave.

"The man who had *her* killed himself?" Lamanon said when the door closed behind her.

Since that night, Lamartinière had caught only fleeting glimpses of the woman when she served them tea in the drawing room, but the awareness of her presence in the house tantalized him in private and buzzed like an unacknowledged background hum between the men whenever they were in the house. Fortunately that was seldom—Lamanon had seen to that—and the two priests' assurances to Sophie seemed to settle any question regarding her. Yet now it turned out Lamanon had been alone in the house with her—had, in fact, *arranged* to be alone with her.

"Lamartinière, my good man." Lamanon stood over him now, grinning with more cheerfulness than was either customary for him or appropriate, given their circumstances. He was wigless under his hat, his face more florid than usual, and his cravat poorly tied, although perhaps it always looked that way. "Apparently our efforts to reason with the commander have been mistaken for insolence," he added.

"Apparently," Lamartinière muttered.

"Don't be downcast," Lamanon said. "We'll talk with our respective captains and have ourselves rowed right back." Then he pointed to his right leg with a rueful expression. It was not the leg he had been favoring as he made his way from the sedan chair just moments earlier. "Would you be so kind—?"

"Oh, do what you like," Lamartinière said, giving up his place on the stool.

"What's wrong?"

"*Unusual rock formation?*"

Lamanon laughed. "Ah, that." He smiled up at his colleague without a hint of embarrassment. "I could hardly tell you what I was really about, could I?" When Lamartinière scowled, he added: "She's available to all of us, my friend."

"Don't be disgusting."

Lamanon laughed again and motioned for Lamartinière to come nearer. When he reluctantly complied, Lamanon whispered, "She offered to show me how to smoke opium. I've read about it, of course, and was curious to document its effects."

Lamartinière peered into Lamanon's broad face, his early training as a doctor reasserting itself. There was no hint of intoxication. The man was wide awake, for one thing. His pupils were not constricted, nor was his speech slurred. His halting gait earlier had looked deliberate, not like the result of drug-induced imbalance.

Lamanon smiled. "She had just set everything up—it's a very elaborate ritual, quite fascinating—when *this* lot showed up." He inclined his head toward the officers and marines. "I couldn't very well be taken back to the *Boussole* in an opium-induced stupor, could I?"

Lamartinière nodded, pleased that they had been interrupted—he disapproved of narcotics of any sort and was abstemious even about wine. But more than that he was relieved to hear the "experiment" was about opium rather than intimacy of another sort. Somehow that was easier to bear.

"But," Lamanon continued, still whispering, "I was so provoked by the effrontery of this *arrest* that I made them wait downstairs while I enjoyed Sophie's other favors."

"*What?*"

Lamanon laughed aloud. "What a jealous prude you are, Lamartinière. Come now, I jest. She only helped me pack my things."

Lamartinière stepped away, face burning, and pretended to look down the promenade for the rest of their party. He was ashamed—of his own jealous feelings, of being caught in that jealousy, of his desire to believe Lamanon had not been with Sophie after all, of the fact that he was, at this precise moment, more distressed by the vision of Lamanon with Sophie than about being arrested. He was also angry—angry that he kept allowing himself to be intimidated by Lamanon, and angrier still that Lamanon, who should at least have felt some kinship with him in their shared predicament, if not outright responsibility for it, should still find it necessary to amuse himself at Lamartinière's expense.

Eventually the last of the officers and accompanying marines arrived, leading Fathers Receveur and Mongez to the landing place. He watched the two priests react to their arrest with neither the injured resentment he felt nor the defiant bombast of Lamanon. They apologized to Lieutenant de Clonard for the trouble they had caused, averred that it had never been their intention to be disrespectful to the commander, and humbly prepared to accept whatever punishment awaited them on their ships.

Father Mongez, slight and balding, joined Lamanon and half of the officers and marines in one sampan headed for the *Boussole*, while Lamartinière followed Father Receveur and the other officers and marines into the second sampan. Once he was out on the water, free of Lamanon's exasperating presence, Lamartinière found his misery over Sophie ease even as his thoughts returned more seriously to what might await him on board. Surely he and Father Receveur wouldn't be . . . *flogged*? No, of course not. They weren't English. And it was hard to imagine Captain de Langle, a man of great dignity, who ruled by quiet persuasion, actually *punishing* them. He was a man of science himself, after all. Then again, it would not be the first time Lamartinière had misjudged the complex, often unspoken, mores that governed life on board. He stared out into the harbor, trying again but still in vain to identify the French frigates, trying to quell his growing anxiety, trying too to ignore the nauseating swaying of the sampan. He had never suffered much on the frigate, but small boats often made him queasy.

Father Receveur was not helping. The *Astrolabe*'s earnest young chaplain

seemed to think it his duty to comfort everyone on board—Lamartinière
for the mortification of being arrested in front of the consul, the marines
for their distress over carrying out an unpleasant duty, the officers for the
time lost when so many more pressing matters awaited. Indeed, Lamartinière thought, if the priest could have comforted the capable, sun-
browned boatwomen who poled them away from shore for the bother of
having to ply their trade, he would have. Lamartinière distracted himself
by imagining the priest falling overboard—the undignified splash, the frantic efforts to get him back aboard, the apologies that would ensue once he
was restored, dripping, to his place. The amusing fantasy kept seasickness
at bay, and before long they arrived at the *Astrolabe*, which loomed so famil-
iarly before them that Lamartinière wondered that he had not recognized
it earlier.

He climbed aboard after Boutin and Father Receveur. Thankfully,
almost no one was on deck; he had dreaded the humiliation of being
censured in front of the crew. He was particularly relieved that none of
his cabinmates was present. Only Lieutenant de Monty, the senior officer
under Captain de Langle, was present to take him and the priest into
custody. Boutin greeted Monty, then announced formally that he had
arrived "to deliver Father Receveur and Monsieur de Lamanon—"

"It's *Lamartinière!*"

"Indeed," Boutin said, not bothering to correct himself. Then, his work in
apprehending the two *Astrolabe* passengers concluded, he nodded perfunc-
torily to his captives, bowed to Monty, and departed over the side.

Lieutenant de Monty, one of the tallest members of the expedition,
looked down at his charges like a headmaster displeased with two errant
pupils. "Father," he said, nodding to the priest, then, with exaggerated
precision, "Monsieur de *Lamartinière.*"

Lamartinière puffed out his cheeks in frustration. Was it really so
unreasonable to insist that people use his proper name?

"The commander believes you have allowed yourselves to be unduly
influenced by Monsieur de Lamanon," Monty said. "Which might be
expected of a young naturalist—" He looked pointedly at Lamartinière.
"But Father—" He tilted his head in Receveur's direction, and the priest
hung his head in rueful acknowledgment. "We'd like to be able to rely
on our chaplains to provide some guidance. Perhaps you've allowed your

otherwise admirable interest in scientific inquiry and fellowship to cloud your thinking. Surely two priests should have been able to urge more moderation, even on an impetuous and headstrong man like Lamanon."

Oh, the man had no idea what he was talking about, Lamartinière thought. Mongez and Receveur, both so mild-mannered and eager to please, were no match for the likes of Lamanon. None of them were.

"Quite right, Monsieur de Monty," Father Receveur said. "I am deeply sensible of my failure in this regard. Please, what is to become of us?"

Monty nodded formally. "First, the official charges," he said, drawing a piece of paper from his coat and unfolding it with exaggerated deliberation. Lamartinière watched with growing irritation. Captain de Langle would not have performed this task with such relish. Monty cleared his throat: "You were absent from the *Astrolabe* without leave," he began. "Further, you failed to make known your whereabouts in Macao. Finally, your communications with Commander de Lapérouse were insolent and inappropriate." He peered down at the prisoners. "I've been instructed by the commander and our captain to consign you to your quarters for a period of twenty-four hours, commencing immediately."

"Oh. That's not so bad," Father Receveur said aloud.

"No, Father, it's not," Monty replied, allowing the cleric a smile.

"Where is Captain de Langle?" Lamartinière ventured.

Monty stiffened. "Monsieur de Lamartinière, did you expect the captain to discipline you *personally*?"

Lamartinière blinked in surprise, then stammered, "No—only—never mind." He *had* expected it, of course. Surely the arrest and incarceration of the ship's chaplain and the expedition's botanist warranted the captain's presence? The captain would have softened the blow. He would have indicated somehow, perhaps by a sardonic raising of his eyebrows—it was something he did—that he was carrying out his superior's orders without agreeing with them.

"The captain's ashore with the commander," Monty said by way of reply. "They're guests of the Portuguese governor and his wife tonight. You might have been invited had you behaved better."

Lamartinière could hardly suppress a smile. In his experience, holders of political appointments were, almost without exception, self-important, pontificating bores. And their wives were even worse—flirtatious leeches with appalling French. They had already endured encounters with several specimens of this genus in Concepción and Monterey. Lamartinière did not mind missing this one. But he knew who *would* mind: Lamanon. That was how the trouble began, after all. Less than a week after moving into the house on Rua de São Lourenço, they learned that the commander and Captain de Langle had been fêted at a reception at the "Casa," a plainly named but lavishly appointed villa that was home to a wealthy senior trader with the British East India Company. Worse than being snubbed was hearing who *had* been in attendance: The commander's good-for-nothing brother-in-law, Broudou, who'd made such an ass of himself in Chile but had, improbably, been promoted to lieutenant after the *Boussole* lost three officers in Alaska. Barthélemy de Lesseps, ostensibly the expedition's Russian translator, but to all appearances the *Astrolabe*'s chief merrymaker. All of the expedition's artists, including that layabout Prévost. *All* the other men of science. Young Collignon, the gardener who should have been Lamartinière's assistant and was being introduced as the *Boussole*'s "botanist." And that petulant poseur Dufresne, who had been begging to leave the expedition for nearly a year and was finally getting his wish, having found a berth on a ship returning to France—even *he* had been there, a soon-to-be *former* member of the expedition!

Lamanon, outraged by the slight, had dashed off a letter of complaint to the commander and insisted they all sign it. The next day they received a response in which the commander said he would have been delighted to invite them to the soirée, and indeed, it was a shame they had missed it, as all of Macao society was in attendance, including many highly placed people interested in science. But since they had declined to inform anyone of their departure from the ships or their address in Macao, he had not known how to find them and, sadly, had had to forego the pleasure of their company at the Casa.

Lamanon had sputtered in fury for a full minute before sitting down at the writing table on the veranda and dashing off a new letter inveighing against the lack of respect shown to the expedition's chief savants. "The most perfunctory effort at determining our whereabouts—the least inquiry at our own consulate!—would have been successful," he wrote. It was true, but it crossed a line, which Lamartinière and the others suspected right away. "Perhaps a more conciliatory approach . . ." Father Receveur gently suggested. "I don't think we should send it," Lamartinière said. He *had* said that aloud, had he not? Not that it mattered. They all signed it in the end and sent it with a messenger to the *Boussole*.

That was yesterday.

Now he and the chaplain were being led to their cabins by marines who made a point of telling them they would remain posted outside their doors all day and all night.

"What for?" Lamartinière retorted. "To make sure we don't *flee*?"

"The lads are only doing their jobs," Father Receveur said.

Lamartinière scowled at the priest before being shut into his cabin, then threw his document case across the room with a yell, belatedly relieved to find none of his cabinmates within. His weeklong absence had not made him any fonder of the "Savants' Quarters." He walked to the far end of the space and flung himself across his hard, narrow bed, banging his head against the wall. He lay back, swearing and massaging his pate while a parade of other, more extreme gestures flitted through his mind: he would destroy the cabin, tear up everyone's bedding, smash and scatter his own specimens and the other men's belongings, pour his ink bottles out over everything, torch the place and himself in it, sink the ship and its inmates. The violent fantasies did not soothe him. He had often indulged such thoughts during the long Pacific crossing. They had not helped then, either. By the time they had dropped anchor in Macao Harbor, he had been spending most of the day either asleep or feigning sleep, and had exchanged scarcely a word with his shipmates for weeks. Father Receveur's unexpected invitation to join him, Lamanon, and Father Mongez in Macao, in a proper house where he would have his own room, away from the fake "savants" with whom he had been trapped for so long, had felt like salvation.

He sat up now, chewing his lower lip, regretting the way he had just left Father Receveur. He leaned over and peeled off his muddied shoes and stockings, wrinkling his nose against the rankness of his still-wet feet. He tossed the shoes across the floor, then shuffled with a groan to his desk. Ignoring the neat, securely arranged boxes of specimens before him, he freed several sheets of paper from the stash he kept dry between layers of oilcloth and sat down to write some letters—one to his brother

Pierre; another to his mentor, André Thouin, the head of the Jardin du Roi; and a third to the Marshal de Castries, minister of marine. What relief to give vent to his feelings! It was with great regret he reported the lack of priority and respect accorded to the pursuit of science—this, on an expedition ostensibly devoted to discovery! Scarcely any time allowed in months for botanizing! Now a trivial misunderstanding had resulted in his incarceration aboard his own ship!

Before he could think better of anything he had written, he sealed the letters and slipped them under the cabin door. He could hear the marine lean over to pick them up, then call to a sailor to deliver them to the officer in charge. Only then did it occur to him that his current situation was largely the result of letters penned and dispatched in high dudgeon and that he might be compounding his difficulties.

A knock at the cabin door interrupted his regret and brought a tray with a lantern and dinner. The meal was a tasty ragout of fowl and a carafe of robust red wine. Ordinarily he would have had only a small glass of wine, but tonight, with no shipmates eager to claim his share, he drank it all. He hated to admit it, but he felt better afterward. It could be vexing, the way the body could overrule the mind. One could be determinedly and quite justifiably aggrieved, only to find a full belly and the sedating effects of alcohol had rendered one's well-tended grievances less grievous. Perhaps, he reflected, the human race needed this faculty for self-deception to survive. Did savages have this same need, or only civilized men? Whatever the answer, it was with some pique that he noted the dulling of his anger and moroseness, and then even that pique became impossible to sustain.

He lit a second candle and turned to the specimens on his desk.

He was primarily a botanist, but tiny animals interested him too, and he was still amazed by what he had discovered on the head of a sunfish the men had caught in Alaska. A keen-eyed sailor had brought it to him. "I saved this from the stewpot, sir," he said, "when I noticed all the worms on it." Sure enough, the head was like a cabinet of curiosities, parasitized by several distinct organisms on and around its gills. The specimens he extracted were now suspended in five alcohol-filled vials secured in a wooden box made specially for the purpose. He opened the box and slid out one vial, then fumbled around himself for a moment in search of his pocket microscope before remembering that he had left it in the house in Macao. Sighing, he held the vial between himself and the candle flame and squinted to see the nearly transparent specimens preserved within.

The sailor who saved the fish head had called the creatures "worms," and indeed, most naturalists did too, but Lamartinière thought they had more in common with insects. To the naked eye, the tiny filaments that protruded from the fish's head and now floated in the vial looked wormy enough, but with a microscope one could clearly see that they had leglike appendages. He had consulted both Fabricius and Linnaeus and felt pretty certain they were parasitic varieties of *Pennatula*. Some of the creatures were buried so deeply and firmly in their host's body that he had trouble extracting them; at least one he had unwittingly beheaded. It was hard to imagine how the soft-bodied creatures had burrowed their way through the fish's scales. Could they have found their hosts early, he wondered, while in some tinier, sharper, juvenile state, then remained headfirst in the fish's body, lodged and fed forever therein as their heads enlarged and their bodies softened and elongated behind them? They also appeared to have eyes, a single compound structure in the middle of their heads, though they hardly had need of them. What a strange life, he thought, with one's head entirely buried in the relative safety of ever-present nutrition while one's back end lay exposed to whatever might befall in the great oceans, including, at the last, the naturalist's indelicate tweezers dragging one out from dark sustenance into light and death.

He had been trying to communicate something of this earlier at the consulate, but it was not an audience given to marveling at anything unless it affected the price of tea or the sale of opium. Perhaps it was just as well he had been interrupted. He retrieved his document case—it had landed on d'Aigremont's side of the partition, narrowly missing a sextant on his desk—and after wiping it clean, pulled out the crude drawings he had made of the creatures. He frowned at his poor draftsmanship, retrospectively relieved that he had not had to show them. Indeed, one of the creatures he had drawn looked for all the world like a striped barber's pole. He had meant to suggest the pumping of the insect's blood, which he had clearly observed while it was alive, but the drawing was not a success. He indulged another flash of annoyance at Prévost for his refusal to do his job. Then reaching again into the case, he pulled out the notes he had made. If he wrote them up into a monograph, he could send it, along with the drawings, to the *Journal de physique* in Paris. What better time than now, when he had nowhere to go and nothing else to do, and ships on their way back to Europe lay at anchor all around them?

The work occupied him until his eyelids grew heavy, then again in the morning after his breakfast tray had come and gone. When the marine knocked on the door the following afternoon to say he was free to leave the cabin, and, indeed, to return to Macao, the manuscript was complete. Only then did he realize that not one of his cabinmates had returned for the night. If he could have enjoyed such privacy even occasionally while at sea, he thought, he might still be on speaking terms with d'Aigremont and Dufresne and—well, probably not with Prévost.

First to greet him on deck was a slicing north wind that nearly took his hat, then, more warmly, Father Receveur. "My dear Lamartinière," the priest said, apparently having forgiven or forgotten the peevishness with which Lamartinière had left him the day before. "You look rather tired but also somewhat pleased."

Lamartinière patted his document case. "I've completed a monograph on the parasites I found in Alaska. I'd like to read it to you all tonight."

The priest smiled. "I'm not going back to Macao."

"You're not?"

"Not today," he said, still smiling, as if he were conveying good news. "I've been neglecting my shipboard duties. I was quite busy with confessions during our little 'incarceration.'"

Lieutenant de Monty, looking less condescending and somehow also less tall than he had the day before, called from the rail: "I'm holding a sampan for you, Monsieur de Lamartinière. The boatwoman is impatient to be off."

Father Receveur put his hands together and bowed to Lamartinière, a rare clerical gesture from him, then added, less clerically, "Don't let Lamanon bully you!" Lamartinière nodded and climbed over the rail, noting as he did that he still had not seen Captain de Langle. Apparently the entire episode would conclude without a word or even an appearance from the captain. The realization left him feeling rather bereft. Especially as he was now returning to Macao alone.

He was not alone, however. In addition to the boatwoman and her child, who was strapped to its mother's back, the sampan contained two marines and Dufresne, the unpopular cabinmate who would soon be leaving the expedition. "Dufresne!" Lamartinière cried out, unable to hide his surprise. "Where have you been?" He looked at the two marines, whom he now recognized as his escorts from the day before, then back at Dufresne. "My God, have they arrested you as well?"

Dufresne cocked his head to one side, a lock of dark hair partially covering his pale face, his expression one of both amusement and annoyance. "Good afternoon, Monsieur de Lamartinière," he said. "I am *not* under arrest."

"No, of course not—forgive me," Lamartinière stammered. "But you weren't—you never came in last night."

"I spent the night ashore as a guest of Monsieur von Stockenström, the head of the Swedish company," Dufresne explained. "I only returned to the frigates this morning to take more of our furs ashore." He pointed to two large bundles next to him, then to the two marines. "These gentlemen are here to make sure they're delivered safely."

"I see," Lamartinière said without understanding. *"Furs?"*

"The otter pelts we got in Alaska," Dufresne said. "We mean to sell them here."

"Otter pelts?"

Dufresne burst out laughing. "Yes, nearly a thousand. One of the voyage's tasks was to determine the feasibility of entering the fur trade between North America and China."

"A *thousand?*" Lamartinière shook his head. How had such an undertaking entirely escaped his notice? Did the expedition have other aims of which he was quite ignorant? "I was rather preoccupied with a sunfish head at the time," he muttered.

"Yes," Dufresne said. "It stank up the whole cabin."

"No doubt it did," Lamartinière said, shrugging apologetically. "And the fur business—*is* it feasible?"

"Not at all," Dufresne replied. "The price has fallen precipitously the last few years. One Portuguese merchant had the temerity to offer to take them off my hands if *I* paid *him!*" He waved his hand dismissively toward the advancing shoreline. "Bloodsuckers, the lot of them," he said, then sighed and added in a lower voice, "And I hardly need mention the unsuitability of the port we explored in Alaska." The two men's eyes locked in shared memory. Dufresne looked away first, gazing eastward toward the hazy Pacific horizon. "That was only six months ago."

"Seems longer, doesn't it?"

"*Much* longer."

"And the Swedish gentleman?" Lamartinière asked after a moment.

Dufresne looked back with a surprised smile, as if he could not account for Lamartinière's continued friendliness. "Yes, Monsieur von Stockenström. He's agreed to store our furs until I can dispose of them. He's been most helpful. Unlike our own officials. They've been worse than useless." His dark eyes danced with judgment. "They know nothing—or pretend to know nothing. Have you met this fellow Vieillard, our consul?" He wheezed in imitation of the man's stertorous breathing.

"I believe he was the gentleman who slept through my abbreviated lecture yesterday," Lamartinière said.

"The man is like a giant barnacle on the ship of state."

Lamartinière laughed. Dufresne had never been so affable before. Perhaps the prospect of going home had cured him of the surliness that had marked him earlier in the voyage. Or perhaps Lamartinière and the others had never given him a chance. Rumor had it he was actually on board at the behest of the Ministry of Finance and not a naturalist at all. Certainly he had little enough acumen for the sciences. He seemed more comfortable now, skewering incompetent officials and discussing the disposition of commodities in a glutted market, than he had ever been on their all-too-infrequent botanizing expeditions. Perhaps the rumors had been right.

The air warmed noticeably as they approached the Praya Grande with its watchful line of European buildings along the waterfront. "And how will you occupy yourself now that you're back in this strange little settlement, Monsieur de Lamartinière?" Dufresne asked.

"Well—" Lamartinière began. "I expect Monsieur de Lamanon will have something planned for us." He frowned, hearing how dependent and ineffectual he sounded, still deferring to Lamanon after what had happened.

"Not tonight, he won't," Dufresne said, smiling. The two marines tittered.

"Why? What's happened?"

"I was on the *Boussole* this morning to collect these two gentlemen and the first of these bundles, and Monsieur de Lamanon was—how to put this?—*expostulating* with Monsieur de Lapérouse."

"A shouting match it was," one of the marines offered.

"A shouting match?" Lamartinière said.

"There was some disagreement over when Monsieur de Lamanon would be permitted to return to shore," Dufresne said.

"Indeed?"

"The commander said Monsieur de Lamanon couldn't leave the *Boussole* until three o'clock," Dufresne explained. "And when Monsieur de Lamanon—uh, *resisted* this notion, the commander said in that case he could stay aboard till tomorrow morning."

"Oh, no," Lamartinière said, trying to sound sorrier than he felt.

"Then it got worse," the other marine said.

"*Worse?*"

Dufresne looked over at the marines with mild disapproval. "Monsieur de Lapérouse tried to mollify Lamanon by inviting him to lunch with the consul"—he inhaled noisily again to indicate Vieillard—"who was coming from Macao with Captain de Langle. But when the party arrived, I'm afraid the consul made the mistake of addressing Lamanon as—well, as *you*."

"As *me*?" Lamartinière felt his face flush. For once it was not an altogether unpleasant sensation.

"I'm afraid so."

"'Good afternoon, Monsieur de Lamartinière, it's a pleasure to see you again, sir,'" the first marine said, imitating the consul's gravelly voice.

"Didn't take it too well, our chevalier," the other one added.

"*Chevalier?*"

"That's what he likes to be called," the marine replied.

Yes, he does, Lamartinière thought, recalling Lamanon's oversize, ornate signature on each of the offending letters: *Chev^{er} de Lamanon*.

"And off he stalked," the same marine said, finishing the story.

"I'm sorry, Lamartinière," Dufresne said, "but you may be quite alone till tomorrow."

"What about Father Mongez?"

"He's staying aboard in . . . unity, I suppose, with his friend," Dufresne said.

"That priest don't do anything without the chevalier's say-so," the first marine said.

"Come now, that's enough," Dufresne said, but he looked back at Lamartinière with an expression that acknowledged the soundness of the marine's judgment.

Lamartinière hardly knew what to think. He had not expected to end up alone in Macao, but the image of Lamanon storming about impotently on board, unable to leave when he saw fit, then subjected to the humiliation of being mistaken for someone he considered a lesser man and savant—oh, he could not help it. He threw back his head and laughed, and, freed by his reaction, the other men joined in.

As soon as the sampan pulled up to the quay, three Chinese porters, drawn by the sight of the bundles next to Dufresne, ran over to vie for their delivery, shouting prices in Portuguese. Dufresne pointed to one man and waved the others off, then joined the chosen porter and the two marines in wrestling the cargo off the boat. Lamartinière stepped ashore behind them, watching the hubbub, trying to catch Dufresne's eye to say goodbye, feeling both pleased and regretful for the late amity that had sprung up between them as they crossed the harbor.

He began to edge away toward the street that would take him to the Rua de São Lourenço, when Dufresne called out: "Lamartinière!"

He turned.

"Will you join me for dinner tonight?"

"Certainly."

They arranged for Dufresne to call on him at seven o'clock, and Lamartinière headed down the street. Till he turned the first corner into a narrow, canyon-like street hemmed in on either side by tall buildings, he could hear Dufresne and the marines and the porter shouting to one another over the furs. What was it about human beings, he wondered, that they thought cultural barriers might be crossed simply by yelling? This was not a trait limited to civilized men. He had seen it everywhere— Spanish colonists, missionaries, soldiers, mestizo servants, Indian guides, Easter Islanders, Alaskan natives, Chinese boatwomen—all shouting to be understood, so angry when communication failed.

These musings brought him to the Rua de São Lourenço and the narrow three-story house he had departed the previous morning, never suspecting he would be away so long. A window above was open, a lace curtain peeking out with the breeze, but he half expected no answer to his knock. With their temporary occupants suddenly gone, the servants were likely to have absconded for the day. The wizened watchman opened the door immediately, however, as if he had been standing on the other side just waiting for someone to return.

"Monsieur Lama!" the man cried.

Lamartinière frowned. *Lama?* "Oh, close enough," he said, following the servant inside. He tried to explain that a friend would be calling at seven, that they were going out for dinner, and that none of the others would be returning before tomorrow. The watchman nodded energetically, but Lamartinière suspected the man had not understood a word.

Upstairs, he was pleased to find his room aired out and fresh water in the ewer next to the basin, and even more pleased to find his belongings exactly as he had left them—his clothes in the massive mahogany wardrobe, his books dusted but otherwise untouched, his pocket microscope undisturbed in its box on the bedside table. Eager to change into fresh clothes, he removed his hat and wig, then his coat and waistcoat, and was undoing his cravat when he heard a hissed conversation outside his room and, opening the door, found Sophie holding a tea tray and the watchman pushing her forward.

Sophie! He had all but forgotten her. She stood before him now in all her languid beauty, swaying slightly, eyes downcast, hair carelessly piled up on her head and half spilling down her neck. She seemed to be wearing only a white silk petticoat, the gauzy fichu thrown over her shoulders quite insufficient to complete the dress. Mesmerized by this vision of alluring dishabille and keenly aware of his own state of partial undress, Lamartinière realized that the old watchman, understanding perfectly that Lamartinière would be alone the rest of the day, was offering the amenities of the house accordingly.

The old man barked something in Chinese and poked Sophie in the back. She took a step into the room, but was so unsteady that Lamartinière rushed forward to relieve her of the tea tray. Setting the tray down on a small walnut table, he led Sophie to the leather-upholstered chair next to it. She fell into it like a dead weight.

"What's wrong with her?" Lamartinière demanded.

"Sophie little sleepy," the watchman said.

"She's not 'sleepy,'" Lamartinière said. He leaned over the chair and tipped her head back. "Sophie, open your eyes." She complied, smiling absently at the sight of his face over hers. Her eyes were so dark it was hard to make out the pupils, but then he saw them, a black pencil dot in the center of each iris. He took a handful of her hair and sniffed it. "She's been smoking opium," he said, recognizing its sweet pungency.

"No, no. Only sleepy," the watchman repeated, then bowed his way out of the room, winking once before shutting the door.

Lamartinière regarded the woman slouched in the chair before him and wavered between anger, repulsion, and lust. What had the watchman been thinking, bringing her to him in this state? It was a terrible imposition. Yet her presence also felt like a gift, some recompense for the vexations he had suffered. He thought too of Lamanon, who might or might not have been with her the day before, and he could scarcely believe the happenstance that now left *him* alone with her.

His fingers were still in her hair, and he could see the slow rise and fall of her breasts beneath the fabric of her shift—the slow breathing another sign of intoxication, but a bewitching one. He sat on the floor next to her and lay his head in her lap, his heart pounding—in sharp contrast to her own slowed pulse, he thought, taking her wrist to check, unable to stop acting the part of medically trained man despite the roar of desire coursing through his body.

He had not touched a woman in two years. Some of the men had consorted with women in Chile or in Alaska, but he had not, constrained by—by *what*, exactly? His own reputation for fussy rectitude, he suspected. He did not have the resourcefulness to seek out such enticements himself, and had never been offered any because his shipmates assumed he would disapprove. They were right: he *did* disapprove. He disapproved mightily even as he allowed one hand to slide down the length of Sophie's leg, caressing it through the silk, then slipping under the skirt and moving back up, this time along the stockinged leg itself, past the garter then along her bare thigh, its warmth and softness overwhelming compunction.

When he tried to put his hand between her legs, she stirred and opened her eyes, looking down at him without recognition, alarm, or pleasure. He gazed into her dark eyes with their opium-pinched pupils and thought of the purposeless eyes of his *Pennatula* in their vials aboard the *Astrolabe*. Perhaps they needed their eyes only long enough to identify their host. He slipped his other hand under the skirt and gently pried her legs apart. She shut her eyes again and offered no resistance. Hosts rarely knew when they were being encroached upon, of course. It was a linchpin of the parasitic relationship. His breath caught in his throat when his fingertips reached the warm, furred center of her. He raised himself to his knees, the better to move himself over her, and pillowed his face against her breasts, still thinking—indeed, unable to *stop* thinking—of the *Pennatula* and his hypothesis that they burrowed into their hosts early on and grew once inside. But now he found his fingers pressing into dry, unyielding flesh. Another symptom of opium use: lack of sexual response. But could one really call it that if the nonresponsive party seemed unaware of the ministrations being applied? He felt himself deflating, body and mind, and tried to rally himself to the task. Reaching behind Sophie, he pulled her forward in the chair, then raised her skirts, the better to see and smell and taste her. A little moisture applied to the right place and he would be able to see it through. But now his head filled with the memory of the difficulty he had had removing the parasites from the sunfish, how he had accidentally beheaded one of them, extracting its back end while leaving the tip buried in the fish, and he drew back with a groan of repugnance and defeat.

The sound—and perhaps the suddenly cooler air around her—roused Sophie from her torpor. "So nice," she said breathily while attempting to straighten her petticoat. The falseness of the sentiment, and her apparent ignorance of what had just happened—or *not* happened—mortified Lamartinière almost as much as the failure itself and elicited another groan from him. "I like too," she said, her words slow and slurred, deepening his misery. She tried to sit up. "I pour you tea."

Lamartinière scrambled up from the floor. "No," he said, placing his hand on the porcelain teapot and wincing at the heat. "You're in no condition to handle hot water. I'll pour it." Stilling his guilty hands by force of will, he poured out a cup of the steaming green liquid. He blew across its surface and brought it to her lips. "Sophie, you must stop using opium," he said.

Her lips fluttered open to take a sip. "Monsieur Telli say so too."

"Monsieur Telli?" He urged another sip.

"Other Frenchman."

"What other Frenchman?" Did she mean Lamanon? One of the priests? She turned to him with drowsy eyes full of sadness, and then he knew: the Frenchman who lived here before, the one who killed himself. He had heard the man's name once—Theiers? Thierry? "Monsieur Thérien?" he whispered, and she nodded.

"This his room," she said.

"What?" He looked around suddenly, knowing alarm to be irrational but feeling alarmed all the same.

She smiled, but not with mirth. "I forget I not suppose to tell." Her accent in French was so odd, neither Portuguese nor Chinese. Sino-Iberian, he thought it could be called.

"I don't mind," Lamartinière assured her. He made her drink more tea, then finished straightening her petticoat for her. "It's not as if Monsieur Thérien died in this room." He noticed her sudden stillness. "Did he?"

She remained motionless, her eyes fixed on the wall just above the headboard of the bed. He saw now that one of the panels was new and did not match the others. But the man had killed himself at the beach; the agent had said so. "Sophie—" No, he would not ask. He did not wish to have his suspicions confirmed.

"He come to Macao very young," she said in her slow, strange French. "Always he want to go back to France but always they say no. Fourteen year they say no, so—he die." Her lips trembled.

"You loved him."

She turned to face him. The bitterness in her expression reminded him of the defiance he had seen in her eyes the first time he saw her. "He leave me," she finally said.

Oh, this was why he had left medicine, he thought, his heart contracting with pity. It was too much, witnessing other people's pain. She had loved an unhappy man, a man who wanted to leave, a man who could not have taken her back with him to France in any case and decided he would rather die than stay in Macao with her. For her part, she had no freedom to leave the house, of course, for she belonged to it, bound to its reminders of the man who wanted to leave, bound now to entertain strange men in the house, even in the room where, perhaps, her lover had shot himself.

No wonder she smoked opium. If she were his patient, he would prescribe laudanum—as much as she wanted.

"Sophie," he finally said. "It's a beautiful afternoon. I'd like to sit on the veranda and correct a manuscript. It will help to read it aloud to someone, though I daresay you'll find it tedious. Will you join me?"

Of the many strange experiences Joseph Hugues de Boissieu de La-martinière would have on the voyage, this would turn out to be the strangest: sitting on a cane chair on the third-floor veranda of a house in Macao, with its view of the Inner Harbor and the forbidding Chinese mountains to the northwest, a beautiful woman installed on a rattan settee opposite while he read aloud his monograph on marine parasites, stopping now and then to make marginal notes, and finding in their odd, transient domesticity the most unexpected happiness. When he finished reading, he found Sophie asleep. He got up; it was time to change for his dinner with Dufresne. But first he lowered the bamboo blinds on the veranda to shield her from the cooling breeze and the slanting rays of the setting sun, then went inside and found a light blanket to place over her.

In the end, he could not rest easy in the bed of a man who might have shot himself in it. He decamped to Lamanon's room for the night, grateful to have another place to sleep and also diverted by the vision of Lamanon returning, like a fairy-tale character, to find his bed had been occupied during his absence.

NINE

DISPATCHES

Russia, September 1787–August 1788

It took more than two years to reach Petropavlovsk and only three weeks to carry out his responsibilities there, translating French into Russian and back again. Then the order came to leave the *Astrolabe*, and Barthélemy de Lesseps thought his heart would break. He had known all along that he would leave the expedition then, but *then* had always seemed so far in the future. He had never guessed how accustomed he would grow to life at sea or how attached he would become to his shipmates. So many of those shipmates now wanted to help see him off that they scarcely fit into the longboat conveying him to shore. The *Boussole* had launched its own longboat as well, crowded with well-wishers calling out to him as everyone rowed toward the official leave-taking onshore.

"This isn't making it easier for me," Lesseps protested.

"You've made many friends," Captain de Langle said.

"I wish the expedition still needed me."

"It does," the captain said, "just not on board."

Lesseps turned to look at the settlement advancing toward them. Petropavlovsk was a rough, modest place, its small wood dwellings clustered in the narrow flats between Avacha Bay and the steep hills beyond, hills that had blazed with autumn when they arrived but had since faded to rust and ocher. The town was not without charm—its tiny churches boasted the steeply tented roofs topped with onion domes and traditional Russian crosses that reminded Lesseps of his childhood in St. Petersburg.

But overshadowing the vista, dwarfing the hills, was Koryakski volcano, as imposing a mountain as he had ever seen, hinting at the wild, forbidding terrain he would be obliged to traverse in the coming months. He turned back. "Monsieur de Lapérouse says the journey will be a good opportunity for me," he said.

Langle nodded. "You'll know the empire better than most Russians."

Too soon, they all scrambled ashore. They were met at the landing place by Igor Golikoff, a soldier the governor-general of Kamchatka had assigned to serve as Lesseps's guide and bodyguard. A few years older than Lesseps, the soldier was tall and serious and a little vain about his fine mustache and beard. He stood respectfully aside as Lapérouse bade farewell to the expedition's Russian translator. Lapérouse praised Lesseps's conduct on the voyage and thanked him for his excellent work in Petropavlovsk. Then he gave him one more task. "Deliver these dispatches to our ambassador in St. Petersburg," he said, holding out a leather-inlaid box. "Should some mischance overtake us, these documents will prove our accomplishments."

Lesseps took the box as if it contained the Holy Grail. "Yes, sir," was all he could say.

"Meanwhile," Lapérouse continued, "learn everything you can about this vast and varied continent. One day you will be the most effective, influential ambassador to Russia France has ever appointed."

"Thank you, sir," Lesseps said. He resisted the urge to throw himself at the commander's feet and beg to be taken back.

"We'll race you home," Lieutenant de Vaujuas quipped.

Everyone laughed, then boisterous, tearful hugs were exchanged, and Lesseps watched, helpless, as they all piled into their longboats and rowed away. They called back and waved wildly until the distance obscured their faces and the bay swallowed their voices. They were the best men he would ever know, and they had all just marooned him at the far end of the world. He felt so bereft he allowed Golikoff, whom he had only met the day before, to hold him as he wept. But after a moment he pulled away, embarrassed.

"Come, *barin*," Golikoff said, using the Russian word for "lord." "I'll take you back to the governor's house."

"I know where he lives," Lesseps said. He walked away, hoping Golikoff wouldn't follow.

"But wait!" Golikoff called. He ran to catch up with his charge. "Your dispatches." He held out the precious box.

Lesseps was too abashed to thank him.

It took three weeks to cross the peninsula to reach the lightly fortified town of Bolsheretsk on the Sea of Okhotsk. The same governor-general with whom Lesseps had stayed in Petropavlovsk had a house here as well, maintained in his absence by a Cossack and his wife. They invited Lesseps and Golikoff to stay with them.

Lesseps had hoped to take a ship across the sea to its namesake port of Okhotsk, but Golikoff said it was too late; the ports were icing over. They would have to go overland, up the length of the Kamchatka Peninsula and around the sea.

"But that will take forever," Lesseps said.

"Some months, yes."

"It's only October. Surely a ship could still—"

"It's almost November," Golikoff countered. A galliot had apparently become trapped in the ice south of town just a few weeks earlier, he explained. The crew had managed to get off with most of its cargo, but there was no hope for the vessel. "Would you like to see it?"

"The wrecked galliot?" Lesseps asked.

"It's become something of a local destination."

They traveled down the Bolshaya River toward the site, taking two small floats and two Kamchadal guides. Eight hours later, the sun was setting and they still hadn't reached the wreck. They took refuge for the night in a wretched shack that kept out neither cold nor rain, then set out again in the morning, fighting rough water and wind as they approached the sea. At last they saw something in the distance—a lighthouse, the guide told them, then pointed out the masts of the doomed vessel, which looked like nothing more than driftwood thrown up on the broken ice.

The cold was unbearable.

"Let's go back," Lesseps said, realizing that none of them wished to continue but that neither Golikoff nor the guides would call off the excursion.

When they turned around, the current was so strong their floats kept filling with water. They made little headway while they bailed, and had to spend another night in the same wretched shelter. Dinner consisted of dried sea wolf and weak tea. The four men huddled together without embarrassment to stay warm.

Shivering, Lesseps thought of the expedition, of the two frigates traveling south, of the men counting on him to deliver their letters and papers. He had abandoned the dispatches for three days, enduring freezing, wet conditions and risking illness and drowning—for what? He hadn't even had a good view of the galliot. What was he doing anyway, seeking out wrecks? It seemed inviting of bad luck to view a shipwreck when all of one's friends were on the high seas.

The next day, his anxiety about the dispatches grew with every league they traveled. What if the box were stolen? Or sent ahead through some misguided attempt to help? What if the house had burned down? They didn't get back to town till evening. He rushed to his quarters, scarcely acknowledging the Cossack and his family's warm welcome, flung open the wardrobe where he had stowed his belongings, unlocked the box, and rummaged through its contents. "Oh, thank God," he cried.

Golikoff was watching him from the doorway. "What's in the box, *barin*?"

"Everything."

"Everything?"

Lesseps sighed with impatience. "The commander's journals, officers' reports, scientific papers, artists' drawings, maps, letters. Yes—*everything*. I have to deliver it to our ambassador in St. Petersburg."

"Your father?"

"No, Golikoff," Lesseps said. "My father is only consul general. The great Count of Ségur is the ambassador."

"But you're going to have his post one day."

"Maybe. My father's not a count." He looked up at the soldier with a self-conscious smile. "Neither am I."

He watched Golikoff's face—would the soldier realize that his charge was not as distinguished as he had been led to believe? But Golikoff nodded thoughtfully and said, "We won't go anywhere again where we can't take your box."

•

Lesseps was frantic to be off again, but they had to wait till winter was advanced enough for dogsleds. First there was not enough snow, then not enough dogsleds, dogs, drivers, provisions. Then *too* much snow, winter gales that lasted for days. He thought his childhood in St. Petersburg had prepared him for Russian winters.

"This isn't a Russian winter," Golikoff said. "It's the devil's own season."

Lesseps spent the days between storms learning to drive a dogsled. Golikoff tried to dissuade him. "If you get hurt, we'll be delayed even longer," he said, and when that didn't work, "If you get hurt, I'll be responsible."

"My dear Golikoff," Lesseps said. "Don't worry." He threw an arm around the soldier and kissed his cheek. Golikoff blushed through his beard.

The Kamchadal guides were happy to let the Frenchman try his hand at driving and showed no concern for his safety, laughing loud and long whenever he fell off or overturned the sled, which was often. But after a month he had become, if not expert, competent enough to join them on a hunt.

They didn't catch much, but they did encounter a sable being chased by a flock of ravens. The animal seemed to be swimming through the snow, poking its head out from a drift, then, menaced by the birds, diving down and reappearing some distance away, only to be set upon again. The Kamchadals released a few of their dogs to chase the birds away, and one of the men devised a small noose to catch the sable. That's never going to work, Lesseps thought, but it did—the man managed after three tries to get the noose around the creature. He presented the defeated animal, squirming dispiritedly in a cloth sack, to Lesseps, and promised to catch another, a female, so he could take a pair back to France.

When he returned to the house that afternoon, Lesseps found Golikoff smoking in the governor's kitchen with the dispatch box at his feet. They had settled into an unspoken arrangement whereby one of them would always have custody of the box. The soldier raised a skeptical eyebrow when introduced to the sable, then left the house and came back with a small wooden cage. When they transferred the sable to the cage, it bit Lesseps, drawing blood.

"Let me see," Golikoff said.

Lesseps sucked on the injured thumb. "It's nothing."

"Let me see."

Golikoff made a very good bandage—secure but not too tight. "My Imperial Army training at your service," he said.

When blizzards trapped them indoors, Lesseps caught up on his journal. He thought he could probably publish it back in France. Mindful of Monsieur de Lapérouse's charge to learn as much as he could, he carefully recorded his observations about the villages he had passed through, how the Russians administered the region, and the behavior of the native Kamchadals, whose population and customs were in obvious decline. He wrote that the men of Kamchatka, natives and Russians alike, were strangely unjealous about their wives, but he really meant just one man— his Cossack host. Lesseps took more pains to hide the affair from Golikoff than from the husband.

Her name was Daria. She was part Kamchadal and had the blackest, most luxuriant hair of any woman he had ever been with. Not that there had been so many—he was only twenty-one, after all. She taught him Kamchadal words that he copied into his journal: *ship, house, family, man, wife, ice.* He loved to lay his head on her belly, softened from bearing four children, and stroke the smooth black hair between her legs. He had never before been with a woman whose hair there was straight. He wondered if it was a characteristic peculiar to the Kamchadals. This detail did not go into his journal. He told her about the accident in Alaska that had taken his best friends on the expedition, two brothers who were around his age. He had not spoken of it in many months. When Daria reached out and stroked his head, he wept like a child. This detail didn't go into the journal either.

Barthélemy de Lesseps departed Bolsheretsk on January 27, 1788, his twenty-second birthday. The party included Golikoff, thirty-five sleds, almost as many guides, a few Russian soldiers, and three hundred dogs. Lesseps drove his own sled, keeping the dispatch box in an enclosure beneath his seat. When they finally stopped for the night, he couldn't sleep—not that night or the next or the next. The dogs howled with hunger, new tempests threatened to blow them away or bury them alive, and all night long his sable rattled in its cage.

The creature had never grown accustomed to captivity; it refused most of the food Lesseps offered and tried to bite him again whenever he approached. Lesseps thought the journey through the snowy wilderness might restore the animal, but it lurked listlessly in a corner of its cage all day and rattled piteously, gnawing on the slats, all night. Perhaps it would settle down if they succeeded in finding a mate for it, he thought. But they didn't, and within a week of their departure, it was dead.

Lesseps's sadness over the animal's loss surprised him; he had not been aware of any attachment to it. Golikoff took the carcass away and returned with the fur. "Give it to your queen as a gift," he said.

Yes, he would do that. But meanwhile he wore it around his neck. At night, trying to fall asleep, he leaned his face against the impossibly soft fur and tried to remember the Kamchadal words Daria had taught him: *sable, woman, hair, love, cage.*

The road north, such as it was, snaked through a birch-filled valley between roughly parallel chains of volcanoes. At first he marveled at the stark beauty of the landscape—the watchful white trees ranged like sentinels in the snow, giving way occasionally to reveal, on a clear day, massive volcanoes smoking benignly against a sky so blue it hurt to look at. But the beauty palled after a while—it was monotonous, unrelenting, and altogether indifferent to their human presence. When they finally reached the Pacific at the coastal village of Nizhne, Lesseps rejoiced to see the ocean again—and experienced a sudden stabbing longing for the friends who were out there somewhere, exploring the same body of water.

In the village itself, Lesseps was shocked to meet nine Japanese mariners, survivors of a shipwreck in the Aleutians who had been rescued by a Russian merchant ship the year before. Lesseps spent an evening with their captain, a short, solid man with a serious, intelligent face who called himself Kodai. He wore his long, straight hair tied French-style at the nape of his neck and smiled when Lesseps pulled off his fur cap and sable cravat to demonstrate the similarity in their coiffures. After eating, a task he accomplished by deftly wielding two polished sticks, Kodai pulled out a kind of notebook and showed Lesseps some Japanese writing. It looked just like Chinese to Lesseps, but he didn't say so, worried the comparison might offend his new friend. "What does it say?" he asked instead. Kodai explained in halting but passable Russian that he was recording their experiences in Kamchatka.

Lesseps undid his deerskin jacket and retrieved from within his own notebook. "I'm doing the same," he said. "It's called a *journal*," he added.

"You will write about us," Kodai said gravely.

Lesseps promised to do so.

Later, when he returned to the fishy, smoky dwelling that was their lodgings for the night, he found Golikoff asleep with his arm around the dispatch box. Lesseps tried to be quiet, but when he started undressing, Golikoff mumbled, "It's very late."

Lesseps pulled on the fur-lined stockings he wore to bed. "Golikoff," he whispered, not wanting to wake the guides sleeping nearby.

"What?"

"Is there any chance for them to get home?"

"Who?"

"The Japanese."

Golikoff opened his eyes and turned toward Lesseps. "Our ships can't get anywhere near their shores," he said. "No captain will risk it. Anyway, we hear they kill their own people who leave then try to come back."

"We've heard that too," Lesseps said, lying down in the space next to Golikoff. He sighed. "Imagine the desolation of being stuck in a place like this with absolutely no hope of getting home."

Golikoff reached out toward Lesseps with one hand, then drew back. "*Barin*, it's my sworn duty to make sure you're not stranded here."

"I know, Golikoff," Lesseps said. "I wasn't really thinking of myself."

Storms assailed them for the next hundred leagues and more. No village, woods, or running water lay in their path to provide shelter or provisions. More than once they were forced to stop overnight in the open with nothing but frozen reindeer to eat. They rationed the dogs to one fish a day. The poor creatures looked thinner under their coats every morning and howled even more piteously at night. Lesseps was so tired and hungry himself that he mostly slept through it.

Every day a few of the dogs would collapse. At first the guides would call a halt, rush over, undo the harness, drag the dog's inert body to the roadside, and shout for the party to move on. But then they started allowing the remaining dogs to eat their fallen comrades. After a few days they abandoned one sled to consolidate the remaining dogs, and two days later, another.

When they ran low on water, Lesseps was incredulous. "How is that possible?" he cried. "We're surrounded by *snow.*"

Golikoff explained that melting enough snow for all the drivers and dogs to drink was impracticable; they needed to find running water.

Later, his throat aflame with thirst, Lesseps stuffed fistfuls of snow in his mouth although Golikoff and the others shouted at him not to. His thirst remained unassuaged, and then he grew terribly chilled. That night he ran a high fever. Golikoff remained at his side, plying him with tea and watching him with concern.

"Go away, Golikoff," Lesseps muttered. "I don't want your face to be the last thing I see."

He woke up shivering the next morning; his fever had broken, but his clothes were soaked. He turned to find Golikoff sitting next to him, sharpening a straight razor. "The doctor on the *Astrolabe* didn't believe in bloodletting," he said.

Golikoff started. *"Barin,"* he cried. "You're alive!"

Lesseps struggled to sit up. "Don't sound so surprised," he said. He trembled violently as he tried to peel off his clothes. "I'm freezing," he said. "Help me out of these and into something dry." He looked over at Golikoff, who was standing over him pressing a cloth to his forearm. "What's the matter?"

Golikoff looked embarrassed. "I nicked myself with my blade just now."

"What?"

Golikoff hastily bandaged his own arm, then made his way to Lesseps's bags. "You surprised me when you suddenly woke up."

Lesseps watched Golikoff fumble for a fresh set of clothes. "Were you about to cut me open?" he asked, his teeth chattering.

"No!" Golikoff cried. He came to Lesseps's side and wrested him out of his clothes, the outermost layers of which were stiff with cold. "I— I was going to shave you, actually," he said, not meeting Lesseps's eyes.

Lesseps ran his hand over the uneven, scraggly growth on his chin and laughed. "Do *not* touch a Frenchman's face while he's sleeping, Golikoff," he said.

Once dressed and warmed by a few sips of tea, he insisted over Golikoff's protests that they press on. "I'm fine," he said. "It's just a cold."

Golikoff shook his head. "Your overconfidence is going to kill you," he barked as he signaled to the rest of the party to move on.

Most of the Kamchadal guides left when they entered the territory of the Koryaks, a people rumored to be restive and bellicose. Lesseps thought they just looked hungry and wary. At the first village they reached, two men appeared and refused to sell the party any food, even though Golikoff offered them an excellent price. When he persisted, the men pulled long knives out. In an instant, Golikoff had a pistol aimed at the younger villager's head. "If you will not sell us any food," he said, "we will take it."

The men cowered and pleaded that they had none to sell or give.

"We'll see," Golikoff said, then instructed the remaining guides to take a few of their stronger and more trustworthy dogs to sniff out the village's stores.

The starving animals immediately led them to a cache buried behind the village's cluster of yurts. Golikoff stood guard while Lesseps and the soldiers loaded dried fish and whale meat onto their sleds. They also found an Imperial Army tent.

"Well," Golikoff said, directing one of the men to add it to their haul, "I think this makes us even."

A low, unearthly wailing, hollow and almost musical, started up around them.

"What is that?" Lesseps cried, the back of his neck creeping.

"Never mind," Golikoff said.

One of the guides pointed toward the yurts. The rest of the villagers were hidden within but were obviously aware of the devastation being wrought upon them.

"Come!" Golikoff shouted to the party.

"How will they survive?" Lesseps asked.

Golikoff's brown eyes, the only part of his face visible from behind the fur hood and chin cloth, glinted hard. "I promised to get you out of here alive no matter what," he said.

That night, three young Koryak men came to their encampment and asked to be taken on as guides. Golikoff assented after searching them and divesting them of their knives.

In mid-March, they reached Penzhina Bay, where Kamchatka joined the mainland, and came upon a large encampment of nomadic Chukchis, a people said to be even fiercer than the Koryaks. The bundles of spears and arrows marking the entrance to each tent seemed to confirm the rumors. Lesseps could see Golikoff, riding in the sled ahead of him, feel for the pistol in his overcoat as they approached. But when their guides explained to the men who barred their way that they were conveying a Frenchman toward St. Petersburg, the party was welcomed with more warmth than they had met anywhere else—offered water and dried reindeer for themselves and their dogs, and invited to spend the night.

"By all means," Lesseps said.

"No, *barin*," Golikoff whispered. "We should pay for the provisions and move on."

"We have nothing to fear," Lesseps said.

"The Imperial Army has waged many wars against these people."

"I'm not the Imperial Army," Lesseps said. "And look at their cheeks, Golikoff, how fat they are. Well-fed people are friendly."

"Is this what your travels have taught you?"

"Yes."

"My travels have taught me that a man will try to kill you for no reason at all."

"Dear Golikoff," Lesseps said. "How very Russian you sound."

The two men pitched the confiscated tent at the edge of the encampment. Golikoff had almost regained his good humor when Lesseps insisted they hide their weapons and refused to let Golikoff stand sentry at the entrance. "It shows we trust them," he said.

"But I *don't* trust them."

Golikoff sat glumly beside Lesseps while the leading men of the encampment crowded into the tent to talk to their exotic visitor. Their solicitousness led Lesseps to suspect that their guide may have introduced him as the French ambassador. He offered them tea and rye biscuits and gifts of tobacco, and tried to satisfy their prodigious curiosity about the world. He tore a page from his journal and drew a rough map of the world on it, showing them the extent of his travels.

"Why have no other Frenchmen come?" one of them asked.

Lesseps smiled. They had no notion of the distances involved, of course. He explained how he had spent two years by sea and six months by land to reach them. But the same man pointed to the place on Lesseps's map that he had identified as England and said, "But we sometimes meet men from this place." Well, of course you do, Lesseps thought peevishly, resenting the English compulsion to go everywhere.

The evening ended with a surprising invitation to choose a companion for the night from among their many wives. When he tried to decline, they pressed him, and the interpreter whispered that it was part of Chukchi hospitality to an honored guest and considered rude to say no.

"In that case," Lesseps said, "perhaps my hosts could choose someone for me."

This satisfied the men, who vied with one another for the honor of offering a woman from his household. "And for your man here?" one of them asked. "He looks like he needs cheering up."

Lesseps turned to look at Golikoff. Indeed, the soldier's face was rigid with disapproval. He refused to speak or to meet Lesseps's inquiring glance.

Two women came to the tent with food and drink and a whale-fat lantern, after which the Chukchi men retired with knowing leers and gestures. One woman was short and round, with dark eyes that disappeared into her face when she smiled. She sat beside Lesseps and plied him with a kind of flower bud steeped in whale fat, tastier than expected. The other woman was taller and more graceful in her movements, but obviously uneasy about being there. She kept her fur hood up so her face remained hidden. A thick braid of black hair was the only visible part of her body. She seated herself next to Golikoff but would not look at him, nor he at her.

The woman who'd chosen Lesseps seemed quite enamored of the brass buttons on his coat. She used gestures to ask for a few of them, and when he said yes, alarmed and tantalized him by biting them off. Removing her many layers of clothes, she revealed without embarrassment a lumpy, middle-aged body that smelled of fish but also demonstrated, Lesseps mused, the extent to which enthusiasm could make up for lack of beauty. He wanted to see what the other woman looked like, but she and Golikoff remained next to each other, not touching.

"I'm going to enjoy myself even if you won't," Lesseps called out.

"Is this how French ambassadors represent the interests of their country abroad?" Golikoff growled. He glanced up and met Lesseps's eyes, then looked away, his face smoldering with—was it anger, or some suppressed longing? It struck Lesseps that the soldier might be a virgin. Was that possible?

"Come, Golikoff," Lesseps said, doffing his jacket and shirt, then helping the round woman undo the buttons of his trousers. "You can insult *me*, but don't insult our hosts."

Golikoff stood and silently removed his hooded fur coat, the cap beneath that, his fox-fur cravat, and his military jacket, throwing each item with vehemence to the floor. When he was down to his chemise, he undid and dropped his trousers, revealing, to Lesseps's astonishment, an advanced state of arousal. Lesseps's partner had pushed him onto the bearskin that served as his bed and climbed on, but he found himself watching, not the woman quite expertly moving over him, but Golikoff. The soldier was pawing clumsily at the other woman, trying to undress her, but she kept pulling away.

"Don't be a bitch," he growled.

The woman looked toward the tent entrance—was someone out there, making sure the women complied with the demands of Chukchi hospitality?—then, as if resigned to her role, knelt before Golikoff and took him in her mouth. Golikoff put his hands around her head—it was still hooded—and groaned in pleasure, then looked defiantly at Lesseps. The two men held each other's gaze, neither saying a word, until Lesseps cried out, at which Golikoff did too.

Afterward the women proffered their visitors a clear brown drink. Golikoff sniffed it and set it down. "It's a mushroom liqueur," he said. "I would advise against drinking it."

"You still think they're trying to kill us?"

"I don't know, but it smells exactly like something we use at home to get rid of insect infestations."

Lesseps tasted the drink with the tip of his tongue, then shuddered and set it down as well. "I don't doubt it. Is it effective?"

"Quite."

"And where's home?"

"Irkutsk."

"Irkutsk?"

"Yes. That's as far as I travel with you."

Lesseps sighed. "That's still a long way from here."

Golikoff sighed too. "It's closer every day."

Spring arrived like another calamity. It continued to snow, a heavy, wet snow that melted during the day, causing the dogs to sink up to their bellies and the sleds to stall. Lesseps suggested they travel at night, when the snow refroze, but the guides didn't want to travel in the dark. He showed them how, using his compass and timepiece, he could accurately calculate direction and distance. The guides appealed to Golikoff, but the soldier raised his hands in resignation. "Who are we to stand in the way of the Frenchman's superior understanding of these regions in which he has never set foot?" he said.

When they arrived—in the dark, through swirling snow—at the fortified town that was their next destination, the guides were impressed, but Golikoff grunted about bastards who were luckier than they deserved.

Night travel couldn't stave off the warming weather for long, however. Eventually the party prevailed on a group of wandering Koryaks to take some of their dogs and food and rubles in exchange for local guides and reindeer. The reindeer, with their longer legs and wider feet, could still pull through the softening snow.

The new guides didn't want to let Lesseps drive the reindeer himself, but after a day of enduring his smiling, confident importunity, they gave in. Driving a pair of reindeer turned out to be quite different from driving six to eight dogs, however. As soon as he took off, his foot got tangled in the trace of the reindeer on the left. Shouting in pain, he let go of the reins and bent over to extricate himself, but the suddenly loose reins made the reindeer start running. Lesseps was flung from the sled, his left foot still caught in the trace. He was dragged a long way, his head banging against the bottom of the sled and in imminent danger of being sliced open by the runners, before the guides could overtake the reindeer and stop them.

Lesseps came to, feeling liquid warmth on his face and aware that Golikoff was holding him and crying. "You arrogant French fuck," he cried when Lesseps opened his eyes. "I thought you had died again."

"*Again?*" Lesseps said weakly.

Golikoff clutched him tighter for a moment.

"My dispatches—"

"Your dispatches are fine, damn you."

Golikoff demonstrated once more his skill with bandaging. Lesseps spent that day and the next strapped down in the sled like a piece of cargo while enduring the worst, most nauseating headache of his life.

On the west coast of the Okhotsk Sea, they were obliged to say goodbye to the Koryaks and their reindeer and revert to using dogs despite the still-warming temperatures. They traveled only at night now, taking advantage of the still-frozen waterways to avoid the more difficult land road. But before long they had to abandon this recourse as well. One fog-shrouded night they crossed a bay whose ice cracked and boomed ominously around them. The guides complained that they could feel the ice moving beneath them.

"Don't be ridiculous," Lesseps called from his sled, urging them onward.

"I feel it too, *barin*," Golikoff said.

"It's because you can't see," Lesseps insisted. "You're associating the sounds with movement."

"No, I'm 'associating' *movement* with movement," Golikoff protested, mimicking Lesseps's accent.

When dawn came, they saw with horror that the sea ahead of them had broken up into giant undulating ice sheets, their edges glinting in the sunlight. The beauty of the sight would have astonished them if it hadn't signaled mortal danger. The party quickly took refuge on a small stony

beach hemmed in by steep promontories while Golikoff and one of the
guides scouted a path ahead. They came back and reported that the only
way forward was a narrow ledge along the cliff wall, a ledge that was broken
in places and suspended over the melting bay, but led to a larger beach
and, beyond, a path into the woods.

"You and your box first," Golikoff said to Lesseps.

When they got to the ledge, Lesseps recoiled. "This isn't a *ledge*,
Golikoff," he said. "It's a crust of ice adhering to the cliff face. It could
shear off any moment."

Golikoff took the box from Lesseps and stepped out onto the ice. "We
have no choice. Follow me."

Lesseps minced his way forward, terrified of slipping, praying the
ledge would hold their combined weight. At times they were obliged to
turn sideways, facing the cliff and proceeding crabwise with no handholds
till the "ledge" widened. There were gaps in the ice, and Lesseps watched
with mounting anxiety as Golikoff stepped over them. Then they came to
a gap that had to be leaped across. Stashing the box in a cleft in the rock
wall, Golikoff jumped over, then motioned for Lesseps to toss the box
across before jumping over himself.

Lesseps studied the turbulent, ice-filled water below them. "If it falls
in, I'm following it," he said.

"Shut up and throw the box," Golikoff called.

He threw the box, crying out in anticipatory anguish, but Golikoff
caught it. Steeling himself against the shaking in his legs, Lesseps followed. When they finally reached the end of the ledge and the wide, rock-
strewn beach that led into a wood, Lesseps fell to his knees, too tired and
too desolated by the prospect of what could have happened to cry or give
thanks or even feel relief.

Golikoff immediately went back for the others. It took seven hours to
unpack the sleds, carry all the cargo to safety, unharness the dogs, drag
the sleds across (one skate hanging off the edge), then cajole the reluctant
animals through. By the end of the ordeal, the ledge had grown narrower
and many of the gaps wider. One dog fell into the icy bay after misjudging
a jump. They could do nothing to save it.

They hadn't slept since the previous day, and the entire party collapsed into exhausted slumber on the beach. But every time he eased
toward sleep, Lesseps would start awake remembering the dog that

drowned, who sometimes looked like his friends who died in Alaska, or imagining that he himself was falling from the ledge, or—most horribly— that he was watching his dispatch box drop away into the sea. Then Golikoff was at his side, offering a flask of brandy.

"I don't like brandy," Lesseps protested.

"But when you don't sleep, *I* don't sleep."

"So why don't *you* drink it?"

Golikoff grunted in annoyance. "Very well," he said.

Later, kept awake by the soldier's low snoring, Lesseps crept out from under his bedding and found the flask by Golikoff's head. He tipped it to his mouth, hoping for a few drops, but there was nothing left. He felt like Romeo left at his lover's bier without a drop of poison for relief. Or was that Juliet?

They reached the port of Okhotsk the first week of May. Built illogically on a long, flat spit of land at the mouth of a treacherous river and its fickle harbor, the town had an air of decline about it, as if it had been born of an old and expired necessity. Nevertheless, it was the first town of any size since Petropavlovsk, and with a return to something that resembled society, the French diplomat's son and his soldier escort went their separate ways, Golikoff lodging with the local garrison while Lesseps took his letter of introduction to the house of the governor-general. This was the same governor whose homes in Petropavlovsk and Bolsheretsk had already hosted Lesseps, but this was the man's real residence, a large, European-style dwelling that was almost grand. The governor was still in Kamchatka, but his very pretty, very upright French-speaking wife and three-year-old daughter, Tasha, were delighted to take him in.

That first night Lesseps nearly wept with the pleasure of sleeping quite alone in a real bed. The next day, free to converse in his native language, he talked more than he had in months, regaling the governor's wife and daughter with stories from his travels. But the morning after he woke late and remembered with dismay how the commander had said, *If some mischance should overtake us.* Oh, what if they had, indeed, come to grief? He still had so far to go before delivering the dispatches. He announced his intention to leave within the week.

"But you just arrived," the governor's wife said.

"It's raining," Tasha said.

Indeed, it had not stopped raining since his arrival. The piles of snow outside grew dirtier and smaller each day. Tasha called him to the window, where they watched a coachman struggle to free his carriage from the mud.

"The roads will be impassable," Golikoff said when Lesseps found him at the garrison.

"We've come all this way on 'impassable' roads," Lesseps said. "I'm leaving on the tenth, with or without you."

At sunset on the appointed day, Golikoff showed up at the governor's house with their old sleds, a complement of dogs, and a Yakut guide. Lesseps bade farewell to Tasha, who was crying, and the governor's wife, who was trying not to.

"Don't be sad, madame," Golikoff called as he helped Lesseps into his sled. "We'll be back."

"Why are you telling them that?" Lesseps said, shrugging off his help. "None of your nay-saying has ever come to pass."

But this time it did. They were back four days later, the dogs caked with mud, the sleds damaged, the guide angry, Golikoff bedraggled and vindicated, and Lesseps bedraggled and depressed. Tasha jumped up and down with glee. The governor's wife invited Golikoff to stay with her as well instead of returning to the garrison while they waited for the spring rains to abate.

"That's really not necessary," Lesseps said.

"But it is," she insisted.

Over dinner—in Russian now, so as to include Golikoff—the governor's wife tried to cheer Lesseps by praising his intrepidity. "Remember how you found that ledge to carry your party past the melting bay," she said.

Golikoff's watchful eyes flicked toward Lesseps, but his expression never faltered. "Indeed, *barin*," he said, raising a glass. "If not for you, we would never have found that ledge."

Lesseps felt his face grow warm. He raised his own glass and drained it. He really should have insisted that Golikoff return to the barracks, he thought.

Smoking in the drawing room after their hostess had gone to bed, Golikoff said, "I knew about Daria."

"*Who?*"

"Daria, the Cossack's wife in Bolsheretsk."

Lesseps's hand stole to his neck, where he still wore the sable fur. He could no longer remember her face or any of the Kamchadal words she'd taught him. The interminability of the trip was crowding out even the memory of pleasure.

He had no interest in seeing the spring breakup of the Okhota River ice. "The thaw is why we're stuck here," he said. "Why would I find it diverting to watch?"

"Because a future ambassador should be interested in the customs of the country to which he's appointed," Golikoff said. "And because your gloomy refusal to leave the house is becoming a burden to the governor's family."

The two men set off and joined townspeople and soldiers and native traders gathered at the eastern extremity of the town, where the Okhota River met the sea. Some years, they learned, the thaw happened so suddenly and with such force that it flooded the town and drowned people. But this year the river seemed more gently inclined. Enormous white sheets floated past, shearing along straight lines whenever they struck one another or something onshore before heading out to sea, a silent, frozen flotilla.

"Beautiful, isn't it?" Golikoff said.

Lesseps shrugged. "It's just as impressive on the Neva," he said, "and the women are better-looking." Seeing Golikoff's stare, he added, "In St. Petersburg."

Golikoff rolled his eyes. "I *know* where the Neva flows, *barin*."

A commotion at the water's edge drew their attention. They made their way through the crowd to find a dozen dogs had somehow ended up on a large ice sheet drifting out to sea. The dogs seemed quite unaware of their danger, placidly looking back toward shore as onlookers added their voices to those of the owners, a Yakut man and woman, who stood on the bank frantically calling to the dogs to jump to safety. Two of the dogs obeyed, leaping into the frigid water and swimming to land. But the others remained on the ice, growing smaller and smaller as they floated away, till in the glare of the rising sun it became impossible to distinguish them from among the thousands of ice rafts around them. They never barked or gave any sign of distress.

"Well," Golikoff said, "is it enough of a spectacle for you *now*?" When

Lesseps didn't reply, he turned around. *"Barin?"* Lesseps shook his head, unable to speak. Golikoff took his arm and drew him away from the crowd. "What is it?"

Lesseps found himself once again standing on a shore weeping in Golikoff's arms.

"You're thinking of your friends on the expedition," Golikoff said.

"Those dogs—" Lesseps said. "It's like another presentiment."

"What are you talking about?"

"The shipwreck in Bolsheretsk, those Japanese mariners, all the dead dogs—"

"You don't believe in presentiments."

"I know. I don't. Yet—I'm starting to think some calamity—"

"Stop," Golikoff said. "Your friends are safer in their ships than you are."

"I know, but— What if I've come through all these dangers for a reason? Maybe I've been kept alive because they—"

"Shh," Golikoff said, touching his hand to Lesseps's lips. "Don't."

Back at the house, Golikoff and the governor's wife insisted that Lesseps take to his bed. A French-speaking Italian doctor who had somehow found himself in Okhotsk came and prescribed him a sleeping draught. Lesseps could hear the three of them conferring outside his door. "I have to get him back on the road," Golikoff was saying. "He won't rest till he's delivered those dispatches."

"I believe you're right, Sergeant," the governor's wife said.

Sergeant? Surely Golikoff had been a corporal when they first met. As he slipped toward unconsciousness, Lesseps wondered when Golikoff had been promoted. Did escorting foreigners earn one higher rank in the Imperial Army?

A month after their first arrival in Okhotsk, on horses still emaciated from their long winter famine, they left the town and headed inland. Lesseps assumed the much-traversed road to Irkutsk, though long, would be easier. It was not. His horse collapsed under him the very first day. Indeed, the roadside was littered with dead horses. Large black flies rose in clouds from the rotting carcasses to buzz in their faces with the stench of death. Then there were the river crossings—terrifying rivers roaring with winter melt. Sometimes they were obliged to use leaky, unstable floats to get across, risking life and cargo as they navigated the surging waters. The sun set late, allowing for long travel days. But with it came heat and biting gnats. Their Yakut guides burned horse dung to keep them away—a smelly but effective recourse.

The only respite was the pleasure of seeing new foliage after so many months of ice and snow. Lesseps felt as if he were seeing the color green for the first time, green in its infinite variety of hue and texture, green with its promise of life and survival. Sometimes, plodding along the muddy road or waiting for a river crossing to commence, assailed by heat and insects, Lesseps would fix his gaze on a spot of green in the distance and surrender every other sensation but that one.

Lesseps and Golikoff took turns carrying the dispatch box in Golikoff's large military satchel. One day, when Golikoff had custody of the box, his horse threw him off and into a large, rock-strewn puddle. He landed right on top of the satchel. He crouched over the road and clutched at his chest, but when Lesseps ran over and tried to loosen his clothing, Golikoff pushed him away. "The box!" he gasped when he recovered his breath. "I broke it." Lesseps reached into the satchel, and indeed—the lid was askew, its lock bent, hinge broken. Golikoff covered his face in shame and wailed.

"It's all right," Lesseps said, showing Golikoff that the contents were safe. "A little carpentry will put everything right. Are you sure you aren't hurt?" It was, he realized, the first time he had had to comfort Golikoff.

When they reached the Lena River at Yakutsk, they left their horses and took to boats, sailing upstream toward Irkutsk, a feat grimly accomplished by the labor of ragged, sullen convicts forced into service as pullers. The Lena and its banks shifted constantly: splitting in two, then splitting again, and again, widening into unnavigable shoals, then noisily converging. They floated through canyons defined by great limestone rock formations that looked like the ruins of some alien race, then through gentler regions of pine-covered hills and rolling grasslands, before finding themselves in barren, flat country between gravelly banks. And then the dramatic cliffs would resume.

Traveling by boat put him in mind of the expedition, of his friends on the *Boussole* and the *Astrolabe*. The commander would have been horrified by the slaves pulling their boats upstream. Monsieur de Lamanon would have loved the geological wonders on display—and taken pains to befriend the native guides. Captain de Langle would somehow have managed to remain clean and well-dressed throughout the ordeal. Lieutenant de Vaujuas would have known where they were, always, just by looking at the sky. He had not thought of them much lately. It was as if the dispatches and their delivery had taken on an urgency of their own, divorced from the actual persons they represented. It was July 1788. Where were his friends right now? What were they doing?

Beyond Kirensk they bade farewell to their Yakut guides and transferred to carriages, a return, at long last, Lesseps thought, to a comfortable, modern mode of travel. But the carriages were old and in disrepair, and the roads full of holes and rocks. Golikoff, still denying he'd been hurt in his fall, clasped his left side for the duration and moaned in pain whenever the carriage suffered a jolt. "This is how rich people travel?" he cried.

"No," Lesseps said. "The rich travel in *good* carriages on *proper* roads." He looked at his companion, whose face was drawn with pain and nausea. "Have you never ridden in a carriage before?"

Golikoff shook his head. "Never."

"Your maiden carriage ride," Lesseps said. "Take heart, Golikoff. It gets better after the first time."

The driver told them they would reach Irkutsk that night. "Do you recognize anything?" Lesseps asked Golikoff. The soldier had grown quieter and quieter as they neared his hometown.

He sat up now and looked out the window. "It's been many years since I was here," he said.

It was nearly midnight when they arrived. As they rolled up to the sentry station at the town's northern entrance, Lesseps felt his heart swell with joy and relief. Considered a small fortified town, Irkutsk nevertheless boasted a cathedral, a palace, and markets filled with tea, silk, and gold. Most important, it was the gateway to Europe. Good carriages could be had for the right price. The still-new Siberian Road would take him to

Moscow, and from there, St. Petersburg. Barring some unforeseeable and unlikely catastrophe, he would make it. He would deliver the dispatches. He would get home. He would be reunited with his friends. He would publish his journal.

"We've done it, Golikoff!" he cried, turning to his companion and grasping his hand.

Golikoff returned the grasp in silence. In the dark it was impossible to read his expression.

Friendly sentries greeted the travelers and directed the carriage to a military lodging house nearby. But the lodgings master, a skinny man with a swollen nose, told them he had no orders to house anyone, and slammed the door.

Golikoff banged on the shut door until a beleaguered servant opened it again. "Excuse me," Golikoff called into the darkness. "I'm Sergeant Igor Golikoff of—"

"Go to hell!" the lodgings master barked back.

"I'm conveying a Frenchman, member of an important expedition—"

"Not important to me!"

The door began to close, but Golikoff stepped up and jammed it open with his foot. "We have letters of introduction from General Kasloff, governor of Kamchatka," he called in a loud voice.

"You can have a letter from the empress for all I care!" came the reply.

"We've come all the way from Petropavlovsk," Golikoff shouted back. "We've been traveling almost a year!"

"Then you can travel a little longer!"

Lights blinked on in windows around them as neighbors woke to the shouting. "It's all right, Golikoff," Lesseps called from the carriage. "We'll find somewhere else to stay."

"No," Golikoff said. He stepped back into the street and yelled, "I have the French ambassador with me! Will no one in this godforsaken town welcome him?"

"Golikoff—what are you doing?" Lesseps cried, cowering in the carriage.

Silence followed. Golikoff leaned against the carriage. "Now watch— something will happen." He laughed mirthlessly. "God, I hate this place," he added.

Another door nearby opened and a stout man with mussed hair stepped into the street. He ran toward them, still buttoning up his uniform. "I'm so sorry," he said. "I'm the commandant here—who did you say you were?"

Lesseps stepped out of the carriage. "My name is Barthélemy de Lesseps," he said. "I'm not the ambassador, but everything else is true."

The commandant's expression sagged only a little. Within an hour, Lesseps and Golikoff were housed in an elegant suite of rooms near the palace.

The dashing young Frenchman was promptly invited to all of the best houses in town. Lesseps was hard-pressed to keep up with social engagements while preparing for the next leg of the journey. For his part, Golikoff spent most of his time in their rooms. One day he reported to the local garrison that would be his home once he saw Lesseps safely on his way to Moscow. Otherwise he remained in the suite with the dispatch box at his side while Lesseps rushed about town securing transportation, obtaining passports and letters of introduction, and playing the part of amiable French diplomat.

"Are you actually from here?" Lesseps asked one night when he returned from yet another dinner and learned Golikoff had not left the building that day.

"Unfortunately, yes."

"Why 'unfortunately'?"

"Never mind why," Golikoff said. Then he laughed and indicated the elegant furnishings around them. "These are the finest rooms I'll ever occupy, *barin*. Forgive me for enjoying them as long as I can."

The night before his departure, Lesseps dined with a wealthy merchant who had agreed to convey most of Lesseps's belongings to St. Petersburg. The two men were finalizing details over a delicate poached fish and a bottle of French wine—the first Lesseps had drunk in almost two years—when a deep rumbling began, first as a sound, its origin unplaceable, then as a sensation visibly rocking the floor beneath them.

Lesseps caught his wineglass before it toppled and got to his feet, simultaneously alarmed and fascinated by the clattering of windows and the violent tinkling of the chandelier overhead. Servants rushed in to keep china and glass from rolling off the table. His host remained seated and unperturbed, silently regarding his pocket watch till the movement subsided.

"Almost one minute in duration," he said, snapping his timepiece shut.

"A *minute*?" cried Lesseps. He sat down and gulped what remained of his wine. "Surely it was longer than that."

"Time seems to stand still during earthquakes," the merchant said, refilling Lesseps's glass. "Any great shock will do that, I find."

They resumed their conversation, and Lesseps felt his pulse gradually return to normal, when another temblor struck, stronger this time. The servants rushed back in, one with the express task of keeping a longcase clock from falling over; the others extinguished all the candles. Riding out the movement in darkness increased its terror, but Lesseps realized the measure was to prevent a house fire from breaking out. He could hear bells pealing angrily through the town, the sound of breaking glass in another part of the house, a woman's shriek, and somewhere distant, a heavy, dull crash.

As soon as the shaking ceased and the safety of the household was assured, Lesseps made his excuses and raced back to his rooms by the palace. People filled the streets, exchanging stories with the exaggerated energy and cheer of near disaster. He overheard snippets about injured neighbors, a kitchen fire, a fallen turret, frightened horses that had run off. And then there was Golikoff, standing before their building, scanning the crowd, the dispatch box cradled like a child in his arms.

"Oh, thank God," Lesseps cried, embracing him. He buried his head on Golikoff's shoulder. That particular combination, not unpleasant, of damp wool, cigar smoke, leather—for as long as he lived, he thought, he would recognize that smell as belonging to Golikoff.

Settled in their drawing room, where a chair had toppled but there was otherwise no sign of disorder, Golikoff poured a glass of clear liquor and handed it to his charge. Lesseps downed it, wincing against the burning sensation.

"Your first earthquake?" Golikoff asked.

"First *and* second," Lesseps said.

"It doesn't improve with practice," Golikoff said.

Lesseps leaned back against the sofa and closed his eyes. "I thought I was finally safe."

"Safety is an illusion."

Lesseps opened his eyes and leaned forward. "You've kept me safe— me and my dispatches—a thousand leagues and more. That's no illusion. *Sergeant.*"

Golikoff blushed, then absentmindedly refilled Lesseps's glass and drank it himself.

Fearing another quake that might send them into the streets, the two men spent the warm night in the drawing room, sleeping fitfully with their boots on, the battered dispatch box in the satchel between them. Lesseps woke at dawn with a headache, his body stiff from being draped over a narrow, too-short giltwood sofa. Golikoff lay on the floor below him next to the satchel and the empty bottle of spirits. He was shirtless. Lesseps could see dark lines of bruising along his ribs.

A few hours later, they were met at the banks of the Angara River by the regional governor, the helpful commandant, and the officer assigned to accompany Lesseps as far as Moscow, a brutally handsome man who waved a large stick he declared was his guarantee of a fast trip. "No one fails to cooperate with this," he said, slapping the stick against the palm of his hand, then stroking its length with a look of satisfaction. Lesseps turned to exchange a disbelieving glance with Golikoff, but Golikoff was looking away. The party took a ferry crowded with merchants and pleasure-seekers across the wide, placid river. The officials spoke light-heartedly of the previous night's earthquakes—a cupola on one of the churches had crashed to the ground, but only minor injuries had occurred, and they knew of no fatalities on account of the temblors.

On the opposite bank, amid the bustle of tea merchants preparing a caravan, a commodious postilion with a smart driver and well-fed horses awaited. Lesseps warmly thanked the governor and commandant for their attentions and stepped up into the carriage, then suddenly stopped. "Where's Golikoff?" he cried.

He found the soldier hiding behind the carriage with his face in his hands. When Lesseps touched his shoulder and called his name, he sank to his knees.

"My dear Golikoff," Lesseps said, torn between embarrassment and sorrow.

His new escort, the officer with the stick, approached to help extricate his charge. Lesseps waved him away. Crouching down, he put his hands on either side of Golikoff's head and raised it. The soldier looked back at him with an expression of such raw longing and grief that Lesseps felt an altogether physical shock. He seemed to be seeing the familiar features— the earnest brown eyes, the neat beard and mustache, the long nose— for the first time.

"I would have died for you," Golikoff said.

Lesseps smiled. "Fortunately that wasn't necessary."

"Do you remember the night you were sick?"

"What night? I was never sick."

A familiar expression of exasperation crossed the soldier's face. "You had a terrible fever. I thought you were dying."

"It was just a cold."

"It wasn't," Golikoff said. "You were raving all night."

"Raving?"

"Then you grew still and quiet. I couldn't find your pulse."

"Pulses are hard to find when it's cold."

Golikoff shook his head. "I made a deal with God."

"What are you talking about?"

Golikoff grabbed Lesseps's hands. "Just listen, for once," he implored. "I made a deal with God. I said if your fever didn't break by morning, I was going to sacrifice myself and then you would live."

"Sacrifice yourself? How?"

"By slitting my wrists."

Lesseps suddenly remembered that winter morning—waking up shivering in sweat-soaked clothes, finding Golikoff next to him with a folding blade, Golikoff bandaging his arm. "You said you'd nicked yourself. You said you were going to shave me."

Golikoff nodded. "You *do* remember."

Lesseps imagined for a moment waking up that morning to find

Golikoff inexplicably dead beside him, his blood frozen where it had spilled on the ground. "How would that have helped me?" he cried, his voice catching.

"We had no shelter, no medicine, no doctor, almost no food or water. There was only God. I was desperate." He shrugged. "And then you woke up. Maybe it was enough for God to see I meant it."

Lesseps shook his head, reeling from the knowledge of what might have been. "All this time I took you for a more sensible man, Igor."

Golikoff tried to smile, but tears spilled from his eyes. "We'll never meet again."

"You don't know that."

"I do know. And so do you."

"My whole future is with Russia and its people," Lesseps said. "You'll visit me in St. Petersburg."

Golikoff shook his head. "What would an ambassador have to do with a soldier from Irkutsk?"

"Everything," Lesseps said, but he knew Golikoff was right.

At length—five minutes later, or perhaps it was an hour—the commandant and the officer came forward and separated the two men. Lesseps had to be helped into the carriage. He was too distraught to look through the window to see how Golikoff fared. Fortunately, his stick-wielding companion remained silent while he wept. The dispatch box sat next to him, still in Golikoff's satchel. He had meant to return the satchel but had forgotten. The sable cravat lay buried in his luggage. It was now too worn to serve as a gift for the queen.

TEN

THE REPORT

Maouna Island, Navigators Archipelago, December 1787

We haul the wounded aboard the frigates—the *Astrolabe* first, then the *Boussole*. We keep our men from shooting the natives. We frighten off the canoes. We count the men who have returned from the cove alive. There are forty-nine. We count again. Forty-nine. Then Monsieur de Lapérouse marches me to his state room, where he asks me to write an official report on what happened. He says to do it right away while my memories are fresh. I remind him that Lieutenant de Boutin is senior to me. You oversaw the retreat, the commander says. But sir, I protest, Monsieur de Boutin has experience writing this kind of report. It's the wrong thing to say, a painful reminder for both of us of last year's calamity in Alaska. The commander draws his eyebrows together and says, his voice low, Vaujuas, Monsieur de Boutin is *injured*. Of course, I say, ashamed. How can I have forgotten? I hauled him up the side myself, held him when he staggered on the deck, blood dripping into his eyes.

Monsieur de Lapérouse toys with a marble bust on his desk. He has two—one of Rousseau and one of Captain Cook. He fingers the base of Rousseau as if he might chip away at the stone. Any more questions? he says. I shake my head, but he is not looking at me. No, I say. Then you may return to your ship, Lieutenant, he says. I leave him, but at the state room door I look back and see him leaning his head against the fingertips of both hands, as if he were holding his skull together.

•

Alone in my cabin on the *Astrolabe*, I find pen and ink but not paper. When was the last time I wrote anything other than a navigational observation in a logbook? Could it be the condolence letter I wrote in Monterey for Jean's family? No—in Macao I wrote several letters to my own family. And sent another, to my mother, with Monsieur de Lesseps when he left us in Kamchatka. That was only a few months ago. Where have I put my writing supplies? I rummage through the clutter I have let pile up on the extra cot, the cot that belonged to Edouard de La Borde. Has everyone else spread out as I have in the spaces vacated by the dead?

I find what I need stashed in a box of books that belonged to Edouard and his brother, books I mean to return to their father once we are back in France. But now it is dark, and I am shaking with headache, hunger, and accumulated grief.

The report can wait until tomorrow.

This morning our surgeon, Monsieur Lavaux, who was struck by a large rock in yesterday's melee, has to be trepanned. I refuse to watch, remaining in my cabin while the operation takes place on the main deck. Unfortunately, I cannot avoid hearing about it—how Lavaux made his own diagnosis; how he directed our botanist, Monsieur de Lamartinière, through the procedure; how dreadfully the hand drill ground against skull bone; how Lavaux remained conscious throughout; how our chaplain, Father Receveur, himself the victim of a vivid black eye, did not; how François, our late captain's servant, calmly cleaned up after the bloodletting.

The men seem only too happy to relinquish their grief for a gory spectacle. I despise them for it. But now, once again, it has grown too quiet on board.

A boat comes from the *Boussole* with a parcel for me. It contains a copy of Boutin's report from last summer, with a note from the commander: *Model your report after this one. Simply begin at the beginning and continue to the point when you returned to the frigates.* He has signed his name "laperouse"—no accent mark, the *l* oversize but not capitalized. I heard once that Lapérouse was not the commander's original name, that his family appended the name when he joined the Navy, to make him sound more aristocratic. The signature is that of a man unimpressed by such things. Undistracted by grief, I am tempted to say, but then I remember the way he held his head in his hands.

Begin at the beginning, he says. Is that half past twelve, when the four boats left the *Astrolabe* for the cove? Or one o'clock, when we landed at the beach? Or later, when I found some shade, and sat down alone, away from the others? Or later still, when the first rock was thrown? Or perhaps earlier, that morning, when our captain, Monsieur de Langle, invited me to join the outing. A walk on dry land will complete your recovery, he said. Perhaps *that* is where the story begins—a month ago, when our descent into this tropical heat left so many of us ill. Monsieur de Langle was a great believer in the benefits of fresh air, clean water, terra firma. He invited the convalescents on both frigates to join his watering expedition. That was how little danger he foresaw. I am not sure how many of us set out. Between sixty and seventy. I will need an official count for the report. Sixty to seventy Frenchmen, but at least twenty of us ill—off duty, unarmed, ambulatory but not strong. This did not help our odds when the crisis came.

Later, tacking in front of the cove, we see our wrecked longboats on the beach. They look like the remains of an old skirmish, not yesterday's, of an encounter gone wrong between the islanders and some other explorers, not us. Amazingly, five or six native canoes come out to trade breadfruit and pigs with us. Does yesterday's catastrophe mean nothing to them? They lost people too. The *Boussole* finally fires one of its guns. The cannonball splashes right in their midst without hitting them, no doubt exactly as the commander has ordered. One canoe capsizes but is quickly righted again, and the natives hurry back to the shore.

Where are the bodies? someone asks. I turn to find Lieutenant de Monty, now acting captain of the *Astrolabe*, standing next to me at the rail. He has always had the stooped shoulders of a young man surprised by growing suddenly tall, but now he also wears the pinched expression of a man who finds his ambitions fulfilled in a way he cannot possibly enjoy.

What? I say, although I heard clearly enough. The bodies, he repeats.

What do you suppose has become of the bodies? I stare out at the beach, at the outlines of our ruined longboats, trying to remember who fell where, while trying not to remember the sickening sound of clubs against flesh—when suddenly I lurch forward. Monsieur de Monty grabs me. I'm sorry, sir, I say, shaking him off and trying to stand up straight. I'm sorry, I repeat. I lost my balance. You're still unwell, Vaujuas, he says. Go below and rest.

After dinner Monsieur de Monty stops at my cabin, ostensibly to ask how my report for the commander is progressing. I tell him I am studying Boutin's report from last year's incident in Alaska, so I can see how it's done. That seems to satisfy him. He pats my shoulder as he leaves, trying out a gesture of Monsieur de Langle's, but we both flinch, and he draws away. When he leaves, I take up Boutin's report, which begins like this:

> On July 13 at 5:50 a.m., I left the Boussole *in the small boat. I was under orders to follow Monsieur d'Escures, who had command of our pinnace.*

I take up my pen, and at the top of a clean sheet of paper I write: *Tuesday, December 11.*
But I cannot tell how to go on. I was not on duty yesterday. I had no orders to follow.

Three days later, and the men are starting to talk again. I wish they would not. They stand in knots of two or three, considering aloud some detail they remember or have learned of the disaster. Even the Chinese sailors we took on in Macao huddle together on deck, and though I cannot understand their unlovely tongue, I know what they are talking about from the way they look at me when I pass. Thank God I am still officially on sick leave, which gives me license to avoid people.
I still need to fix the number of men who were at the cove, however, and this requires conversation. It's awkward: I was the most senior of the *Astrolabe*'s officers to survive that day, but I was not on duty. That distinc-

tion belongs to Pierre Le Gobien, the midshipman who joined the *Astrolabe* eight months ago, when we met up with the *Subtile* in the Philippines. He should have the figures I need; he would have overseen the loading of our two boats that day. I saw him in the wardroom just this morning, and he looked up at me with a quick, sad smile, expecting me to speak to him. I nodded back but said nothing. I saw in his face a first experience of real grief, a yearning to draw someone into his confidence, and I recoiled. I cannot play the consoler, not for this. I write Le Gobien a note and leave it under his cabin door. Monsieur de Langle would disapprove. He always insisted that his men speak face-to-face.

I send a similar note to the *Boussole* for Boutin, asking for an accounting of who went on the expedition from his ship and who returned. I hear that although he is still recovering from his injuries, he insists on aiding me with the report. Do I feel grateful or put upon by his interest? Perhaps he believes he should be writing it instead. I wish to God he were.

We have finally sailed away from the island. Monsieur de Monty says it is called Maouna, but the men are calling it Massacre Island. I hope they are calling it Massacre Island still in a hundred years. Nine leagues away we encounter another island that looks much the same. We are surrounded by canoes that look just like the canoes we scared off two days ago, canoes filled with breadfruit and bananas and natives who look just like the treacherous natives we left behind. Some of our men claim to recognize a few of the murderers and are ready to open fire, but Monsieur de Monty has strict orders from the commander. We are not to fire upon anyone without cause, we are not to allow any natives on board, we are not to anchor till we reach Botany Bay. We trade by raising and lowering a canvas between the deck and the canoes. I see one native attempt to scale the side of the *Boussole*. He is beaten back with a long oar and falls screaming into the sea—a sight and sound that fills me with horror and pleasure both.

In the morning Pierre Le Gobien comes in reply to my note. He knocks tentatively, and I can hear him breathing on the other side of my cabin door. But I keep very still, and at length he leans over to push a note under the door. The boyishness of his handwriting surprises me. Later, in a more practiced hand, a note from the *Boussole*, from Boutin. I copy out their figures in my notebook:

SET OUT FROM THE BOUSSOLE:	LOSSES, BOUSSOLE:
1 *longboat*	1 *longboat*
1 *small boat*	—
13 *water casks*	11 *water casks*
28 *men*	4 *men*

SET OUT FROM THE ASTROLABE:	LOSSES, ASTROLABE:
1 *longboat*	1 *longboat*
1 *small boat*	—
15 *water casks*	14 *water casks*
33 *men*	7 *men*

There is satisfaction in the making of lists and the doing of sums, a satisfaction that even tragedy cannot quite erase. The numbers impress on me both the enormity of our loss as well as our relative good fortune. Eleven good men gone, our two longboats destroyed, days' worth of water storage lost—I wonder that the voyage can continue. On the other hand, it could have been worse, much worse. I recall the deafening hail of stones on the beach and am amazed any of us left the cove alive. We managed to hold on to the two small boats, and forty-nine of us lived. Forty-nine out of sixty-one. But wait—*wait*. Forty-nine and eleven add up to sixty. We left with sixty-one. We have counted someone twice. Or someone among the dead is missing.

Dead calm today. Sweltering belowdecks and sunburn above. Monsieur de Monty, bending his tall frame into my cabin, asks again about the report. I tell him I am still assembling the pertinent facts. I do not mention the discrepancy in the numbers. He says, Bear in mind, Vaujuas, that Monsieur de Lapérouse will include his own account of events in his journal. Yes? I say, not understanding, and Monsieur de Monty says, A man's account always tends to exonerate him. But the commander wasn't even there, I say. Monsieur de Monty cocks his head. Vaujuas, he says, as if recalling me to sense. Vaujuas, he repeats, the commander authorized the expedition; he's undoubtedly wishing he had not. The commander hadn't liked the idea from the outset, he goes on. He and Monsieur de Langle, they argued about it the night before. The commander only relented after our captain said it would be the commander's fault if scurvy broke out on the frigates for lack of fresh water. Were they angry? I ask, and Monsieur de Monty says, Oh, yes, voices were raised. You were there? I say, and then he draws his head back and says well, no, he'd heard the story from an officer on the *Boussole*. He urges me to complete the report as soon as possible, then leaves for his cabin. He still sleeps in his old cabin off the council room. He only uses Monsieur de Langle's cabin during the day.

I complete the first sentence of my report:

> *Tuesday, December 11th, at eleven o'clock in the morning, Monsieur de Lapérouse sent his longboat and his small boat, loaded with water casks, and a detachment of soldiers, to form part of an expedition under the command of Monsieur de Langle.*

The humidity makes writing difficult. The ink grows viscous, the paper sticks to my hand.

I write an entire page of my report and feel pleased by my progress until I review my work and see that all I have done is describe four boats and sixty-one men—or is it sixty?—headed for a watering place in a cove three-quarters of a league from the frigates.

Was the tragedy already inevitable at that point?

The only thing I remember from the trip to the cove is Monsieur de Lamanon. He arrived that afternoon in the *Boussole*'s small boat, wearing a preposterous straw hat he had purchased in Macao, his torso criss-crossed with the straps of leather specimen pouches. When his boat pulled up alongside the *Astrolabe,* he clambered into our longboat, nearly toppling several crewmen in the process. He declined to help row and spent the trip complaining to Monsieur de Langle about the commander's lack of sympathy for the *Boussole*'s savants. He regretted very much that he'd not been assigned to the *Astrolabe,* with its more sympathetic captain. He regretted too that the commander had not come along today to see for himself how superior these natives were to most so-called civilized men. Monsieur de Langle laughed. You forget, Monsieur de Lamanon, he said, that Monsieur de Lapérouse is not only my commanding officer, but one of my dearest friends. I know, Lamanon said, I swear I cannot account for it at all.

What *I* still cannot account for is Monsieur de Langle's tolerance of Lamanon. The man complained so much the officers on the *Boussole* called him Monsieur de Lamentation. He would seize any excuse to have himself rowed over to the *Astrolabe* for dinner with Monsieur de Langle, and then pontificate the evening away while the captain looked on with amused interest. One evening, after Lamanon had intruded on one of our officers-only dinners, Monsieur de Langle laughed at our pique. Of course the man has no manners, he said. He's a genius, he has no time for manners. One day his journals will make our voyage famous, he added, and you'll all be claiming him as a friend.

We have sighted a large island. I ask Monsieur de Monty what island it is, but he does not know. I'm not as well-read in the travel accounts as Monsieur de Langle, he adds. The men want to know if they can go ashore, but Monsieur de Monty says the commander will not allow it. Why not? one crewman calls back, and I swat the back of the man's head. Show some respect, I cry. Monsieur de Monty's your captain now.

I am back on duty, my greatly accelerated recovery one strange outcome of the disaster. Perhaps some constant level of energy operates among us, so that when some of us fall others inherit their strength. I do not know whether to credit science or Providence for this. I do know there is comfort in the performance of the myriad duties of shipboard life. I am especially glad to resume the astronomical observations, which I have overseen for most of the voyage, our astronomer having proved too seasick

to continue past Tenerife. I am pleased by the reliability of our chronom-
eter, pleased by the smooth workings of our English sextant, pleased by
the neatness of my own hand as I take down my readings of the sky.

I have been thinking about Lamanon and what he said in the longboat
about wishing the commander could be there to see how delightful the
natives were. I remember now what he said next. He smiled under his
straw hat, pointed aft, and said, See how their innocent curiosity draws
them to us. Monsieur de Langle, who had the tiller, turned around and
swore. Scores of canoes were following us into the cove. He gave the order
to pull in the sail as we were approaching the reef. There are too many of
them, he said, then concentrated on steering us through the narrow channel
into the cove.

Hundreds following us into the cove, hundreds already gathered on
the beach when we arrived: I wonder now that we did not take alarm and
turn around. Especially when Monsieur de Langle realized that the tide
was out. The longboats touched bottom a musket shot away from the
watering place. Why did we not turn around then? Why did no one realize that we would have to wade knee-deep through the water to reach the
shore? That our weapons would get wet? That the water casks would be
heavy after filling and would weigh down the already grounded boats?
Some of the natives on the beach threw branches out into the water at
our approach, and Lamanon said it was a sign of friendship. Monsieur de
Langle said he was heartily glad to know it. But I think friendship may
not be possible between three score and a thousand, even when some of
the three score are armed with muskets.

I write:

*When we neared our destination, we saw with concern that a large
number of canoes was following us and coming to the same cove.*

Ten days since the massacre. Monsieur de Monty calls me to the captain's state room. I begin a rehearsed plea for more time for the report,
but he raises a hand to silence me and asks me to help him complete a
map of the cove.

The map covers the captain's table. Fine dots for sand, thick dots for forest, thin lines for elevation, *x*'s for reef. Monsieur de Monty points to one spot on the map and says, I understand there was only the narrowest channel through the reef. Yes, I say, it complicated our retreat. I assure him the map is fine, better than fine. It conveys everything: the shape of the shoreline, the reef-choked cove and its narrow entrance, the thin slip of beach, the watering place, the hills that blocked the frigates' view of us.

Monsieur de Monty clears his throat. We need to draw the boats in as well, he says, then quickly adds, Monsieur de Lapérouse requests it. He opens his hand and holds out two breadfruit seeds and two grains of rice. The seeds are the longboats, he says, and the rice— The small boats, I say, taking the seeds from his palm. His hand is sweaty. I put one seed down on the map, just to the right of where the stream empties into the cove. The longboat from the *Boussole*, I say. I set the *Astrolabe*'s longboat next to it, then line the grains of rice under the longboats. I run my finger down the vertical gap between the two sets of boats. Most of the men who managed to get between the longboats had scrambled to the safety of the small boats, even some who had been struck in the head by rocks, like Boutin, whom I dragged bleeding out of the water. This was not true of the men who ended up in or on either side of the longboats. How was it we failed to notice all the natives armed with clubs?

Excuse me, Monsieur de Vaujuas, Monsieur de Monty says, but which of the small boats is which? I point to the grain of rice on the right. This one is ours, I say. The one you commanded to safety, he says. Yes, I say, the one I brought back.

I have gone over and over the lists from Boutin and Le Gobien, and I still cannot reconcile the numbers: sixty-one men off the frigates, forty-nine returned, eleven dead. I write another note to Boutin and send it to the *Boussole* by small boat. I slip another note under Le Gobien's door.

For two days now I have written nothing. I tell myself I need to be sure of the numbers, but I suspect this is no more than an excuse. The crisis—I have not yet described it, and it looms before me like an impossible thing. I cannot get beyond this, the last line I wrote:

*Among the natives were some women and girls who offered them-
selves to us in the most indecent manner, and not all of the men
rejected their advances.*

I only noticed the women because I was off duty and not part of the
line of men busy with the water casks. Light-headed from the heat and
lingering illness, I sat down in the shade and hoped I would not be dashed
in the head by a falling coconut. I wondered if such things ever occurred.
Then I heard the laughter of women behind me and turned to watch
as they lured a few of our crewmen into the forest. They disappeared
into the undergrowth, but I could hear them well enough, the forced,
lewd cries of the women and the men's piglike grunting.

I leaned my head back and closed my eyes, and when I opened them
I found an older native woman pushing a most reluctant girl toward me. I
shook my head but reached into my satchel and handed a glass bead each
to the girl and to the woman, whom I supposed to be her mother. The
woman began raising up the girl's skirt while the girl tried to get away,
and I shook my head again, trying to explain through gestures that I was
sick and unable to do more. I was sorry for it, indeed I was; the girl had
lustrous black hair that fell like a silk curtain over her breasts. My spirit
was willing, but the flesh was weak, as the apostle says, although I believe
he meant it differently.

When the girl realized she would not have to go through with what
had been expected of her, she smiled and ran off. But a few minutes later
she returned with a friend, and I was obliged to give her a bead as well.
And not ten minutes later three more girls appeared.

I am mindful of what Monsieur de Monty said—how my account will
stand next to the commander's. I remember too his story about the disagreement between the commander and Monsieur de Langle the night before the watering expedition. I wonder what the commander has written in
his journal. Would I write differently if I knew? Perhaps it does not matter
what I write. I have been given an order, that is all. Completion is the thing.

I need say no more about the island women, but the beads I cannot
ignore:

*As we filled up the water casks, more natives arrived, and the crowd
grew restless. Monsieur de Langle abandoned his plan to trade with
them and gave the order to return to the boats. But first, and this, I
believe, to be the primary cause of our misfortune, he gave beads to
some of the chiefs. These gifts, distributed to five or six individuals,
provoked the others.*

We left France with a million glass beads. They are not Venetian beads,
nor even the finest French beads, but they are pretty, with smooth, milky
surfaces—milky blue, milky green, milky white. They are supposed to help
us establish friendly relations with the natives.

Yesterday we sighted Traitors Island, and today we are hove to outside a
large bay on its west side. Why is it called Traitors Island? I ask. Monsieur
de Monty shrugs. When we get to Botany Bay, he says, I'm transferring to
the *Boussole*. I am surprised, and for one dizzying moment I imagine
myself captain of the *Astrolabe*, until he says, quite evenly, Monsieur de
Clonard will be transferred from the *Boussole* to assume command. Ah, I
say, that makes sense, he is senior to you. And then I should have said, I'll
miss you, sir, or It's been a pleasure to serve under you, sir, or almost anything at all, but I say nothing, and Monsieur de Monty says, It's time you
finished that report of yours, Vaujuas, and walks away.

The natives of Traitors Island come out in their canoes and trade with
us in good faith, apparently unaware of the name given them by a previous explorer. They do not have much to trade, but we procure coconuts,
bananas, some yams and grapefruit, a pig, and three hens. They like the
beads but are also interested in our iron, which bespeaks a better breed of
native, more practical and hardworking. Still, we never let down our guard
and not one is allowed on board. One of our men notices that nearly all of
them have one or two joints of the little finger of their left hand cut off.
We have not seen this before.

Tonight Monsieur de Monty and our savants are having dinner on the
Boussole with the commander and their savants. I have assigned Le Gobien
to the watch and now sit at the council room table to work uninterrupted

on my report. Reviewing the completed pages, I come to the point where I left off: *These gifts, distributed to five or six individuals, provoked the others.*

Somehow I have to get from gift beads to rocks being thrown; from an orderly line of sailors to dozens of men flailing and screaming in the water; from a beach full of curious natives to a mob of deadly savages. I write:

There arose at that point a general murmur, and we were no longer able to control the islanders.

This will not do at all. But from this point I can only remember my own actions, and I cannot—must not—write of myself. I could say that I stayed by Monsieur de Langle as he tried to distribute the beads. That when he saw me, he shouted, What are you doing, Vaujuas? and ordered me back to the boats. That rushing across the beach and into the water, weaving my way through the natives, I felt a surge of panicked vitality that was the first sign I had of a return to health. That I saw that the *Astrolabe's* small boat had no officer aboard, and decided to wade toward it. But no—this is not a personal account. I write:

Although they let us return to our boats, one group of islanders followed us into the water, while others gathered stones from the shore.

Monsieur de Monty returns from dinner flushed with wine. I learned why it's called Traitors Island, he says. Schouten and Le Maire were attacked by the islanders here one hundred and fifty years ago. It had to be something like that, I say. He also learned about the islanders' strange habit of severing their fingertips. They cut them off to pray for an ailing friend or relative, or grieve a lost one, he tells me. I look up from my report. You and I should have no fingers left at all, then, should we? I say. Monsieur de Monty smiles sadly. I'm not sure Monsieur de Lapérouse will recover from this, he says. I look down, remembering again my last sight of the commander in his cabin. He blames Lamanon, Monsieur de Monty adds. He says Lamanon's absurd ideas about savages caused Monsieur de Langle to let go his customary caution. I'm not sure that's what happened, I say. The lieutenant strides to the doorway as if suddenly aware that such informality is no longer appropriate between us. Finish the report, Monsieur de Vaujuas, he says, then perhaps we can all learn what *did* happen. But a moment later he is back, embarrassed, an envelope in his hand. I forgot, he says. From Monsieur de Boutin.

Thank you for asking after me, M. de Vaujuas, Boutin writes. *I am very nearly recovered, and the rest of our injured are mending as well. Lieutenant Colinet, who was unconscious by the time we brought him back to the* Boussole, *sustained a broken arm and several gashes on his head but is already back at work . . .* I shut my eyes, oppressed by these confidences. I asked about the *dead*, not the living. I turn the page to read the end: *As I said in my first note, we lost four from the* Boussole. And then a list, very neat, in rank order, with names in full:

> *Jean-Honoré-Robert de Paul de Lamanon, physicist*
> *Pierre Talin, master-at-arms*
> *André Roth, fusilier*
> *Joseph Rais, soldier*

During the night Le Gobien slips his reply under my door: *I can account for only the seven I reported earlier.*

There is nothing for it but to tour the frigates, question every company, account for every person. I leave my cabin with a lead pencil and a piece of paper, and begin at the stern deck, where I write:

> *Paul-Antoine-Marie Fleuriot, Viscount de Langle, captain*

Who would have believed, before December 11, that muskets and swivel guns were no match against rocks? But muskets must be understood to be feared, and they must be used to be understood. They must also be dry to be usable, and then must be reloaded, a difficult matter when wading through water, or crouched in a pitching boat filled with bleeding and panicked sailors, or cowering under a hail of rocks.

Monsieur de Langle was doomed by his moderation. He somehow made it back to our longboat and ordered the grapnel raised, but several of the islanders held the cablet to prevent our leaving. Instead of firing at them, Monsieur de Langle fired in the air, which, rather than frightening the natives, worked like a signal for a general attack. If we had not been the intended target, we should have been most impressed by their surprising skill and strength in throwing rocks. Had he survived, Lamanon would have found a perfect marriage of physics and mineralogy in calculating the velocities and trajectories of the natives' missiles.

Monsieur de Langle was knocked over in the first volley, falling across our longboat's thwart and then into the water on the port side, where the natives set upon him with clubs. A similar fate awaited everyone who remained in the longboats. For every native who fell to a successfully discharged musket, there seemed to be ten to take his place. I got the *Astrolabe*'s small boat to the reef and, looking back, saw that an officer from the *Boussole* had command of their small boat. We began dumping the water casks overboard to make room for the men who swam out to us. The last I saw of my captain, the natives had hauled his bloodied body out of the water and were tying one limp arm to a tholepin on the *Boussole*'s longboat.

I go belowdecks to talk to the seamen. Don't forget my brother, a man growls from his hammock. I make my way toward him and ask him his name. Jean Hamon, he says. And your brother? Yves, he says. Why aren't you up, Hamon? I ask. My legs, he replies, they're swollen. I feel a chill at this revelation. I ask if he has seen Monsieur Lavaux. He doesn't answer. His friends, who have gathered around, tell me he figures it's judgment for what happened at the cove. What do you mean? I demand. The men look at one another, then one whispers, Well, sir, some of us who were there, we became friendly with the women, and Jean here thinks we might've caused some unpleasantness that led to the fighting that killed his brother. Not one of you is to blame for what happened, do you hear me? I say. I point to one seaman: Go tell Monsieur Lavaux about Hamon's legs. I ask the others, Who else did you lose down here? They crowd around, watching me write in the dim light.

Yves Hamon, sailor
Jean Nedellec, sailor
François Foret, sailor
Laurent Robin, sailor

Next I find the chief gunner. He scowls. It's been nearly three weeks, he says, you're only now getting around to figuring out who's dead? Just tell me who you lost, I say. He walks away as I write:

Louis David, fusilier

I then make my way to the galley, where I find Monsieur de Langle's servant, François, and his suspiciously thin cook, Deveau. Deveau hears my errand and says, Of course you've counted our captain, God rest his soul, and François repeats, his voice breaking, God rest his soul. I suspect they've been drinking. What about the servants? I ask, returning to the task at hand. Deveau says, There was poor Geraud, and François echoes, Poor Geraud.

Jean Geraud, servant

With that I have the seven Le Gobien listed for me. Who else can there be? I wonder, shaking the list in my hand. François says, Sir, didn't we lose one of the Chinese out there? A Chinese? I say. Yes, a Chinese, Deveau says, nodding with approval at François before saying to me, You forgot about them, didn't you, sir?

I go up on deck and find Le Gobien. I have so successfully avoided seeing him that I am shocked by the large scab on his forehead and his still blackened eye. He had been the last to leave our longboat alive. What is it, sir? he says, looking at the list in my hand. Is it possible, I ask, that one of the Chinese was killed in that cove? He clicks his tongue and draws in a long breath. Yes, he says, we did lose one of them, now that you mention it. Had he a name? I ask. No doubt he did, Le Gobien says, but I'm damned if I know it. I stare hard at him, and he adds, *Sir.* I complete my list as he walks away:

a Chinese

Next I find Monsieur de Monty. We may have scurvy aboard, I say, then tell him about Hamon's legs. Also, I suggest, we should assign some meaningful tasks to François. Like what? Monsieur de Monty asks. *Any-*

thing, I say. Deveau is turning the lad into a drunkard. And then I return to the council room, where I am now, where I am prepared to stay till I have written my way through the disaster. I thought I had only been pretending that the discrepancy in the numbers was an obstacle to completing the report, but the freedom I feel now is not imaginary. My mind is easier. The missing man was not even French.

It is nearly dawn before I finish describing our retreat from the cove and our arrival back at the frigates, and I am wondering again why the natives did not massacre all of us. Their canoes were faster than our small boats under any conditions, much less laden, as we were with forty-nine men, only a few of us uninjured enough to work the oars. They could easily have prevented our leaving the cove, but they did not. We rowed back through the channel in the reef and only a few canoes followed us, heckling us but careful to keep a safe distance from our muskets, whose power they now understood.

When we came in sight of the frigates it was as though nothing had happened, as if we had passed through a nightmare world and would now wake to the safety of our lives aboard the ships. Scores of canoes still surrounded the frigates, and we could see natives on deck visiting and trading with our people. No one on board even noticed us or our distress till we were quite close. We reached the *Astrolabe* first and delivered the injured, then made our way to the *Boussole.* Boutin and I fairly crawled up the side. At any moment I feared one or the other of us might faint and plunge into the sea. He was bleeding from the head and very pale. Later I would discover a gash on my own head, but whether the injury was caused by one of the native's rocks or sustained during our frantic escape, I cannot say.

Once on deck, Boutin saw the commander and cried out, We were attacked, then dropped to his knees. I tried to hold him up, but he is larger than I am and dragged me to the deck with him. An angry cry came from the men, and they ran for their weapons—soldiers for muskets, gunners to their cannons. The commander stood in shocked silence for a moment, then called out, No! Do not fire! Seeing one of the men grab a native on deck, he shouted to let him go, whereupon the frightened native leaped overboard and swam away, followed by the other natives on

board. The commander took his trumpet and called over to the *Astrolabe*:
Do not fire! I repeat, do not fire! He ordered the survivors brought up
from the boats below, had Boutin taken to the sick bay, then turned to me
and fixed my face between his hands. What happened? he said. They
killed him, I cried. Who? the commander said. The captain, I said, it was
the beads, he was trying to help. The commander shook me. Where is
Monsieur de Langle? he shouted. He told me to go back to the boats, I
said, so I did. Then the commander's face crumpled in grief. No, he said,
no, not him, not like this, and I cannot say now whether he held me or I
held him, and whether the sobs I heard were mine alone.

New Year's Day, 1788. I have completed the report. Monsieur de Monty
insists I deliver it in person, so I put on my dress uniform and am rowed
to the *Boussole*, the first time I have left the *Astrolabe* since the disaster. Boutin, his head bald in patches, greets me at the deck with such
warmth that I draw away. He sees my embarrassment and steps back.
Monsieur de Lapérouse is waiting for you below, he says, his voice now
formal.

There are few agonies worse than watching someone read your writing. I stand before the commander as he reads my report and think of a
dozen sentences I should have rewritten. I also see how the commander's
uniform hangs loose from his shoulders. At the beginning of the voyage,
some of the younger officers and I called him Commander de La Paunch.
It seems like an ancient memory. At last he looks up and says, It's a good
report, Monsieur de Vaujuas; you've been most fair to all concerned. I
have been holding my breath, and gasp out, Thank you, sir. I particularly
appreciate the ending, he says, then reads aloud:

> *Everyone who was there can attest, with me, that no violence or im-*
> *prudence on our part preceded the savages' attack. Monsieur de*
> *Langle had given us the strictest orders in this regard, and no one*
> *disobeyed them.*

I thought it might be important to emphasize that, I say. You can
scarcely imagine how important, the commander says, the color rising in

his face. Critics at home are always ready to blame the explorer when there's trouble with natives, he adds.

He looks back down at the report, then says, Do you have any idea how many natives died? No, I reply, surprised. There were shots fired, were there not? he says, then presses: You must have seen natives fall during the battle. Who suffered more losses? I take a deep breath before answering. Proportionally, sir, I say, we did, of course, by far. But in total numbers, perhaps they did. I'd like to think we killed at least thirty or forty. But it's only a supposition. Should I have included that in the report?

No, the commander says, shaking his head. Then, his voice low and cold, he adds: How very surprised Lamanon must have been. I have never heard the commander speak with such bitterness before. But his voice breaks as he asks, Did you see—do you remember—how Monsieur de Lamanon fell? Like all of them, sir, I say. He climbed into the *Boussole's* longboat after Captain de Langle and was struck down by rocks, then dragged out of the boat and set upon with clubs. The commander closes his eyes against the words. No one deserves such a death, he finally mutters. No, sir, I say. No one.

He remains silent for so long that I wonder if I should leave. But then he opens his eyes and looks up at me. Do you remember the last thing Monsieur de Langle said to you? he says. Yes, sir, I say, he told me to go back to the boats. I mean before that, the commander says, the last real conversation you had with him. He looks so expectantly at me and so dejected for himself, and I remember that he and Monsieur de Langle argued the last time they saw each other. Yes, I say after a moment, yes, at the cove, he joined me for a time beneath a pine tree— A *pine* tree? the commander asks. A *palm* tree, I correct myself, then go on: Monsieur de Langle turned to me and said, Take a good look, Vaujuas, remember everything—when we get back to Europe this will all seem a dream. The commander nods mournfully, and I want to say, Sir, it's no use dwelling on the last words exchanged. But it is not my place to say so.

Monsieur de Langle did join me once beneath a tree. He said everything I reported to the commander. But it was not at the cove on Massacre Island; it was not in the South Seas at all. It was over a year ago, and we were sitting under a cypress tree, not a palm, on a point overlooking Monterey Bay, in California. Lamanon was arguing in Latin with one of the Spanish priests. Can you understand what they're saying, sir? I asked the captain. I believe Monsieur de Lamanon is trying to persuade our host that there is no God, Monsieur de Langle said, and when I frowned, he laughed. Take a good look around, Monsieur de Vaujuas, he said, Try to remember everything. I did as he bid. The fog was receding. Sea otters played in the water below us. Stretching out into whiteness beyond was the great expanse of the Pacific. When we get back to Europe, Monsieur de Langle added, this will all seem a dream.

A dream: native girls crowd around me, their brown fingers reaching for my pouch, calling out for beads. Word has spread, apparently, of a man who will give you a bead for nothing. I get to my feet when they will not leave, and waver where I stand, lightheaded from hunger and fever. No more, I say to them, holding the pouch over my head, beyond their reach. One girl jumps up and snatches off my hat, and another grabs at my jacket, trying to twist off the buttons. Stop! I shout, trying to shake them off. I slap at one with my free arm and she jumps back with a cry into the arms of a naked, tattooed man who might be her father. He growls in my direction, and several other native men come forward. An older woman appears and orders the girls away. They slink off, pouting and grumbling, a few stopping to shout back an insult. The men begin to circle me. *What are you doing, Vaujuas?* Monsieur de Langle cries, leaving the watering line and advancing toward me. He grabs the pouch from my hand. *Get back to the boats!* I do as he bids, I hurry to the water's edge and walk in up to my knees, then turn back. He is trying to distribute what is left of my beads. I see our unattended launch, and plunge into the water after it.

ELEVEN

AMONG THE MANGROVES

Botany Bay, New Holland, February 17, 1788

Midafternoon, but looks later. Heavy rain with occasional thunder and lightning. In the bay, two frigates at anchor. On the northern shore, near a place the inhabitants of the area call Kooriwall but that the English will call "Frenchman's Gardens," a hectic, temporary settlement: makeshift tents, an observatory, a palisade, dozens of men hunched over against the rain, working, trying to work, giving up on work. In one tent, Jean-François de Galaup de Lapérouse, captain and commander, sits on a rough wooden bench, as individuals are brought before him to tell him what they know. Everyone shouts to be heard over the rain and thunder.

PAUL-MÉRAULT DE MONNERON, chief engineer of the *Boussole*:
Yes, sir, I found the body. Monsieur Charron and I had taken a boat a few leagues west to look for trees to fell, and— Sir, I've never believed in premonitions, but perhaps our misfortunes have made me superstitious, for I felt a kind of cold misgiving all morning. We entered a small inlet with particularly large mangroves when we found him lying facedown in a shallow pool below a cluster of trees. I thought at first it must be one of the English convicts, escaped from their settlement and come to grief in the wild. But we turned him over and could see straightaway that it was the *Astrolabe*'s chaplain, Father Receveur.

I immediately surmised that he'd been killed by the savages—struck by one of their barbed spears. No, there was no spear—they must have taken it. But it's the only thing that could explain the damage to his head.

And why most of his belongings were missing—food, water, tools. They'd even taken his shoes. No, he was otherwise still clothed. They also left his hat. I found it hanging on a low branch above his body.

He hadn't been dead very long. His limbs were still pliable. He wasn't yet cold. I feared the savages might still be nearby, ready to attack again, so I drew out my pistol. Then Monsieur Broudou suddenly appeared, which startled us extremely. Yes, alone and on foot, soaked to the knees. You'll have to ask him, sir, but I believe he was hunting—he had a rifle. And about half an hour earlier, Monsieur Charron and I had heard a gunshot. I asked Monsieur Broudou if he had discharged his weapon, but—well, he said it was none of my concern.

Could Father Receveur have been *shot*? I suppose so. Accidentally, of course. But—that wouldn't explain the missing belongings. Surely Monsieur Broudou wouldn't have—of course not.

We *had* seen a few of the savages when we set out this morning— mostly women fishing from canoes. But none after we found the body. It was as if they knew to keep out of sight. And it's just as well they did, sir. I can no longer promise to behave with moderation toward them. What kind of men attack an unarmed man peaceably studying *plants*? Can such men even be called human?

Monsieur Charron? Yes, we're friendly enough, I suppose. He's nearly completed a new longboat. He was dissatisfied with the quality of wood he's had to work with, however, and asked me to accompany him upstream to see if we could locate more suitable trees—which I'm pleased to report we did. My task was to figure out how to fell them and float them back here. We obviously abandoned that part of the mission when we found Father Receveur.

PIERRE CHARRON, head carpenter on the *Boussole*:
I actually saw him first, sir, meaning no disrespect to Monsieur de Monneron.

We found these great mangrove trees, just the thing for our purpose— the wood is dense and doesn't rot in saltwater, you see—and I'd climbed out of our boat onto the lower-down branches of one specimen and was making my way round it when I saw the poor abbé, God rest his soul, lying there dead. I called to Paul—Monsieur de Monneron, that is—who tied up the boat and joined me.

What a shock, the sight of the abbé's mangled face! I'll never forget it, sir. What was he doing out there all by himself—botanizing? It's just my opinion, sir, but he should've stuck to his priestly duties and left the botanizing alone. He'd still be alive, wouldn't he? Yes, sir, I know it's not my place, but—

Oh, I expect he was shot by mistake. We heard the shot—*two*, I think—only a few minutes before. And then Monsieur Broudou shows up, panting and pale, with a hot rifle over his shoulder. How he frightened us—and we him! I expect he was looking for his quarry and found he'd shot a priest instead. He didn't say a word all the way back in the boat. Nor did we, of course, we were that distressed.

As for the abbé's belongings, I don't know, sir. Maybe someone else found the body before us and took them. Maybe that someone was someone who'd shot a priest by mistake and wanted it to *look* like an attack, then hid in the underbrush till he heard our voices. No, sir, I'm not accusing Monsieur Broudou of anything—I speak only of possibilities.

Killed by a native? I don't think so. We didn't see any. I expect they've mostly fled well inland now that the English have dumped all their undesirables on the continent.

Monsieur de Monneron—oh, yes, we've been friends since Chile. We built that giant tent together—the one for the great dinner on the beach—remember, sir? Of course you do. Anyway, Paul—Monsieur de Monneron—heard me complaining about the wood—meaning no disrespect to the men, sir, but it's as if I've been asking for kindling rather than timber. Anyway, he offered to help me look for better trees. I believe Monsieur de—what's his name, the *Astrolabe*'s plant man?—I keep wanting to call him Monsieur de Lamanon, but that was *our* learned gentleman that was killed at Massacre Island—Lamartinière? right, that's him—he told us we might find larger mangroves upstream, where the water isn't as salty, and he was right.

Oh, we've been on several such outings now, Monsieur de Monneron and I. Today we were finally ready to fell a tree and drag it back when we found the abbé. I suppose it's a good thing we were there, sir, or the poor man might have languished in that spot with no proper burial and none of us ever knowing what had become of him.

FRÉDÉRIC BROUDOU, lieutenant on the *Boussole* and brother-in-law to Commander de Lapérouse:

I know, I *know*—I wasn't supposed to be away from the encampment. I'm sorry, brother—*Captain*. I wanted to be alone for a while, go hunting, bring back something other than kangaroo to eat. Is that so terrible?

I did *not* shoot the priest. A rifle shot wouldn't result in anything like what happened to that poor man's face. I did shoot—once, at a bird. I thought I'd hit it and was looking for it when I heard voices. When I heard French, I made myself known. I'm lucky your dear Monneron didn't shoot *me*. He had his pistol out. And the carpenter looked at me like I was Satan's own son. He probably came in here and said *I'd* shot the priest, didn't he?

How long between my shot and when I found them with the priest's body? I don't know—maybe fifteen minutes?

Killed by natives: Whose theory is that? Monneron's? I was in the area all morning and never saw or heard a single native. Oh, come, brother— it's rubbish, this notion that natives can slink about silently and unseen. Monneron's just trying to justify his own panic—as we were leaving, he shot his pistol two or three times, firing at phantoms.

Oh, but I didn't say the priest wasn't murdered. He was murdered. Just not by natives. Look what I found floating in the water next to the body: a woman's hair ribbon. Dirty, but recognizably pink and European. I think we can agree it's an odd thing to find in these parts, especially in the vicinity of a cleric. And it just so happens that this morning, heading out from camp, I saw our dead priest, still alive, talking to a man and a woman, both European. Escaped English convicts, of course.

No, I didn't approach them. I wasn't supposed to be there, remember? I slunk off as quietly as I could. As quietly as a native, you might say. Now I see I should have intervened, as I expect they lured him into the woods, then bashed him in the head with a sharp rock and robbed him. The woman probably lost her ribbon in all the excitement.

Where are these convicts now? How should I know? You should send some of your more reliable armed men out there to look.

But if you dislike my theory, *Captain*—or is it *Count* these days?— maybe you should look closer to home. Oh, I don't know—Monneron and that carpenter—they spend an awful lot of time together. "Tree-hunting." Is that what they call it these days? Maybe our priest surprised *them*.

Have I been drinking? Yes. Yes, I have. As have you. What other remedy is there while we're killed off one after another on the far side of the world?

I know, I know—we've done this before. You want me back on the ship. I'm going. And there I'll remain till your shorthandedness inclines you once more to let me ashore.

Joseph Hugues de Boissieu de Lamartinière, botanist on the *Astrolabe*:

Oh, sir—I cannot believe it! He invited me to go with him today—and I declined. I've been unwell. No, nothing like that. Just fatigue. But I should have gone—he shouldn't have been alone. He's had terrible headaches and fits of dizziness lately.

I don't know, sir. He'd sustained that blow over his left eye in the unfortunate incident at Maouna, but he seemed wholly recovered by the time we arrived here. Yet the last few weeks he's complained of a return of vertigo and of terrible pain on that side of his face. I advised him to consult with Monsieur Lavaux, but I don't know if he did.

Yes, sir, I have some medical training as well, but— Yes, under duress, I did perform surgery on Monsieur Lavaux. But Monsieur Lavaux is largely recovered now and is by far the more able medical man. But yes—I worried there might be some latent swelling or internal bleeding connected to Father Receveur's earlier injury. And to be so grievously injured in that exact part of his head— Yes, it *could* be a coincidence, but a very strange sort of coincidence, is it not?

I *did* try to dissuade him from the outing, but he insisted. He said he'd heard the same petty confessions from everyone twice over, and it was time to discover some new plants.

Yes, I saw him go, just after dawn. What did he have with him? The usual—walking stick, leather satchel— It's *missing*? Oh, no. Well, it's nothing compared to the loss of his life, of course, but—I'd lent him my handheld microscope. It would have been in a small wooden box—it wasn't on him?

A hat? Yes, a straw hat he bought in Macao, he and Monsieur de Lamanon both. No, sir, that's not it. He didn't have a hat like that. Although I *did* see that hat today. Not on him. It was on Monsieur Broudou, actually.

I—well, no sooner had Father Receveur left the camp than I changed my mind and decided to join him. By the time I was ready, he was gone, of course. But I walked into the woods a little ways to see if I could catch up, and—I thought I saw Monsieur Broudou, in that hat.

Yes, no doubt Monsieur Broudou would normally wear a tricorne. I may be mistaken, of course. Perhaps it was someone else. But the man I saw was wearing a gray felt hat just like this, and appeared to be in conversation with two bedraggled English convicts, a man and a woman. No, I don't believe they saw me. I couldn't hear them, not even to determine what language they were speaking. I wished to have nothing to do with it and returned to camp as quickly as I could.

Oh, I'm absolutely certain it wasn't Father Receveur. The man I saw was too tall to have been the chaplain. And as I said, he didn't have a hat like this. He was inordinately attached to that straw hat. Lamanon was too. And now both of them—

I just hope the end was quick and painless. Sometimes it feels like we're each simply waiting our turn, and that a death with little suffering is all we have left to wish for.

SIMON-PIERRE LAVAUX, surgeon on the *Astrolabe*:
He wasn't shot, Commander. Of that I'm certain. There's no exit wound, for one. And the damage to his face—I don't believe a gunshot caused that. The wound is too—*irregular.*

I'm not sure of anything else, however.

Yes, I knew about the headaches. He'd come to see me last week. All I had to give him was laudanum, but it seemed to help. I meant to ask him today if he needed more. Yes, I suspect it was connected in some way to the contusion he received in the Navigators. But how, or what his prognosis was, I can't say.

Certainly if I'd known he was contemplating a trip into the woods alone, I would have forbidden it, sir. What a shame that Monsieur de Lamartinière had neither the good sense nor strength of will to stop him or accompany him. Although if it's true he was attacked, I suppose we might have lost two men of science today rather than just one.

Well, it does seem most likely, doesn't it, sir? The missing belongings certainly suggest foul play. Who would want to attack him? *Anyone*—a native with a spear, an English convict with a knife, one of our own with an unknown grudge. Perhaps even a wild animal.

It's possible the thefts occurred ex post facto, of course. Perhaps one of his headaches came on while he was out there, and he fell and impaled himself on something. He liked to climb—he might have been up in a tree and lost his balance. I understand he was found facedown in the water—he might even have drowned after the initial injury. Or—this is horrible to contemplate and rather unlikely, but he might have inflicted the injury himself. I once had a patient prone to such agonizing headaches that he tried to scalp himself in a misguided attempt to relieve the pain.

We'll have to wait till morning to bury him, sir. It's raining so hard now the men are having trouble digging a proper grave. But Monsieur Charron and his assistant are completing a casket, Father Mongez is inscribing a wooden plaque, and I'll join his other friends to prepare his body. He'll be the only one of us—thus far—to have a proper burial, on land.

I'm much improved, sir—thank you for asking. I do wish the *Boussole*'s surgeon could have performed the surgery rather than a botanist more accustomed to slicing up plants, but it could not be helped. No doubt Monsieur de Lamartinière did his best.

ANNE GEORGES AUGUSTIN DE MONTY, lieutenant, lately transferred to the *Boussole*:

Sir, we just apprehended two escaped English convicts a half league west of here, a man and a woman. We discovered them in possession of a straw hat, a pair of boots, a walking stick, a canteen, and a partially consumed loaf of bread. Monsieur de Lamartinière has identified several of these as belonging to Father Receveur. No, no satchel. Monsieur de Lamartinière asked as well—no microscopes or scientific tools of any kind, no journal.

Sir, I believe these two individuals approached our men a week ago seeking passage on our ships. They look very much worse for wear, sir—my guess is they've been hiding in the woods since we turned them away. Nevertheless, they were recognized by several men, including Monsieur de Lamartinière, who said he saw them outside the camp just this morning.

It's my belief, sir, that after more than a week in the woods without food or shelter, they grew desperate, and when they saw Father Receveur venturing out alone this morning, they set upon him in order to rob him of food and clothing.

We did find a large hunting knife on the man. Neither Monsieur de Lamartinière nor Monsieur Lavaux recognized it as belonging to Father Receveur. It's very clean, sir—as if it were recently cleaned, if you understand me.

They refuse to answer our questions. The sailors who recognized them from last week say the man could speak French when he was here before. Shall I find someone who speaks English? Monsieur de Monneron? Yes, sir, I'll ask him in. And Monsieur Broudou as well? He's returned to the *Boussole*, sir. Shall I—? No? Very well, sir.

MONSIEUR DE MONNERON, interpreting for the escaped English convicts: Sir, this man calls himself Peter Paris. The woman claims to be his wife, Ann, but Mr. Paris insists that they aren't married and that her name is Ann Smith. He says that his father was French and a rogue, and that we've proven ourselves no better, so he'd prefer to speak his adopted language.

They admit that they came here eight days ago to seek passage back to Europe and were turned away. They were loath to return to the English settlement—sir, I'll spare you the invective Mr. Paris uses in referring to his English masters. They apparently remained nearby, hoping to find a sympathetic crew member to ferry them to one of our ships after nightfall. Obviously they did not, and the state you see them in now is the result of a week spent out of doors.

This morning they met Father Receveur as he left the encampment. He told them that he couldn't sneak them on board, but they claim that he gave them his bread. They also say that they then met another Frenchman whose name they don't know but who was wearing a gray hat. Yes—just like that one, apparently. This man offered to help them, but only if the woman would submit to certain . . . *favors*. They—well, she's saying that she refused, while he says she was willing enough—

Marine—separate them and keep them apart, please.

Sir—whatever transpired with this man they claim to have met, they then hid in the woods for some time before hearing a gunshot. Afraid they were being hunted by the English, they went deeper into the woods, where, they say, they found the priest they'd met earlier, fallen among a clump of trees and being preyed upon by a wild dog. They threw rocks at the dog to scare it away, but the priest was already dead. They insist they would never have taken anything off a dead man's body, especially a man who had been kind to them in life. They claim, rather improbably, sir, that the boots Mr. Paris was caught wearing they found resting in a crook of the tree.

They're emphatic that there was no leather satchel—and point out that if they'd seen one, they certainly would have taken it. They didn't return to report the priest's death because they feared they would be blamed for it. They then left the area and saw no one until they met Lieutenant de Monty and his men just now. They didn't venture farther into the woods because they were afraid of being set upon by wild dogs.

The woman denies any knowledge of the ribbon, but Mr. Paris is shouting that she knows very well it's hers and that the man in the gray hat pulled it out of her hair during—during their "encounter." She says if that's so, he placed it in the water himself in order to lay the blame for the priest's death upon them. As for the gray hat, she's quite sure it wasn't in the tree when they found the body. But sir—*I'm* quite sure it *was* in the tree when *I* found the body.

Monsieur Broudou? No—he arrived bareheaded.

Sorry, sir? Did *I* discharge my weapon? Well, yes, but only after we found Father Receveur. As we were preparing to carry his body to the boat, I shot once into the woods to warn any savages against approaching. And a second time, from our boat—I thought I heard a dog bark onshore, and I know the savages travel with dogs. I didn't want one of their spears flying at us through the woods, sir.

What shall we do with the captives, sir?

Sir, if I may—if we take them aboard our ship, we'll be acquiescing to their original request, a request they may now have achieved by killing one of our men. Yes, sir. Very well. I'll call Monsieur de Monty to take them.

Meanwhile, on a wooded path near the village of the Kameygal (Spear Clan), two young men, running from opposite directions, stop short when they see each other. They are both out of breath. The men are brothers. Both bear

*symmetrical white markings on their faces and chests, although the older
brother's are more elaborate. The younger one carries a leather satchel. The
older brother draws his brother toward a shallow cave to get out of the down-
pour. "Where have you been?" he demands.*

Nowhere. I was just out looking for eggs. No, I didn't find any. I found
this instead.

No, I didn't steal it. What? No! I didn't kill anyone for it. And I didn't
go into their camp either. I'm not stupid.

I wouldn't call it a *gift* exactly. But the man who had it doesn't need it
anymore. How do I know? Because . . . he's dead. No! I did *not* kill him.
He was *already* dead, all right? I was out hunting for eggs, and I found a
dead man. And I brought this with me because it's useful and he doesn't
need it anymore. That's the whole story.

Yes, I'm sure. He was facedown in the water by a clump of mangroves.
I don't know. Back there somewhere, by the bay.

How did he die? How would I know? There was blood in the water
around his head, but I didn't roll him over to see. No, of course I didn't
touch him. You really think I'm stupid, don't you?

I don't know. Maybe his own people killed him. I heard their weapons
a couple of times before I found him. Maybe they knocked him right out
of a tree. No, I don't *know* that he was up in a tree. But you've seen those
coverings they wear on their feet? Well, this man didn't have any. I found
something that might have been his foot coverings in the crotch of the
tree he was under. My guess is he took them off to climb. No! I didn't
take them. They stank.

Maybe his people mistook him for a possum or something. Of *course*
people don't look or sound like possums. You and I know that. But it wouldn't
be the first stupid thing *they've* done.

What stupid thing did *I* do? Taking this? That wasn't stupid; it was
smart. Look—you can carry whatever you need for the whole day, and the
inside stays dry. Put your hand in and see. What's inside? I haven't really
had a chance to look till now, but it's all harmless. Look—I think this
might be a drawing stick. Because here's something with pictures of trees
and birds inside. Go ahead, take it. It's not going to bite you. What are you
afraid of? How could it be dangerous? They're not going to come looking
for it. Oh! Now it's in the mud. What did you do that for?

What? Why was I running just now? Because after I left the dead man, I heard their weapons again, and I didn't want to get hit.

You still think I did it, don't you? Why would I kill one of them? To take their things? *You're* the one who wants to drive them away. Why were *you* running? In fact, you were supposed to be hunting today. Where's your spear? And where's the dog? She ran away when the weapon went off? Oh, so you heard that too.

Why didn't you say so?

Maybe you're trying to blame me for something you did.

I did *not* kill him.

I *didn't*.

Did *you*?

Final page of the journal of Claude-François-Joseph de Receveur, chaplain of the Astrolabe:

. . . from Lavaux does alleviate the pain, but I distrust how much I enjoy the stupefaction. I begin almost to long for the first twinge of pain so I can indulge in its remedy. I am afraid to ask him for more—and afraid not to.

I invited Lamartinière to accompany me today, but could not persuade him. Poor anxious man. Exploring in the wild like this is, I suppose, an act of faith. I mean to enjoy it. And to find something new. Sir Joseph Banks discovered a hundred plants when he came to this place with Cook—is it vain to hope he left one or two species for me?

On my way, I met an Englishman and woman, two wretched souls who had run away from the convicts' settlement just north of here. Her name was Ann Smith; he called himself Peter Paris and spoke a very odd sort of French. He said they didn't know where to go, as they had been rejected by us some days before but hated the colony and feared the natives. When I told them I could not possibly help them aboard, they asked me to marry them. "So we may finish whatever life we have left with God's blessing," the man said.

It was unorthodox in every way, of course, but God forgive me, I consented. Which is to say I mumbled what I could remember of a service I have had no need to perform for years. Then I gave them my bread, as they looked famished.

And now I am comfortably ensconced in a great mangrove tree, on a large limb shaped by nature into a perfect seat. I have discovered that the undersides of the mangrove leaves are gritty with salt. This remarkable species appears to excrete salt through its leaves; thus it survives the salinity of the water in which it grows. If only men could do this—shed from their bodies and their selves the things that would destroy them.

TWELVE

SKULL HOUSE

Vanikoro, Solomon Islands, August 1791

Captain Edward Edwards stands on the deck of the HMS *Pandora*, looking at a small island to the northwest. The island is steep and densely forested. Even the sides and summit of its one abrupt mountain are thickly covered with trees. The *Pandora* lies less than a mile from the reef that tightly girdles the island, but a low haze obscures the shoreline, and Edwards cannot make out anything like boats or houses. He knows it is inhabited, however, for a narrow plume of white smoke rises from the island's western side. It rises over the haze, over the abundant trees, and into the hot tropical sky.

Edwards wonders briefly about the smoke and whose fire it might be. He has fourteen prisoners on board—*Bounty* mutineers he captured in Tahiti—and more remain at large somewhere in this endless Pacific. But it has been three months since Tahiti, stopping at one island after another, and he has found no trace of the other mutineers. He can hardly stop at every speck of land rising out of the deep. If he needed wood or water, that would be different. But he does not. It is time to make haste. Time to return to England, to deliver for trial the mutineers he has. He directs one of his lieutenants to determine the island's longitude and latitude and decides to call it Pitt's Island, in honor of the prime minister. And then he orders the *Pandora* to proceed on its westerly course—toward, as it happens, shipwreck on the Great Barrier Reef just two weeks hence; a terrible open-boat voyage to Batavia; court-martial back in England;

criticism for his cruelty to the prisoners, most of whom are acquitted; and
the rest of his life spent on land and the half-pay list.

If only Captain Edwards had stopped at the island that day! He would
have been astounded to discover a Frenchman there, a lone survivor of
the Lapérouse expedition, missing for three years. If Edwards had rescued this man, if he had been the one to discover what had become of the
voyage, he would be known today as more than the unhappy captor of
Bounty mutineers. He might have been awarded a knighthood, or even
the Légion d'honneur, and come down to us as Sir or Chevalier Edward
Edwards. He would surely have received another command at sea. And
he would figure more prominently in our tale. But he did not stop, and we
must proceed on that basis.

Edwards did not see any people when he passed the island, but the islanders could see him—or rather, they could see the *Pandora*. They did
not call their home Pitt's Island, of course. They called it—they *still*
call it—Vanikoro, and it is, in fact, *two* islands, one small and one even
smaller, a fact not visible from the deck of the *Pandora*. The Vanikorans
understood their island to be one of many that made up the world.
Theirs was a half-day sail by canoe to their nearest neighbor, Utupua; a
day's sail to Ndeni beyond it; and two days to Tikopia, a trading neighbor in the direction of the rising sun. They rarely had the need or desire to sail out any farther. A three days' sail was usually the result of
bad weather or errors in judgment. Four days' sail was their name for
suicide.

In the village of Paeu on the island's western flank, the sight of the
Pandora created a commotion. In fact, the smoke Edwards saw from the
island—the smoke that told him it was inhabited, the smoke he briefly
wondered about—had been set in order to attract his attention. That it
failed to do so caused one person on the island to despair, brought relief
to another, and gave the rest something to talk about for several days.

The children had seen the ship first. Old enough to wander away from
mothers but too young to help all day with chores, they spent their
time fearlessly climbing for coconuts and diving for seashells, and one
of them—there was considerable disagreement later as to *which* one of

them—saw the frigate as it approached from the east. The older children knew what it was, for they could remember the last time they had seen a ship. Actually, it had been *two* ships, and their arrival had caused trouble, although the children did not know exactly what *sort* of trouble. Now here was another one. After a moment of silent surprise, the children raced from the beach to tell the others.

Most of the men of Paeu were fishing on the north side of the island that morning and never saw the ship, only learning of it later, when they returned to the village. So when the children ran to spread the news, most ran to the women, who were inland, tending to infants or vegetable gardens or bead making. A few of the children ran to the chief elder, who was too old to fish and spent most of his time chewing betel nuts and bothering his wife. And Alu, who was the fastest boy, ran to get the man they called Vo.

Vo was young enough and strong enough to fish with the other men, but had never been expected to and accompanied them only occasionally. He was the only man left on the island from the two ships that had come before. When Alu came running up from the beach, Vo was outside his sago-palm-thatched house, sharpening a knife while seated on a round stone that had come from his ship. His wife, Oriela, was frowning over a patch of taro plants that had unaccountably wilted overnight. Their child, slung to Oriela's back, greeted Alu's breathless arrival with an open-mouthed grin.

"*Vaso! Vaso!*" Alu shouted. Vo set the knife down and looked up at the excited boy. He could not remember what *vaso* meant, but he liked Alu and allowed the boy to drag him away toward the beach. No doubt he was required for one of the children's games. It happened often enough.

Oriela knew it was no game, for she remembered what *vaso* meant. She straightened up and noisily exhaled, as if she had been holding her breath a long time in anticipation of this exact moment. She watched Alu take her husband away, then followed them down the same worn path toward the water.

When Vo saw the *Pandora* lying just offshore, he remembered. *Vaso* was his word; he had taught it to them.

"See?" Alu was shouting. "Just like your *vaso.*"

Not *just* like, Vo thought, trying to make out the ship's details through the hazy noon glare. But like enough. It was a frigate. Was it French? He squinted, trying to make out the flags and wishing, not for the first or last time, that he had managed to save a spyglass for himself.

Not anything like, Oriela thought. This one sat tall and bold on the ocean as if it were king of all the *vaso*. It was so large it made the horizon look closer, as though the world had shrunk. Giant cloths billowed out from three great pillars, perfectly straight, that stood up from its middle. Along the side ran a line of black holes that seemed to stare across the distance like hard eyes. If she had not known better, she would have been afraid, she would have thought only a mighty spirit could command such a vessel.

But she did know better; they all did.

The two *vaso* that had brought Vo and the others had not looked proud at all. They had been thrown around in the big storm like uprooted huts, tossed horribly for half a day before collapsing on the reef, belching out their contents over half the island. Much of what washed ashore was wood—an entire forest's worth, it seemed, wood of all sizes and shapes, jagged splinters and smooth planks, solid blocks and tall posts, some of them decorated with pictures and some so elaborately carved or impossibly bent that they could not have been made by ordinary people. The rest of the debris was even stranger—spoiled meat spilling from cracked earthen containers; small tools shaped from shiny, malleable rock; beads made of something harder than seashell that light passed through; hollow objects the height of a small child but so heavy they required two or three villagers to move. And then men, of course, although at first the villagers didn't recognize them as men. Pale, sodden men with wild hair and wilder eyes, men arriving in strange battered canoes or hanging to slabs of wood or flailing themselves through the surge, raging and moaning unintelligibly. And later, for days afterward, the dead, with their distended bellies, blue-gray skin, empty eyes, and bodies ravaged by reef and sharks and seawater.

Now the other villagers—mostly women, drawn to the beach by children, grandchildren, and younger siblings—came to see the *vaso*. The head elder came too, hurrying to the beach with the help of a walking stick. He stood away from Vo and Oriela, and looked out at the ocean. His betel nut–stained fingers tugged at the grizzled hair on his chin. "They have come for revenge," he said.

"Revenge for what?" Vo said. He was staring at the *vaso*, so he did not notice the way everyone stopped moving or breathing. Even the wind died, as if the spirits themselves were listening for what would happen next.

"Perhaps they have come to take you home," the elder finally said, and the beach returned to life, everyone breathing again—in, out, stirring up the island breeze. Only Oriela remained still, breath held, till a restless kick from the baby surprised her into taking a step toward Vo.

He had pinched his thumbs and forefingers together and was looking out through the tiny opening between his fingertips. "They're not my people," he said.

"Who are they?" Oriela asked.

He turned to her in surprise. "Oriela." It sounded like an apology. He reached out toward the baby. She chirped at him, and he clucked back at her.

"Who are they?" Oriela repeated.

"*On-lay,*" he said, or something like it.

"Are they friends of your people?"

Vo laughed. "Sometimes." He looked back at the *vaso* through his fingertip peephole. "They're not sending anyone," he said. His face grew blotchy with unhappiness. "*Meh-du,*" he muttered; it was a word he used when he was frustrated or angry.

Oriela watched as his eyes darted from beach to horizon, back to the swaying tops of the palm trees, then out toward the midday sun, lips moving all the while. He looked as if he were chanting, calling a blessing or a curse down on the beach, and the villagers followed his movements, anxious that it be the blessing and not the curse. Oriela could guess what he was doing, for the great *vaso* was drifting away. He was looking for a canoe to take out and wondering if the wind and the tide would help or hinder him. He had told her once that he had been the one on his *vaso* responsible for figuring out where to go. She sometimes wondered how this could be; why would the others have left such an important person behind? But their house was filled with objects he had saved from the broken *vaso*, tools and parts of tools that he told her had once helped him measure the sun and the stars, so maybe it was true. Her people also looked at the sky for help in sailing around the island, and even to neighboring islands and back. But they had no need of these tools, so heavy and so breakable. Anyway, none of that could help him now. Most of the men were out fishing on the other side of the island. The only canoe on the beach was the head elder's, a delicate, decorated vessel used only for ceremonies. It was never taken out past the reef.

Vo looked around at the villagers. "I need a fire," he said, "a big one. Maybe they'll see the smoke."

Alu understood first and sprinted into the woods. The other boys followed, hollering in excitement, spreading the news to the rest of the village, that a *vaso* had come for Vo. They returned with armloads of sticks and leaves, friends who wanted to join the fun, and an old woman who brought a white-hot coal from her underground oven. In an instant the fire blazed skyward, the air around it watery with heat and acrid with the smell of burned pandan and banana leaves, the white smoke calling to the *vaso* to come back.

The bustle around the fire separated Oriela from Vo, and then she found herself driven farther away by the heat. The baby, hungry and tired, began to fuss against her, so she retreated to the shade of a young palm and drew the baby around to her front. She nursed the child and watched Vo, struck by the way he expected the others to tend the fire while he stared out at the escaping *vaso*. He was used to giving commands and being obeyed. Had he always been like this, she wondered, or was it a habit he had grown into here? She knew he had not been a chief to his people. He had said so. But it had been obvious enough: here he remained, after the others sailed off in that shabby canoe.

The baby's suckling slowed, then stopped. Oriela tried gently to shake her awake, but the child's mouth went slack, and she popped off the nipple like a sated starfish. Oriela frowned. *Meh-du*, she thought. She disliked the lopsidedness of having one breast empty and the other full, and had meant to switch sides before the baby fell asleep. She brushed a fly from the baby's head and ran her fingers through her hair, soft brown ringlets tipped with sun-yellow. No one could resist touching it—not Oriela, not Vo, not the villagers. With that magical hair, her light brown skin, and dolphin-colored eyes, the child looked like neither Oriela nor Vo, but like something entirely her own, as if she belonged to no one.

A cry came from the other side of the fire, and Oriela looked up to find Vo running along the beach, shouting words she did not know, calling out to the *vaso* as it floated away. He ran into the water, and for a terrible moment Oriela thought he might try to swim out to the *On-lay*, the sometime friends of his people. But he got in only to midcalf before falling to his knees, then sank back onto his heels. He struck at the water swirling around him and howled in grief, and Oriela could hear an answering cry leave her own lips. The baby's eyes stayed shut, but her body started at the sound, short arms flying up as if to protect her own head.

The villagers stopped tending the fire and looked at Vo. They were not used to seeing outbursts like this, not from grown men, not unless someone had died. They began to scatter, looking for a return to the ordinary—the head elder to his favorite shady spot, the few young men to the repair of fishing nets or traps, the women back to babies and vegetable gardens, with just a few children staying to poke at the shrinking fire. Waves broke over Vo's bent and whimpering figure, buffeting his sorrow, wearing it down. By the time the last fingers of smoke drifted up from the blackened heap of sticks and leaves, he was silent. He lay down in the surf, looking nearly as he had when he first arrived, washed up on the beach after his *vaso* had destroyed itself on the reef. Not that Oriela remembered him from that day. They had all looked the same then, like beached jellyfish—monstrous, howling, storm-bringing jellyfish. It was not till later that she began to recognize Vo. He was one of the few survivors who ventured outside the enclosure they built for themselves from pieces of the wrecked *vaso*. He was the only one who tried to learn their language. And he was the only one she saw up close who did not repel her with his ugliness.

The shrill rattle of a kingfisher overhead woke the baby. Oriela entertained her with a string of seashells and watched the tide start to draw in around Vo. With the *vaso* gone, the world seemed to spread itself back out, the deep blue of the ocean beyond the reef disappearing once more into the unseeable distance. Even the space between her and Vo—it could not have been more than twenty paces—seemed great and impassable. It was not until she saw the men's canoes returning, threading their way through the openings in the reef, that she gathered up the baby and went to collect Vo.

"Come, Vo," she said. The canoes drew closer to the beach, and in a terrible flash she imagined the men coming ashore and finding him there, another great jellyfish spit out by the sea, and falling on him with their oars. She could still remember the terrible thudding of clubs against skulls and the doomed men's screams. "Quick, get up," she said now, jabbing Vo's side with her foot.

He looked up, his face swollen with sadness, his eyes pinched with aggrieved surprise that she had kicked him. Nevertheless he obeyed, getting up without a word and walking home after her like a tired child.

There was no time for baking yam or grilling fish, so she split a small coconut, mashed some of its flesh for the baby, and arranged larger pieces of the fruit on a few broad leaves alongside pieces of banana and mango. She placed the leaves before her fishing spirit, a kauri-wood carving she kept on an altar against the back wall. Above the carving was a pair of sticks Vo had tied together with strips of bark and insisted on fixing to the wall over her altar. He had told her that it was a spirit more powerful than hers, but she did not believe it. Two sticks tied together, something the smallest child might manage—how could it have any power over her fishing spirit with his shell ornaments and headdress made of real hair? She bent her head and thanked the fishing spirit for their meal, then added: "Please keep the *vaso* away." She hoped the fishing spirit heard her. He had thornlike hooks from his wrists and ankles, hooks that meant he was a skilled fisherman. "Take good care of him," Old Talimba had said when she gave Oriela the carving, "and he will catch for you whatever you need."

Oriela called to Vo, then put the baby on her lap and tried to entice her with the mashed coconut. The baby opened her mouth eagerly for every morsel, but ended up pushing most of it back out with her tongue. Vo watched the baby and smiled at her efforts, but said nothing. Eventually Oriela wiped away the white mash that had collected on the baby's chin and chest, set her down on the reed mat, and brought Vo the food from the altar. He shook his head and motioned for her to have it. Usually he left exactly half of his meal for her, a habit their neighbors found funny. "He spoils you," they told her. "You get fat while Vo gets skinny." It was true, she thought, eating up first all of the mango, then the bananas, and finally the coconut. She had been sticklike when she moved in with

Vo, but now her arms and legs were fleshy and strong, and she had grown round and solid, like a young tree.

The baby was trying to pull herself across the mat toward Vo. He leaned over and patted her head, bouncing the ringlets of hair against his palm, then said something to her in his language. Oriela did not know what he called the baby. There was no word he always used, at least not one Oriela recognized. It was strange that they had never talked about a name. She knew Vo's people loved names. He sometimes amused her by saying the names of people he had known, and then she would make him laugh by trying to repeat them. The only one she could really say was *Jah-lafo*, a man who had sickened and died during their journey. Vo was still sad about him even though the man had just been his slave. He had explained to her that people of higher rank had longer names. Vo himself had a long and unsayable name, or so he claimed. "Vo" was the only part of it any of them could manage.

Maybe his people did not name children until they survived infancy or did something nameable. Or maybe the *mothers* named the children. Oriela liked that idea—her own choice for a name would have been Iri. But that was not the way here, and without Vo's announcement of a name for the baby, the villagers had settled on one for themselves. Someone called her "Half-Child" after she was born, and to Oriela's dismay, the name had stuck. Every time she heard it she remembered a baby born on the island a long time ago, a sad creature with no arms and legs. *That* was the half-child, she thought. But that baby had never been called anything. It had simply disappeared—thrown to sharks, perhaps, or abandoned on the mountain, or smothered by its father and buried under the house. No one spoke of it.

She stepped outside to toss the scraps from their meal, then lingered in the doorway to admire the sunset. It looked as if a giant parrot had spread its many-colored feathers across the sky, filling her with both joy and sadness. Behind her she could still hear Vo talking. When she had first heard his language spoken among the survivors of the wreck, she had thought it the worst collection of sounds, all snorting and swallowed, as if they had something to hide. But now she could not imagine the sound gone from her life. She ran one heel across the rough surface of the round stone where Vo liked to sit when he was outside. He had told her the stone was used to grind food on their *vaso*. Reaching up, she gently tapped a hollow bowl-like thing, an object from the *vaso* that Vo had hung upside down from the roof beams of their hut. It made a lovely *teen-teen* sound against her fingernail, and was the perfect accompaniment to the shifting colors of the sky and the lilting murmur of Vo's voice as he told his secrets to their daughter.

By the time Oriela stepped back inside, the hut was silent and growing dark. She lay down between the baby and Vo, eager to claim sleep at the end of such a strange day. But Vo turned to her, his narrow face filled with longing, though not, she saw, longing for her.

"Perhaps it's good," she said. "Perhaps your people are now at war with their people."

"I would gladly have gone as their captive," Vo said.

Oriela shut her eyes tight. It was not dark enough to hear this. She did not need to ask, *What about me? What about our child?* He would have left them behind, and she would not have asked to go with him. She was curious about his part of the world, a place where everyone was pale like him and where they were forever making new and larger and more complicated things. But curiosity was different from desire. She did not wish to leave the island. Little good had ever come of people leaving the island. Still, she wished to be wanted. And finding herself unwanted, she wished to injure him.

"The *vaso* was not looking for you," she said.

"You don't know that," he said.

"My poor Vo." The pity in her voice was not false. If someone were looking for him, it would mean the other survivors had made it home. But that was impossible. "Your friends—"

"Yes?"

"You *saw* the canoe."

"I helped make it."

When she said nothing, his brow creased in anger and he turned away. Vo and the other survivors had built the canoe out of wood and parts culled from their broken *vaso*. They had worked for days and days, but when they dismantled their enclosure and dragged their creation to the water, the islanders had stared in horror. One of the village men had said, "We might as well have killed them all if they're going to kill themselves." The others shushed him, but they had all been thinking something like it, for a sadder canoe it was difficult to imagine—unstable, cramped, open to the sky.

Two men had had to be left behind because there was no room for them—Vo and another, younger man. The head elder had taken a liking to Vo and offered him protection, the house, and then Oriela. The younger man had foolishly attached himself to an unlucky rival elder who was later driven to the other side of the island. Oriela assumed the young man had gone with him, but for all she knew he was dead. Perhaps his blood had been exacted to spare the life of the rival elder.

Vo said nothing more, and Oriela began to ease toward sleep. There was no happiness in learning that one's husband would leave if given the chance, but how likely was that chance to come again? The other survivors must have perished of thirst or, if they were lucky, drowned, taking with them the news of Vo's whereabouts. The *On-lay* who skimmed their horizon that morning were far away by now, no doubt satisfying their curiosity about the world, as Vo and his friends once had. She and Vo should not have spoken of it. From now on, she told herself, she must let Vo believe that his friends had found their way home. It was not such a hard thing to do.

Then Vo, his voice loud in the darkness, asked, "Oriela, who do you belong to here?"

She came fully awake, her stomach flipping like a trapped fish. The baby stirred, and Oriela turned toward her. But Vo held her by the shoulder, his thumb pressing into her upper arm. It hurt, and she knew the baby's snuffling would soon turn into real crying if ignored.

"I'll tell you if you let go," she said.

He released her and she rolled over, taking the baby to her just as the child opened her mouth to wail. Oriela tried to lose herself in the baby's fierce suckling and its strange mix of pain and pleasure, but Vo pressed a finger against her back to prod her.

"I don't belong to anyone . . ." she said. The words felt like swallowed fish bones in her throat. "I don't know. There are just stories."

"*Stories?*"

She drew in a long breath, the way the island boys did before diving off a high cliff. "My mother may have been the head elder's wife."

"Head elder?" Vo said. "The same head elder you have now?"

"I don't know," Oriela said, although she was pretty sure she did know. She knew from the way the elder so carefully ignored her. The only time he had spoken to her was when he brought her to live with Vo, and then he had been too cheerful, too loud, giddy with the relief of solving an old problem.

"What happened to her?"

"My mother? Well . . ." Now that she had begun, it was easier to continue. She told Vo what she had learned from all the whispered conversations around her—whispers she was not supposed to listen to but was nevertheless meant to hear. That her mother had been taken away by raiders from another island. That later she was rescued or returned, or maybe had managed to escape. That she came back pregnant, and that her husband, the elder, had rejected her and the baby. In despair, she had taken the infant in her arms and walked into the ocean. Oriela had washed ashore alive, but her mother was never seen again.

"But other people tell it differently," Oriela said. She had simply washed ashore one day, her origins unknown, or no, she had been stolen from the enemy in retaliation for the taking of the elder's wife. And yet others whispered that she *was* the head elder's child—but by his sister, not his wife.

Vo listened in silence, then said nothing for a long time, so long that Oriela wondered if he had understood. Perhaps she had spoken too quickly or used words he did not know. His fingers traced lines in her back—along her shoulder blades, and then each notch in her backbone. "Who raised you?" he said.

"She was called Talimba. She lost her own baby, so she took me." That answer would have sufficed with her own people, but Vo would want to know more, so she added: "She used to dream all the time about her dead baby telling her things. People came from all over the island to tell her their dreams, and she would help them. I got the fishing spirit from her."

"Is she dead?"

"Yes. It was before you came."

He sighed, then said, "When they first brought you to me, I thought you were the daughter of a chief." He sounded angry, as if he had discovered her in a lie.

Oriela opened her mouth, then closed it, not sure whether to laugh or weep at his pride and disappointment. She remembered his delight with her in those early days, a delight she had attributed to his being so long without female company, and to his need for comfort after being left behind. He had been hungry for her then—for her body, for the food she prepared, for the words she taught him. It had never occurred to her that he had also thought himself honored by the union. A helpless man with no skin color, washed ashore in a storm, then left behind by his longer-named friends, given to the daughter of a chief? Did all the men from his land think so much of themselves? What trouble there must be among them!

"But later," Vo continued, "I saw how people were around you, and I knew something was wrong—you were sick, or crazy. Or something about your family." His finger stopped at a point in her midback, as if he had discovered the source of her malady. "That's why they gave you to me. Because you belong to no one. Like me. And no one else would have you." He lifted his hand away, and she felt a chill spread from the spot.

The baby had fallen asleep again, so Oriela pried her off. Her chest was damp from its contact with the baby's face, and she rolled onto her back to cool off. Staring up, she felt like she was falling, the barely visible roof above her receding. She knew she could right herself by turning toward Vo and offering herself to him. They would then pass from sadness to pleasure to sleep. Instead, she said, "There's a house full of skulls behind the village. Some of your people are there." So many unsayable things had been said already. Why not that?

Vo sat up. "What?"

"A skull house." Oriela could feel the ceiling swim back into place. The scrabbling of a rat on the roof sounded just the right distance away.

"We buried all the bodies," Vo said.

"The bodies you found."

"I don't understand."

She sat up too and faced him, although it was utterly dark now and they could not make out each other's expressions. "The big storm was terrible for us too," she said. "It took trees down all over the island, every village lost houses, people were swept out to sea. When your people started coming ashore, wet and raving and so white, everyone was terrified. We thought you had brought the storm."

Silence. Then Vo said, "You killed them."

"Our men did, yes."

"How many did you kill?"

"I don't know. Ten. Sixteen. Maybe more."

"Why didn't you kill all of us?"

Why did he keep saying *you*? It made her want to scream. "The men who drowned began washing ashore," she said, "and then the things from your *vaso*, and we saw that you were just men suffering from the storm, like us. The head elder made them stop."

"But I've been all over the island. I've never seen this—what did you call it?—*bone* house?"

"Skull house. We've kept you from it."

He went still; she could not even hear him breathe. But she could sense him remembering all the times he had walked through the steep wooded interior of the island, and how someone, often Alu, always happened by to distract him with some marvelous thing—a flycatcher's nest, a new spear, a waterfall great for diving. He lay back down.

"I wonder who you killed."

She pulled at her hair, hard, to keep from shouting, *I didn't kill anyone!* "Who were your best swimmers?" she said.

From the sharp intake of breath next to her, she could tell that Vo had thought of someone, or maybe several people—men he had not buried, men whose bodies he had assumed till then had been lost in the ocean.

She felt suddenly heavy, with a deep-down tiredness that pressed behind her eyes and drained through her body, demanding and refusing sleep at the same time. She had been awake this far into the night only twice before. Once as a girl she had been sick all night after eating a spoiled fish. The other time was the long night of birth pangs with the baby. Terrible nights, both of them, but they had ended, and light and life had returned in the morning. And so they would again. It was not sleep that made morning come. Morning arrived each day, guided by its own kind spirits.

When she opened her eyes, however, she knew right away she was wrong—wrong about not falling asleep and wrong that morning would restore the ordinary. She knew it from the relative coolness of one less body in the hut and from the extra layer of quiet beside her. She sat up and looked around. The gray light before dawn was just seeping into the house, but she could see that the heavy ax that hung from the opposite wall was gone. Fear spilled over her. Had he taken it and killed the men in the village? But no—there would have been shouts, an uproar that would have wakened her. The skull house—perhaps he had gone in search of it. What would he do if he found it? She strained to hear the angry sound of splintering wood, even though she knew the dense, green distance between the skull house and the village would swallow up any noise.

She got to her feet. One of her baskets was missing, along with two water gourds, and a few of the coconuts she had lined up along one wall. Then she knew. He must have taken one of the canoes. She stood before the altar, regarding it with both relief and dismay. He had taken neither his own stick spirit nor her hooked fishing spirit, which meant he was out in the ocean with no protection at all. Not that either spirit had impressed her lately. Maybe they were trapped in combat with each other and had no power to spare for her or for Vo. She plucked Vo's feeble sticks from the wall, snapped them in one hand, and dropped the pieces to the floor. She should have done it long ago.

She moved to the ledge where Vo stored his old tools, and suddenly she understood: here were the spirits Vo truly revered. He had taken every-thing except for a small, round object he said was broken. It housed a shiny little needle which spun over a bottom painted with strange mark-ings. The needle was supposed to point in the same direction all the time, "so you can tell where you're going," Vo had said. Oriela had twirled around with it once, watching the needle spin in her hand. But no matter how she held it or where she stood, it always pointed back at her.

"See, it's no good," Vo had said, laughing.

"It likes me," Oriela had said.

Had he left it behind to please her? Or was it to make sure he did not rely on a spirit that would steer him back to her?

Oriela returned to the mat and leaned over her sleeping child. The baby's lips were moist and slightly parted, like a hibiscus about to open. Oriela hated to think of her waking up fatherless and abandoned, and now she sensed the truth of her own mother's story. She knew how easy it would be to walk into the ocean with the baby. Gently she scooped up the child, noticing as she did so that a fistful of ringlets had been clumsily cut from one side of her head. Oriela rubbed her hand over the cut hair, feeling the blunt ends between her fingers. What did it mean? Was it a mark of shame, of rejection? Or had Vo loved the child and wanted something to remember her by? Oh, she had not known him at all, she thought with bitterness. Not even after all the secrets traded during the night. Weeping, she tied the still sleeping baby to her back, then left the hut and padded silently toward the beach.

And there he was, just offshore, struggling against the wind and tide, unable to get past the reef. Oriela stared in amazement, forgetting for a moment her own misery. If he had taken one of the smaller fishing canoes, he would have made it, might already have been beyond her sight. But he had taken the head elder's ceremonial canoe, the least seaworthy in the village and nearly impossible to manage without other rowers. Why? Had he not wanted to trouble anyone by taking a working canoe? Or was he making a claim? *I know now you may be my father-in-law, so you won't mind if I take this.* Or, *I know you married me to the village outcast, so now I'll have your canoe.* Or maybe it was to make sure everyone knew: *I would rather die than stay with people who killed my friends.* But now, fighting uselessly against the water and the wind, he only looked foolish. Oriela did not know whether she felt more relieved or embarrassed as she stood on the beach and waited for him to notice her. When he finally did, his shoulders fell in surrender. Bringing up the oars, he allowed the current and the morning breeze to carry him ashore.

As the first rays of sunlight washed over them, Vo and Oriela dragged the ceremonial canoe to its accustomed place on the beach, then carried everything back to the house—the ax, the gourds and coconuts, the navigational instruments. They worked in silence, shyly, not looking at each other, as if they had just met. Luckily, no one from the village had seen them, or so it appeared, as they saw and heard no one. The baby did not wake till they had put everything away. Sitting in the doorway of their house, Oriela nursed the child and said, "I want to call her Iri."

"What?" Vo raised his head from where he lay facedown on the mat.

"Our child. I want to call her Iri."

"Iri," Vo repeated. "That's pretty."

"You have to tell everyone."

Vo's eyes widened in alarm. "Tell everyone *what*?"

"That her name is Iri."

His tired, lined face relaxed, and he lay his head back down, then suddenly laughed. "Yes, of course. I'll tell everyone." Then, not looking at her: "Will you take me to the skull house?"

Oriela said nothing and Vo did not repeat the question. Before long, she could hear that he had fallen asleep. When the child finished nursing, Oriela retied her to her back, then shook Vo by the shoulder. "Come," she said when he opened his eyes. He looked confused, but stretched himself noisily and followed her out. She led him inland, behind their house, behind the village, uphill along a familiar path, to a dense wall of vines he had walked past hundreds of times. She pointed to it. "Only a priest or elder can go," she said, then walked away, her footfalls swallowed up by the forest.

What looked like a wall was really just a thick curtain and parted easily at his touch, revealing a path beyond. Stepping through, he felt like the prince in the story of Sleeping Beauty. But no castle of enchanted sleepers awaited at the end—just a humble leaf-and-wood structure smaller than the hut he shared with Oriela. He ducked into its entrance and stood, listening to the dense silence while his eyes adjusted to the darkness. And then he saw them—shelf upon shelf of skulls, arranged in tidy rows from floor to ceiling, some forty or fifty altogether, joined in the unbreakable spell of death.

Everything about the place surprised him—its nearness to the village; the care with which the structure was maintained; the deliberation with which each skull, some decorated with seashell rings, had been placed within; the ease with which he was able to identify the fourteen newest skulls, nestled on their own shelf, as belonging to his shipmates. Most were cracked or broken, evidence of the violent ends they had met. He wondered for one pulse-racing moment if honor required him to avenge their deaths, even if it meant, as it surely would, that he too would die. He recoiled at the thought of what this would mean for Oriela, for Iri, for his friends on the island, like Alu. Then he noticed that many of the other skulls in the house were marked by similar injuries, and he began to understand that this was where the villagers placed those who had fallen in battle, friends and enemies alike.

He did not tell Oriela what he had seen, and she did not ask. He asked no more about Oriela's parentage. He never mentioned the broken cross, which he never replaced. Oriela never asked about Iri's hair. He did announce his daughter's name, and the villagers stopped calling her Half-Child. He would continue to hope for rescue, to long for a return to France, but neither he nor Oriela spoke again of the English frigate that had sailed past the island. No other ship returned during their lifetime.

Their Paeu neighbors knew everything, of course. They knew Vo had tried to make off with the head elder's canoe, a story that became funnier with each retelling. They knew Vo had learned about the skull house. At first they feared he might try to avenge his people, but after a few restless nights, the men sleeping with knives under their mats, the fear spent itself, and then it seemed laughable to think that the pale, skinny man who had agreed to take Oriela might act against them. For a few days, little work got done as everyone ignored their weaving and fish traps and taro patches to watch the ocean for another ship. But before long, they resumed their more pressing occupations and amusements. One of the boys thought it would be funny to shout *"Vaso!"* and watch everyone come running, but after the third time he did it, his older sister pinched him very hard, and he never did it again.

THIRTEEN

PERMISSION

Villefranche-de-Rouergue, France, April 1816

Isn't it enough to bear the twin indignities of womanhood and old age without also having to fix the mistakes of men? Take, for instance, the mishandling of my late brother's name. How many different governments have we petitioned for permission to use it? Now the permission is finally granted, but the name is misspelled. My husband, our eldest son, Victor, and our youngest son, François, attended the tribunal at city hall where the name change was officially registered—and didn't even notice! Indeed, they returned in high spirits, my husband shouting to the household to come greet the "Messieurs Dalmas de Lapérouse!" I was the only one who heard—I'd banished the four visiting grandchildren to the garden—and after making my way to the library, I find the three of them practicing their new names on the expensive writing paper.

Pierre-Jean-Antoine Dalmas de Lapeyrouse
Pierre-Antoine-Victor Dalmas de Lapeyrouse
Philippe-François Dalmas de Lapeyrouse

"There's no *y*," I say.

"What do you mean, my dear?" my husband asks. He peers at me through a fringe of thick hair like a graying schoolboy.

"It should be an *e* with an accent." I draw the letter in the air before them.

Antoine and our sons look at one another, then Victor points to the paper before them. "Mother, this is the official spelling," he says. "The magistrate at the tribunal—he showed us."

I turn to my husband. "How could you fail to notice it was misspelled?"

"Lapérouse with an *e*, Lapeyrouse with a *y*," Antoine says. "What difference does it make?"

"It makes a great deal of difference."

"How?"

"One is correct and the other is not."

Antoine raises his hands in a familiar gesture of exasperation.

"And I thought we were dropping 'Dalmas,'" I add, knowing I'm going too far but unable to resist.

"Oh, now you're ashamed of my name?" he says, then strides from the room. I watch him go, jealous of his still youthful gait.

My sons look at me reproachfully. "Why do you do that, Mother?" François says. "We thought you would be pleased. Isn't this what you wanted, you and Aunt Victoire?"

I pick up the piece of paper on which my husband has been practicing his new, misspelled name. "This is not how we wrote it," I say. The sheet flutters in my hand, evidence of an intermittent palsy that began a few years ago, after my seventieth birthday.

"Don't you mean this is not how you've *been* writing it?" Victor says.

"What are you talking about?"

He takes my hand and stills it, then extricates the sheet from between my fingers. His own hands are large and rough and unexpected: the hands not just of a grown man, but of a man no longer young. "Mother," he says, "we all know that whenever you're back in Albi with Aunt Victoire—or anywhere away from the rest of us—or with your fellow Pénitents Bleus— you call yourself Madame de Lapérouse."

"And why shouldn't I?"

Victor exchanges a glance with François, then looks pointedly back at me, as if he can think of any number of reasons why I shouldn't. "Well, now you're officially Madame *Dalmas* de *Lapeyrouse*," he says, holding the page before me. "Does the exact spelling really matter?"

I think of the many letters I wrote to my brother over the years, addressed at first to *Jean-François de Galaup de Lapérouse, marine,* and later, *ensign*, then years later, in quick succession, *lieutenant, captain, commodore*. At some point, although he never officially received the title, we began referring to him as Count. The Count de Lapérouse. That's what most people say nowadays when they speak of him. Jean-François himself was careless about spelling, signing his name as one word or two, with or without the accent, ignoring capitalization, just as he pleased. But I was always careful. The name had been my idea, after all. No one remembers this now, but it's true. "Jean-François needs a finer name," I said one night after we knew he was going to the naval school in Brest. And so it was. After my father wrote to the right people and paid the right fee, Jean-François de Galaup became Jean-François de Galaup de Lapérouse, ready to hold his own among the sons of the best families in France.

"Of *course* it matters," I say to Victor, snatching back the paper.

The children rush in at this moment—Antoine has apparently gone outside and instructed them to see their grandmother straightaway about their new names. I hate being accosted by the children, and Antoine knows it. But perhaps I deserve this. In our long marriage, we have both come to excel at the small, tailored acts of revenge.

"We have a new name?" Victor's daughter Delphine shouts, standing too close. "Is it Lapérouse? It is, isn't it? I knew it!" At eleven years old, she's already taller than I am. Her brown ringlets dance in my face. The other children crowd around as well, bouncing and hollering. Someone is stepping on my dress.

"Victor!" I call over their heads. "Make them settle down."

"Where is their nursemaid?" he asks. So typical—a man's first impulse when asked to help in a domestic matter is to see if there isn't someone else on whom he can fob off the task.

"She's *sick*!"

He frowns as if it's *my* fault that the woman I hired to help look after his daughter is ill, and it's François, my unmarried, childless son, who intervenes. "Delphine," he calls, drawing his niece away. "You're quite right. You are now Mademoiselle Delphine Dalmas de Lapérouse."

"Oh!" she cries, pleased by the additional syllables in her name. And she's right: "Dalmas de Lapérouse" has a wonderful, patrician ring.

Her twelve-year-old cousin, Martiane, our second son Léon's child, visiting from Vannes, cries, "And *me*, Uncle?"

He pats her pretty blond head. "You are now Mademoiselle Martiane Dalmas de Lapérouse."

"And *me*?" her younger brother Émile asks.

"You, my lad, are Émile Dalmas de Lapérouse."

There is more bouncing and jollity. I take refuge in a nearby armchair, but the seat cushion is soft and my hip aches as I ease myself down. It will hurt even more when I get up.

"What about me, Uncle? What about me?" squeals the youngest, seven-year-old Pierre, my daughter Julie's son.

François purses his lips thoughtfully. "Well, Pierre," he says, "you are still Pierre Louvain-Pescheloche."

"Why? Why can't I be Lapérouse too?"

"Because Louvain-Pescheloche is your father's name."

"But I want to be Lapérouse too!" he whines.

"You *can't*, Pierre," Martiane scolds. "Don't be a baby." She sounds just like her mother, Léon's carping wife, Jeanne.

I have no time to retreat before Pierre throws himself at me, sobbing aloud that he wants to be a Lapérouse too. "Don't be silly, Pierre," I say, trying to pry him off of me, but my arthritic fingers are no match for his strong, plump hands.

"It's not fair!" he cries, burying his head in my lap.

I have seven living grandchildren, and only Pierre is openly affectionate. Somehow he alone has failed to learn—or doesn't care—that I have no habit of tenderness.

I try to reason with him. I remind him that children get their names from their fathers, which for his cousins was, till today, Dalmas, and for him, Louvain-Pescheloche. He follows me thus far, and nods through my recitation of the familiar story of his great-uncle Jean-François, who died while commanding a great voyage of exploration for the glory of France and had no children to carry on his name. But when I get to the part about how Grandfather and I petitioned the king for permission to use the name so it wouldn't die out, Pierre refuses to understand why it can only be appended to the name Dalmas.

"Because," I say, "the permission was granted to the sisters of Lapérouse— that's me and your great-aunt Victoire—and to their husbands and sons."

"Aunt Victoire?" Pierre says. "*She's* not a Dalmas."

"No, she has her late husband's name, Barthès."

"Then why—?"

"Because Jean-François was *our* brother, mine and hers."

He falls silent, but his large brown eyes look off into the distance, following some line of argument. It makes me nervous, watching him think. "So," he says at length, "you and Aunt Victoire get the name—and give it to your husbands—and they give it to their sons."

"Something like that."

"Then why do Delphine and Martiane get the name?" he asks. "They're not sons."

"Well, they have their father's names till they marry."

He looks at the ceiling, thinking again. "Then," he says deliberately, "why can't my mother get the name from Grandfather, like Delphine and Martiane from *their* fathers, then give it to *my* father, like you are giving the name to Grandfather?" A triumphant smile spreads over his tear-stained face.

"*What?* No, Pierre, that's not how it's done."

"Why not?" he cries, more in anger than sorrow.

"Oh, that's enough," I say. "You're giving me a headache." I sweep him off my lap, then try to get up to call for the maid.

Antoine has returned to the library and is watching me, amused as always by my discomfiture. "Madame Dalmas de Lapérouse," he says, pulling the bell he knows I was trying to reach, then bowing with a show at gallantry. "Come, children," he calls, making his way back to the writing desk. "Let's practice writing our new names. Your grandmother has one way of writing it, but the gentleman at city hall showed us another, which will suit us just as well."

This draws the three older children away but unleashes a new wave of misery from Pierre, who clings once more to my skirts. "You're too old for this!" I cry, pushing him away. "Stop sniveling!" Even a seventy-four-year-old woman may have a favorite dress she wishes to keep safe from the depredations of a grandchild's runny nose.

When the maid finally arrives, I instruct her to take Pierre away and divert him for at least an hour. Leaning back in the armchair, I close my eyes against Pierre's receding wails and the boisterous, inky enjoyment of the other grandchildren with their new names. Antoine always says I should be grateful for the clamor of children. "It's a sign of *life*, Jacquette," he used to tell me when our own children were small and loud. And when I complain now about noisy grandchildren, he says, "My dear, we have *descendants*." I know he's right, but—well, can one be grateful for a thing without *liking* it?

My own childhood was so quiet, I never learned to tolerate the ordinary din of family life. We were nearly always in mourning. Jean-François was the eldest, and I was next, and Victoire the youngest, but between me and Victoire there had been seven others—four sisters and three brothers—all dead by eighteen. And then Jean-François, to disappear like that, he and all his men, somewhere in the trackless South Pacific—

I know how and where my other siblings died. And my own dear child Louis, gone after only a year. And Victor's middle two, both boys, between his oldest son and Delphine. I know where they're buried, I can lay flowers at their headstones if I wish, and I don't feel so sad about them anymore. But of Jean-François I know nothing, nothing at all. And I can never completely surrender to grief, because even after a quarter century, there's still a fool's hope that he may return. This—this is mourning that never quite begins and therefore never ends.

Ten of us, and only Victoire and I are still alive, with families of our own. Yes, I'm grateful. Of *course* I am. But perhaps I may be excused for preferring quiet.

After dinner, Antoine retires to the library to read, Victor and Delphine return to their home on the rue du Marteau, and François entertains the other children. I believe he's teaching them how to play faro for small coins. I don't like gambling, but I'm too tired to disapprove, so retreat to my own room to write a letter to Victoire. I can't make too much of the misspelling: if I do, she'll try to persuade me that it's not important. But by casually mentioning it—"By the way, the name has been recorded as 'Lapeyrouse'"—I'm sure of securing her as an ally in my outrage. In this way I've managed my younger sister for more than fifty years.

After I finish the letter, my maid Thérèse comes in to help me undress. I send her away before she can start brushing my hair. She's too rough—the brush is always cobwebbed with silver afterward. But even passing the brush gently over my own head does little to stem the thinning. Antoine, three years my senior, has more hair now than I do; he's not even had the decency to gray completely. It's terrible to look older than one's husband. On Sundays after Mass at our chapel, I endure the greetings of scores of female parishioners, members, all of them, of our lay confraternal association, the Pénitents Bleus, their eyes lingering over Antoine's still-youthful face and figure while darting resentfully in my direction, wondering that I am still alive. The widows and spinsters are the worst, but married women do it too, and occasionally, a man.

Peering into the dressing table mirror, I try drawing what hair I have back over my forehead, and suddenly remember, with a stab of envy, Jean-François's wife, Éléonore. His *widow*, I should say, though she never called herself that, even after she'd given up hoping for his return. His *late* widow, actually. She died—it must be nine or ten years ago, in Paris, where she'd moved to be closer to news of Jean-François. News that never arrived, of course. A genteel woman, despite the disadvantages of her birth. She used to wear her hair pulled back. It was so thick it added a handbreadth to her height. When she powdered it, people told her she looked like the queen. That was before the queen lost her own head, of course. When Éléonore herself was still young, before she'd stopped waiting for Jean-François, when she still hoped to have children of her own one day.

I lean toward the glass and try again to arrange my hair the way she once did. But on me, the effect is ghoulish. I blow out the candle to erase the image, then grope my way in the darkness toward bed and forgetting, not even bothering to say my prayers.

"Good morning, Madame Dalmas de Lapérouse," Antoine says with a grin when I come down the next day. I can't tell if he's trying to restore harmony between us by addressing me this way—or making sure he fires the first salvo in an ongoing clash. Another symptom of long marriage: every statement may be taken kindly or unkindly.

"I wish to go to the civil records office this morning," I announce. It's worth saying just to see my husband's smile vanish.

"What for, my dear?"

I sit down. A servant brings me coffee. I blow lightly over the surface and take a sip. "Too much chicory," I call to the retreating servant, then look across at Antoine. "I wish to see for myself how the name is written."

He sets down his own coffee with a show of exaggerated patience. "I can't take you today," he says. "I have too much to do. Remember we're leaving for La Bessière tomorrow."

So we are. That's why the children are here, to accompany us to the country estate of my husband's family. A long day's coach ride to the southeast, La Bessière is a dull, restful place, perfect for cows, sheep, and children. Ordinarily I welcome the temporary respite from the narrow streets, petty town gossip, and love-starved penitents of Villefranche-de-Rouergue. I also look forward to the company of Jacques, our Bordeaux mastiff, a large, tranquil animal quite devoted to me. But we're likely to be at La Bessière till the end of May. I can't wait that long.

"I'll go to the office myself," I say.

"I need the carriage."

"I'll walk."

"*Jacquette*. You can scarcely make it to the end of the street."

I look away, not wishing to give him the satisfaction of knowing he's hurt me. Nor do I wish to be accused of manipulating him with womanly emotions. A hasty, scorching gulp of coffee brings more excusable tears to my eyes. "I'm going *today*," I say, waving my hand before my scalded mouth.

The reception room to which we're conveyed appears designed to make the perusal of government records as difficult and unpleasant as possible. The room manages to be both airless and cold, the light dim, the long oak table too high, the chairs hard and too low, the registry book a dense, cube-like tome, hard to open, and the handwriting in it crabbed and spidery. I end up standing and leaning over the table to get the proper distance from the page. My right hip aches with the effort.

"Are you the one who wrote this?" I demand of the pimply young man who brought us the registry and stands fidgeting while we examine it.

"I'm not sure, madame," he says. "There are several clerks here." He nervously pinches a bit of skin at his throat.

I point to the entry. "This judgment was entered *yesterday*. The ink is barely dry. Don't you recognize your own hand?"

He peers down at the book, then clears his throat, pulling harder at his throat, as if that might help. "Yes, I—I believe that was me."

"Do you realize that you've written our name three times in three different ways?"

"Madame?"

"Look," I command. He bends over the page. "Here, it's 'Lapeyrouse' with a *y*. And here, 'Lapeirouse' with an *i*. And finally, here"—I jab the page—"it's 'La Peyrouse,' two words. As it happens, not one of these is correct."

"I'm—I'm sorry," he stammers. "I'm always very careful, and—"

"And?"

"And I very much need this position, madame."

"What did the official decree from the king say?"

"It says exactly what this says."

"The *king's decree* also wrote the name three different ways?"

"No, madame—I'm sure it did not."

"I would like to see it."

"Pardon me?"

"If you show us the decree, I will not complain to the head clerk about your orthographic inconstancy."

The young man, whose neck now sports an angry red welt, excuses himself from the room.

Antoine, seated at the table, sighs. "Is this really necessary?"

I ignore him, watching instead a cloud of motes swirling in a weak shaft of light coming through a high window. Does the light make visible the dust already present in the air, I wonder, or is the dust attracted to the light? As a child I used to ask such questions all the time. It drove my poor mother to distraction. But Jean-François would gamely try to satisfy my curiosity. "It's too bad you're not a boy, Jacquette," he told me once. "You could become a great savant and make speeches before the Academy of Sciences." The old questions still intrigue me, but I've stopped asking them aloud, much less expecting any answers.

The young man returns with a superior, an entirely bald individual carrying a thin document case. Though obviously older than the first clerk, his age is impossible to guess: he might be an old man with an unlined face or a still-young man who's lost his hair early.

"Do you know who we are?" I ask him. Antoine stirs discontentedly beside me but says nothing.

"Yes," the bald man says. "Madame Dalmas. Your brother was the great navigator Lapérouse who was tragically lost at sea."

"Exactly. We've waited many years for permission to use his name."

"Yes, madame." He coughs. "Now, how is it you believe the name *ought* to be written?"

I spell it out for him: *L-A-P-É-R-O-U-S-E.* "That is how we spelled it when my brother was alive."

"I see." He pulls a sheet from the document holder. "Now, as you'll see from this copy of the royal decree, that is not the spelling authorized by His Majesty."

I hold it at arm's length and read while Antoine looks over my shoulder:

Louis, by the grace of God, King of France and Navarre, ordains the following: That the honorable Pierre-Jean-Antoine Dalmas, Philippe-François Dalmas, François-Marie-Léon Dalmas, Pierre-Antoine-Victor Dalmas, and Jean-François-Charles-Salvy de Bar-thès, be permitted to add to their names that of La Peyrouse.
                    Paris, Tuileries Chateau, signed, Louis

Well, there it is: La Peyrouse with a *y*, two words. And appended to—not in place of—our current family name. Did the spelling change every time a new person encountered it—or, in the case of our pimply clerk, every time it was encountered? Oh, how many men worked in mindless concert over a quarter century to mistake my lost brother's name?

But that isn't all. I actually find myself preoccupied less with the name itself than with the list of people authorized to use it. It shouldn't surprise me, of course—there they are, my husband, our three sons, and Victoire's son, Charles. I know how the world works; I was just explaining it to Pierre yesterday. Names belong to men, while women belong to names. Yet I *am* surprised—and dismayed—to find myself and Victoire entirely absent from the judgment. Isn't it by virtue of their connection to *us*, Jean-François's sisters, that the men in our lives are permitted to take on his name? I can't stifle a sigh as I hand the document back to the bald clerk.

"Madame," he says, "if I may make so bold, it is my belief that this spelling, with the *y*, is more in keeping with the family's Languedocian roots."

I stare hard at him until he blushes right to the top of his smooth pate.

"Of course, the family may submit a petition asking that the spelling be altered," he quickly adds. "But that may take some time."

Sometimes a husband knows when to remain silent: an occasional gift of long marriage. Antoine says nothing as we drive, nothing when we stop before our house on the rue Basse Saint-Jean, nothing as he helps me down from the carriage and to our front door, only squeezing my hand by way of farewell before setting off on his errands.

In the drawing room, the three older grandchildren look up with entirely-too-innocent faces from what looks like a hastily arranged game of piquet. "Grandmother!" Martiane calls out much too brightly. "Will you play with us?"

"Where's nurse?" I ask.

"She still has a headache," Delphine says.

Still? She's altogether too prone to headaches, this nurse.

"And Pierre?" I ask.

All three children shrug and won't meet my eyes.

"What happened?" I demand.

"Nothing—" Delphine begins, but I put up my hand to silence her and point to Émile. At ten, he's less practiced at dissembling than his older sister and cousin. Right now he's visibly wriggling behind the hand he's been dealt.

"I don't know," the boy mumbles, fanning and unfanning his cards. "He's just crying."

"And the three of you had nothing to do with that, I suppose."

Another collective shrug.

I find Pierre sniffling in a far corner of the library, where he's pulled several volumes of Diderot's *Encyclopedia* from the shelves and is bent over an illustration showing two men fencing. "Are you going to challenge your cousins to a duel?" I ask.

"Grandmother!" he cries. "Where were you?"

I lower myself into a tufted settee. "City hall."

He sets the books aside and climbs up next to me. "They chased me and called me 'Levain Pêche-louche.'"

"What for?"

He slaps a fist against the cushion in frustration. "They're making fun of me because I can't be a Lapérouse."

"I see." Pierre Louvain-Pescheloche. *Levain Pêche-louche.* Suspicious sourdough fishing? "It's not a very imaginative insult," I say.

He folds his arms and pouts beside me. I can't remember my siblings and me—or our cousins—teasing one another as much as my grandchildren do. Perhaps we were too busy trying not to die to indulge in such play. We had our nicknames, of course. As a small child, I'd been unable to pronounce "Jean-François." "Sois, Sois, Sois," I used to call him, following him around our house in Albi, commanding him to be. He in turn took to calling me by the last syllable of *my* name—"Quette," or sometimes "Quette-quette." Even when we were older, both married, he would call me that if we chanced to be alone.

"Next time they make fun of you," I say to Pierre, "tell them their name is wrong."

He looks up at me. "Wrong?"

"It's misspelled."

"Is that why you went to city hall?"

"It is."

"And did you fix it?"

His big round eyes are still watery but no longer sad. I never cease to be amazed by the rapidity with which children's feelings change. Was I like this as a child—morose one moment and hopeful the next? "We have to ask the king to fix it," I explain.

"So why don't you?"

"We can, Pierre. But it may take a very long time." Indeed, it exhausts me just thinking of it. Our original petition was sent to King Louis XVI. Then resubmitted to the National Assembly. Then Emperor Napoleon. And finally, after the Restoration, to the current king, Louis XVIII. "It took twenty-five years to get permission to use the name in the first place," I muse aloud. "How many years will it take to fix the spelling?"

"I don't know," Pierre says. "How many?"

I shrug, conscious of imitating the other grandchildren.

"Another twenty-five years?" he says.

"Could be."

"How old will I be then?"

"You tell me, Pierre."

He doesn't have to think long. He may be tiresome, but at least he's not stupid. "Thirty-two!"

"You'll be a grown man."

"And how old will *you* be?"

"Me?" I laugh. "I'll be long dead."

Pierre falls silent for a moment, then tugs at my sleeve. I expect him to say something sentimental and childish—perhaps expressing the hope that I will never die. Or making an outrageous guess at my age: *"Two hundred?"* But instead he says, "Grandmother, did you find out if you could give me the name too?"

"Oh, child," I say, my heart pulled between impatience and sympathy. "It's not mine to give. The king didn't grant me or Aunt Victoire permission to use the name. That went only to our husbands and sons."

"But you said—"

"Enough talk of names," I say. I haul myself to my feet, groaning with the effort. Every day it gets a little harder to stand up from a chair, to raise myself out of bed, to fight the downward pull of the earth.

After lunch, I send for a cab, no mean task in our town. When it finally arrives, it's an equipage so shabby I'm embarrassed to be seen in it. But it can't be helped. "Take me to the chapel of the Pénitents Bleus," I tell the driver, a droopy man who bears an alarming resemblance to his horse. When we get to the chapel entrance on the rue du Sénéchal, I instruct him to ring at the side door and tell Père Armand that Madame de Lapérouse is there.

The chapel looks much like other such chapels—a simple rectangular box symmetrically punctuated by stained-glass windows and topped with a lanterned dome. Antoine and I owned the building for a time, acquiring it in 1796—the Year Four, we were obliged to call it then—when the misbegotten Republic was filling its empty coffers by selling off church properties. I had joined the lay order after marrying Antoine and moving to Villefranche-de-Rouergue, and hated to think of the building being turned into a theater or tavern—or worse, falling into the hands of our rivals, the upstart Pénitents Noirs. After the horrors of the Revolution finally abated, we had the building restored, then donated it to the association. It flourishes in its way—we have our own priest who reads Mass once daily and twice on Sundays, and every September our people lead the procession on the feast day of St. Jerome. Last year I was named the chapel's "prioress," which sounds very ecclesiastical and even a little nunnish but really just means I have the thankless task of collecting dues from wealthy-enough members who seem to believe that the Christian duty of stewardship does not apply to them. When some of these same individuals fawn over my husband after Mass, it's all I can do to keep from flinging my missal at their heads.

I compensate myself for these vexations by coming to the chapel whenever I need solitude. Père Armand and I have an understanding about this. And indeed, here he is, coming through the double front doors and bounding down the steps to help me out of the shabby carriage. I lean on his shoulder as I step out, struck as always by the firmness of the muscles I can feel through his brown serge.

"I'm delighted to see you, Madame de Lapérouse," he says. A clever young man who knows exactly where his stipend comes from, Père Armand has always called me Madame de Lapérouse in private and Madame Dalmas in front of my family.

"It's now Madame *Dalmas* de Lapérouse," I tell him.

"Indeed?" He takes my arm to help me up the four shallow steps to the entrance. "It's official, then?"

"Yes," I say. "Not so much a name *change* as a name . . . *enhancement*, as it turns out. And they've misspelled Lapérouse." I try to say this lightly, but my voice unaccountably catches.

"Oh, madame."

The sympathy in his voice nearly makes me burst into tears. "It's nothing," I say as briskly as I can manage. "What can one expect, after all? We had our little revolution, but they killed all the wrong people. The bureaucrats remain our oppressors."

He guides me up the remaining steps and into the building. The place never fails to soothe me. It's the resonant silence of the long, narrow sanctuary with its unadorned stone walls. It's the tamed light streaming through the eight hexagonal stained-glass windows. It's the satisfaction of knowing that something pleasing in the world exists because of my money and my effort. It's also the sureness of the young priest's hand under my elbow as he escorts me to the tiny side-chapel at the back of the nave, my favorite spot in the building. It's the comfort of having someone in my life who knows what I need without being asked.

Père Armand helps me to the iron rail, waits while I light a candle, then leads me to the small wooden stool kept there for my especial use. I shut my eyes against the pain in my hip as I ease myself down. At home, this ache is a depressing reminder of my physical deterioration, but here it feels more purposeful, as if it were part of my devotional practice. When it subsides, I open my eyes. I can hear Armand's footfalls receding as he retreats to the apse. Before me, a simple white vase filled with jonquils graces the plain oak altar. No doubt left over from Easter Sunday, the bright yellow flowers seem to emit their own light and warmth.

Éléonore would love this, I think, my mind turning again, unbidden, to Jean-François's wife. She had excelled at the simple flower arrangement. Whenever I visited her in Albi, she had something in every room—a glassful of woodland flowers she'd picked on a walk, a bouquet of roses spilling from a pitcher, camellia blossoms floating in a bowl. Not that I visited all that often. Villefranche-de-Rouergue is a half-day's journey from Albi. And we were never intimate, she and I. None of us had approved of the marriage, of course. She didn't hold that against us, for she wasn't a resentful person, and anyway, she could hardly blame us. She was a Creole, for goodness' sake—the daughter of a hospital administrator in Île de France. Once Jean-François left, the distance between all of us became harder to ignore. When she eventually decamped for Paris, we were relieved, I think Éléonore not least of all.

I last saw her in 1803, back in Albi, on the occasion of my niece's marriage. I hadn't seen Éléonore in some years and was shocked by the change in her appearance. She'd grown skinny and pale, her steps slow, her breathing labored. She wasn't yet fifty but looked older. It rather confirmed a theory I had, that while childbirth aged women in their earlier years, women who'd never had children more than made up for it later. It's not an idea I dwell on much these days; a woman who's survived to seventy looks old regardless.

Weddings don't, as a rule, allow for much in the way of meaningful conversation with others. I spent most of that week managing Victoire's nerves by pretending to care about every little setback; in mollifying me, the mother of the bride rose above each problem, a model of calm and grace. But one afternoon, Éléonore and I found ourselves alone and un-occupied in my sister's drawing room. After dispensing with pointless pleasantries about the bride and groom's prospects for lasting happiness, an awkward silence fell between us, broken even more awkwardly when a maid appeared with a tea tray and said, "I thought you might like some tea, Madame de Lapérouse," and we both said, "Thank you."

Éléonore looked up, her blue eyes regarding me with a kind of sur-prised empathy. I'd never told her that Victoire and I had petitioned to use Jean-François's name, much less that we'd already started using it in Albi, where people knew us first as Jean-François's sisters and secondarily as our husbands' wives. Antoine said we ought to seek Éléonore's blessing before submitting the petition, but I hadn't seen the need for that. It was only her name by marriage, and a brief enough marriage at that.

I met her glance with equanimity. She poured out a cup of tea and handed it to me, then said, "Do you think Jean-François could still be alive?"

Well, this was unexpected. He'd been gone—eighteen years. The ex-pedition had been declared lost for thirteen. I stared at my sister-in-law, quite unable to formulate a reply.

"Over the years I've met some of the other wives," Éléonore went on. "Many of them said they *knew* their husbands were still alive."

"Hope fed by desperation," I said.

"A few of them seemed equally sure that their men were dead."

"The less happily married ones," I suggested.

Éléonore laughed at this, a small trilling laugh that reminded me of her cheerfulness when she'd first come to Albi as Jean-François's bride, a cheerfulness that seemed immune to our collective disapproval. But now the laugh turned into a dry, papery cough. When it subsided, she said, her voice quieter: "Do you think there can be such bonds between people? Bonds so strong they can communicate over vast distances?"

"It seems a question for a philosopher," I said.

"I've never had any sense of Jean-François's fate," she said. "I thought that you—" She pressed her lips together before going on. "You may re-member that I also lost a brother in the expedition."

I clinked the spoon against the side of my teacup. I'd forgotten about her brother and was not pleased by the reminder. He'd been arrested for assaulting their sister, then given a choice between going to prison or accompanying Jean-François as a volunteer. He should have chosen prison, I thought. He could have spent the ensuing decade happily assaulting aristocrats. "I'm sorry, Éléonore," I said, then thought about why she'd mentioned him. "Are you saying you know what befell your brother?"

She looked away, embarrassed. "I don't *know*, of course," she said. "But I do have an inkling—or I did, early on—that Frédéric might still be alive. Now, of course, it's been so long . . ." Her voice trailed off, then she looked directly at me. "You are Jean-François's sister and knew him the longest," she said. "If he were able to convey his fate to anyone, it would be you."

I shook my head and said nothing. Her unjealous, clear-eyed sadness was more painful to me than an undisciplined episode of tears would have been. I kept my lips shut tight, fearful of revealing the raw anguish I felt welling up inside. As soon as I could manage, I made my excuses and got up.

"Madame Dalmas," Éléonore said, also rising. "I would be very happy, and honored, if your family were to adopt the name Lapérouse. It would be an enormous comfort to me, in fact."

I left the room. My niece was married the next day. Éléonore returned to Paris, where, I learned later, she successfully petitioned Napoleon for a small pension. I never saw her again.

You were his sister and knew him the longest.

And what was it that I knew? That Jean-François was a man maddeningly indifferent to society and his status in it. That he would have found my adoption of his name amusing and my distress over its misspelling incomprehensible. That he would have delighted in the noisiness of children. That the fading and early death of Éléonore would have broken his heart.

I also knew that he had never communicated his fate to me—or if he had, I had been too insensible to hear him. Every year it grows more certain, not only that he will not return, but that I will go to my grave not knowing what happened to him or to the expedition that bears his name. His name is all I have left of him. An old woman may be forgiven, I think, for hoarding a few things over which she may still exercise some sway.

I turn at the sound of a footstep—not Armand's. It's my husband, hat and cane in hand, standing just outside the side-chapel and regarding me with a look of patient indulgence. *What are you doing here?* I want to cry. But that hardly seems an appropriate utterance in church, even if the church is a private chapel one used to own. Anyway, it's entirely obvious Antoine has come to take me home.

"Monsieur Dalmas de Lapérouse," I say.

His face opens into an expression I have not seen in a long time, an expression of pleased surprise and gratitude. I'm reminded of him as a younger man and younger husband, and the heat rises to my face as I realize: he's been waiting two days to hear me call him "Monsieur Dalmas de Lapérouse." It would be so easy—it's so tempting—to quash his pleasure, to say, *How considerate of Jean-François to disappear so you could improve your name.* But—well, we're still in church, so I let him help me up, and I wave my farewell to Père Armand as my husband escorts me outside.

Helping me down the steps, Antoine says, "Victor and François and I have written to Paris about the name, Jacquette. And we've written to Léon to get his help. With his connections, he may be able to see it through better than we can." Léon, Martiane and Émile's father, is a naval commissary in Vannes.

When I say nothing, he adds: "We may not live to see it fixed, Jacquette. But our children will. And I predict that within a generation or two, they will drop the 'Dalmas' and call themselves only 'Lapérouse.'"

I pause at the bottom of the steps and look up into the face of the man who has been my husband for fifty-one years. "Won't that bother you?"

"Only a little."

At the carriage, I'm startled by Pierre's impish face grinning at me from the window.

"Oh, what did you bring *him* for?" I ask.

"Because he's your favorite."

"He most certainly is not."

"Then you may believe I've brought him to punish you for the trouble of having to collect you," he says, helping me in.

"Grandmother!" Pierre cries when I seat myself opposite him. Quite heedless of my frown, he leaves his seat and sits next to me, then takes my hand. I've never liked holding hands. And his fingers are damp and sticky—no doubt he's eaten something sweet and not washed afterward. But as I said earlier, his hands are stronger than mine, so I let him.

FOURTEEN

RELICS

Hôtel de La Marine, Paris, March 1829

Spoon & Fork

Barthélemy de Lesseps picked up the spoon and fork, one in each hand, and held them flat against his palms as if weighing them. Peter Dillon watched the Frenchman with a mixture of admiration and anxiety. "The islanders had lots of silver," he found himself explaining. "But most of it they'd beat into wires for rings and bracelets and the like. These few we found intact in their original forms."

He knew Lesseps was sixty-three, but the man looked younger, too young to have been a grown man forty years earlier. Perhaps it was his clothes: fashionable blue coat worn over white waistcoat, cambric shirt, neat gray breeches. He was also thin and agile, with a full head of barely graying hair and clear blue eyes. He'd been introduced to Dillon as "Monsieur de Lesseps, our consul general in Portugal," but Dillon wondered if he could get away with calling him *Viscount* de Lesseps in his book. This aristocratic gentleman was the perfect figure for the narrative's triumphant conclusion in Paris.

But those clear blue eyes were now examining, with an expression of careful detachment, the utensils Dillon had brought back from the island of Vanikoro in the South Pacific. The well-fed and medal-bedecked Baron Hyde de Neuville, minister of the Navy and the man who'd arranged this meeting, stood by watching his countryman with a kind of pompous intensity. Dillon had thought of this meeting with Lesseps, taking place in the most ornate room he'd ever set foot in, as simply the crowning formality to cap his achievements. But he realized now that that wasn't how the two Frenchmen saw it. For them, it wasn't a meeting so much as a *test.* A test he could fail. Even though his discoveries had been touted in newspapers in Sydney, Calcutta, and London. Despite his audience with His Majesty King Charles X. Notwithstanding the Légion d'honneur he'd been promised, or the monetary reward for information on the missing frigates, or the annuity of four thousand francs. None of that mattered—all of it could be rescinded, in fact—if this man, the only known survivor of the Lapérouse expedition, missing these forty years, declined to confirm his findings.

For his part, Barthélemy de Lesseps wished the tall, red-headed Irishman would not stand so very close. The man's recently re-dyed coat and resoled shoes fairly exuded, not just the smell of dye and glue, but an anxious wish to please and be liked. Lesseps had heard rumors about Dillon—that he was a fearless and skilled ship captain, a savvy trader in sandalwood and native artifacts, a man well-versed in the cultures and languages of the South Seas. But he was also known as a brute who dragged his wife along on his travels, beat her when he got drunk, and carried on liaisons with island women at every port of call. The missionaries hated him, as did many of his former associates, who tended to regard him, not as fearless and skilled, but as foolhardy and very, very lucky. Odd how meek the man seemed now, Lesseps thought. He'd met such men before: tyrannical in their own spheres but timid, even obsequious, before men they believed to be their social betters.

He looked at the silver utensils in his hand and sighed. When the minister's letter came, asking him back to France to examine objects recovered from the South Pacific, objects suggesting that the final resting place of the *Boussole* and the *Astrolabe* had at last been discovered, he'd departed on the first ship out of Lisbon and hired the fastest postilions out of Marseilles to convey him to Paris. For wasn't it *this* for which he'd been granted long life through such dangerous times? He'd sat forward in the carriage seat, willing the horses to go faster, impelled by a sense of destiny.

But now he couldn't help it: he wished someone else—someone with more dignity, someone more, well, *French*—had solved the mystery, not this gruff Irishman of uncertain parentage and little education. What could a scarred spoon or tarnished fork prove, anyway? They looked like items one might find anywhere.

"It is hard to say," he said at last, diffident about his English but aware that both Dillon and the minister were waiting for him to speak. He turned the spoon over, then moved to one of the room's tall, recessed windows to examine it more closely. At the base of the bowl he could just make out a worn design—a seashell, perhaps—and experienced a frisson of familiarity, a memory of elegant officers' dinners aboard the *Astrolabe*, wineglasses glinting in candlelight, meals served on china and eaten with polished utensils. The back of the fork seemed to have a similar design. He ran his thumb over the ribbed silver, then turned to Dillon: "We did have forks and spoons like these."

Dillon exhaled noisily and Lesseps stepped back, put off by an unpleasant mix of fish and tobacco that wafted his way. "Though I suppose such spoons are common enough," he added, setting the items down. He heard Dillon inhale sharply and wondered if he might control the man's respiration by alternating encouraging comments with dismissive ones.

Fleur-de-Lis

Unnerved, Dillon led the way to the next item—a decayed fir plank that one of his men had found in the threshold of a hut in Vanikoro. The hut's owner had not been home at the time, but an elderly man who claimed to be the village chief had been pleased to receive one of Dillon's hatchets in exchange for the post. It had been their most successful day on the island: a village full of objects related to the wrecks, most of the villagers away on a fishing expedition, and the "chief" only too happy to enrich himself at his neighbors' expense. Afterward Dillon had amused himself imagining the villagers' reactions when they returned home to discover most of their prized possessions gone.

But Monsieur de Lesseps was regarding the board skeptically, tilting his elegant head, first to one side, then the other. Dillon rushed forward. "See?" he said, pointing to one end of the plank. "Right here."

Lesseps leaned in and squinted, then suddenly widened his eyes. "A fleur-de-lis?"

"Still visible after all this time," the minister said helpfully. He spoke English with an American accent, a particular quite at odds with his aristocratic dress and demeanor.

Lesseps replied in French. His neutral expression made it impossible for Dillon to guess what he was saying. Perhaps he suspected the item was fake—a weathered board on which someone had painted the outline of a fleur-de-lis. Dillon wanted to interject, to tell Lesseps about Monsieur Chaigneau, the French attaché who'd accompanied the expedition and witnessed the retrieval and inventory of every item. The minister knew about Chaigneau; surely he would defend Dillon's methods and the authenticity of the post.

"We wondered the same thing, Monsieur de Lesseps," the minister said in English. "But we know of no other French voyage lost in that part of the world."

So *that* was Lesseps's question. An intelligent question. Dillon was relieved he hadn't interjected.

Lesseps nodded, then switched back to English himself: "There were many fleurs-de-lis on both vessels, of course. But this—" He reached out and ran a finger along the rough surface. "It might have been a—how do you say?—*ornamentation* on the *Boussole*'s stern."

Not that he'd had such intimate knowledge of the ships' architecture, especially the *Boussole*, which he'd been on board only twice in his two years with the expedition. The truth was he'd spent most of his time on the voyage on the *Astrolabe*, playing cards with anyone off duty, reading other men's books, drinking other men's wine. As the expedition's Russian interpreter, he'd had nothing official to do till they reached Petropavlovsk. The first year of the voyage he'd befriended the two La Borde brothers, the younger of whom was a cabinmate. The brothers had begun teaching him navigation. "We're going to make you useful yet, Lesseps," they said. But a violent tidal current one unforeseen summer morning in Alaska had taken the brothers and ended Lesseps's career as a navigator. It had been his first lesson in the cruel unpredictability of life. No loss since then—not even the deaths of two of his own children—had shocked him in the same way. The memory of the La Borde brothers still stung, as if the losses sustained in his youth, before he'd learned to protect himself from attachment, would never quite heal.

"Monsieur de Lesseps?" the minister called from behind. "May I interest you in some cannons?"

Presumably the minister insisted on speaking in English for Dillon's sake. Lesseps found it incredibly irritating. "Are they for sale?" he asked in French.

Brass Guns

The cannons, four quite large and three smaller, had been placed on wooden pallets to protect the room's marble floors. Of all the items the minister had chosen to show Lesseps, these guns, it seemed to Dillon, were the most generic and therefore least likely to create a clear association with the expedition. He thought of other items he'd salvaged—an ornate silver candelabra, tarnished and bent but very distinctive, came immediately to mind—that might have compelled the inscrutable Monsieur de Lesseps to say, "Why, yes! This is the very one Monsieur de Lapérouse had in his quarters . . ."

But he hadn't been consulted about which items would be displayed— an oversight that, it now occurred to Dillon, suggested the minister considered him a mere transporter of *stuff* rather than the knowledgeable explorer who'd recognized the items' importance and successfully negotiated the myriad difficulties involved in effecting their recovery. It was a sour realization, one of many that had steadily eroded the elation of the initial discovery three years before. He reflected, not for the first time, that Fortune was indeed a bitch. A man could fulfill his most cherished dreams—and hadn't he plied the waters of the South Pacific for decades hoping to discover the traces of Lapérouse and his frigates?—yet find himself still subject to petty indignities from men of "superior" birth.

Lesseps approached the pallet, reached out to touch the worn and oxidized surface of one of the larger guns, and said with a boyish grin, "I never dared touch any of the cannons, but I always wanted to."

The man's good cheer intensified Dillon's annoyance. Surely the iden-
tification of items from a lost expedition—an expedition whose loss you'd
been mercifully spared—deserved some gravity? "Touch them all you like
now, Monsieur de Lesseps," Dillon couldn't stop himself from barking.
"There's no one to say aught."

Lesseps turned to look at Dillon. Had he offended somehow? Might they
now be treated to a display of the Irishman's famous temper? He had a
sudden urge to climb onto the pallet and straddle one of the cannons—
see how that deflated the man's self-importance. But of course he'd never
do such a thing—not in front of Baron Hyde de Neuville, whose good
graces still mattered. And not even in front of this humorless Irish trader,
who was probably writing a book about his adventures. It wouldn't do to
appear in such an account as an antic fool.

He drew himself up and spoke with as much formality as he could
muster. "We had cannons like these on both ships," he said, indicating
the larger ones. "They were never fired—not in anger, that is," he said,
remembering a salvo before the launch of a hot-air balloon in Concepción
and formal gun salutes on entering the harbors in Monterey and Macao
and Petropavlovsk. "Not while I was with them," he added, remembering
what happened in the Navigators. Not that he *remembered*—the massacre happened after he left the expedition. But he remembered getting the
terrible news, and he wondered again how it could have happened, for—
pointing to the smaller cannons—"We had guns just like this mounted to
the bows of each of our landing boats." He heard Dillon exhale again with
relief, but he was no longer inclined to make fun of the man. For really—
how *was* it that four boats, so equipped, and manned, moreover, by armed
officers and marines, could not overpower islanders with *rocks*? Captain
de Langle had died in the battle, as had eleven other men, including
Monsieur de Lamanon, whose sardonic pomposity Lesseps had always
found more amusing than annoying, and a fusilier named Louis David
who'd made a small fortune at cards.

Their deaths had never seemed quite real—*paper* deaths, he thought
of them, their only proof the reports sent back from Botany Bay. Even less
real, of course, were the deaths of the rest of them—*air* deaths, he regarded

them, deaths by supposition. He'd refused to succumb to sorrow while hope remained of the expedition's eventual return, but as hope faded, grief had not taken its place—as if grief had its appointed season beyond which it became unavailable to experience.

"Are you all right, Monsieur de Lesseps?" Dillon asked.

He'd been unconsciously holding his hand against his left side, site of a chronic, hollow pain. "I'm fine," he said, dropping his hand. "What is next?"

Sword Guard & Grip

Dillon moved toward a sword guard and handle displayed on a red velvet cloth. "This was the first thing we found," he said, picking up the sword guard. He raised the other piece. "The handle we found later but it obviously belonged to the same sword." He brought the pieces together to show how they fit. Lesseps nodded his appreciation.

"This was what began it all," Dillon continued, separating the pieces and holding up the guard again. He explained how he'd found it on Tikopia, a tiny outlier of the Solomon Islands, where it was discovered hanging around the neck of a lascar who called himself Joe. Joe told Dillon he'd procured the item in Vanikoro, an island two days' sail west, a place filled with such objects, the detritus of two European ships that had been wrecked there many years before. Joe claimed an old white man, a survivor of the wreck, had sold it to him.

Dillon paused. It was clear from the perfunctory way Lesseps was nodding that he had heard the story already. The minister and the king had both nodded in the same way in his meetings with them. Dillon set the pieces down and stifled a groan. When he'd so readily shared his story with every newspaper that approached him, he hadn't anticipated the way the story would get ahead of him. His discoveries had been widely reported in France before he ever set foot in the country, picked up from Australian and Indian and English accounts. The advance fame had opened every door in Paris for him, of course. But now that he was *here*, in France, where he'd most looked forward to telling his story, he discovered that everyone already knew it.

Not that he'd revealed *everything*, of course. No one knew, for instance,

that it was impossible for him to see the sword guard without resenting
Joe all over again for refusing to accompany his expedition. The lascar
spoke both English and Tikopian quite well; he would have been an able
interpreter. Instead, Dillon had had to make do with Martin Buschart, a
flabby, tattooed alcoholic Prussian who spoke neither language properly,
despite having lived on Tikopia for a decade after deserting an American
whaler. And then there was Rathea, the Tikopian who claimed he'd just
returned from a two-year stay on Vanikoro. But when they finally got to
Vanikoro, no one recognized him or could make any sense of his speech,
which sounded to Dillon suspiciously like Fijian. The ineffective chain of
translation from Dillon to Buschart to Rathea to the Vanikorans and back
would have been comical had it not been so entirely exasperating.

It meant he was unsure of the account he was giving of the wrecks,
especially regarding any survivors. He reported that a storm had driven
the frigates onto the reef, that a group of Frenchmen had made it ashore,
that from the ships' wreckage they'd crafted a small boat, and that most
of them had sailed away in it, promising to return. This was largely Joe's
account, however, and although Joe had seemed a credible enough fellow,
he wasn't an eyewitness. It had proved impossible to confirm the story in
Vanikoro. The only thing Dillon knew for sure was that no Frenchman—
or European of any kind—remained on the island.

"Mr. Dillon," the baron said. "Monsieur de Lesseps was just saying
that all the officers on the voyage carried swords like this."

"Indeed?" Dillon looked at Lesseps. The older man was looking intently at the sword guard and grip. Dillon suddenly understood: Lesseps
wasn't here to discredit Dillon; he *wanted* to believe the mystery solved.
And why shouldn't he? No doubt it had gnawed at him these forty years.

Lesseps lifted the guard and grip and held them against each other as
Dillon had. With no side rings or loops or much in the way of a pommel,
the guard itself fashioned with a pattern of woven silver, it had been the
elegant and simple hilt of an elegant and simple sword. He'd had one just
like it but had left it behind on the *Astrolabe* when he disembarked, taking
only essentials for the long trip across Russia. He remembered missing it
one night when he and Igor Golikoff, the Russian officer who'd accompa-

nied him as far as Irkutsk, had been stuck in a filthy yurt waiting for a blizzard to pass. They had nothing but frozen reindeer to eat and only Golikoff's dull saber with which to slice it. They tried to thaw and cook the shredded slices, but the fire just filled the yurt with smoke, and in the end they'd simply eaten the slices raw, then dispensed with slicing and chewed directly on the slabs. Afterward, cold and nauseated, they'd clung together for warmth among a pile of smelly furs in the middle of the yurt.

"This could have been *my* sword," Lesseps said in English, as much to end the memory as to return to the task at hand. "I left a sword behind when I disembarked."

"What an extraordinary thing that would be," Dillon said, his eyes wide.

Lesseps felt the first inkling of something like sympathy with the Irishman. "Yes," he said. "Quite extraordinary." To think he might be reunited with an object he'd left behind forty-two years ago on a ship off the coast of Kamchatka—after it was recovered from a South Pacific island where he'd never set foot! He examined the pieces again, admiring the handiwork, still evident despite the wear. One rarely saw craftsmanship like this anymore, he thought, but he didn't say so aloud. He never expressed any yearning for the past. It was the primary lesson of his eventful life, seeing him safely through the upheavals of the Revolution and the Terror, the ascendancy and fall of Napoleon, the restoration of the monarchy.

He was equally careful about expressing enthusiasm for the status quo. The current ultraroyalist regime, for instance, could not last. This year or next, Charles X would fall. The self-satisfied baron standing next to him would lose his position and return to exile, perhaps back in America, where he'd spent the years of Napoleon's rule—a fitting end for the obdurate monarchist. But Lesseps didn't share these predictions with anyone. A change in government wouldn't affect him. In a few days, he'd leave once more for Lisbon, where he'd continue as consul general, probably until he died. This was the other lesson of survival as a modern Frenchman: make oneself useful outside the country.

Not that he'd expected to end up in Portugal. Almost from infancy he'd been groomed to become the French ambassador to Russia. When he told Golikoff that they would meet again, he'd been *certain*—not that he would see Golikoff again but that he would return to Russia. Yet other men, less well acquainted with Russia and Russian and Russians but better connected at home, kept winning the post over him. By way of consolation he'd been appointed secretary of the embassy in Constantinople, only to end up imprisoned there for three years—he and his growing family—thanks to Napoleon's invasion of Egypt. When they were finally released, a rumor that their ship had lepers on board forced them to remain in quarantine for a month off the coast of Marseilles, biding their time in a moldering, leaky ship filled with refugees.

So when Napoleon invited him to join his suite with the Grand Armée in 1812, he was thrilled—thrilled to be back in service, thrilled to be close to the center of power, thrilled most of all to be going back to Russia. It couldn't turn out worse than Constantinople, he reasoned. Oh, how that misapprehension would return to him in all its bitter irony through the calamities that followed—the bloodbaths at Smolensk and Borodino, the terrifying Moscow fire, the horrors of the retreat! He'd kept thinking he saw Golikoff—in the light cavalry that harassed them as they fled, in the ruined faces of the peasants whose food they stole, in the hunched postures of their own soldiers, plodding slowly forward or stopped on the roadside, sleeping or dying or already dead. Everyone had something—a cut of military jacket, a mustache still neatly trimmed, a stolidity of expression, a whiff of tobacco smoke—that reminded him of his old companion.

After the peace, he'd petitioned Emperor Alexander and, after Alexander's death, his brother, Emperor Nicholas, for clemency and permission to return to Russia, but to no avail.

"Monsieur de Lesseps?"

Lesseps looked around at Dillon and the minister and laughed. "I was just recalling the days when fashionable young Frenchmen carried swords instead of canes," he said airily.

Millstone

The last item was a small millstone, broken in two, lying on a heavy floorcloth. Dillon explained, trying not to sound too shamefaced, that it had split in half when they rolled it over in Vanikoro. "We found it in the same village as the post with the fleur-de-lis," he added. He didn't add that they'd faced such rough seas returning to the ship that night that he'd nearly heaved it over the side of the boat. Or that it should have broken into more pieces when they hauled it aboard; his men, tired and storm-tossed, had dropped it, crushing Rathea's right foot. The Tikopian had hollered so loud and so long that Dillon finally threatened to tie him to the stone and throw him overboard.

Poor Rathea. Dillon couldn't remember the wiry old islander without a simultaneous upwelling of rage and grief and guilt. Rathea hadn't belonged on the expedition. He was just an old man talking big before the white man who paid so generously for the Vanikoran trinkets. Once the initial excitement abated, he'd tried to back out of the expedition. Dillon, desperate for an interpreter, had compelled him to remain, first by promising that Rathea would return to Tikopia laden with riches, and when that didn't work, by pretending he'd had dreams filled with portents should Rathea fail to cooperate. But he underestimated—by over a year, as it turned out—how long the voyage would take. It wasn't his fault. A leaky ship, uncooperative weather, unexpected detours, legal and bureaucratic difficulties, incompetent officers, troublesome passengers, outbreaks of illness—all conspired to create delay after delay after delay. It was too much for Rathea. Dillon had seen men die of many things—tropical fevers, accidents, drowning, scurvy, suicide. Rathea died of homesickness— only four days before the brig assigned to take him and Buschart back to Tikopia set sail.

And now here was Lesseps, crouched in judgmental silence before the millstone that had cost Dillon so much trouble. His mood darkened by memories of Rathea, Dillon now wondered wretchedly if he'd brought back a native tool. Had he taken some island woman's grinding stone for no reason? But then Lesseps put one hand over his mouth and said in a hoarse whisper, "This is the best thing you have."

Dillon stepped forward and helped Lesseps back to his feet. He was surprised by how bony the Frenchman felt through his coat sleeve.

"We had two millstones on the *Astrolabe*," Lesseps said. He explained that the stone had been connected to an ingenious windmill Captain de Langle had set up on the decks of both frigates to provide fresh flour. Dillon had read the published accounts of the voyage and knew this but remained silent, holding in check his mounting elation over Lesseps's recognition of the stone. "We always had fresh bread on board," Lesseps added. "It astonished every European we met." He paused. "We gave a spare stone to the priests in Monterey for the native women to grind corn," he went on. "It looked exactly like this. Only—not broken, of course."

Silence fell over the three men. Dillon could hear the asynchronous ticking of two clocks—a longcase clock in the corner, its wooden housing topped with a gold finial, and a second clock on the mantel, its plain white face peeking out from an absurdly embellished gold setting. If he only listened hard enough, he thought, he might compel the clocks to tick together, and all would be well with the world.

"Mr. Dillon," the minister finally said, coming forward to shake his hand. "I congratulate you. We were already quite sure of your achievement, of course, as evidenced by the honors our government has bestowed on you. But Monsieur de Lesseps's testimony has confirmed it. You will be remembered forever as the man who discovered the wrecks of the Lapérouse expedition."

Dillon wanted to shout, to embrace the minister, to pick up Lesseps and twirl him around. He'd done it! He would collect the reward money. He would finish his book, which would be published to great acclaim. Learned societies throughout Europe would seek him out. He could retire from trading and sailing, perhaps pick up a diplomatic post somewhere. His children, the sons and daughter of the *Chevalier* Dillon, would marry well and assume their proper places in society. *They* would not be cowed by golden rooms and overdressed barons.

But then he saw the way Lesseps's face had collapsed at the word "wrecks," and he restrained himself. He grasped the older man's hand. "Monsieur," he said, "my great regret is that I could not bring back any survivors."

Lesseps nodded and returned Dillon's grasp. He could see the elation in the Irishman's eyes and the effort it took to contain it, and he felt something almost like regard for the man. For Dillon seemed to understand the way his success had, finally and definitively, consigned to their deaths nearly two hundred men, the companions of Lesseps's youth. And if his fate was to bear the doomed expedition's documents safely back to France and then, years later, to identify remnants from the wrecks—what remained for him to do in this world? He felt depleted and old, and he must have shown it, for here was the minister helping him into a chair.

He sat before the broken millstone. Grooves remained visible on its weathered surface. He'd probably eaten bread made from flour ground on this very stone. He suddenly remembered a fig tart served on a beach in Chile: the crust, delectable in its buttery, crumbly perfection, might have originated from this stone as well. Funny to recall that after so long. Over the years his memories of the expedition hadn't just dimmed, as memories do; they'd lost the pressure of authenticity. More and more they seemed like someone else's memories. Or like something he'd read in a book. Occasionally he would find himself stopping short and wondering if any of it had actually happened.

This had come to him most forcefully some ten years earlier when a Monsieur Dufresne called on him during a rare furlough in Paris. Thin and stooped, with unkempt white hair that fell over his eyes, Dufresne had perched on the edge of a chair and breathlessly related the ups and downs—mostly downs—that had befallen him since leaving the expedition in Macao. He'd apparently bounced between various posts in the controller's office of the Navy, lost all his family wealth during the Revolution, and shown an unusual aptitude for attaching himself to men about to lose their influence, their money, or their heads. He asked Lesseps for help securing a post, and when Lesseps demurred, asked for a loan. Afterward, Lesseps stood at the window watching the man's retreating gray figure and reflected that although the visit should have confirmed for him the reality of the expedition, it had done the opposite. For he'd had absolutely no recollection whatsoever of the man who introduced himself as his onetime shipmate on the *Astrolabe*.

Yet here, before him, carefully laid out on tables and over the floor, was tangible evidence that it *had* happened. Perhaps even evidence that *he* had been there. It grieved him. It comforted him. He allowed a tear to fall—it seemed the polite thing to do, given Dillon's show of restraint. And wouldn't it be a nice detail for Dillon's book?

He stood up and held out his hand. "Congratulations, Mr. Dillon," he said.

EPILOGUE:
FOLIE À PLUSIEURS

We were explorers on a voyage of discovery. Our charge from His Majesty, God rest his soul, was to complete and perfect the globe. We understood that to mean finding new places. Naturally, along the way it might fall to us to fix the coordinates of locations that lesser navigators had mismapped. We might fill in the dotted shorelines that others had seen but dimly, hampered by winds or fog or laziness. We might even disprove the existence of islands reported long ago and drawn ever since on our maps though never confirmed. But the real excitement, the promise of *glory*, lay in discovering places no European had ever seen, places that had been empty on the world's maps—terra incognita or blank expanses of ocean—until *we* found and measured and named them.

We were patient. It took a long time to get anywhere that hadn't been traversed by scores of expeditions before us. We knew the work of that first year would consist mostly of fixing rather than discovering. Our first task was to locate Isle Grande in the South Atlantic, reported by La Roche more than a hundred years earlier and not seen since. La Roche had described a large, uninhabited island supplied with trees and water and fish and an excellent port on its east coast—an ideal base for French whaling ships. Forty days we looked for it—forty days of heavy seas and gales and squall after squall during which we forgot what it meant to be dry or warm. We called our captain Noah behind his back and referred to our ship as the Ark. We cursed La Roche for his fanciful sighting.

Wishful Thinking Island, we began to call our quarry. It was with relief more than disappointment that we declared the island imaginary and made for Cape Horn.

Less arduous was dispatching that persistent myth of a "Davis Land" off the coast of Chile. That one had been cluttering up charts of the southeast Pacific for two hundred years, ever since some English pirate named Davis claimed to see a low, sandy island five hundred leagues offshore and named it after himself. We wondered about men like La Roche and Davis. Were they liars or bad navigators? Forgers or confused observers? Maybe they'd mistaken cloud banks or fog for landmasses, some of us suggested. Others scoffed at this—surely any shipload of seasoned sailors can tell the difference between a cloud and terra firma. We argued for a while, but it was good-natured debate. For we were now sailing into the open and, we believed, still explorable Pacific, and we were ready to discover—ready below with maps outspread and the journals of our predecessors open to the relevant pages, ready on deck and aloft with our keen young eyes and burnished telescopes.

Only there was almost nothing left to find. Captain Cook, that greedy bastard, had made off with most of what was left besides Antarctica. We surveyed the Hawaiian Islands—we called them the Sandwich Isles back then—and created our own charts, but they didn't improve much on the existing ones. We did land on Maui, the first Europeans to do so, and that bay still bears our captain's name—La Perouse Bay. We pressed him to claim the island in the name of France. Claiming territory for our king seemed very much of a piece with completing the globe for him— especially territory the English had seen first but not bothered to walk around upon. Our captain declined, however. "Who are we to take possession of this place?" he said. "These people have lived here for hundreds of years. Do they have no rights, simply because we have muskets?" We felt chastened and puzzled and, to be frank, a little cheated by this response.

Making charts that just confirmed the greatness of Cook's accomplishments didn't quite fit our notions of fulfilling work either. Not that Cook's work was perfect. His people had charted Pylstaert Island, a tiny outlier of the Friendly Archipelago first spotted by Abel Tasman in 1643, and placed it almost two leagues too far south. We set that to rights, of course. The Friendly Isles did very well by us, in fact, for we also corrected the location of Vava'u, one of its biggest islands, a place with a decent harbor and fresh water. A Spanish captain, Francisco Mourelle, had discovered it just a few years earlier but located it six degrees too far west. A mistake of that magnitude could consign one to sailing a long time in vain in search of safe anchorage and refreshment. We were forever correcting the work of the Spaniards, who for all their colonies and missions and galleons seemed unable or unwilling to create an accurate chart.

But who among us aspires to be the great cavilers and naysayers of the high seas? We began with Isle Grande and proceeded to erase more from the world's maps than we added. It was one thing to be rid of Davis Land—the name itself lacked inspiration. And it's true most geographers were already suspicious of Nuestra Señora de La Gorta, an island no respectable eighteenth-century sailor had ever seen. But what a pity to lose Los Mojos—or was it Los Majos, Las Mojas, or Los Mauges? We sank not only the islands but the entertaining controversy over their proper name. And when we expunged Rica de Oro and Rica de Plata, said to be wealthy islands inhabited by civilized and friendly white people, east of Japan—at that point we weren't in the business of completing the globe so much as laying waste to dreams. We lost a man during that search—a young sailor from Saint-Brieuc who fell into the sea from the fore-topmast, drawn there, like so many of us, by the captain's promise of a reward for the first man to sight land. It was a shame to lose him. And the islands. "Rich with Gold." "Rich with Silver." Every map should offer a few such temptations. Sometimes we felt less like explorers than like inquisitors rooting out cartographic heresy.

Do not misunderstand. We did make some discoveries of our own. Like Frenchman's Bay in southeast Alaska, though it's not called that any longer, a terrible place where an errant tidal current swept twenty-one of us away, the first calamity of the expedition. And Necker Island, a tumorous, uninhabited rock outcropping northwest of Hawaii, which we found one moonlit November evening. Two nights later, we veered away just in time from a mostly submerged atoll that our captain called—and which we are pleased to say are *still* called—the French Frigate Shoals. And Moneron Island, a tiny speck off the southern tip of Sakhalin, all steep cliffs and raucous birds and sea lions. We also added a few pieces to the

Samoan archipelago (we called them the Navigators), site of our second
calamity, twelve of us massacred by natives. Still we hoped to find something wondrous, a large landmass with people, a place to rival Tahiti or
Hawaii or New Zealand. We discovered Vanikoro, of course, one of the
Solomons, although no one would know that for many years. No sooner
had we seen it than our third and final calamity was upon us.

Perhaps it was our passion for discovery that doomed us, drawing us
too close to the Vanikoran reefs when the weatherglass was falling and
the sky boiling with storm. Making us beat into the wind when we should
have borne away. Inuring us to risk. Wasn't it what had led twenty-one
men to their watery deaths while surveying a new bay? And tempted a
young sailor too far out a yardarm? And blinded a watering party to the
hostility of the islanders? Our immoderate desire eroded caution.

But we are getting ahead of ourselves.

For before our undoing in Vanikoro, before the melee in Samoa, there
was the hallucination.

It was June 16, 1787. We had come north through the Sea of Japan and
were exploring the Strait of Tartary. Fog obscured the continent, but
around us, the day was clear and pleasantly warm, with a cooperative
breeze. Around four in the afternoon, the lookout cried that he spied
land, and there in the south appeared a great landmass lying nearly per-
pendicular to the mainland, the gap between them very narrow. Drawing
nearer, we could make out every detail of its terrain—mountains, ravines,
coast, even curls of smoke that spoke of human habitation. Our hearts
soared. Perhaps here—*west* of Japan, not east—was the fabled island of
wealth and white people. Most likely it was nothing so wonderful. But
surely it would be a discovery to rival any of Cook's. We held to the wind
and made for the south-southeast. As we approached, however, the island
began to shift, its forms and colors blending into one another, peaks swirling skyward, mountainsides collapsing into canyons, the shoreline draining
into the ocean. We watched, despairing, as our discovery resolved itself
into the most extraordinary fog bank any of us had ever seen, and then it
dissipated like a conjurer's trick, leaving empty blue water and a clear view
of the Tartary coast. We sailed all night in the ocean space our phantom
island had seemed to occupy, though there was no need to confirm its
nonexistence. It was a sad, defeated exercise, like trying to console oneself while holding a dead lover's dress.

The illusion was complete and shared by us all. So was the disillusion. Something faltered that day in the Strait of Tartary. For it turned out we were no better than the La Roches and Davises whose cartographic fantasies we'd laughed off the world map. And if nearly two hundred experienced sailors could mistake mist for land, then there was no misapprehension to which we were not vulnerable. Suddenly, every outcome seemed equally possible and equally unreal. So when we first spied Vanikoro between the angry dark of sea and sky, a ribbon of green that appeared on no charts in our possession, we didn't know whether to believe our eyes. When the full power of the storm fell on us, we were loath to accept its lashing reality; it could so easily have gone the other way. We were still in doubt as the waters closed over us, the globe we had tried so hard to complete swallowing us whole.

AFTERWORD

Peter Dillon was only the first of many to begin unraveling the mystery of the Lapérouse expedition's disappearance. The Dumont-d'Urville expedition arrived in Vanikoro just a few months after Dillon, collecting more artifacts from the wrecks and largely corroborating what Dillon had learned from the islanders. For the next century and a half, most expeditions to Vanikoro were undertaken by missionaries, some of whom suggested on entirely paltry evidence that the survivors of the wrecks had been cannibalized by the islanders—a "fact" that got repeated over and over, even in otherwise careful treatments of the Lapérouse expedition, well into the twentieth century.

It wasn't until the late 1950s, when scuba diving technology had advanced sufficiently to allow for sustained and more mobile underwater explorations, that substantial new relics of the shipwrecks were recovered from the ocean floor. In the decades since, numerous expeditions, some mounted by the French Navy and the Association Salomon in Nouméa, New Caledonia, have turned up more and more evidence about where and how the *Boussole* and the *Astrolabe* came to grief.

I relied on the work of numerous scholars to piece together the factual elements of this story. The single most important source was *The Journal of Jean-François de Galaup de La Pérouse, 1785–1788*, translated and edited by John Dunmore and published by the Hakluyt Society in two volumes in 1994. Dunmore's comprehensive introduction and footnotes provided historical context and suggested many of the ideas for the tales in this book.

The most helpful source in French, besides the French-language edition of the journal itself, was Catherine Gaziello's exhaustive 1984 study of the expedition, *L'Expedition de Lapérouse 1785–1788*, published by Comité des Travaux Historiques et Scientifiques. The Musée Lapérouse in Albi, France, and the relevant rooms in the Musée National de La Marine in Paris also provided helpful facts and visuals. The curious and compulsive reader may find a more comprehensive bibliography for this project at my website: www.naomijwilliams.com.

I am, of course, indebted to numerous individuals and organizations for their artistic, material, professional, and moral support of this project and its creator. Thanks first and foremost to my agent, the warm, witty, and wise Nicole Aragi, and to my gently persistent editor, Eric Chinski. Also thanks to Duvall Osteen at Aragi, Inc.; Peng Shepherd, Frieda Duggan, Sarah Scire, and everyone at FSG; Clare Smith, Rachel Wilkie, and everyone at Little, Brown, UK; and the excellent people at the Abner Stein Agency and the Marsh Agency.

Many teachers and mentors have helped light the way for this book. Thank you, Lucy Corin, Karen Joy Fowler, Lynn Freed, Pam Houston, Alessa Johns, Yiyun Li, Kevin "Mc" McIlvoy, Elissa Schappell, and Jim Shepard.

I am indebted to several organizations and individuals for their generous support of my work. I completed a first draft of this book while a student in the UC Davis Masters in Creative Writing program. Hedgebrook provided me with the incomparable gift of a month's residency in 2010. A 2013 Promise Grant from the Sustainable Arts Foundation allowed me to devote time to completing the manuscript. The Maurice Prize, established and funded by John Lescroart, has been a great boon to emerging writers from UC Davis for many years. Thank you, all.

My heartfelt gratitude, collectively, to everyone who has read and commented on parts of this book over the years: the Davis Writers Group; participants in the Sacramento Master Writers weekend workshops; the brilliant and supportive women I met at Hedgebrook; my wonderful classmates at UC Davis; the regulars at Don Schwartz's Tuesday night creative writing class at the Davis Art Center; the ASH Writing Group; and fellow workshoppers at Squaw Valley and Tin House. For assistance with research questions, thank you, Eric Berti, Sarah Curtis, Rachel Fuchs, Judy

Kalb, Ricardo Lezama, Lynda Newman, Jesper Olsson, and Dimitri Salichon. Any historical inaccuracies are obviously my fault alone.

For support of the variously moral, literary, and culinary varieties, thank you, Carlos Davidson, Valerie Fioravanti, Teresa Herlinger, Cynthia Kaufman, Marian Mabel, Jen Marlowe, Linda Matthew, Paul Rauber, Erica Lorraine Scheidt, Cora Stryker, Josh Weil, and Elise Winn. Chris Chang and Rae Gouirand offered not only their warm and indispensable friendship but the gift of undistracted writing time in their homes. Thank you, thank you. And I owe a particular debt of gratitude to Susan Wolbarst, who read nearly every page of this novel, many of them more than once, including hundreds of pages I ultimately discarded. Greater love hath no writer friend than this.

I am inordinately lucky when it comes to family. My mother, Atsuko Williams, and my sister, Mari McQuaid, always expressed confidence that I would publish a book, even through the long decades when there was little evidence to support their faith. My in-laws, Norman and Rachel Fuchs, offered unflagging moral support, bought references for me, and funded a research trip to Paris and Albi. My children, Julian Fuchs and Eliot Williams, can scarcely remember a time when their mother was not working on this book. Thank you, guys, for your patience, your love, and your always insightful and timely encouragement. My husband, Dan Fuchs, has been chief breadwinner, co-parent extraordinaire, head chef, and first reader. Your love and your belief in me have made my entire adult life possible. And now this.